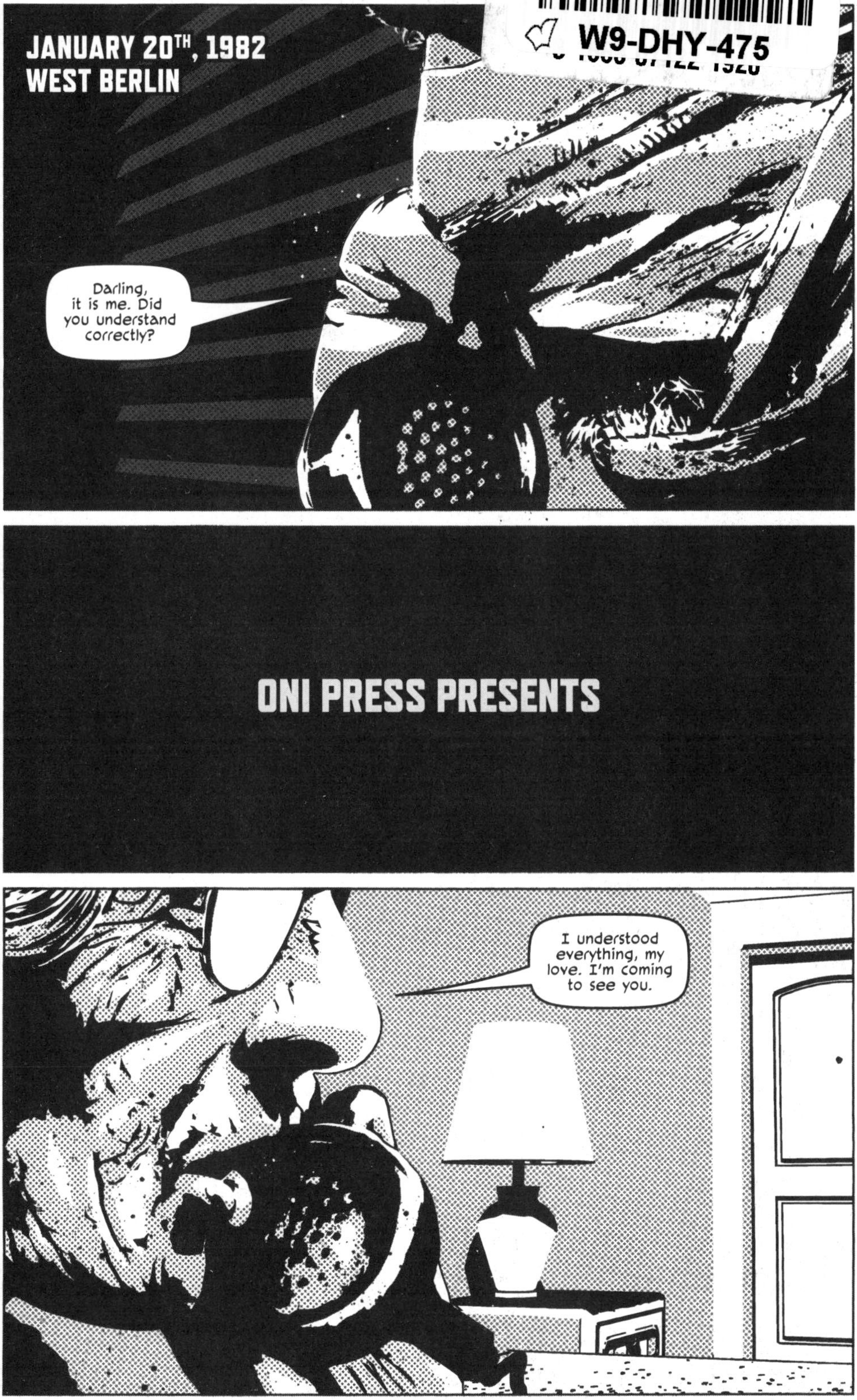
JANUARY 20TH, 1982
WEST BERLIN
Darling, it is me. Did you understand correctly?
ONI PRESS PRESENTS
I understood everything, my love. I'm coming to see you.

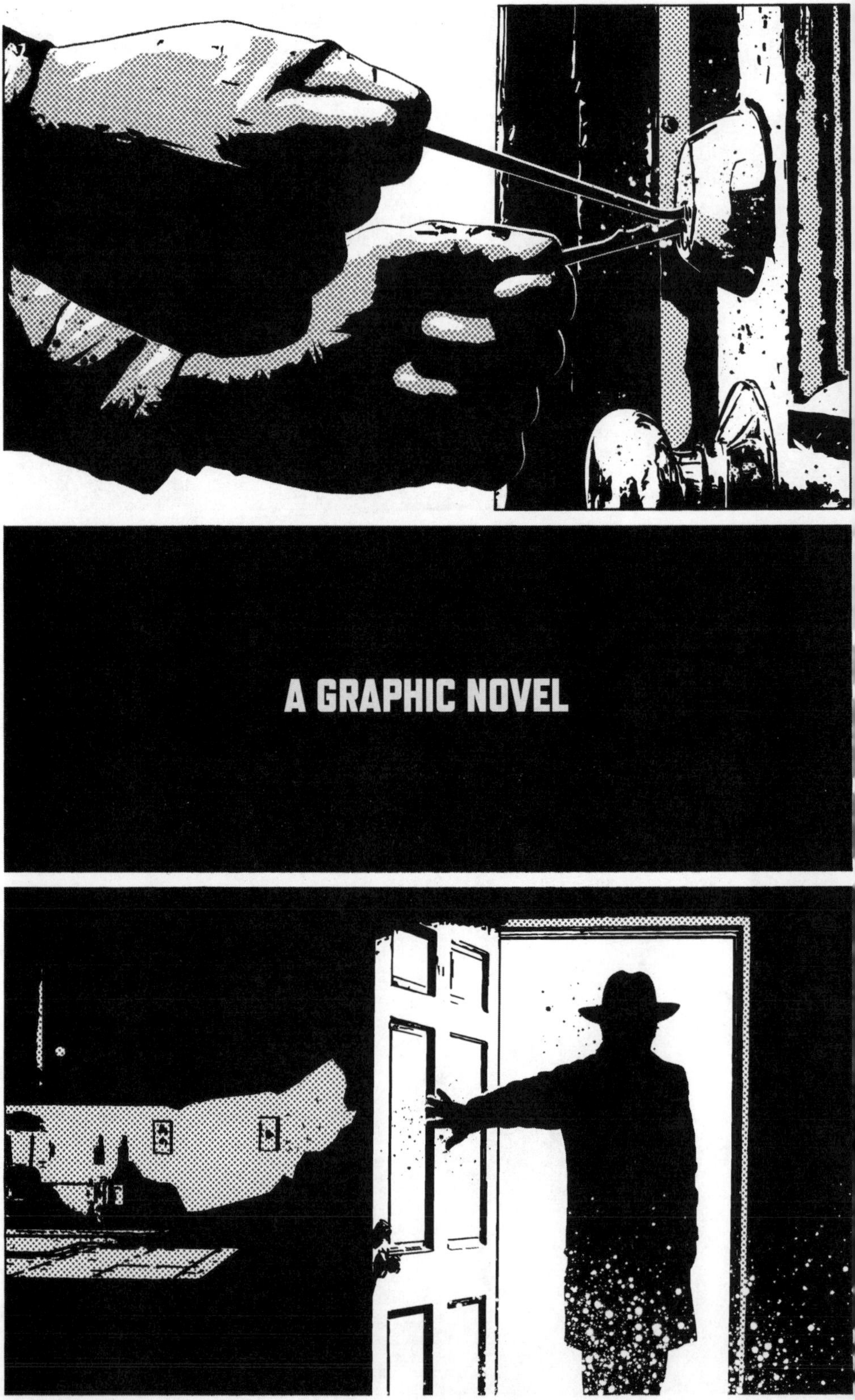
A GRAPHIC NOVEL

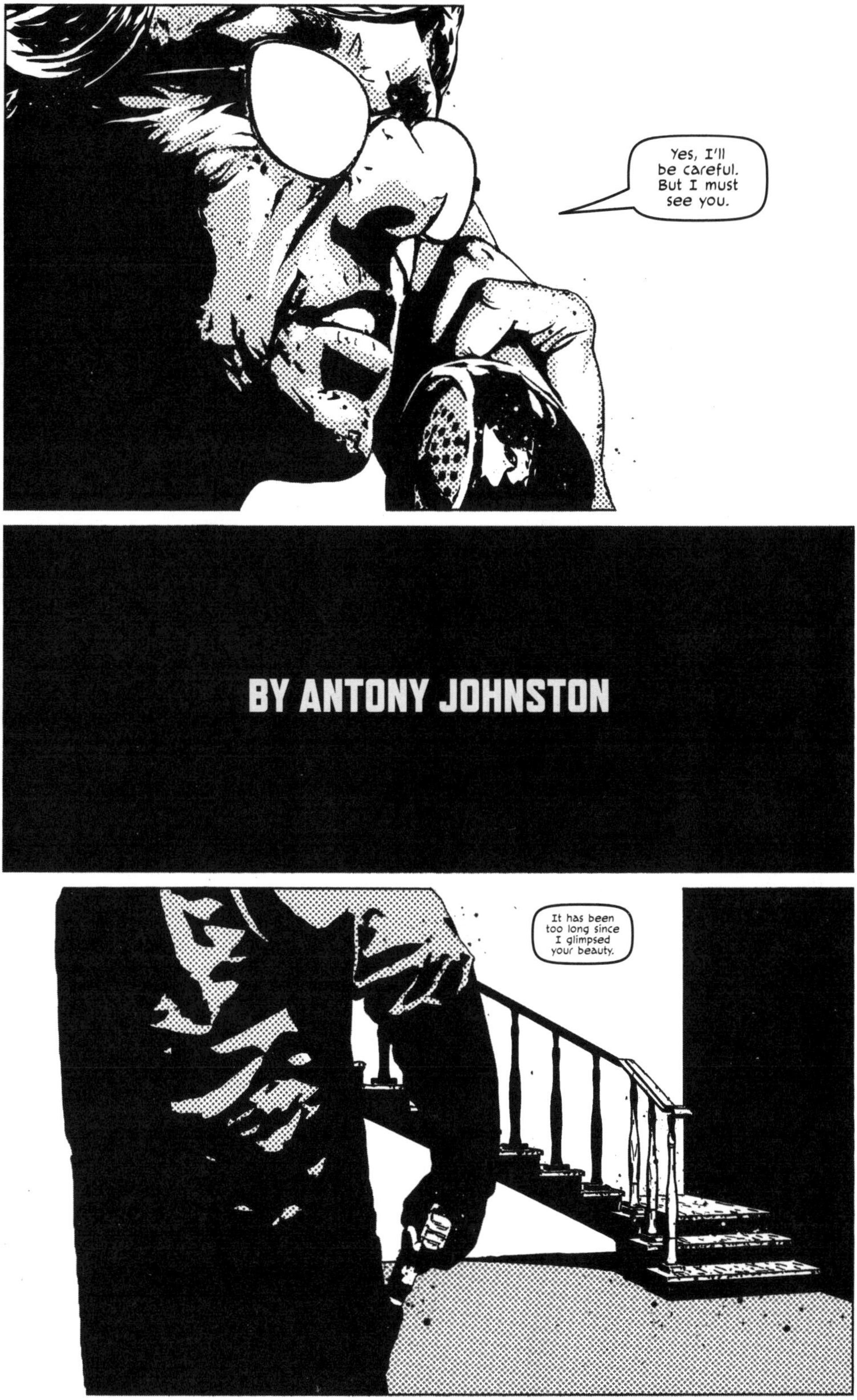
Yes, I'll be careful. But I must see you.
BY ANTONY JOHNSTON
It has been too long since I glimpsed your beauty.

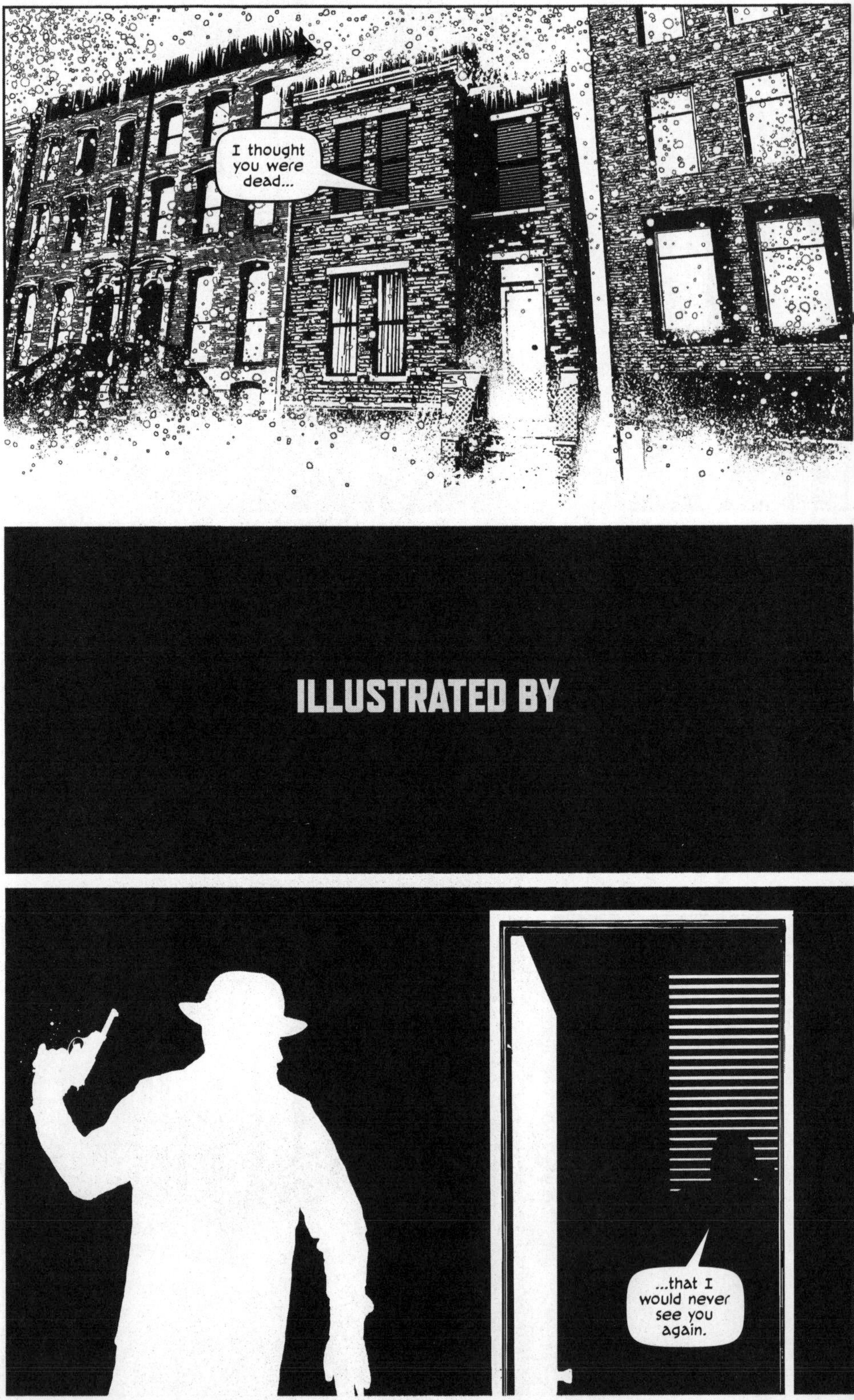
I thought you were dead...
ILLUSTRATED BY
...that I would never see you again.

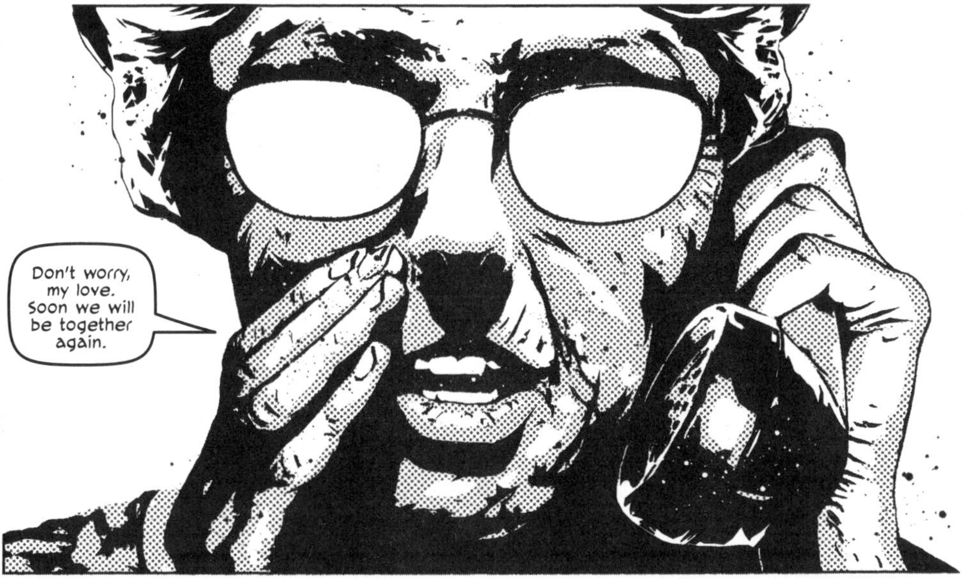
Don't worry, my love. Soon we will be together again.

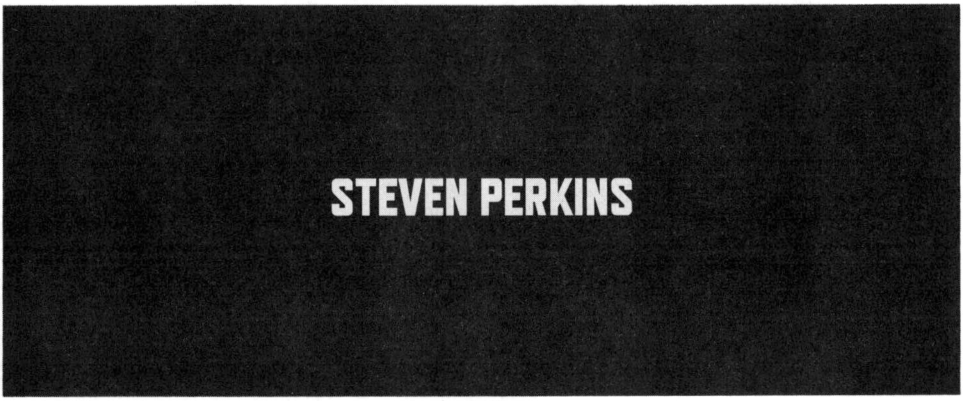
STEVEN PERKINS

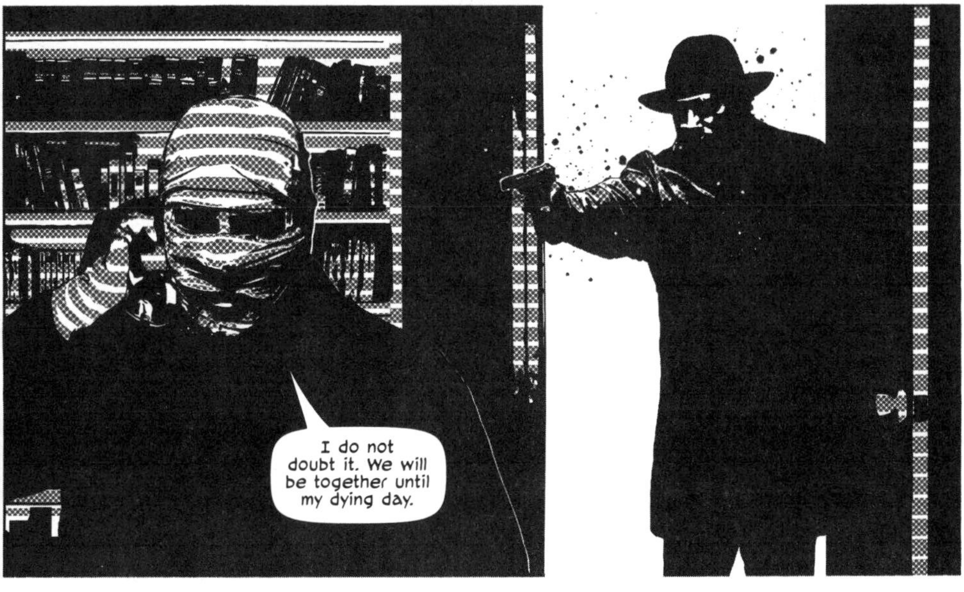
I do not doubt it. We will be together until my dying day.

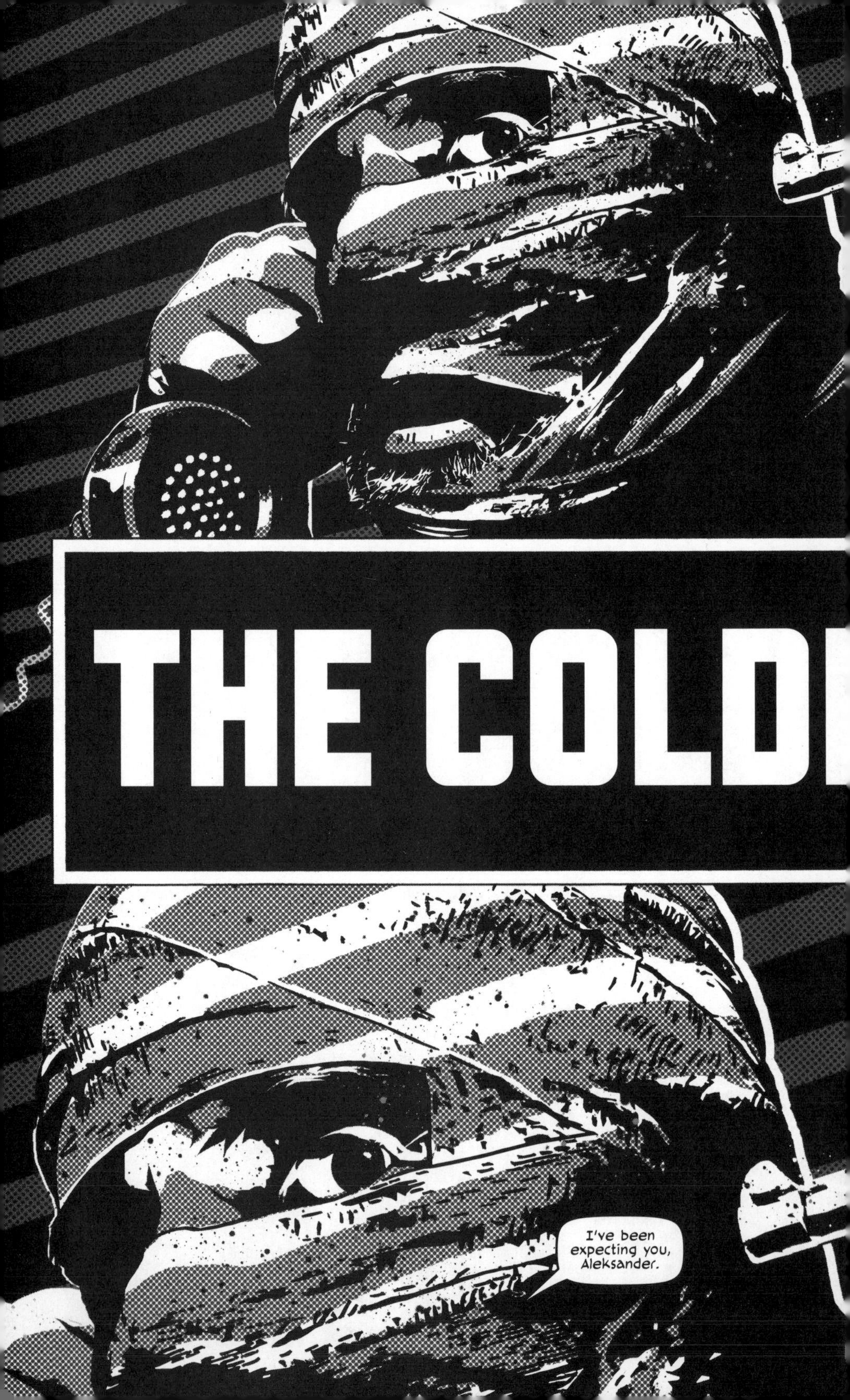
THE COLD
I've been expecting you, Aleksander.

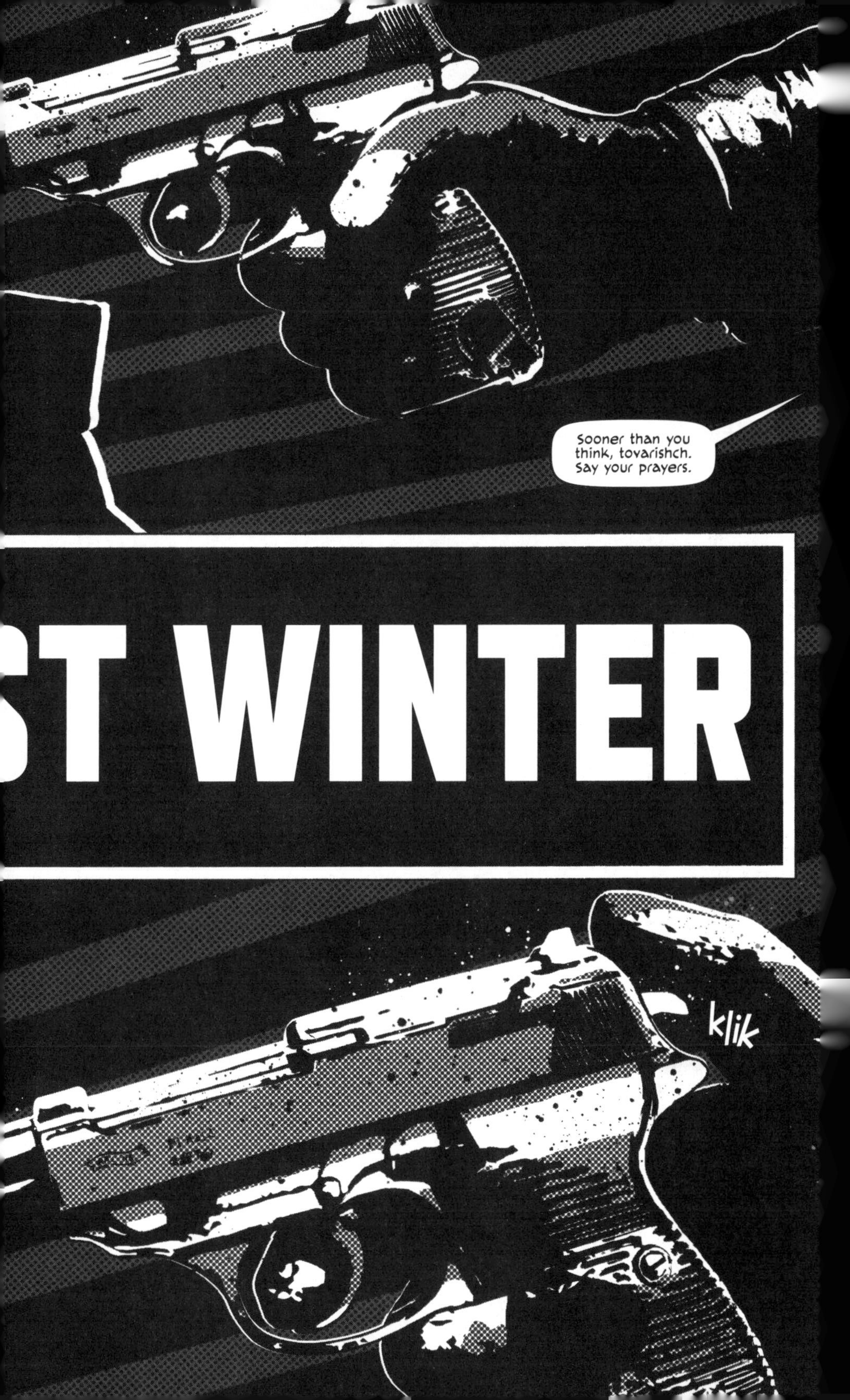
Sooner than you think, tovarishch. Say your prayers.
ST WINTER
klik

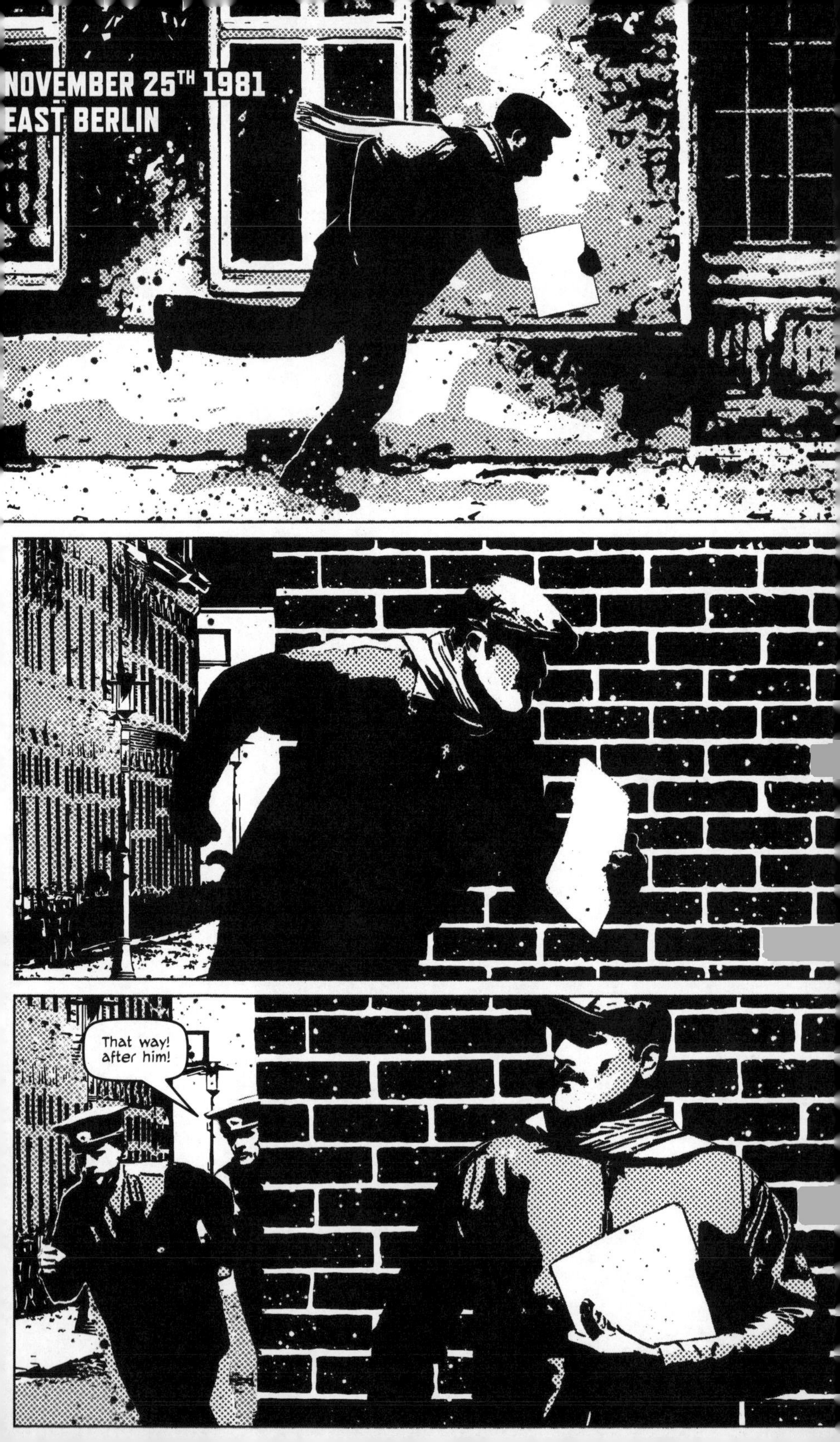
NOVEMBER 25TH 1981
EAST BERLIN
That way! after him!

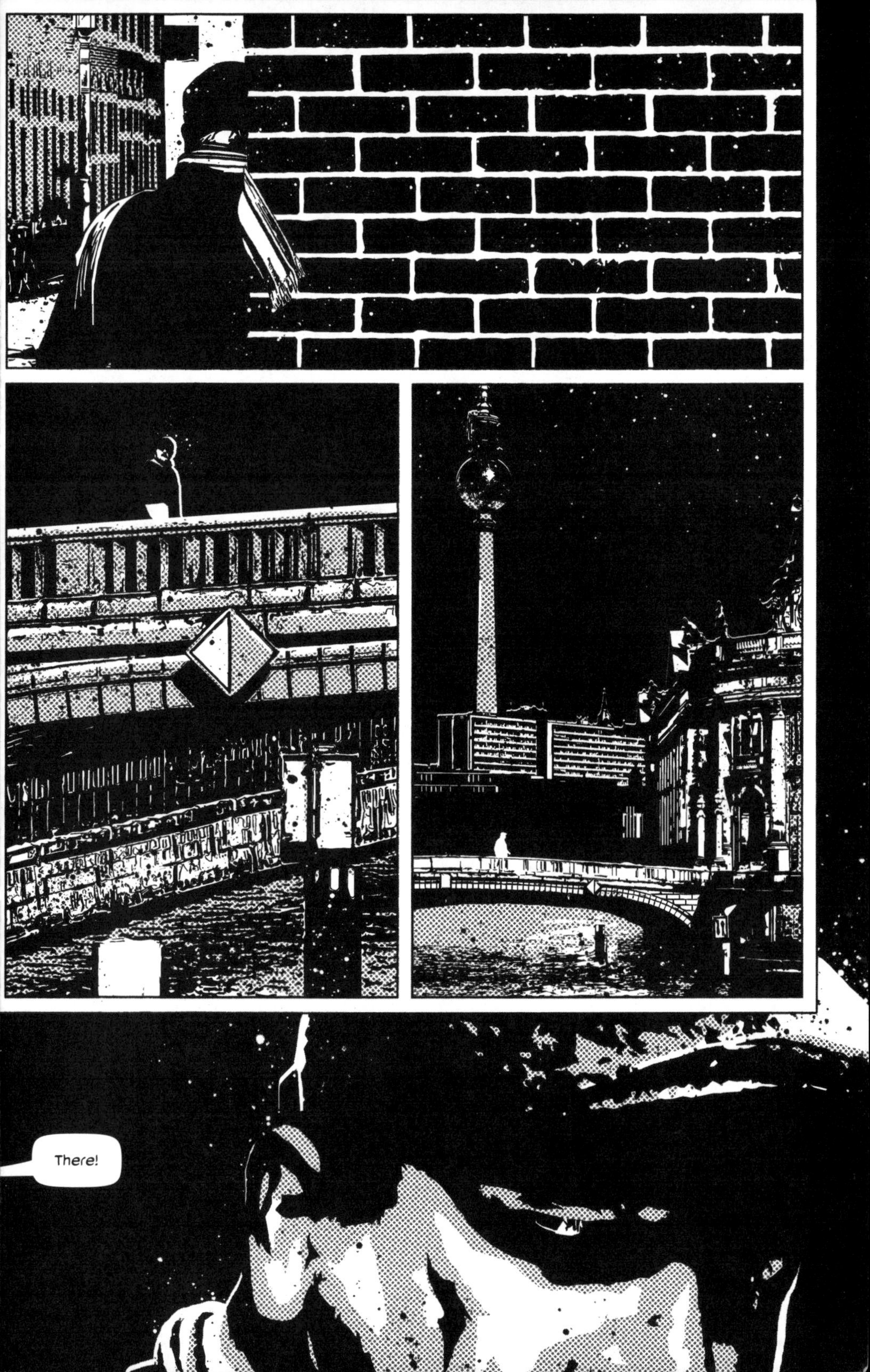
There!

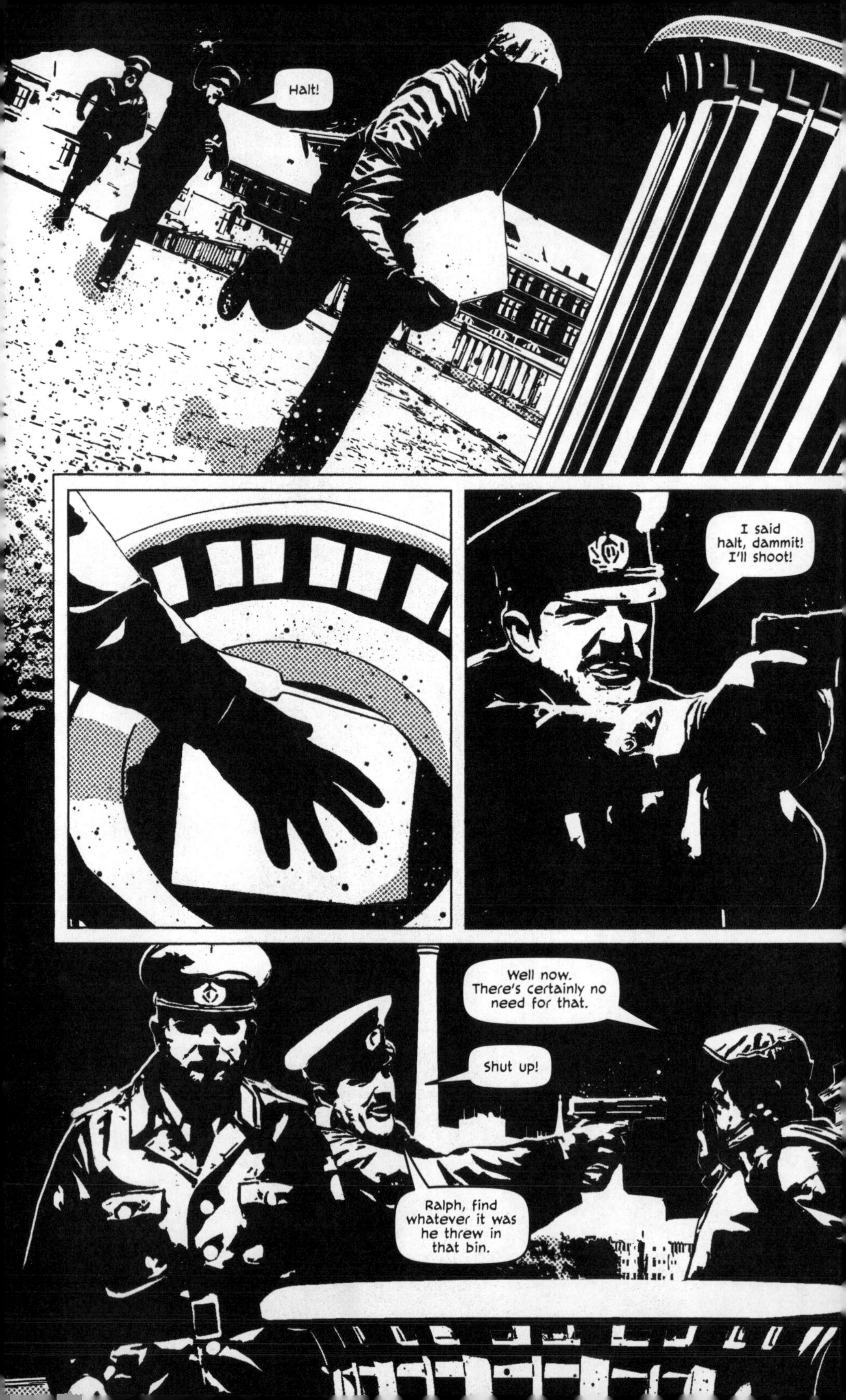
Halt!
I said halt, dammit! I'll shoot!
Well now. There's certainly no need for that.
Shut up!
Ralph, find whatever it was he threw in that bin.

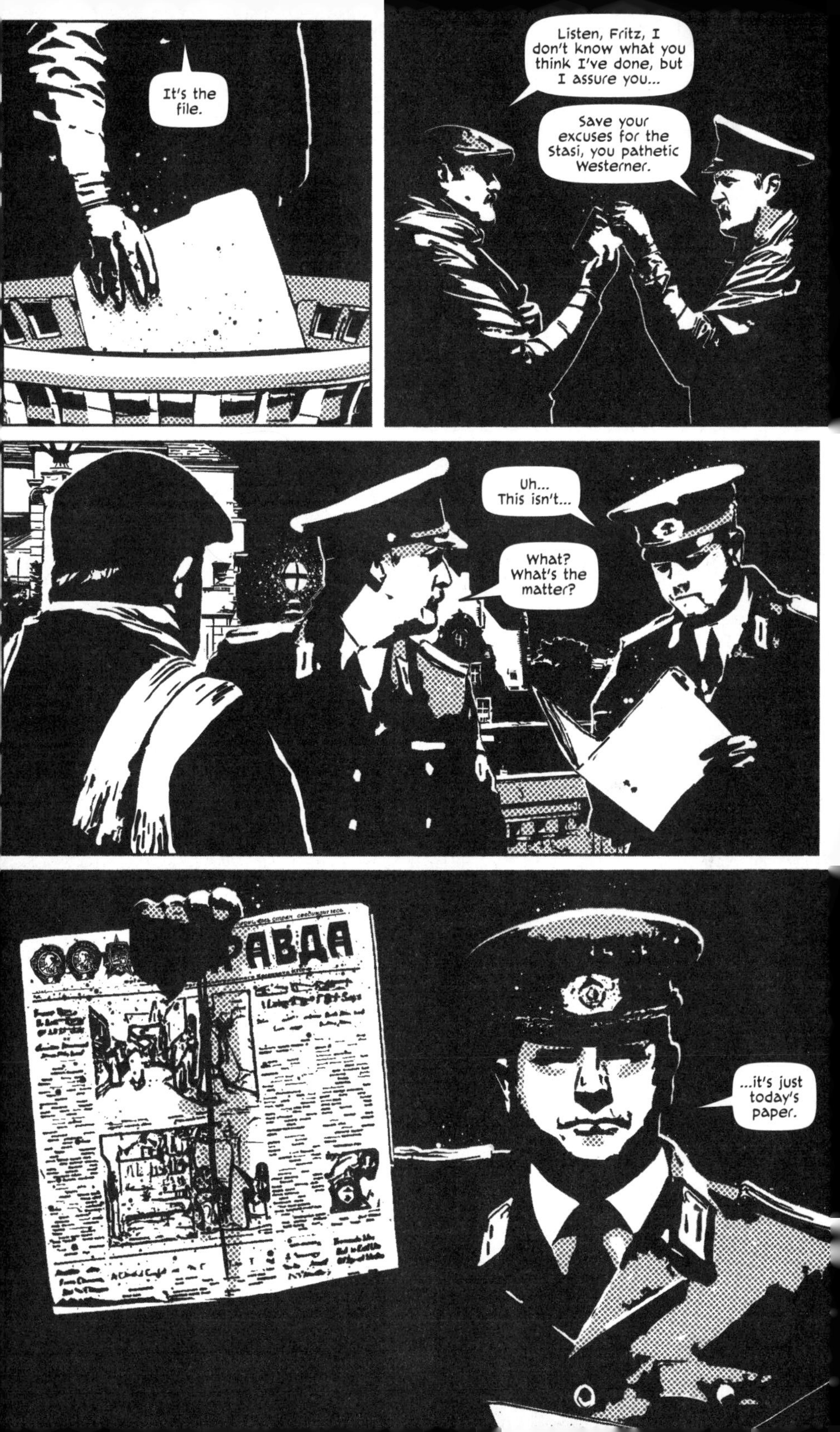
It's the file.
Listen, Fritz, I don't know what you think I've done, but I assure you...
Save your excuses for the Stasi, you pathetic Westerner.
Uh... This isn't...
What? What's the matter?
...it's just today's paper.

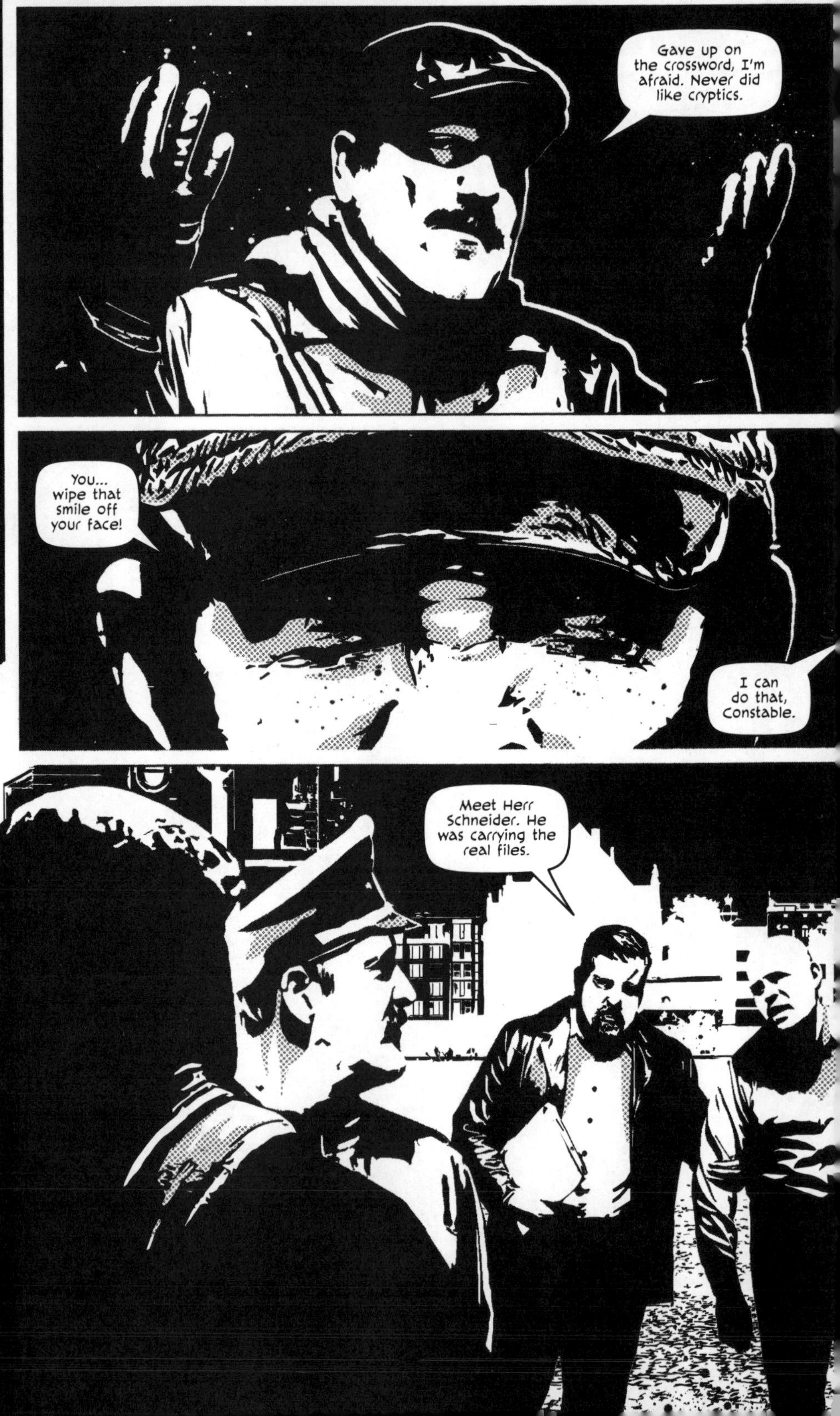
Gave up on the crossword, I'm afraid. Never did like cryptics.
You... wipe that smile off your face!
I can do that, Constable.
Meet Herr Schneider. He was carrying the real files.

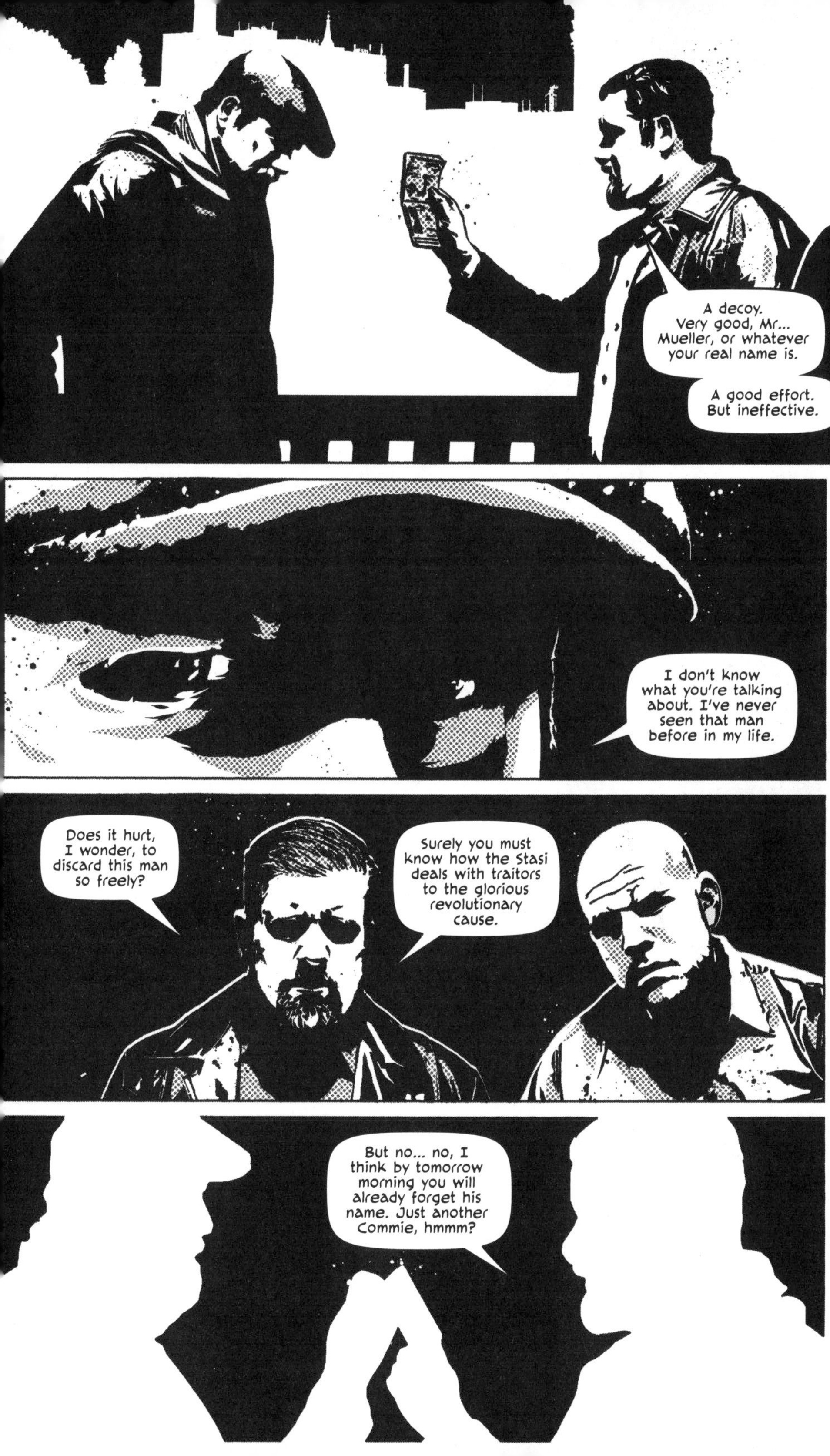
A decoy. Very good, Mr... Mueller, or whatever your real name is.
A good effort. But ineffective.
I don't know what you're talking about. I've never seen that man before in my life.
Does it hurt, I wonder, to discard this man so freely?
Surely you must know how the Stasi deals with traitors to the glorious revolutionary cause.
But no... no, I think by tomorrow morning you will already forget his name. Just another Commie, hmmm?

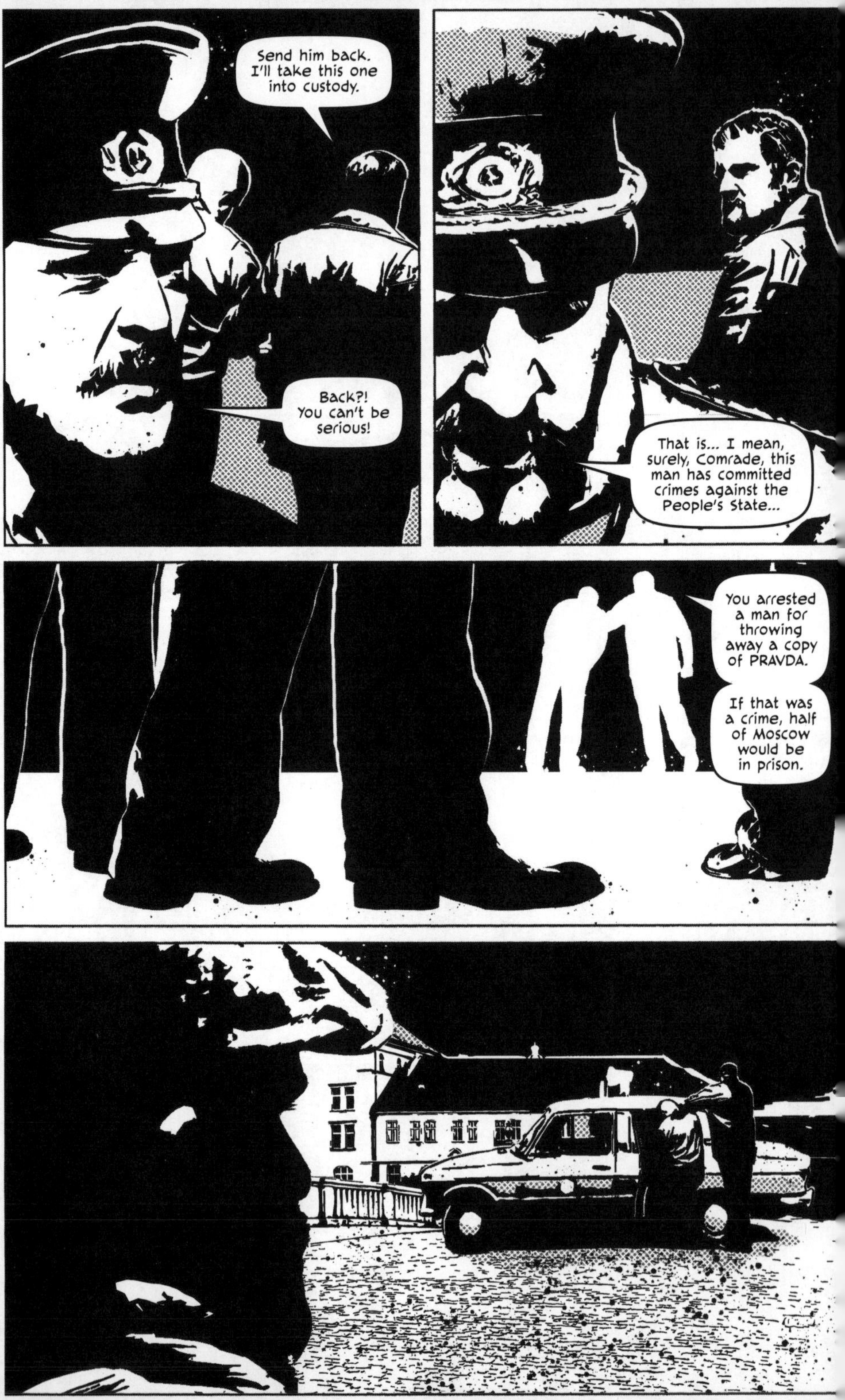

Send him back. I'll take this one into custody.
Back?! You can't be serious!
That is... I mean, surely, Comrade, this man has committed crimes against the People's State...
You arrested a man for throwing away a copy of PRAVDA.
If that was a crime, half of Moscow would be in prison.

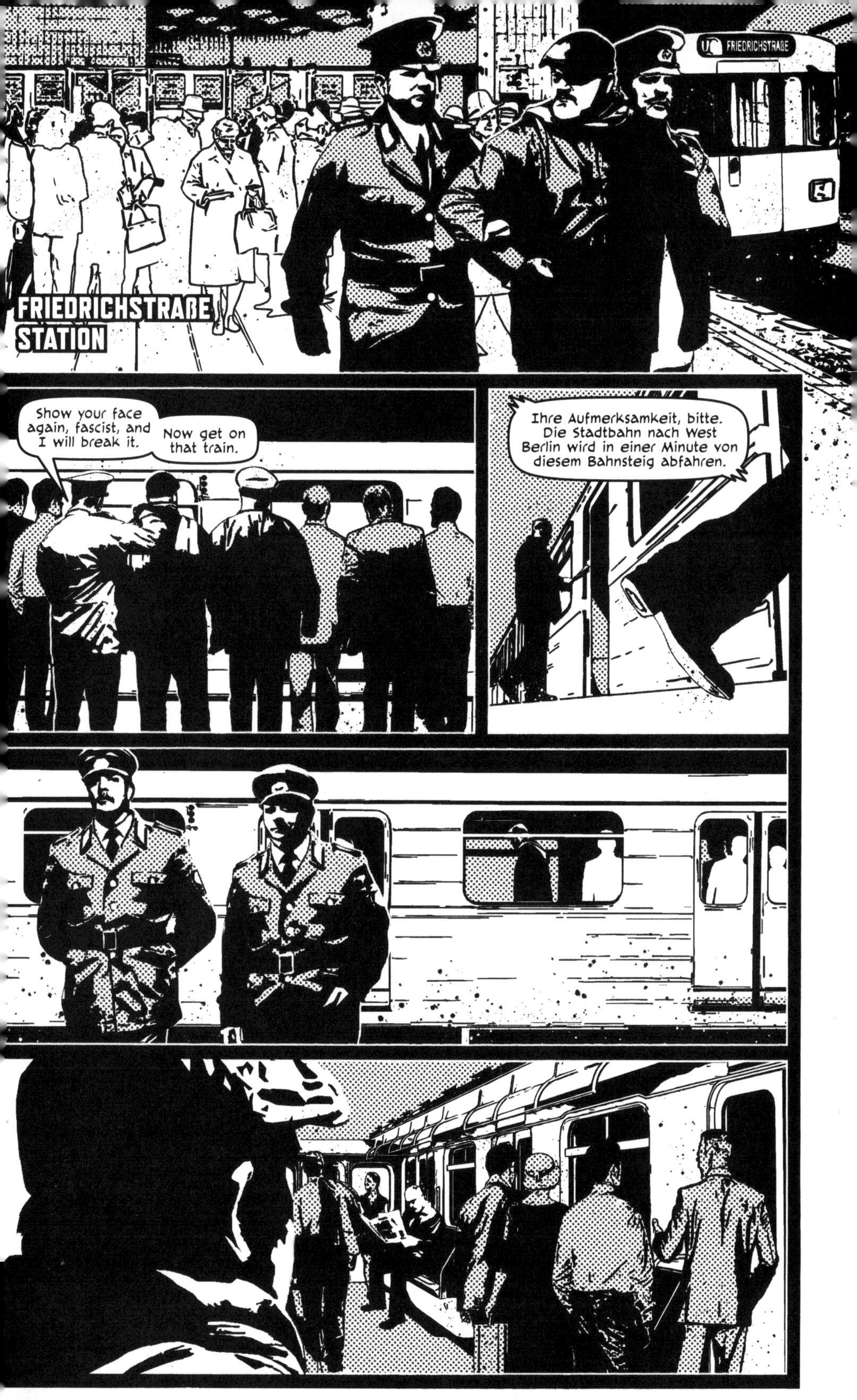

FRIEDRICHSTRAßE
FRIEDRICHSTRAßE STATION
Show your face again, fascist, and I will break it.
Now get on that train.
Ihre Aufmerksamkeit, bitte. Die Stadtbahn nach West Berlin wird in einer Minute von diesem Bahnsteig abfahren.

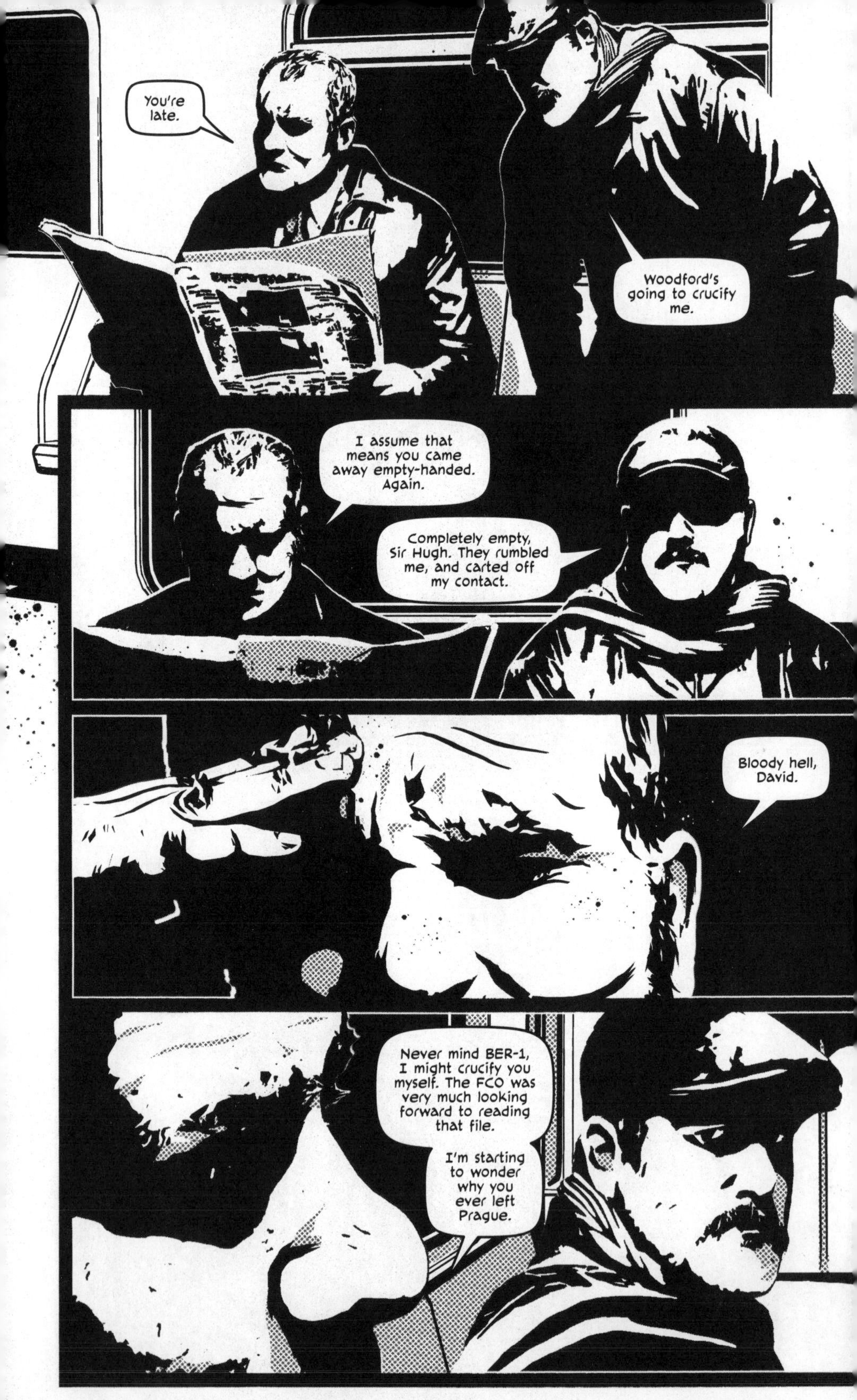
You're late.
Woodford's going to crucify me.
I assume that means you came away empty-handed. Again.
Completely empty, Sir Hugh. They rumbled me, and carted off my contact.
Bloody hell, David.
Never mind BER-1, I might crucify you myself. The FCO was very much looking forward to reading that file.
I'm starting to wonder why you ever left Prague.

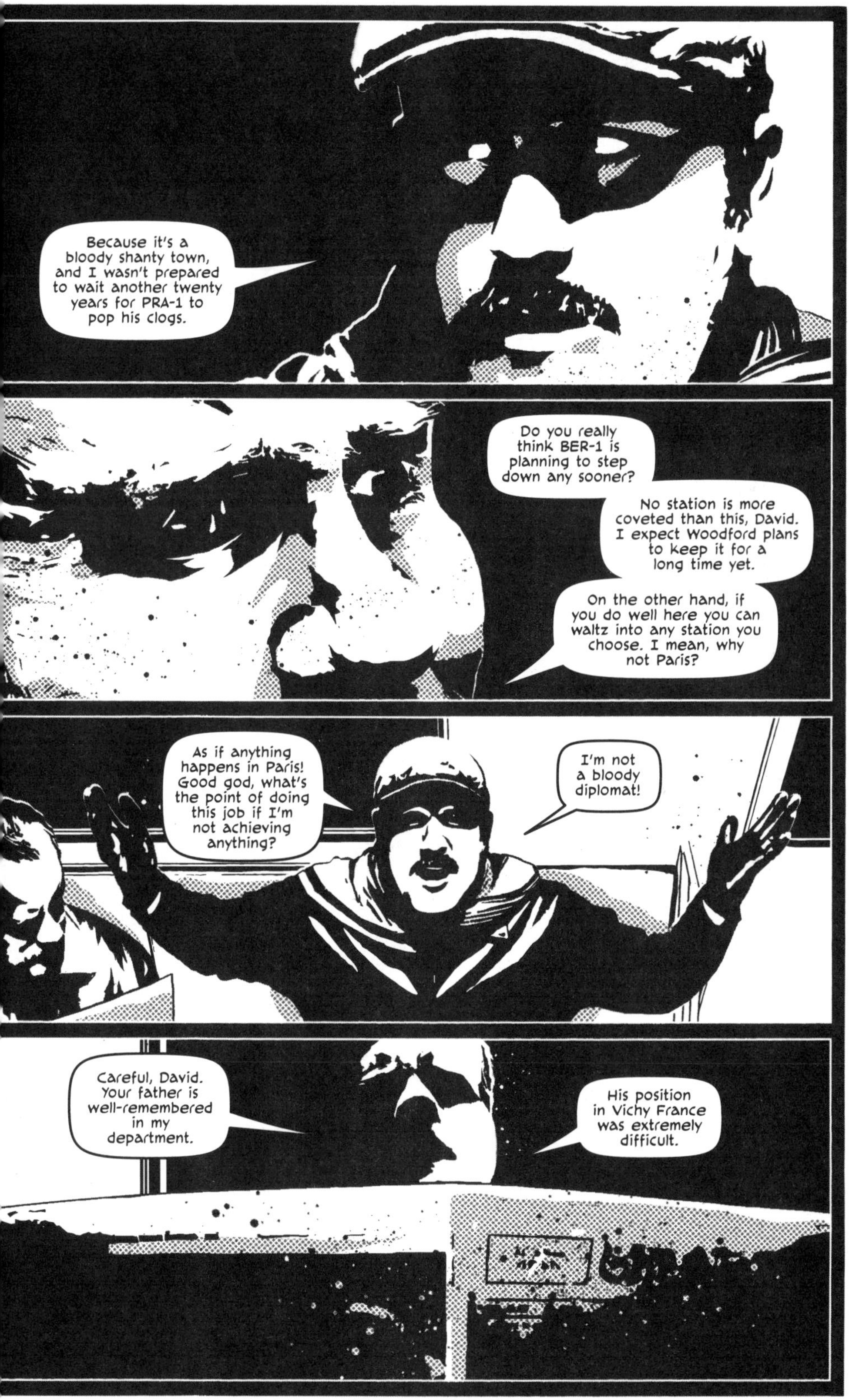
Because it's a bloody shanty town, and I wasn't prepared to wait another twenty years for PRA-1 to pop his clogs.
Do you really think BER-1 is planning to step down any sooner?
No station is more coveted than this, David. I expect Woodford plans to keep it for a long time yet.
On the other hand, if you do well here you can waltz into any station you choose. I mean, why not Paris?
As if anything happens in Paris! Good god, what's the point of doing this job if I'm not achieving anything?
I'm not a bloody diplomat!
Careful, David. Your father is well-remembered in my department.
His position in Vichy France was extremely difficult.

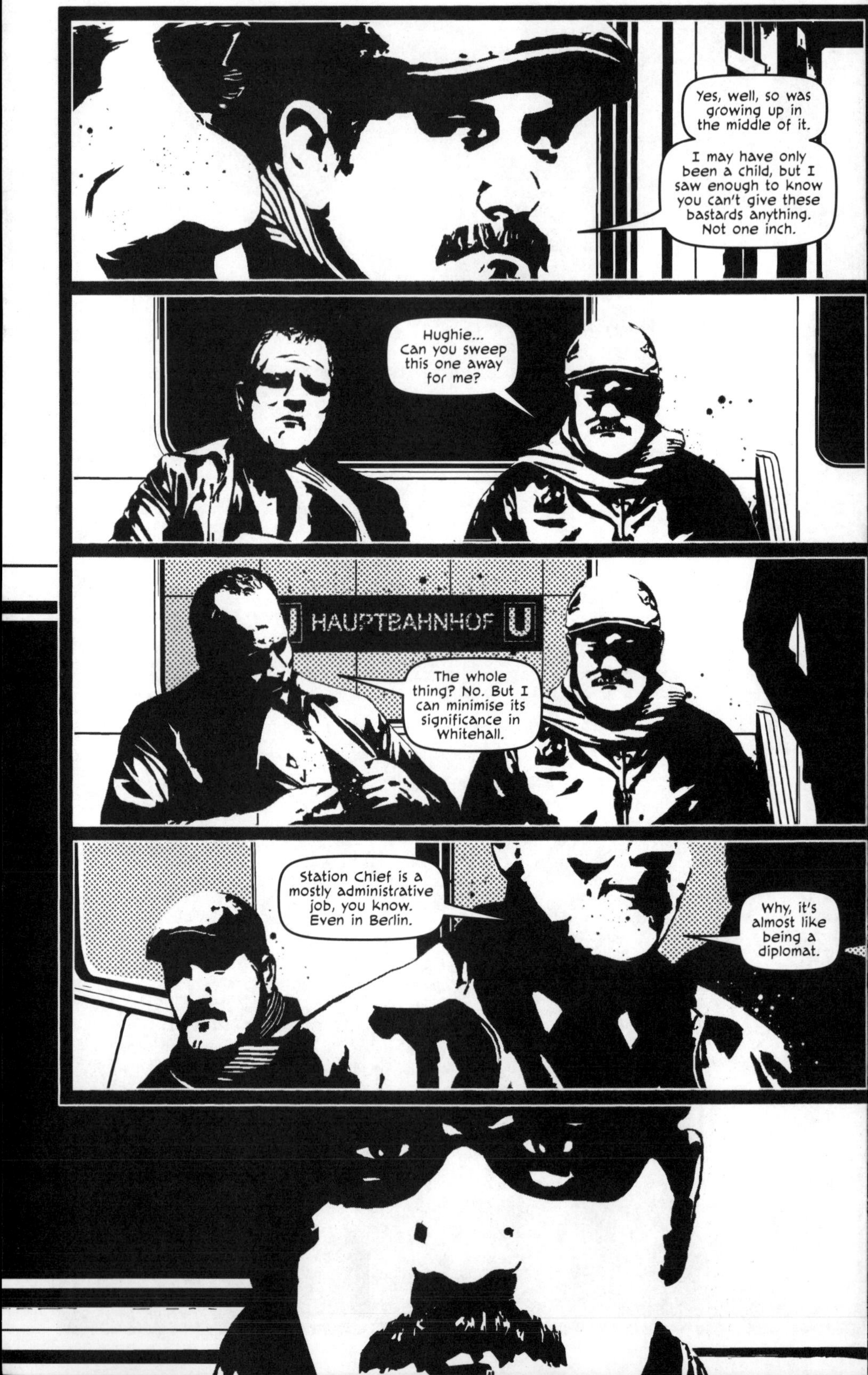
Yes, well, so was growing up in the middle of it.
I may have only been a child, but I saw enough to know you can't give these bastards anything. Not one inch.
Hughie... Can you sweep this one away for me?
HAUPTBAHNHOF
The whole thing? No. But I can minimise its significance in Whitehall.
Station Chief is a mostly administrative job, you know. Even in Berlin.
Why, it's almost like being a diplomat.

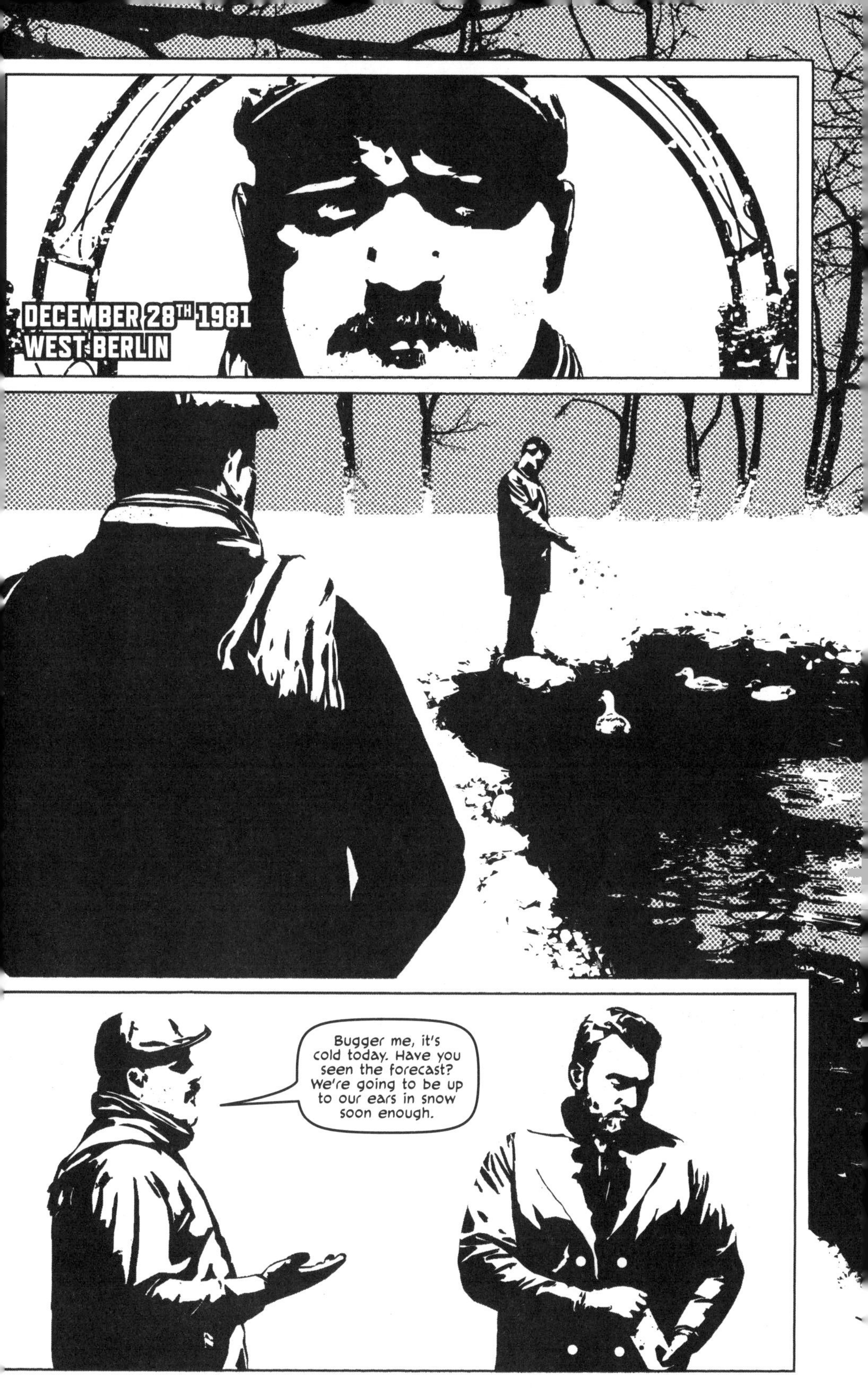
DECEMBER 28TH 1981
WEST BERLIN
Bugger me, it's cold today. Have you seen the forecast? We're going to be up to our ears in snow soon enough.

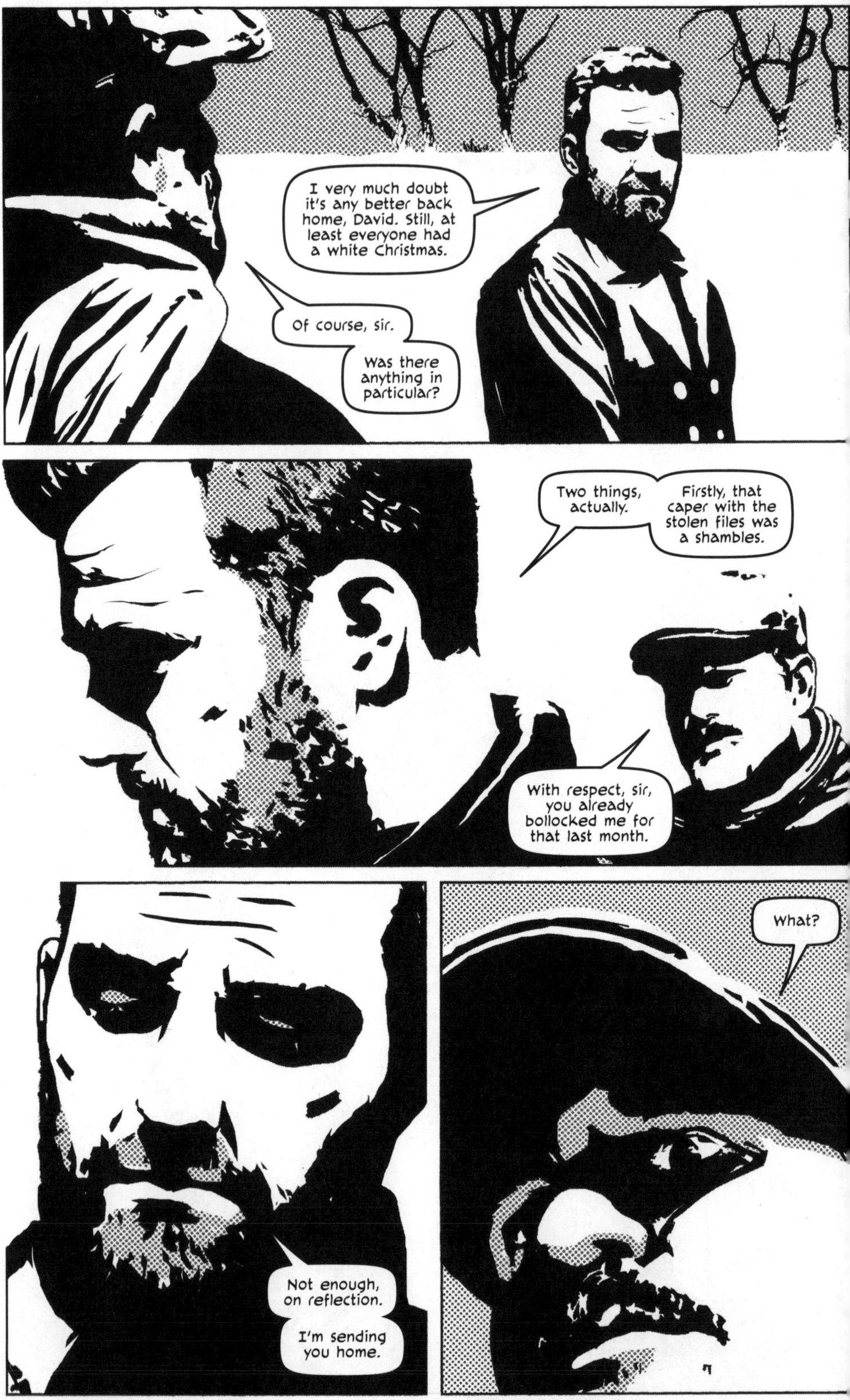
I very much doubt it's any better back home, David. Still, at least everyone had a white Christmas.
Of course, sir.
Was there anything in particular?
Two things, actually.
Firstly, that caper with the stolen files was a shambles.
With respect, sir, you already bollocked me for that last month.
Not enough, on reflection.
I'm sending you home.
What?

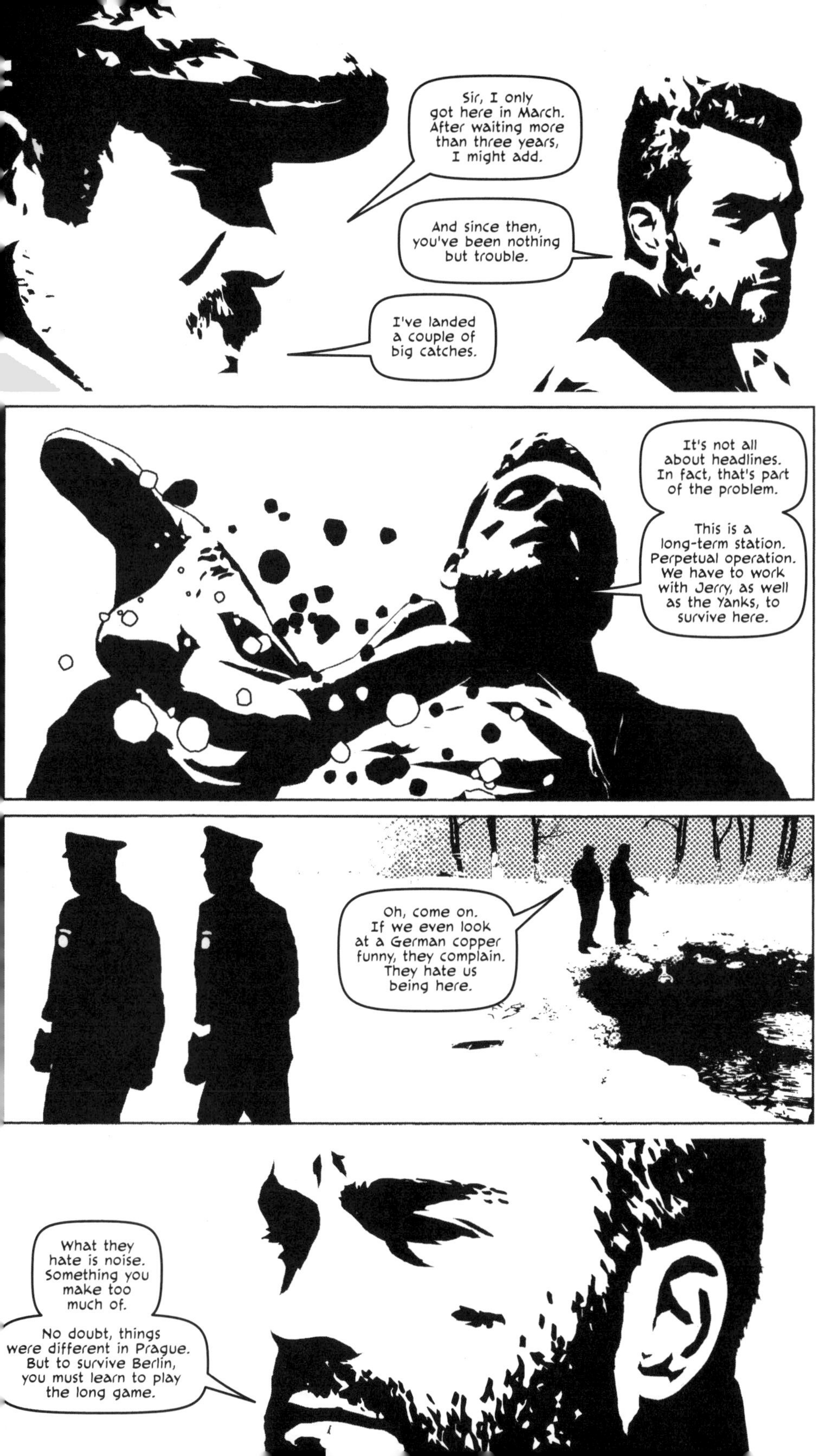
Sir, I only got here in March. After waiting more than three years, I might add.
And since then, you've been nothing but trouble.
I've landed a couple of big catches.
It's not all about headlines. In fact, that's part of the problem.
This is a long-term station. Perpetual operation. We have to work with Jerry, as well as the Yanks, to survive here.
Oh, come on. If we even look at a German copper funny, they complain. They hate us being here.
What they hate is noise. Something you make too much of.
No doubt, things were different in Prague. But to survive Berlin, you must learn to play the long game.

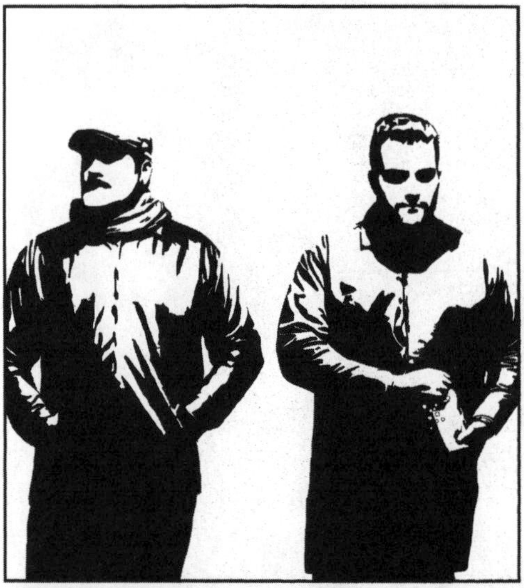

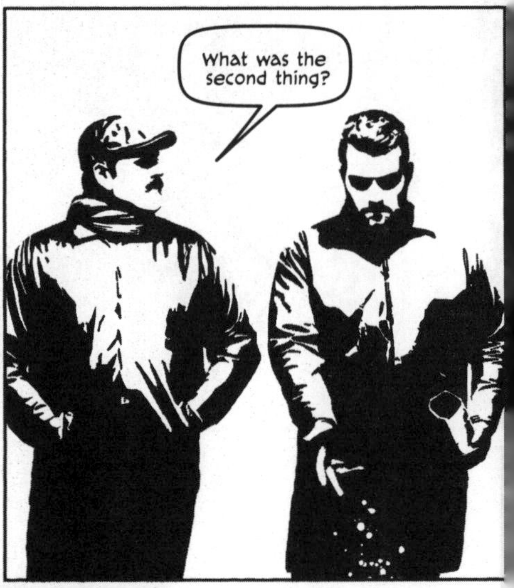
What was the second thing?

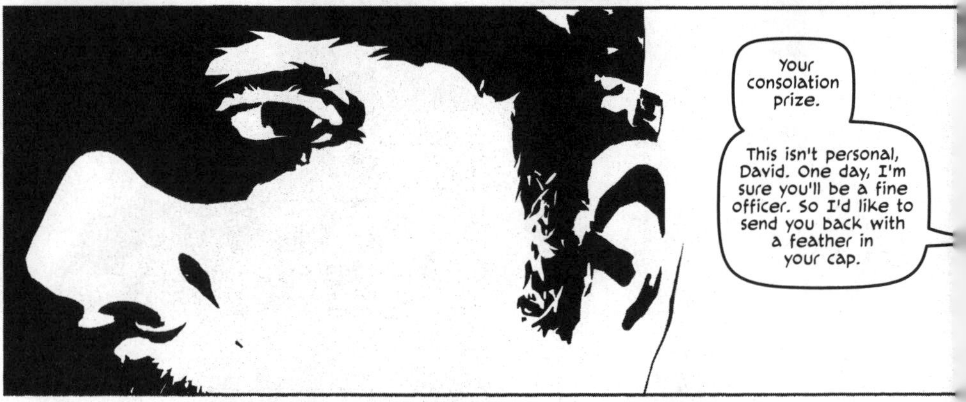
Your consolation prize.
This isn't personal, David. One day, I'm sure you'll be a fine officer. So I'd like to send you back with a feather in your cap.

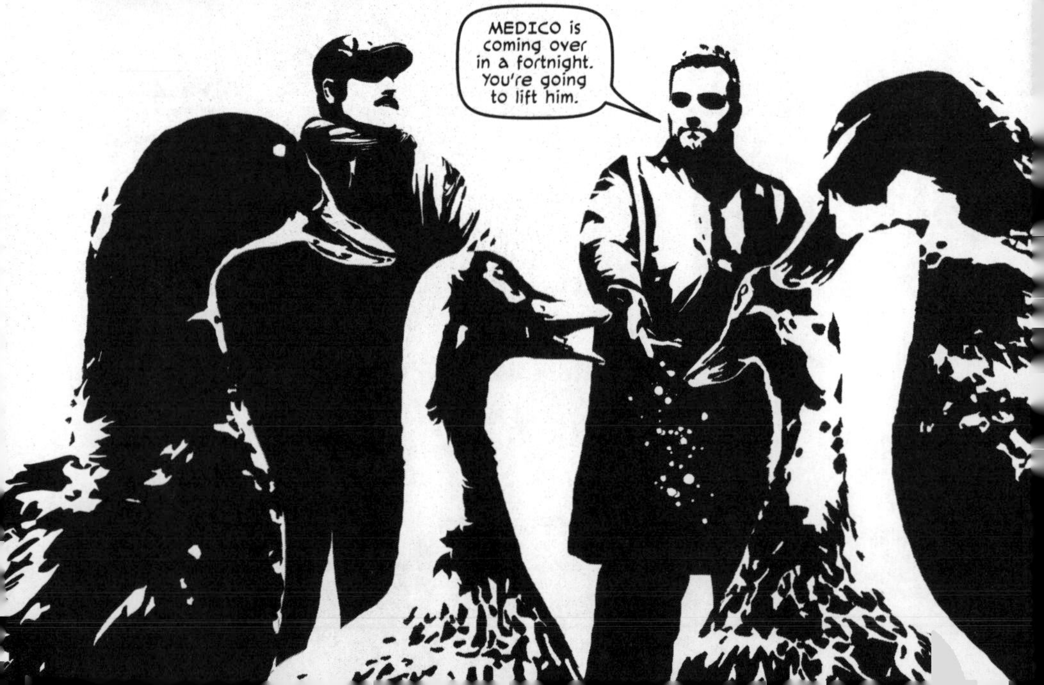
MEDICO is coming over in a fortnight. You're going to lift him.

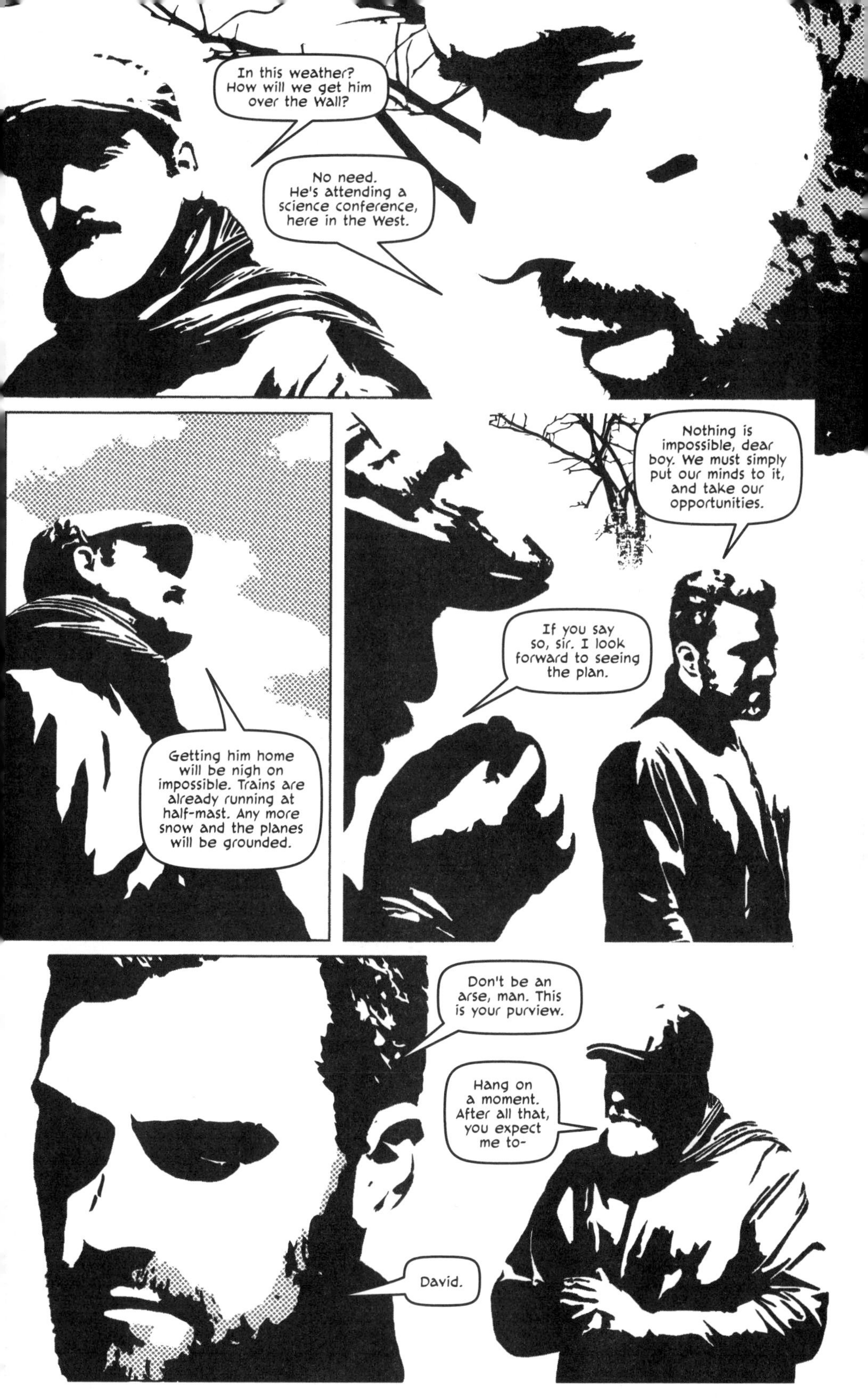
In this weather? How will we get him over the Wall?
No need. He's attending a science conference, here in the West.
Getting him home will be nigh on impossible. Trains are already running at half-mast. Any more snow and the planes will be grounded.
Nothing is impossible, dear boy. We must simply put our minds to it, and take our opportunities.
If you say so, sir. I look forward to seeing the plan.
Don't be an arse, man. This is your purview.
Hang on a moment. After all that, you expect me to-
David.

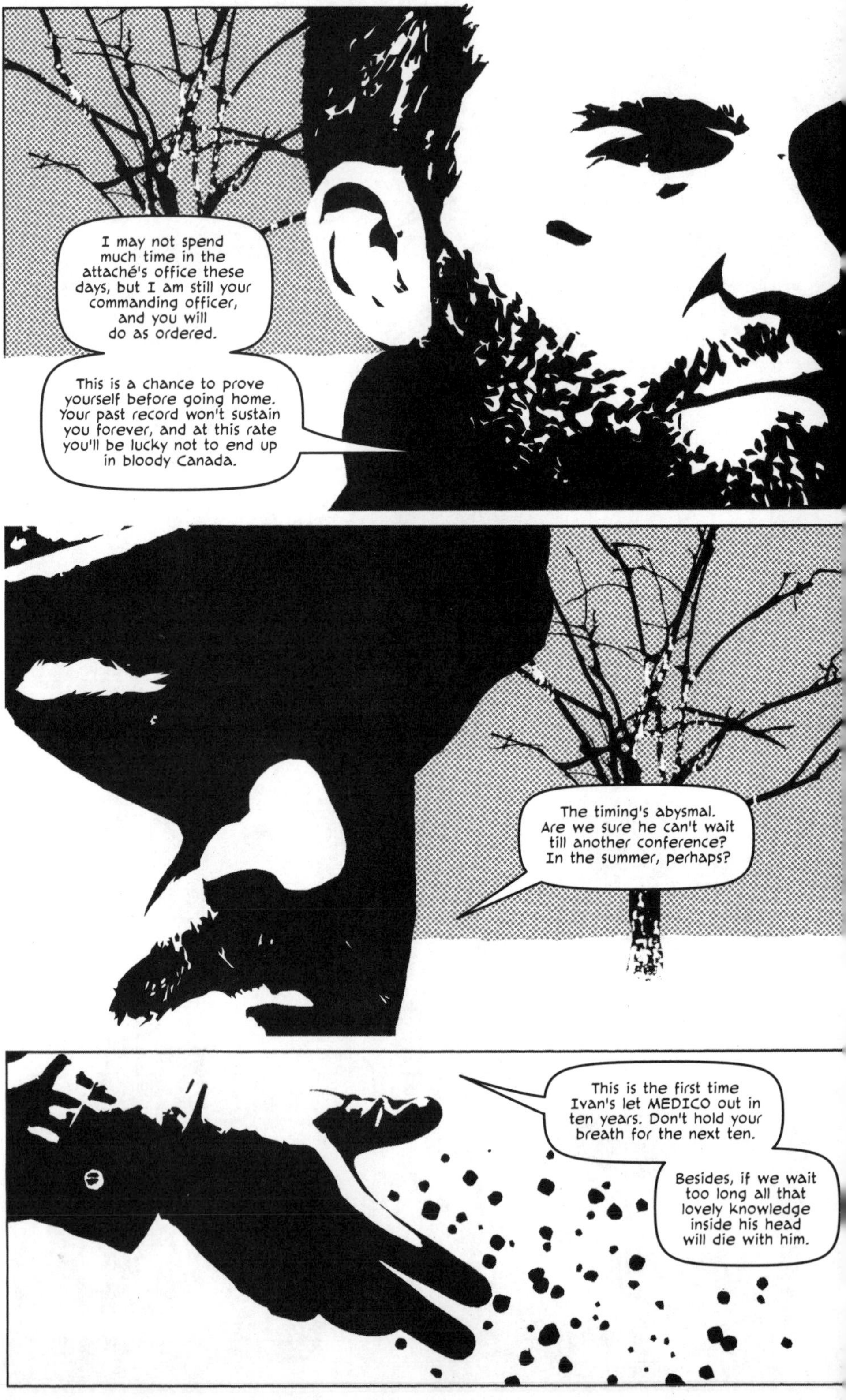
I may not spend much time in the attaché's office these days, but I am still your commanding officer, and you will do as ordered.
This is a chance to prove yourself before going home. Your past record won't sustain you forever, and at this rate you'll be lucky not to end up in bloody Canada.
The timing's abysmal. Are we sure he can't wait till another conference? In the summer, perhaps?
This is the first time Ivan's let MEDICO out in ten years. Don't hold your breath for the next ten.
Besides, if we wait too long all that lovely knowledge inside his head will die with him.

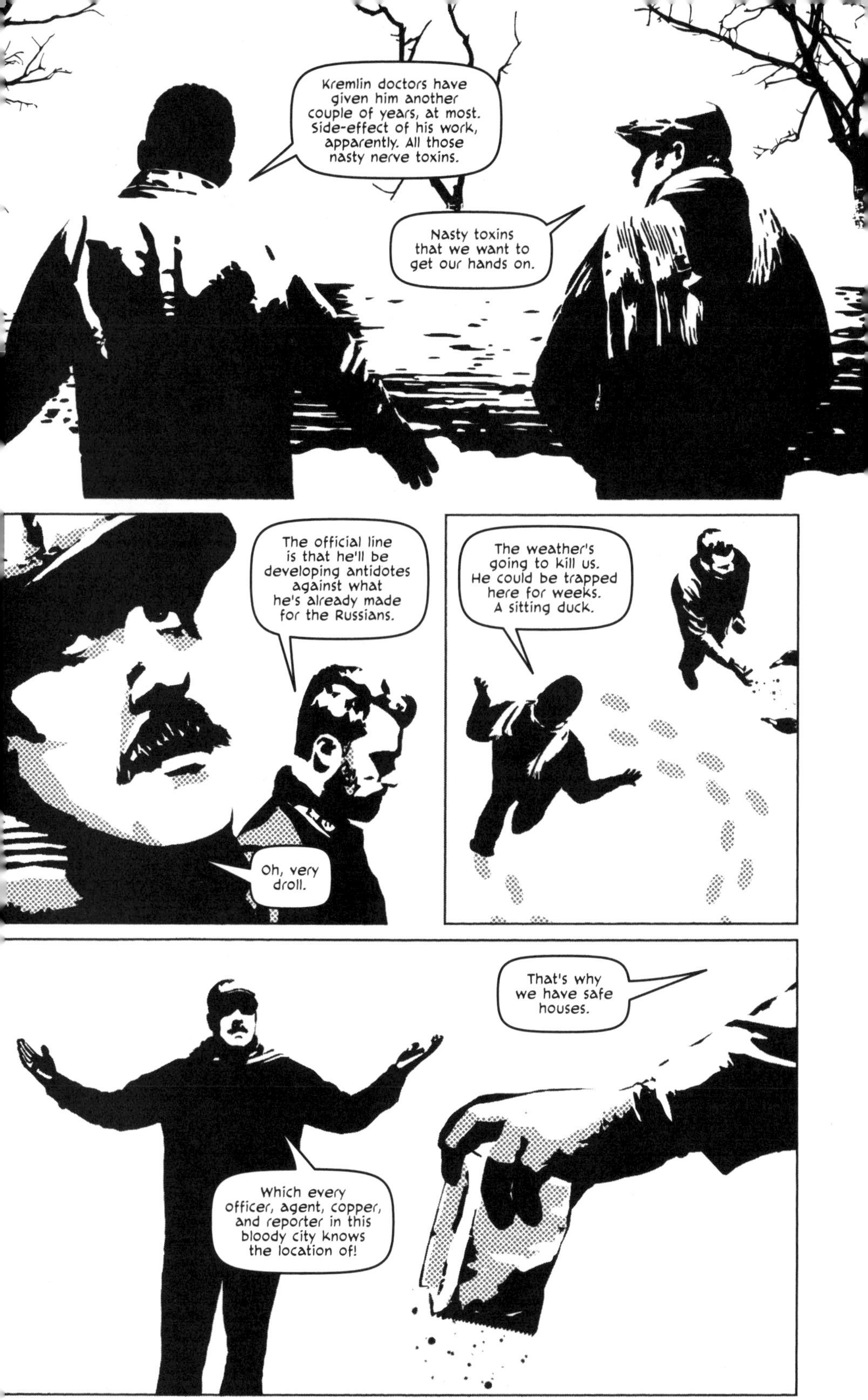
Kremlin doctors have given him another couple of years, at most. Side-effect of his work, apparently. All those nasty nerve toxins.
Nasty toxins that we want to get our hands on.
The official line is that he'll be developing antidotes against what he's already made for the Russians.
Oh, very droll.
The weather's going to kill us. He could be trapped here for weeks. A sitting duck.
That's why we have safe houses.
Which every officer, agent, copper, and reporter in this bloody city knows the location of!

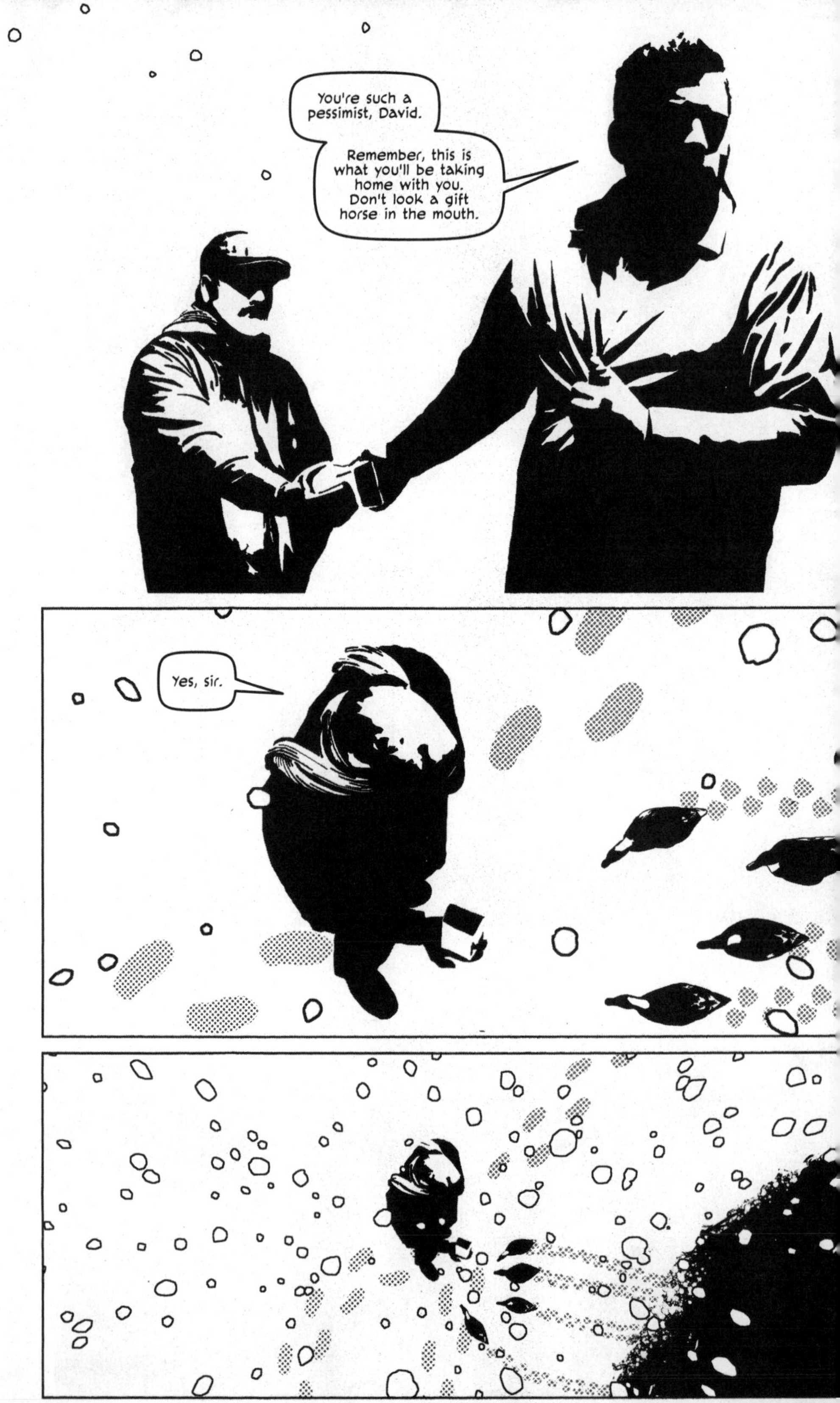
You're such a pessimist, David.
Remember, this is what you'll be taking home with you. Don't look a gift horse in the mouth.
Yes, sir.

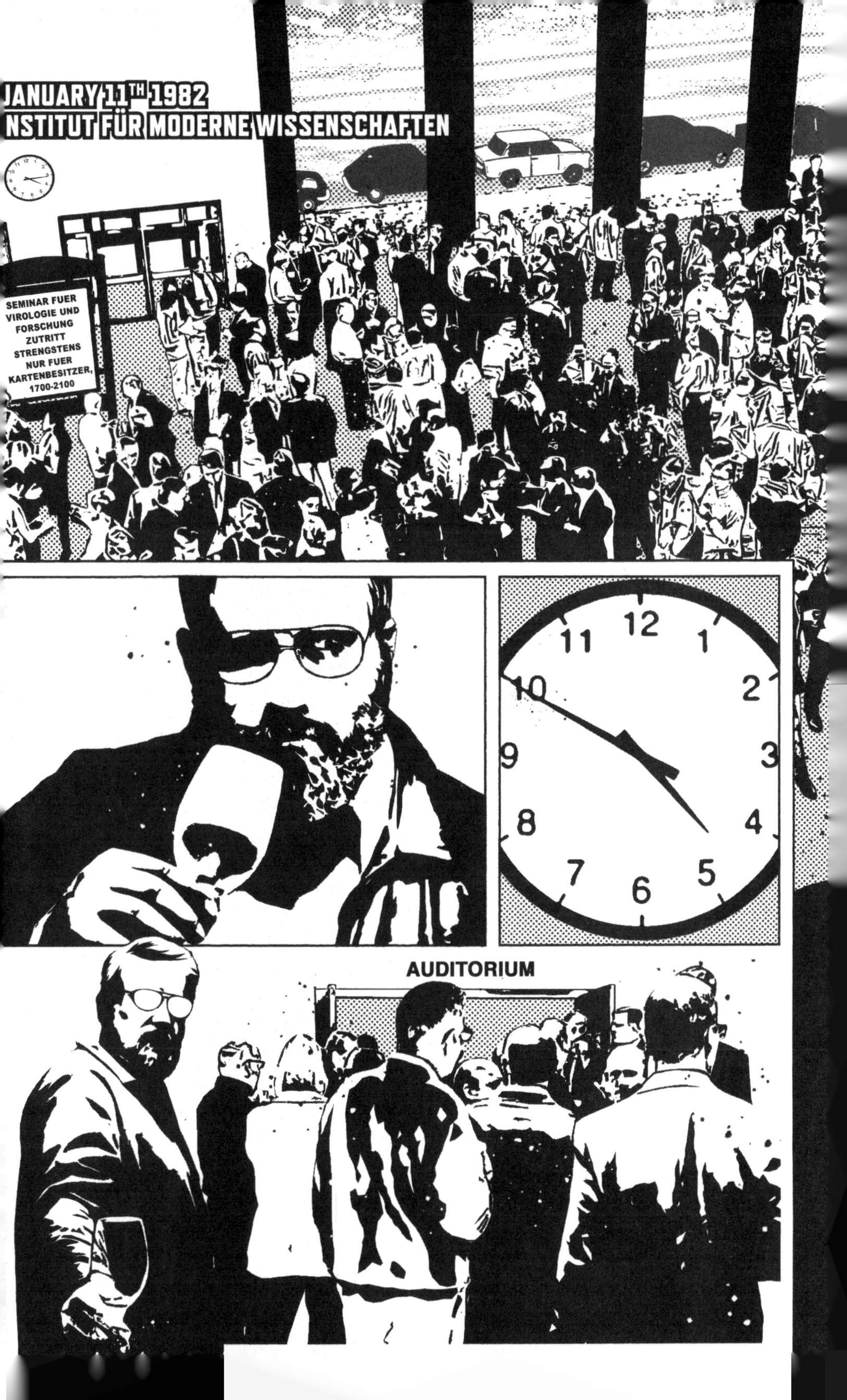
JANUARY 11TH 1982
NSTITUT FÜR MODERNE WISSENSCHAFTEN
SEMINAR FUER VIROLOGIE UND FORSCHUNG ZUTRITT STRENGSTENS NUR FUER KARTENBESITZER, 1700-2100
AUDITORIUM

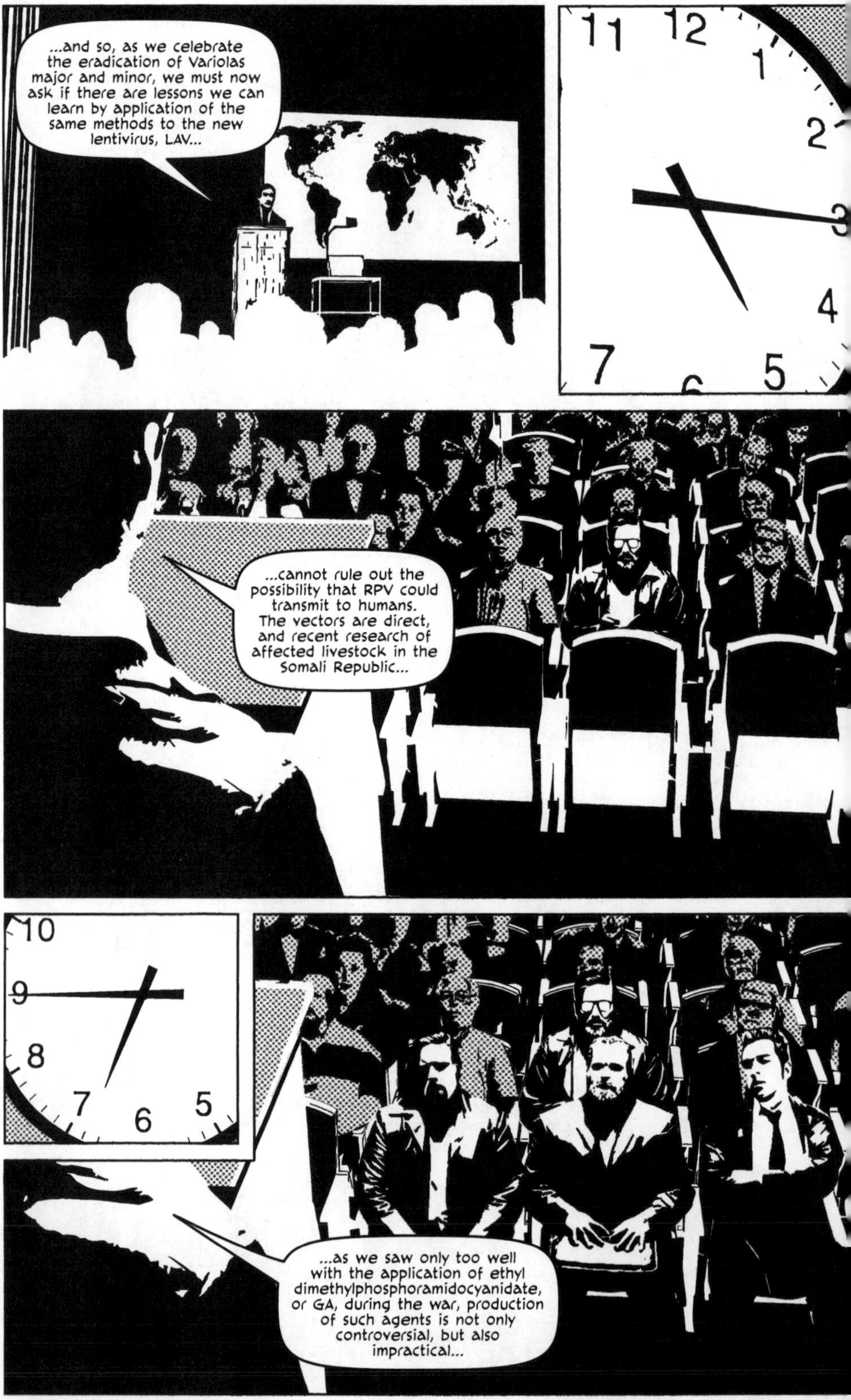
...and so, as we celebrate the eradication of Variolas major and minor, we must now ask if there are lessons we can learn by application of the same methods to the new lentivirus, LAV...
11 12 1 2 3 4 5 7
...cannot rule out the possibility that RPV could transmit to humans. The vectors are direct, and recent research of affected livestock in the Somali Republic...
10 9 8 7 6 5
...as we saw only too well with the application of ethyl dimethylphosphoramidocyanidate, or GA, during the war, production of such agents is not only controversial, but also impractical...

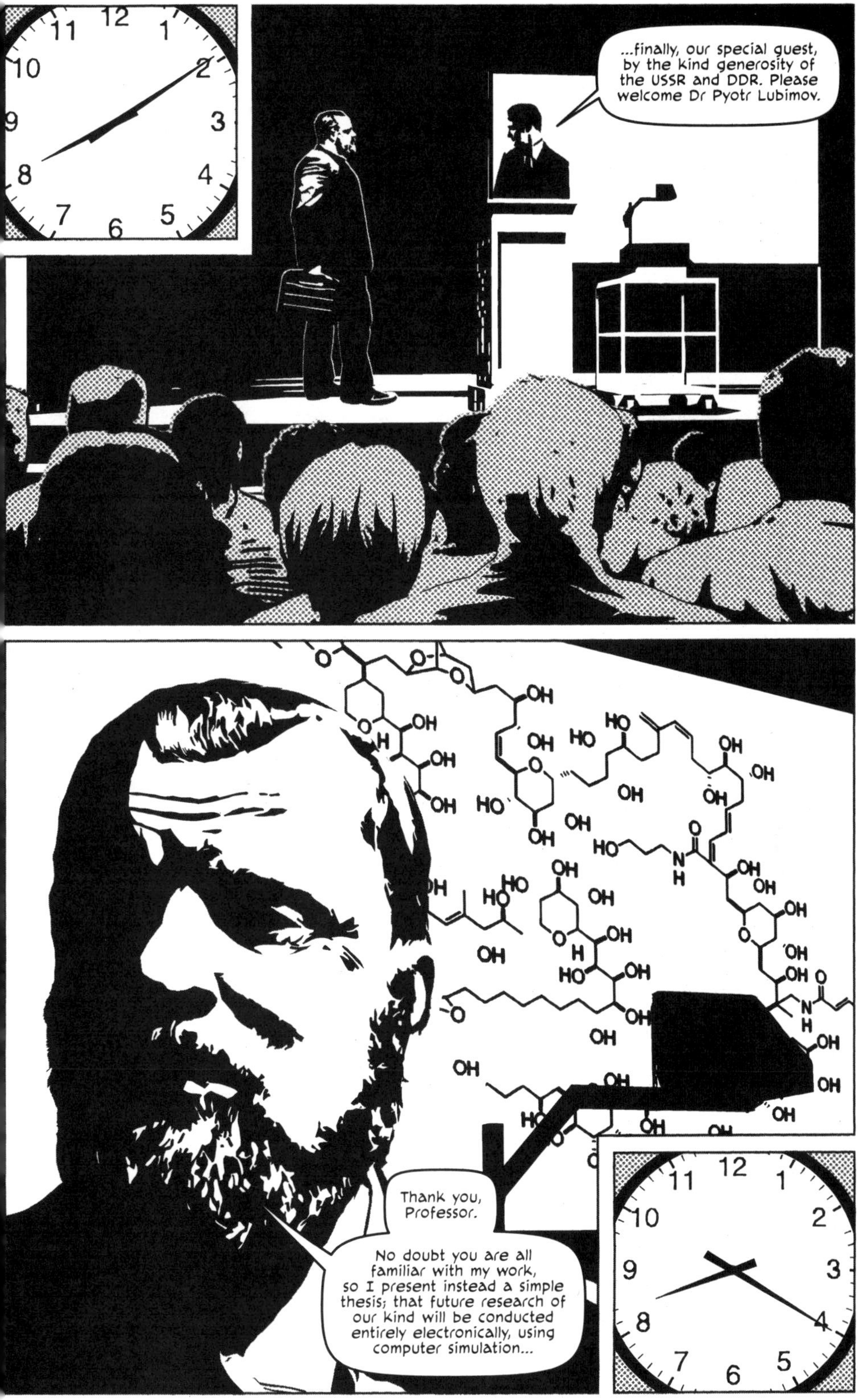
...finally, our special guest, by the kind generosity of the USSR and DDR. Please welcome Dr Pyotr Lubimov.
Thank you, Professor.
No doubt you are all familiar with my work, so I present instead a simple thesis; that future research of our kind will be conducted entirely electronically, using computer simulation...

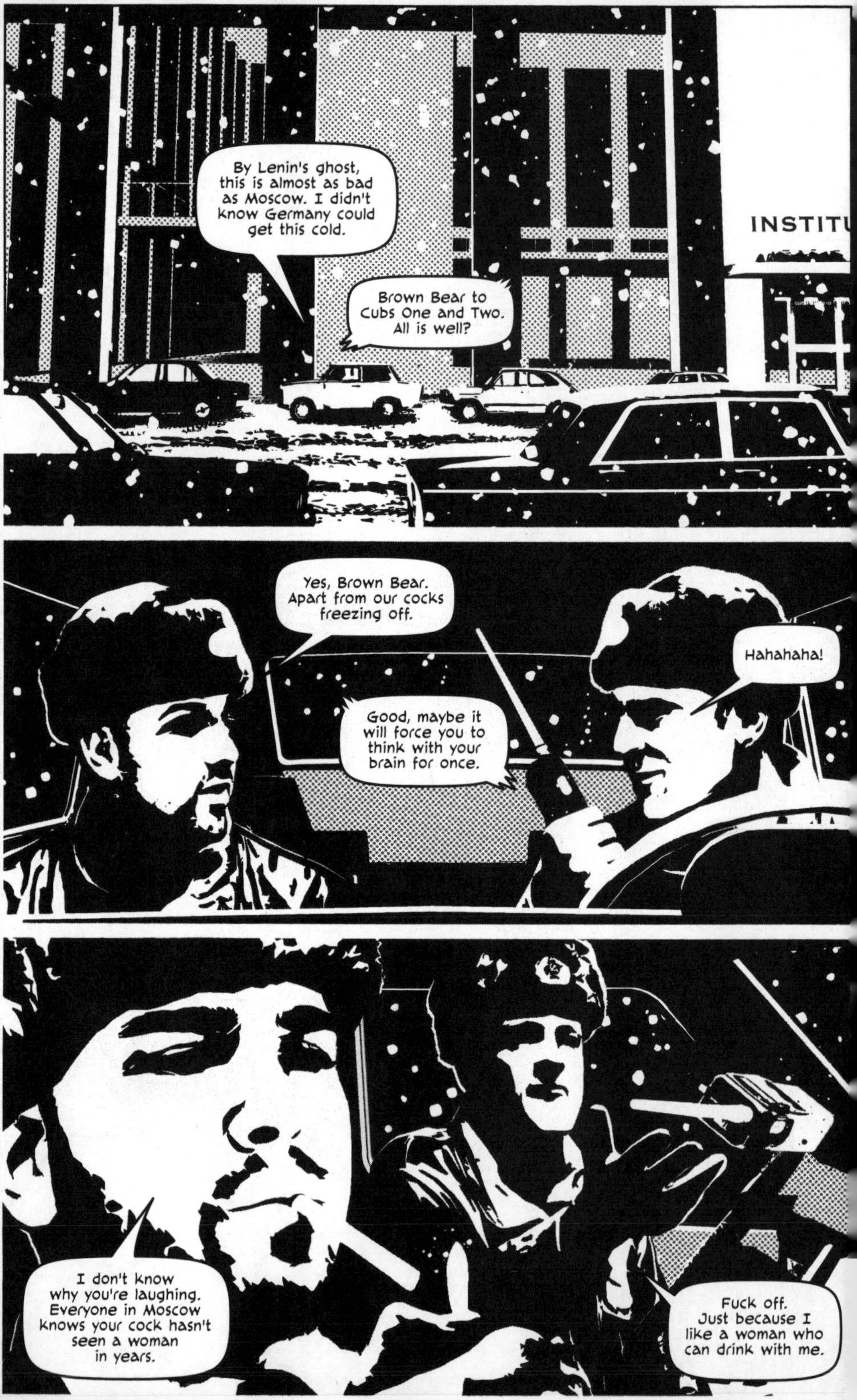
INSTITU
By Lenin's ghost, this is almost as bad as Moscow. I didn't know Germany could get this cold.
Brown Bear to Cubs One and Two. All is well?
Yes, Brown Bear. Apart from our cocks freezing off.
Hahahaha!
Good, maybe it will force you to think with your brain for once.
I don't know why you're laughing. Everyone in Moscow knows your cock hasn't seen a woman in years.
Fuck off. Just because I like a woman who can drink with me.

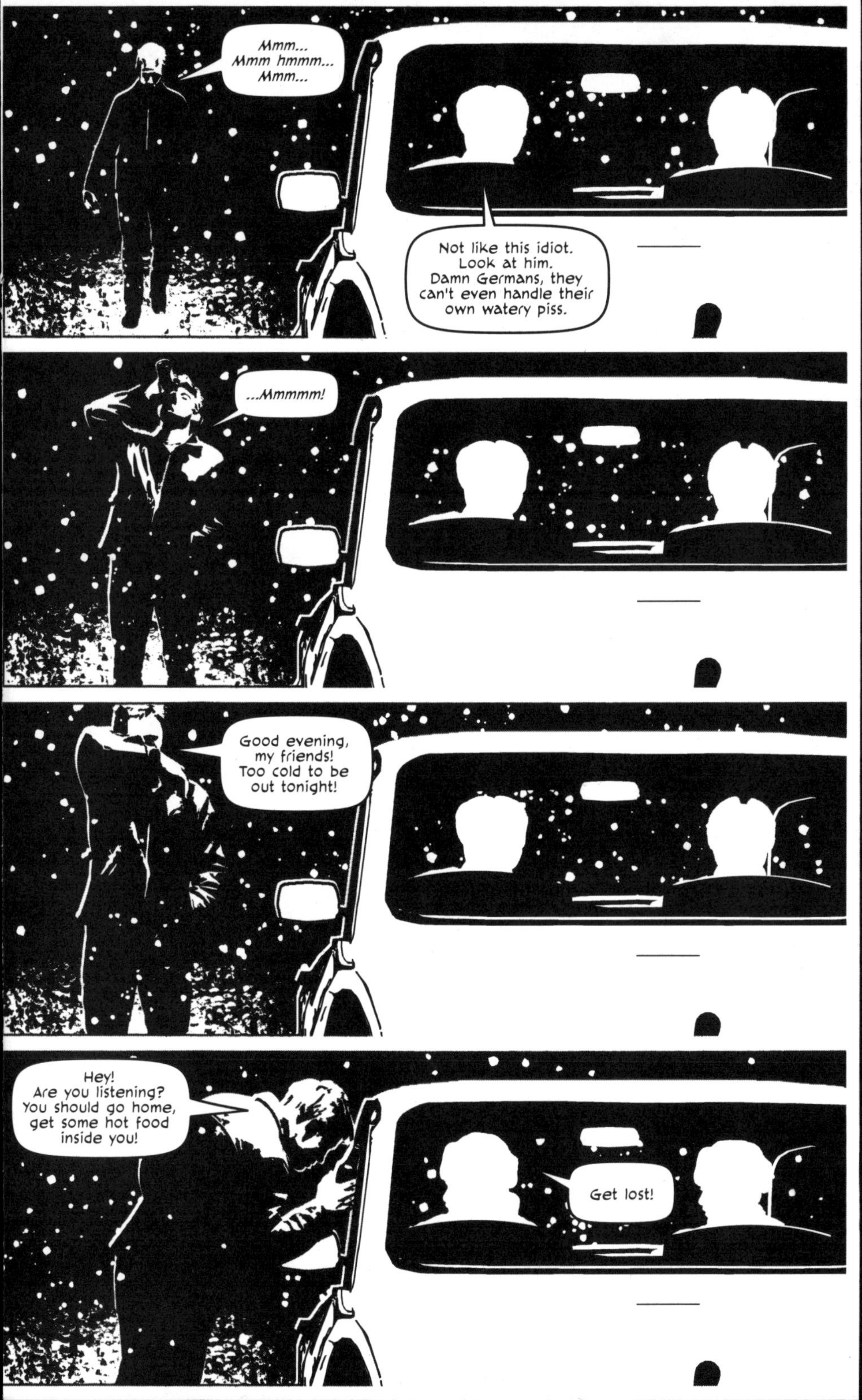
Mmm... Mmm hmmm... Mmm...
Not like this idiot. Look at him. Damn Germans, they can't even handle their own watery piss.
...Mmmmm!
Good evening, my friends! Too cold to be out tonight!
Hey! Are you listening? You should go home, get some hot food inside you!
Get lost!

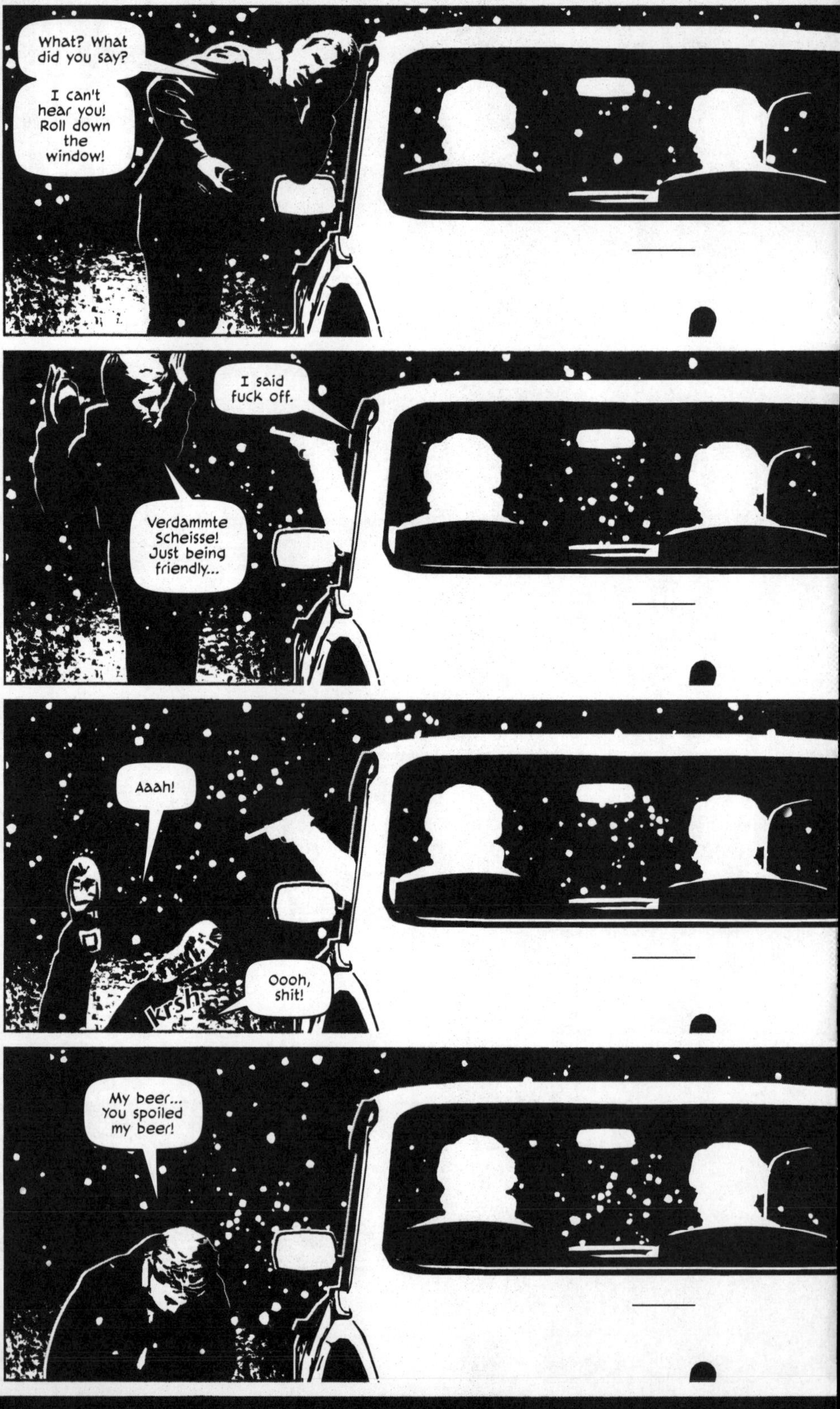
What? What did you say?
I can't hear you! Roll down the window!
I said fuck off.
Verdammte Scheisse! Just being friendly...
Aaah!
krsh
Oooh, shit!
My beer... You spoiled my beer!

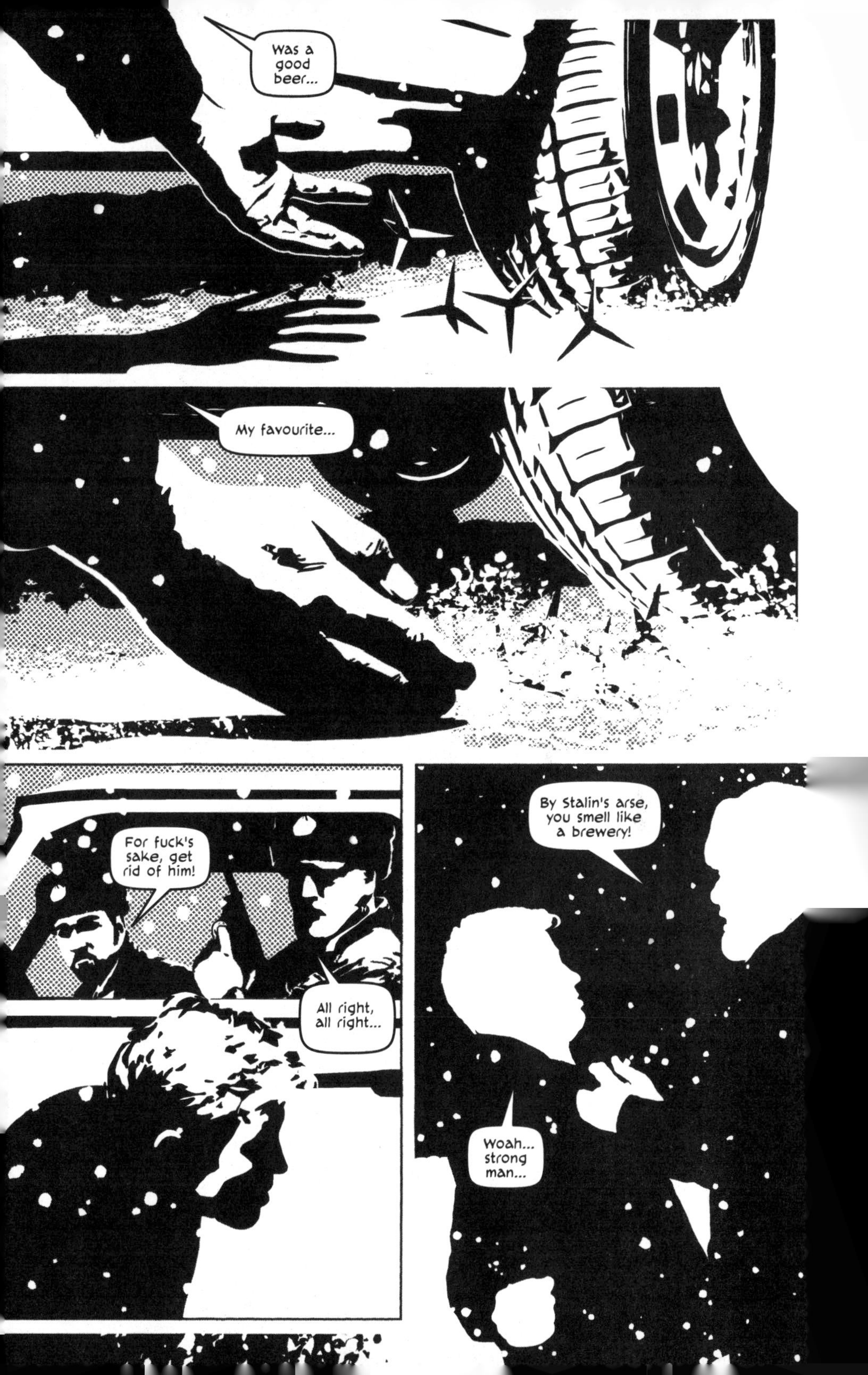
Was a good beer...
My favourite...
For fuck's sake, get rid of him!
All right, all right...
By Stalin's arse, you smell like a brewery!
Woah... strong man...

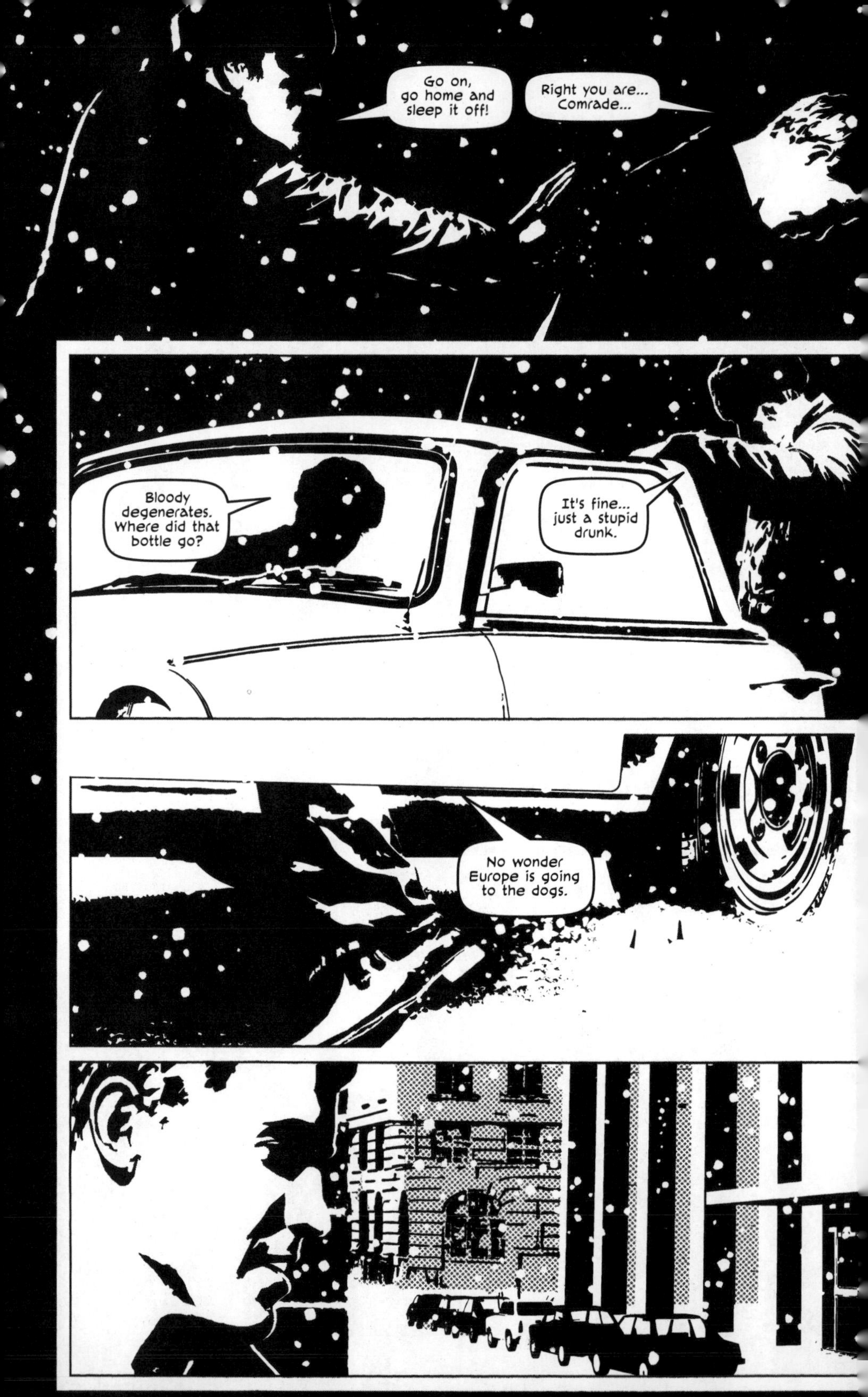

Go on, go home and sleep it off!
Right you are... Comrade...
Bloody degenerates. Where did that bottle go?
It's fine... just a stupid drunk.
No wonder Europe is going to the dogs.

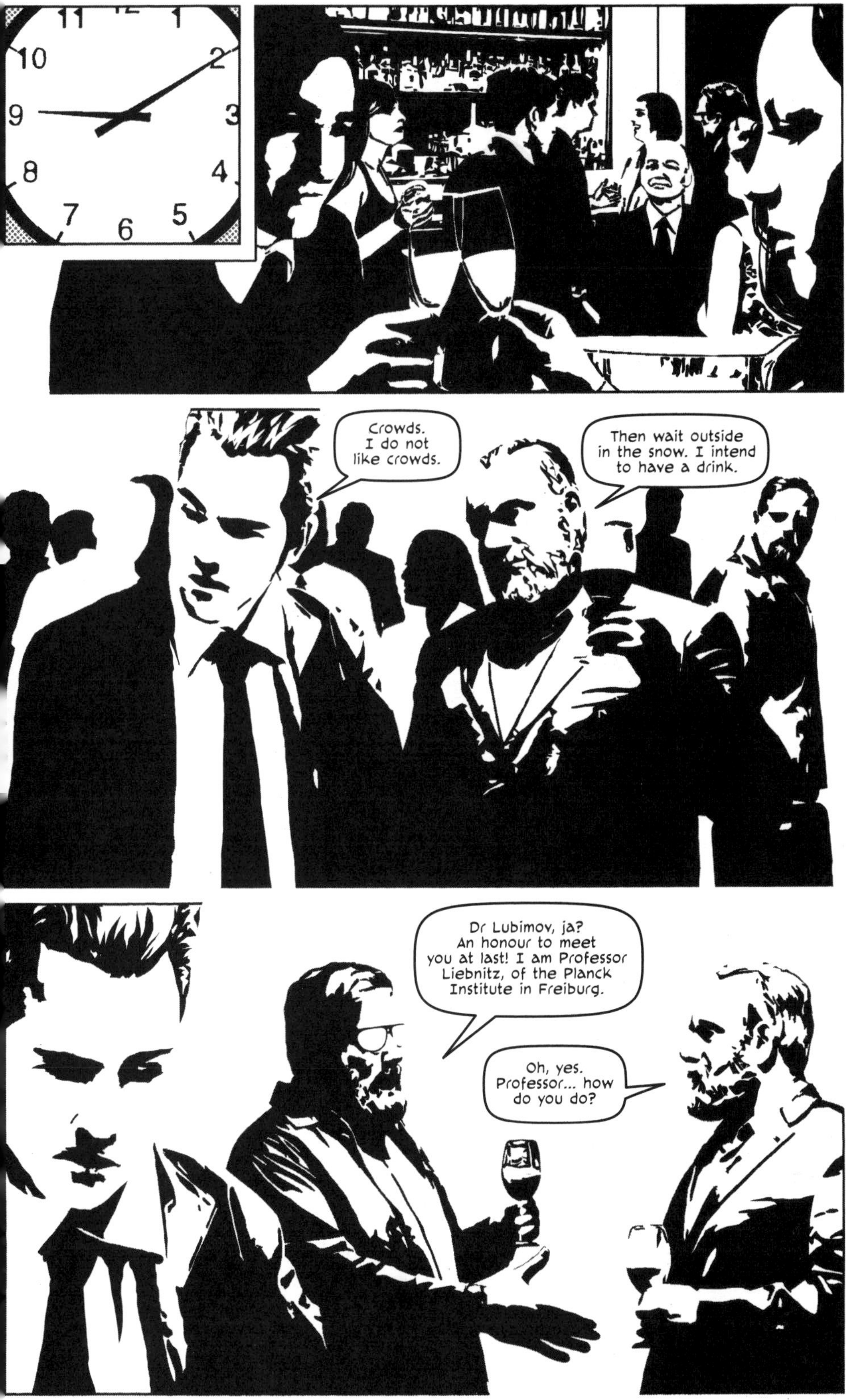

Crowds. I do not like crowds.
Then wait outside in the snow. I intend to have a drink.
Dr Lubimov, ja? An honour to meet you at last! I am Professor Liebnitz, of the Planck Institute in Freiburg.
Oh, yes. Professor... how do you do?

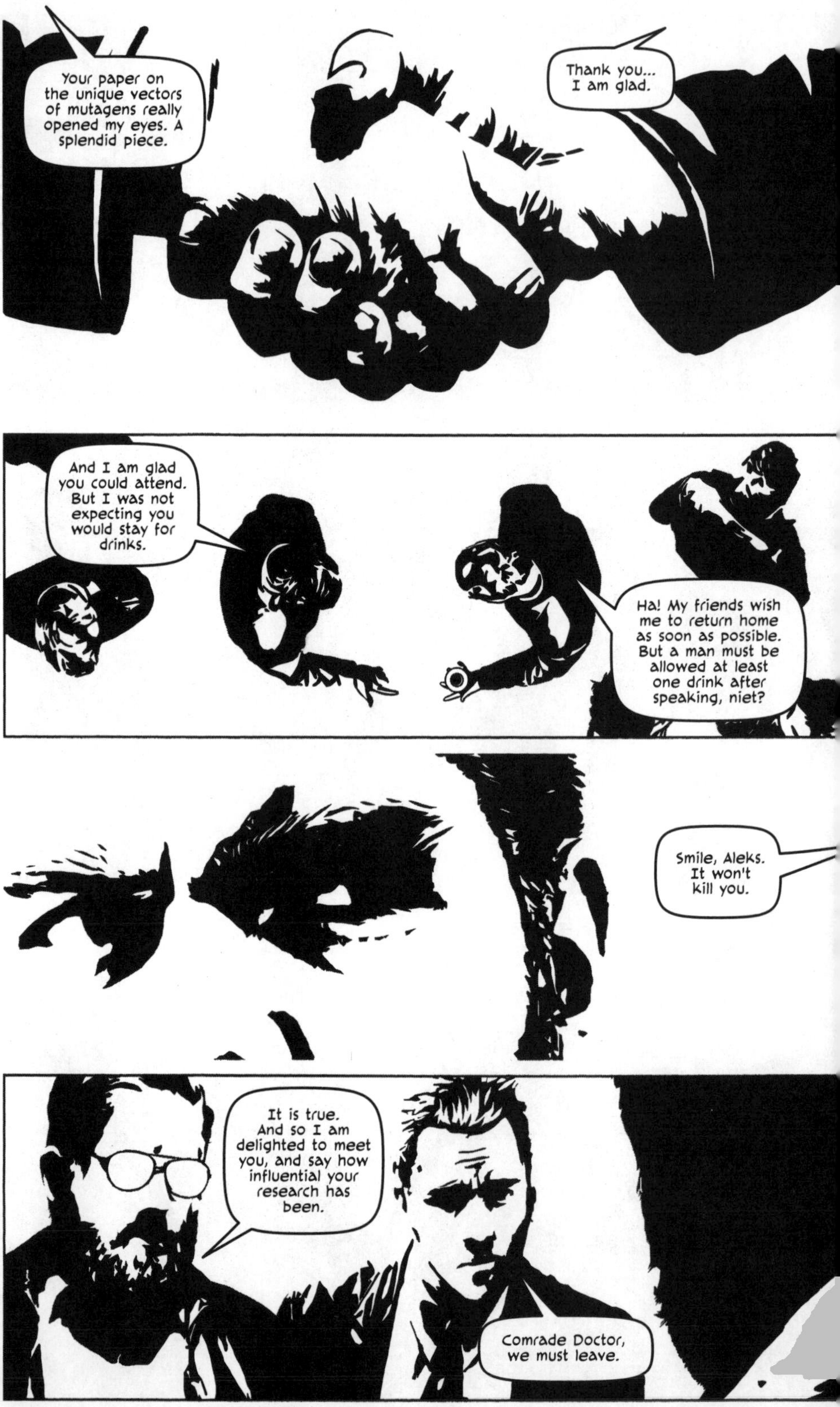
Your paper on the unique vectors of mutagens really opened my eyes. A splendid piece.
Thank you... I am glad.
And I am glad you could attend. But I was not expecting you would stay for drinks.
Ha! My friends wish me to return home as soon as possible. But a man must be allowed at least one drink after speaking, niet?
Smile, Aleks. It won't kill you.
It is true. And so I am delighted to meet you, and say how influential your research has been.
Comrade Doctor, we must leave.

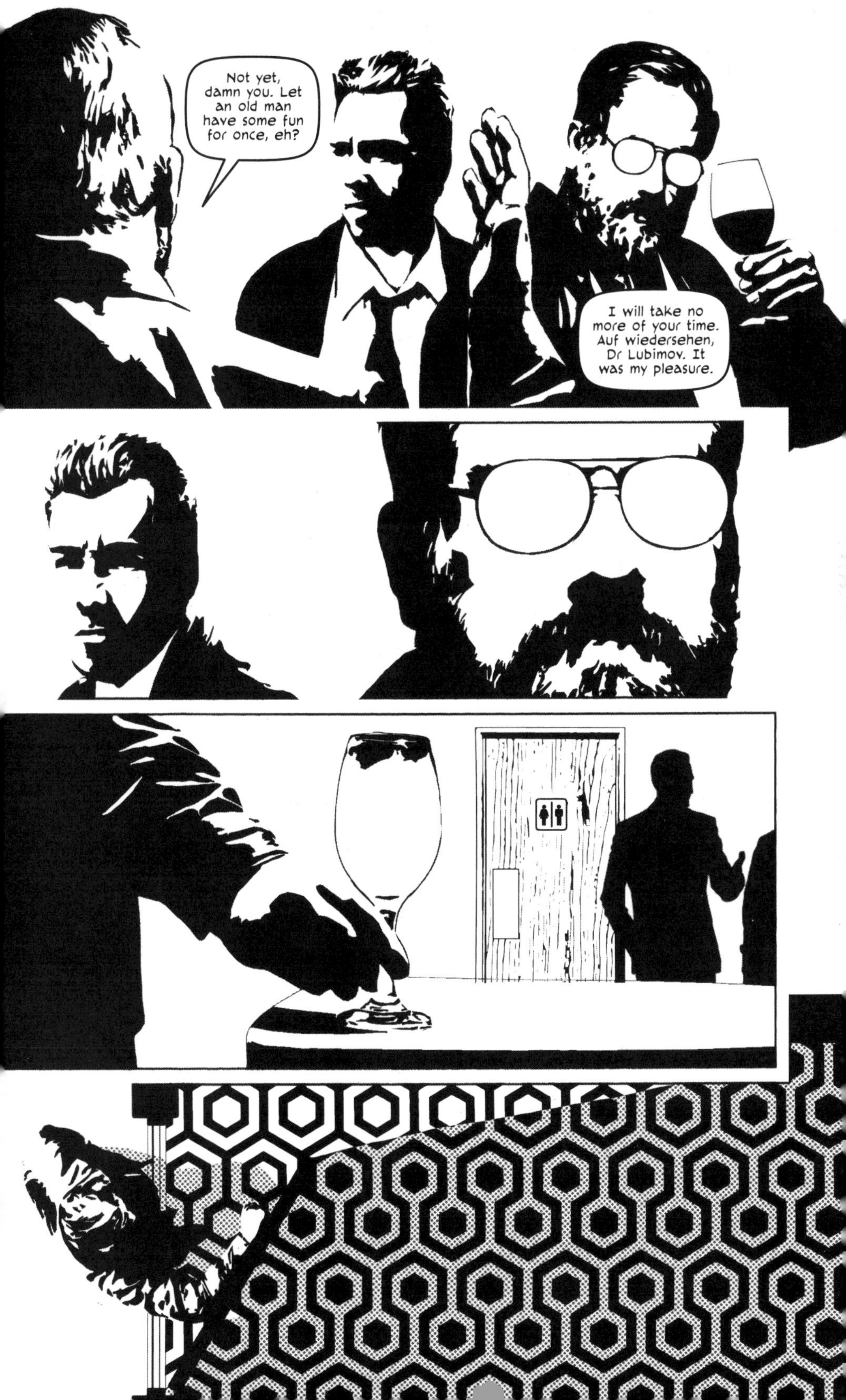

Not yet, damn you. Let an old man have some fun for once, eh?
I will take no more of your time. Auf wiedersehen, Dr Lubimov. It was my pleasure.

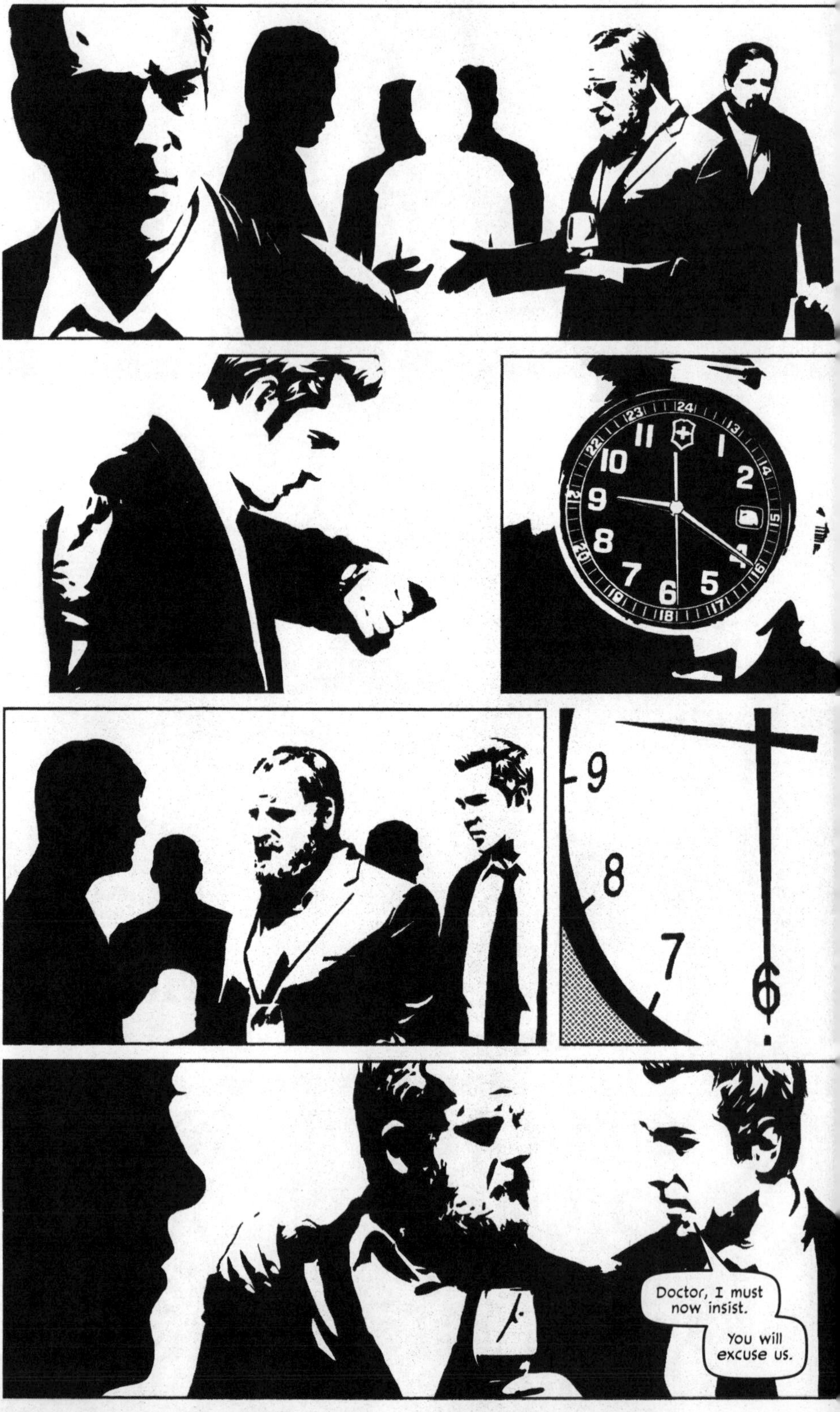

Doctor, I must now insist.
You will excuse us.

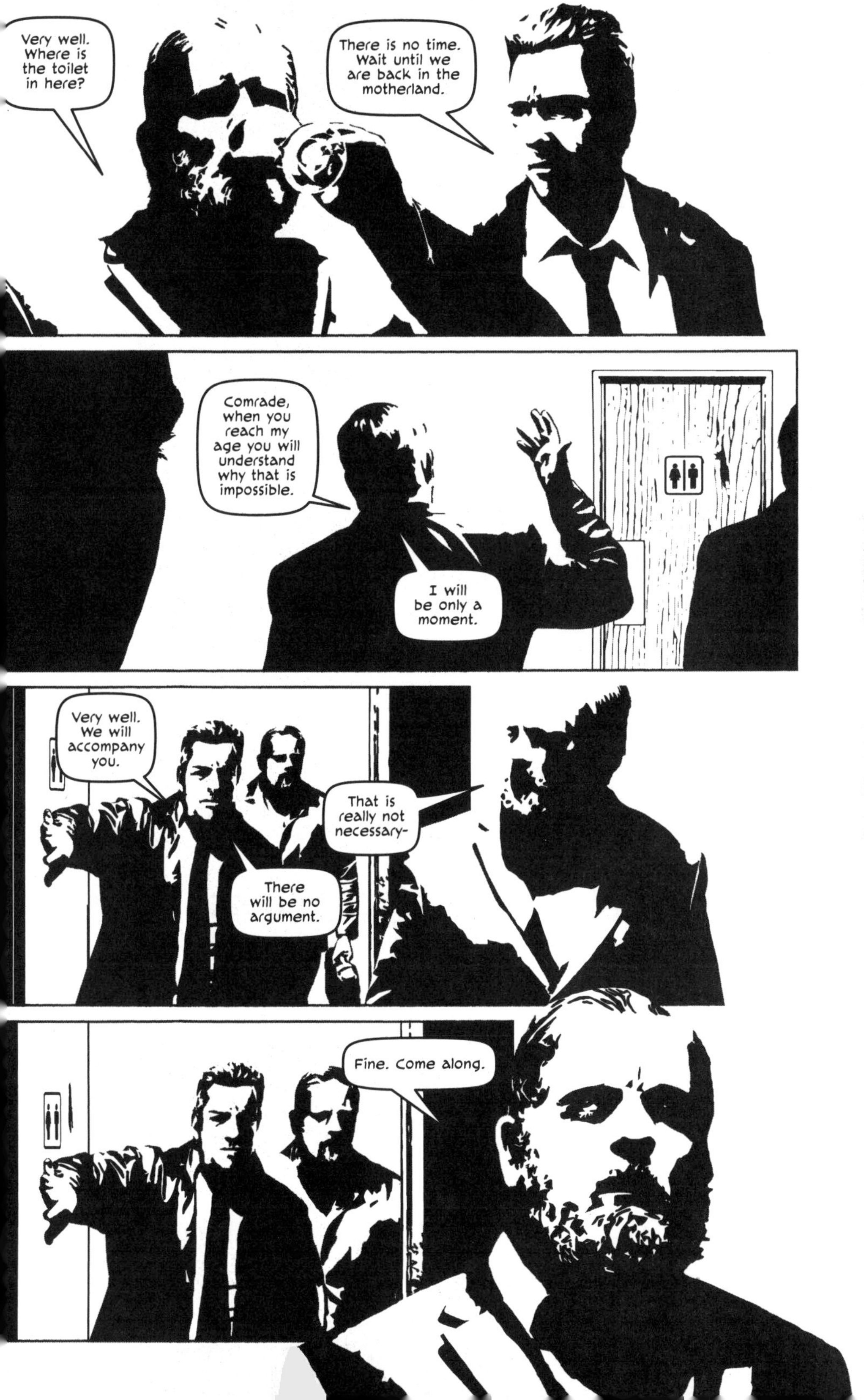
Very well. Where is the toilet in here?
There is no time. Wait until we are back in the motherland.
Comrade, when you reach my age you will understand why that is impossible.
I will be only a moment.
Very well. We will accompany you.
That is really not necessary-
There will be no argument.
Fine. Come along.

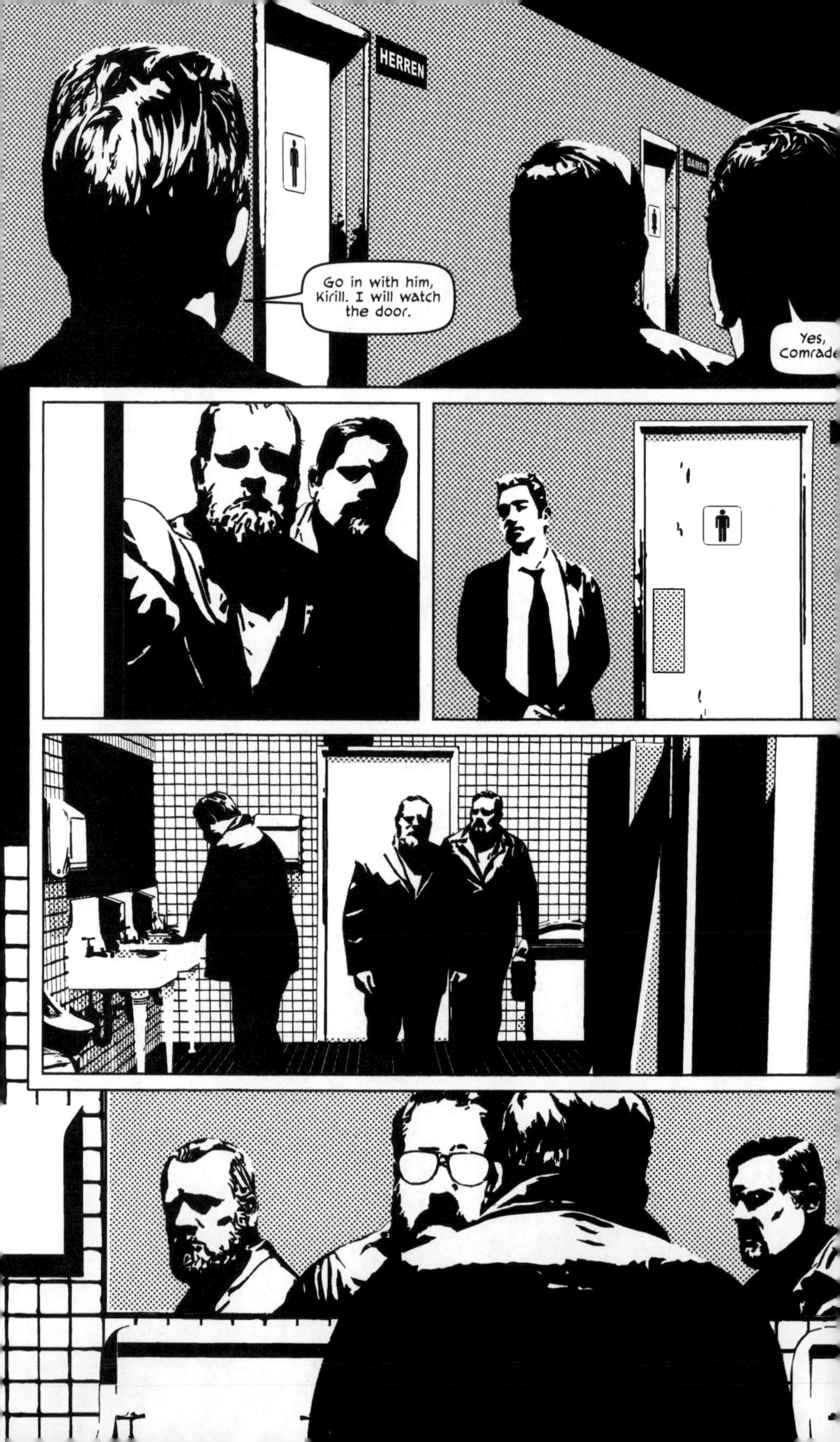
HERREN
DAMEN
Go in with him, Kirill. I will watch the door.
Yes, Comrade

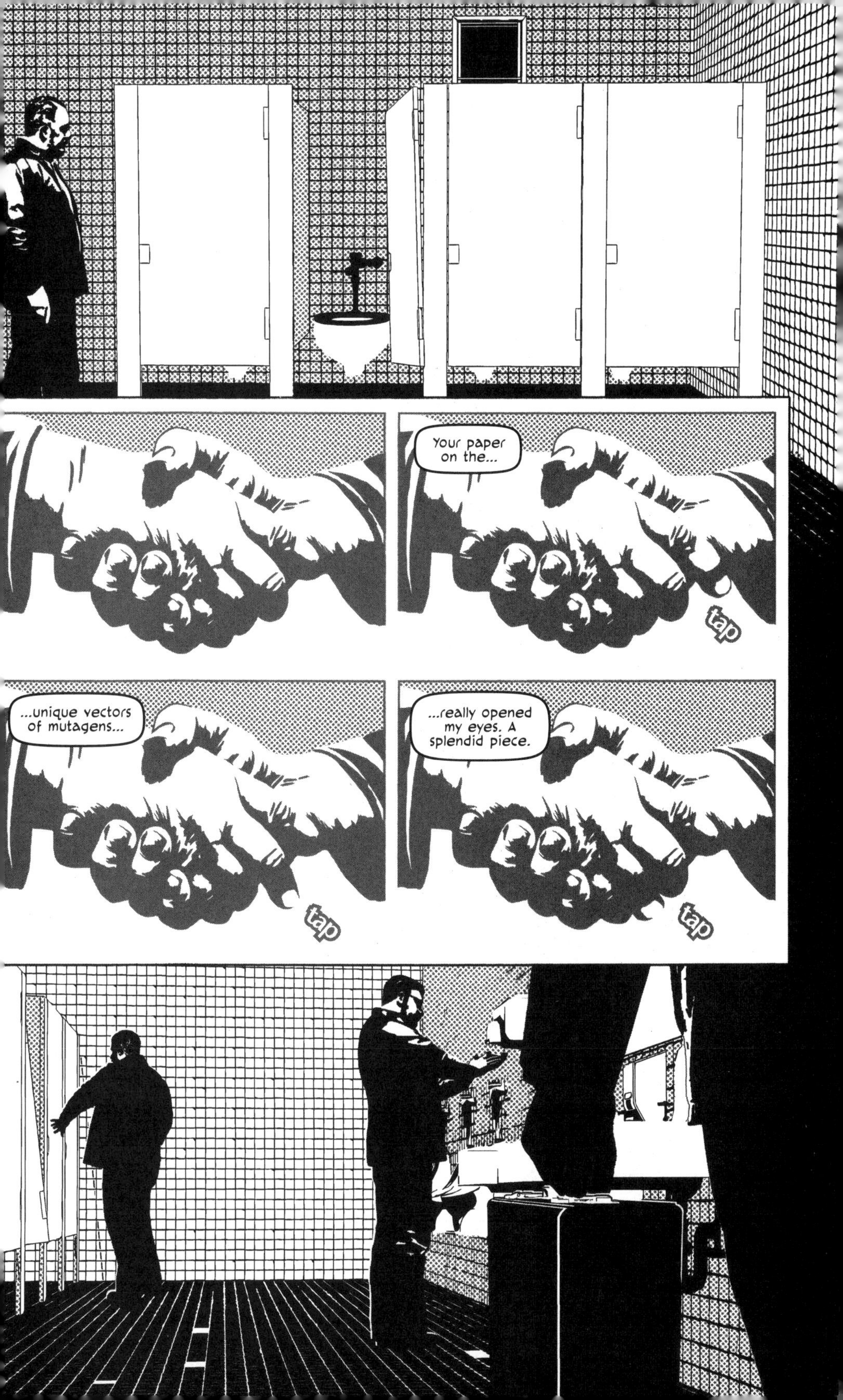
Your paper on the...
tap
...unique vectors of mutagens...
tap
...really opened my eyes. A splendid piece.
tap

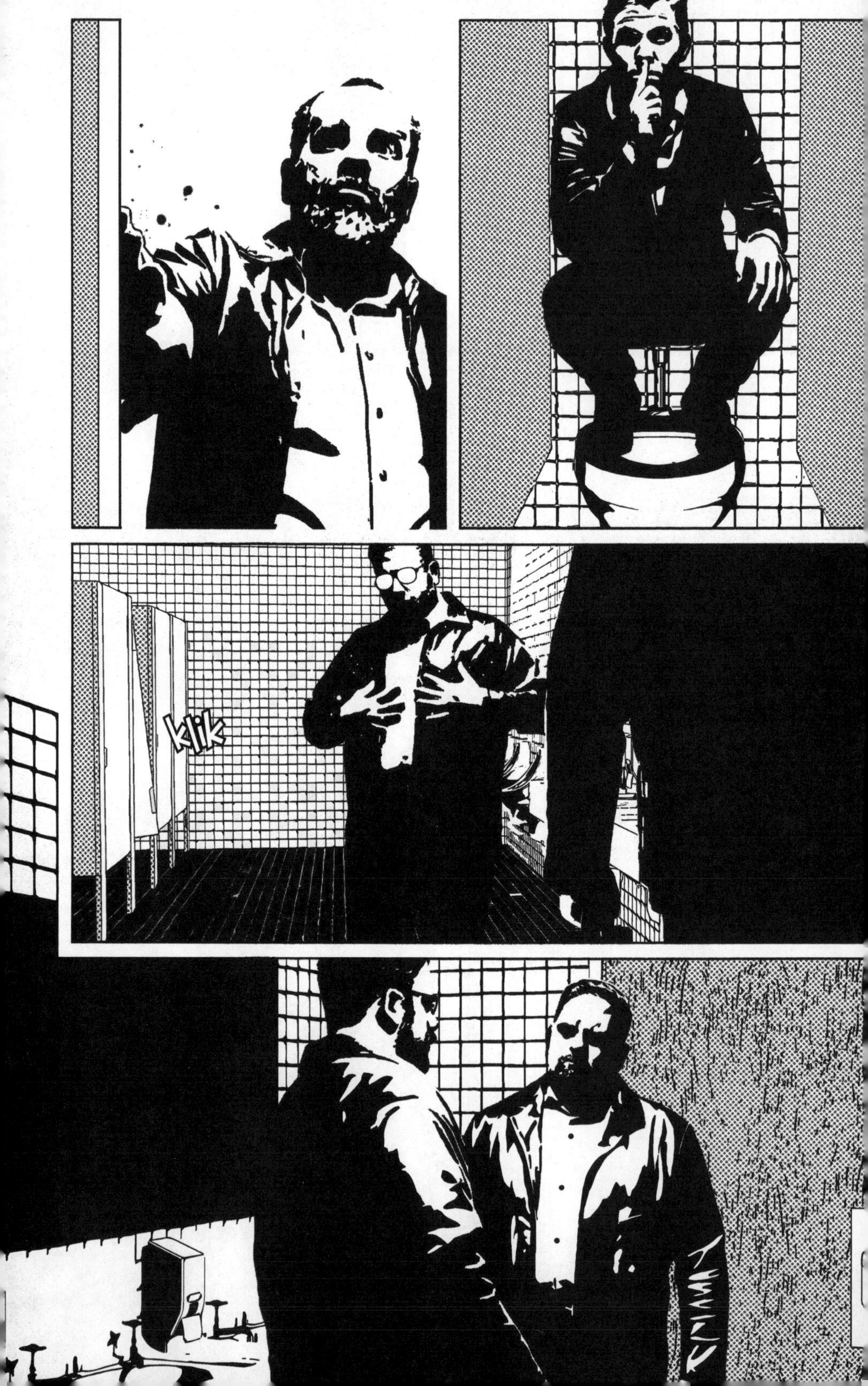
klik

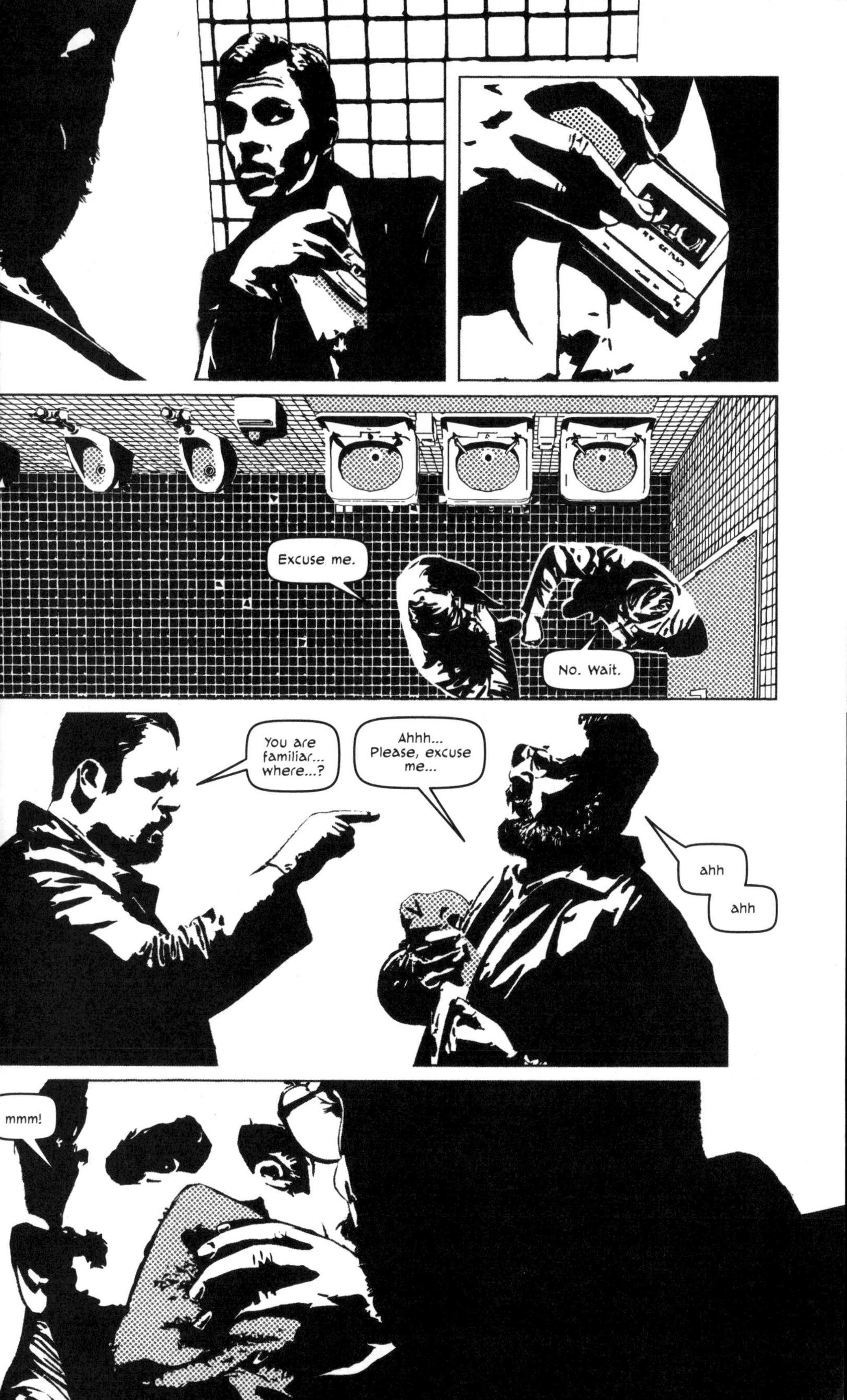
Excuse me.
No. Wait.
You are familiar... where...?
Ahhh... Please, excuse me...
ahh
ahh
mmm!

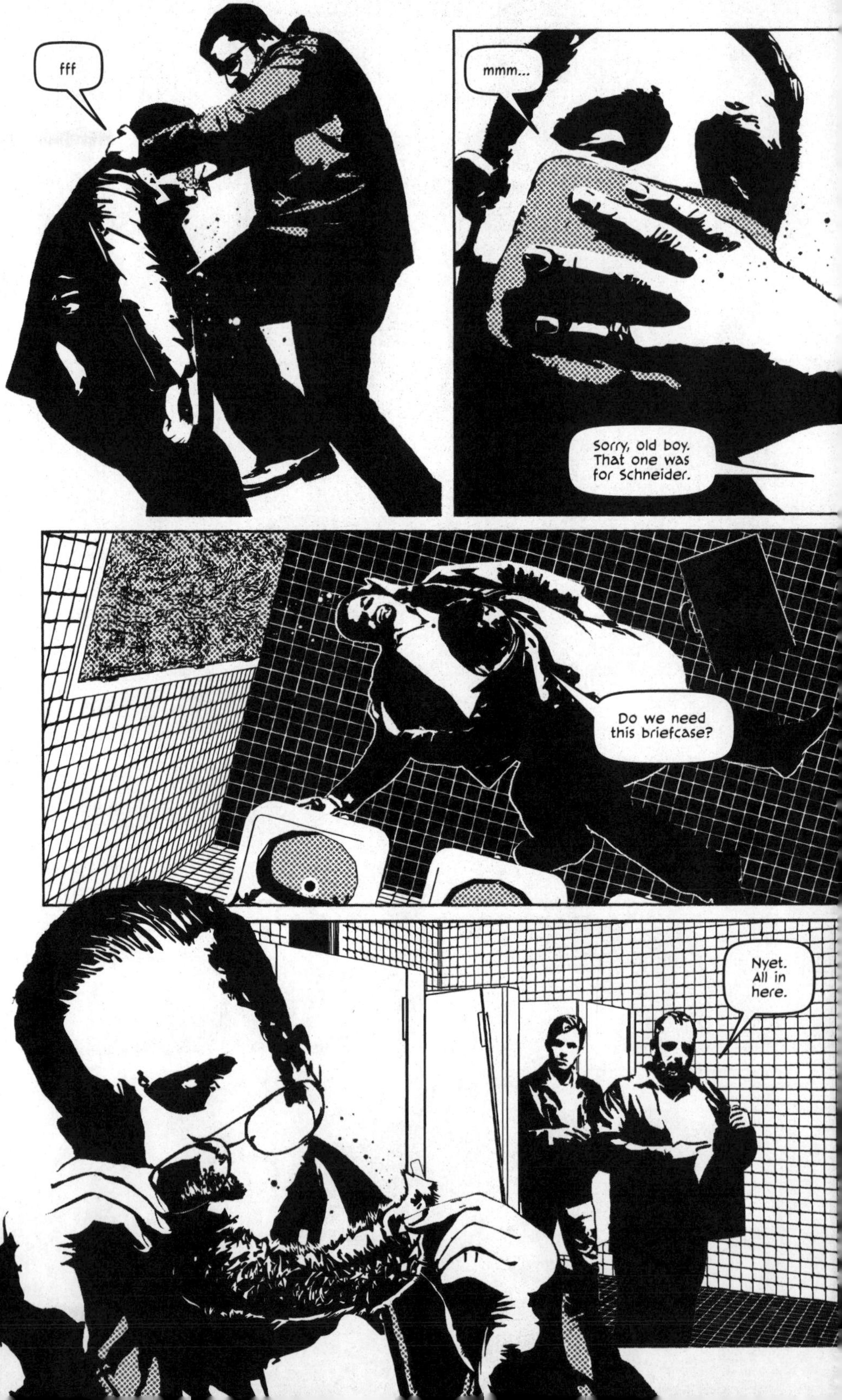
fff
mmm...
Sorry, old boy. That one was for Schneider.
Do we need this briefcase?
Nyet. All in here.

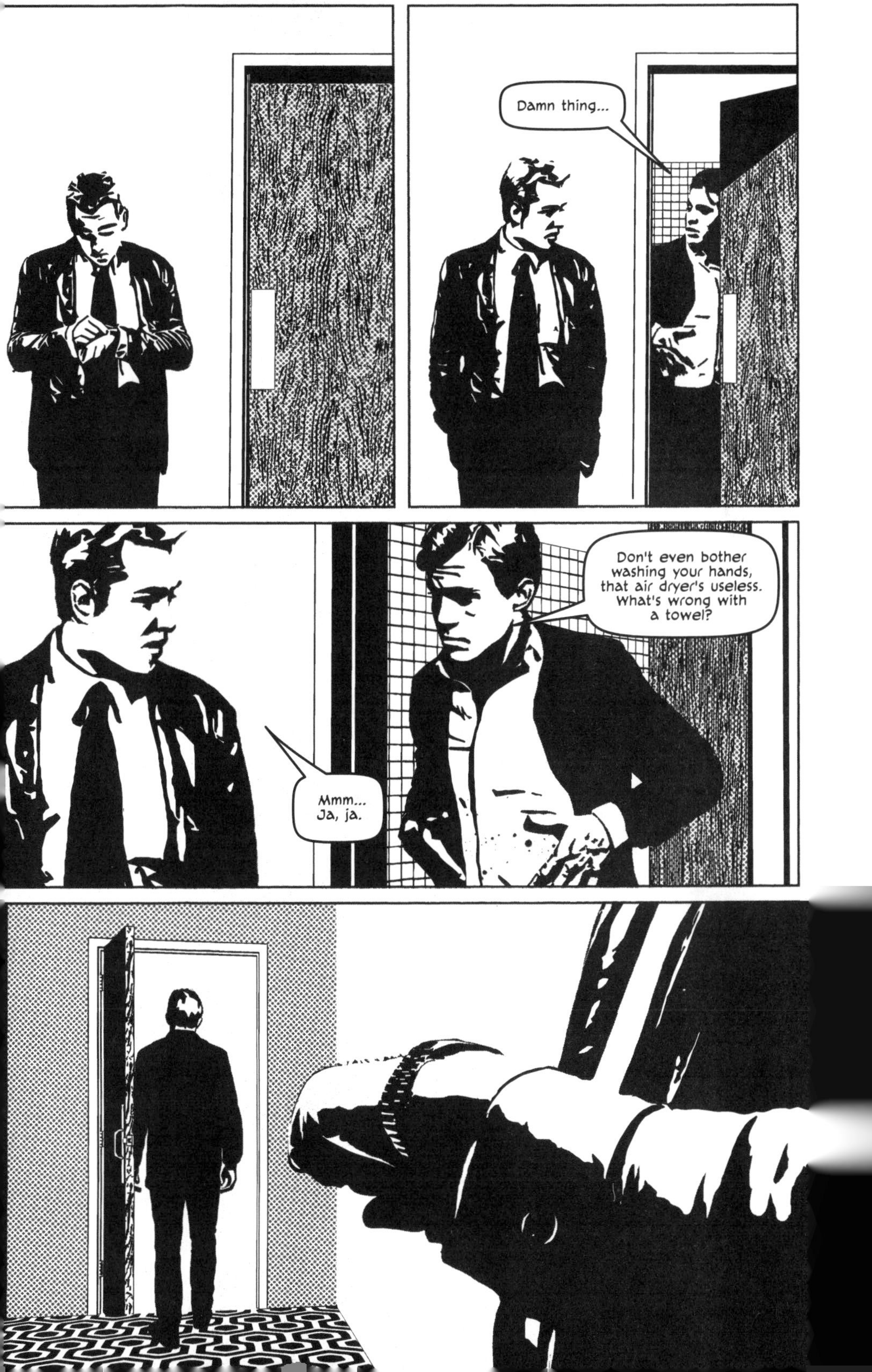
Damn thing...
Don't even bother washing your hands, that air dryer's useless. What's wrong with a towel?
Mmm... Ja, ja.

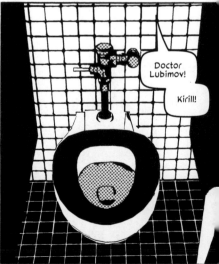

Doctor Lubimov!

Kirill!

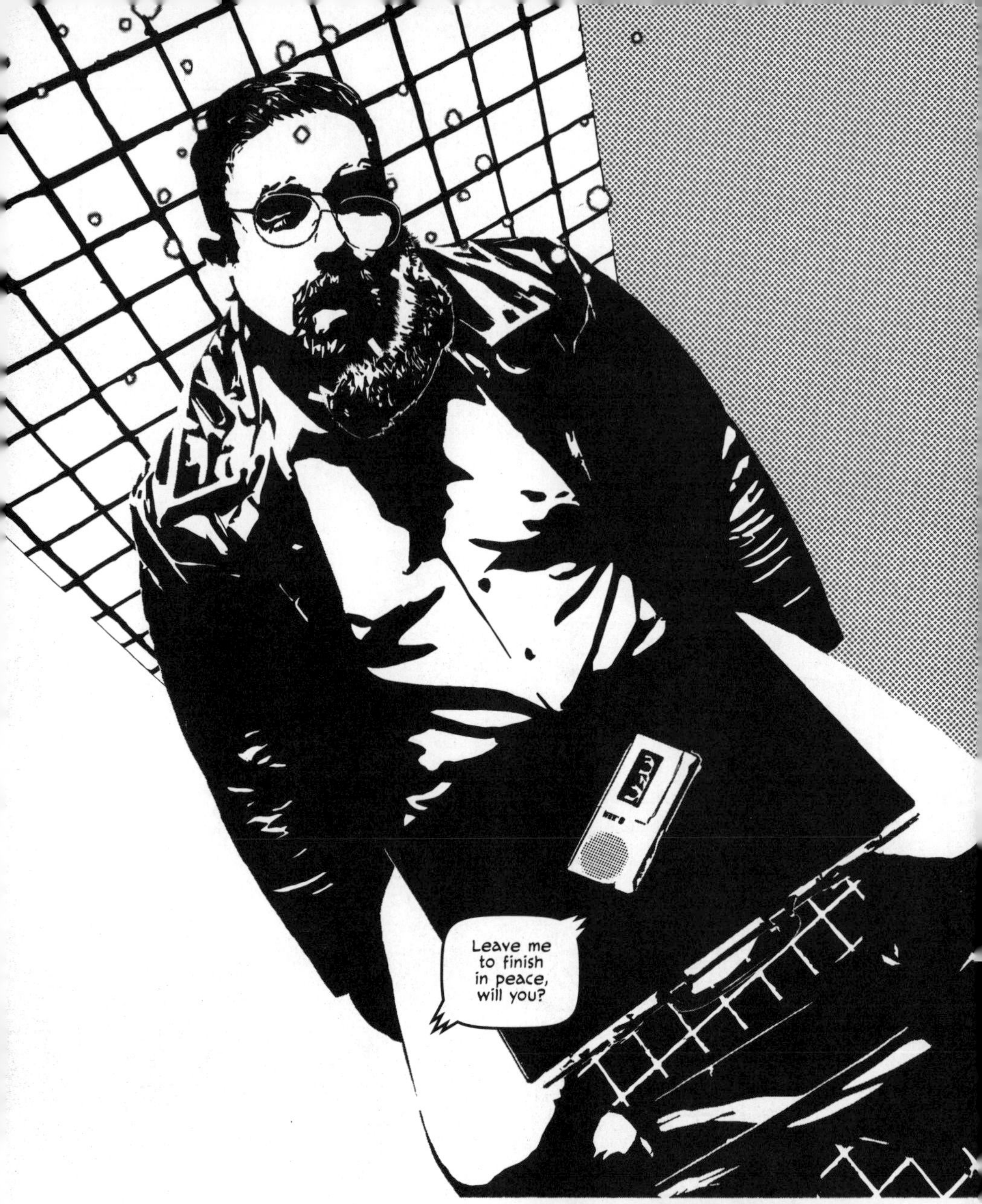
Leave me to finish in peace, will you?

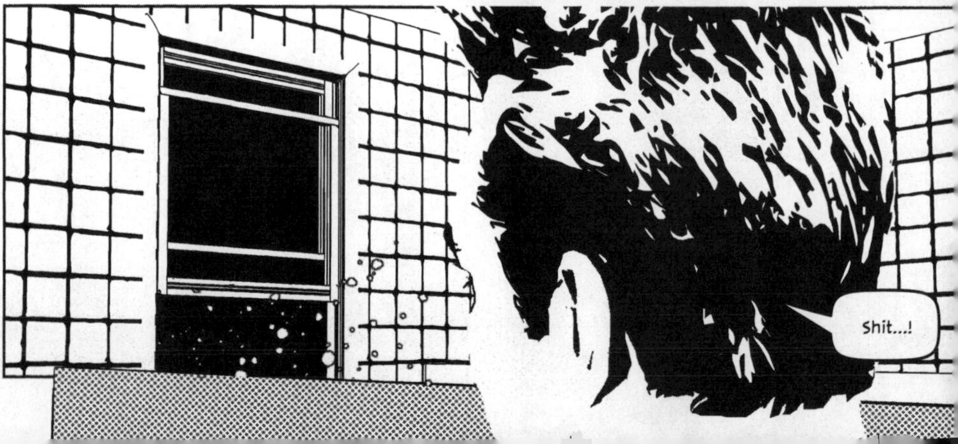
Shit...!

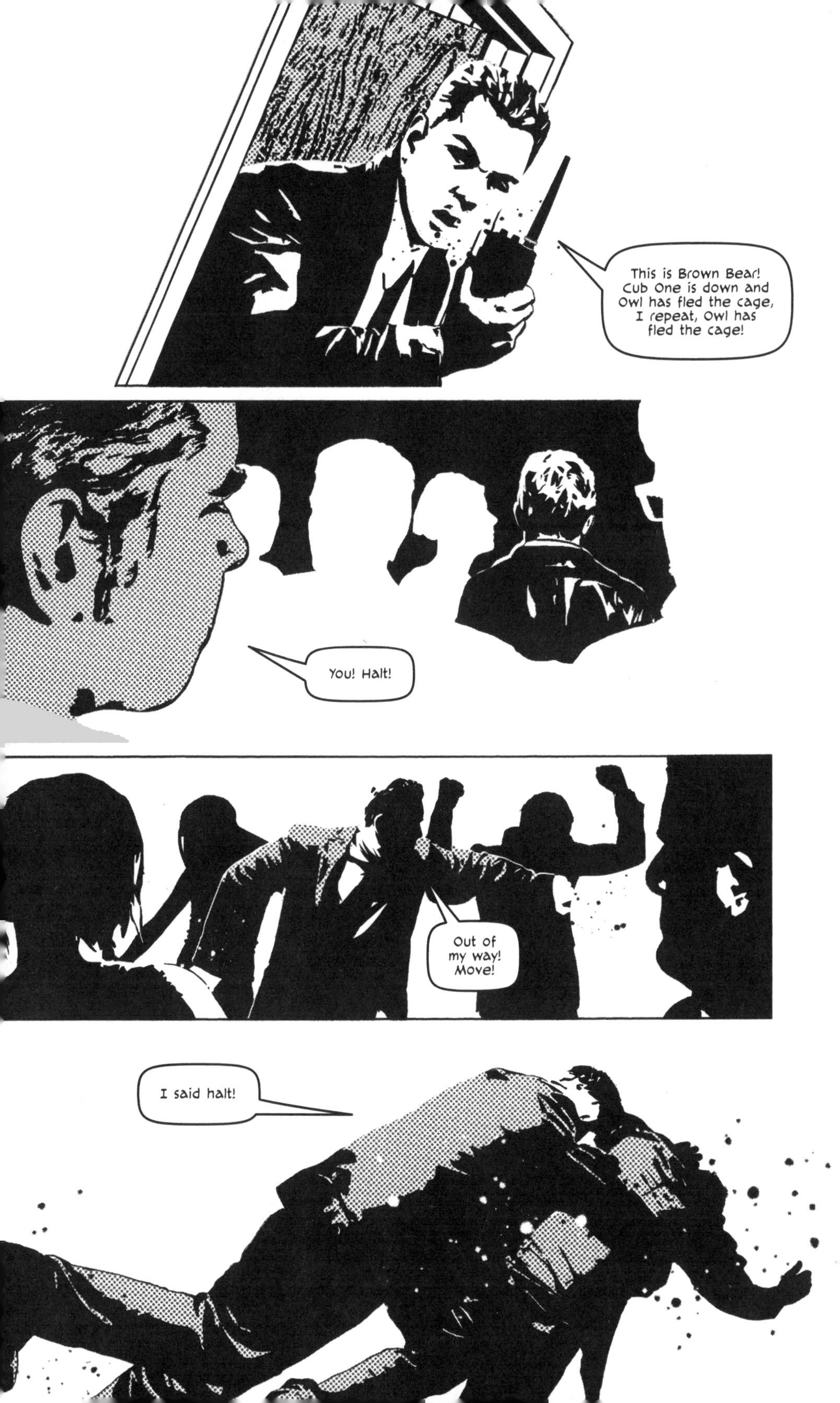
This is Brown Bear! Cub One is down and Owl has fled the cage, I repeat, Owl has fled the cage!
You! Halt!
Out of my way! Move!
I said halt!

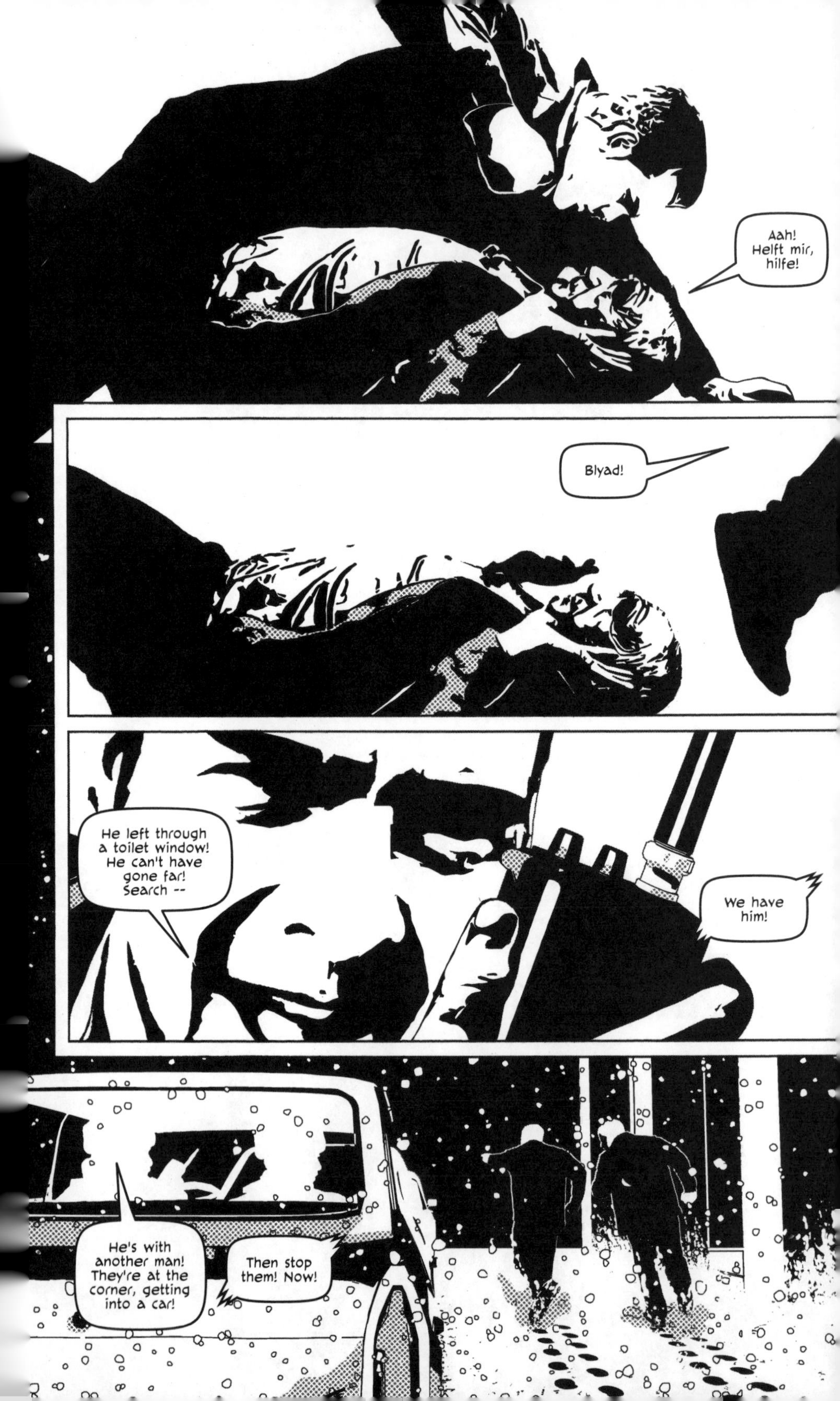
Aah! Helft mir, hilfe!
Blyad!
He left through a toilet window! He can't have gone far! Search --
We have him!
He's with another man! They're at the corner, getting into a car!
Then stop them! Now!

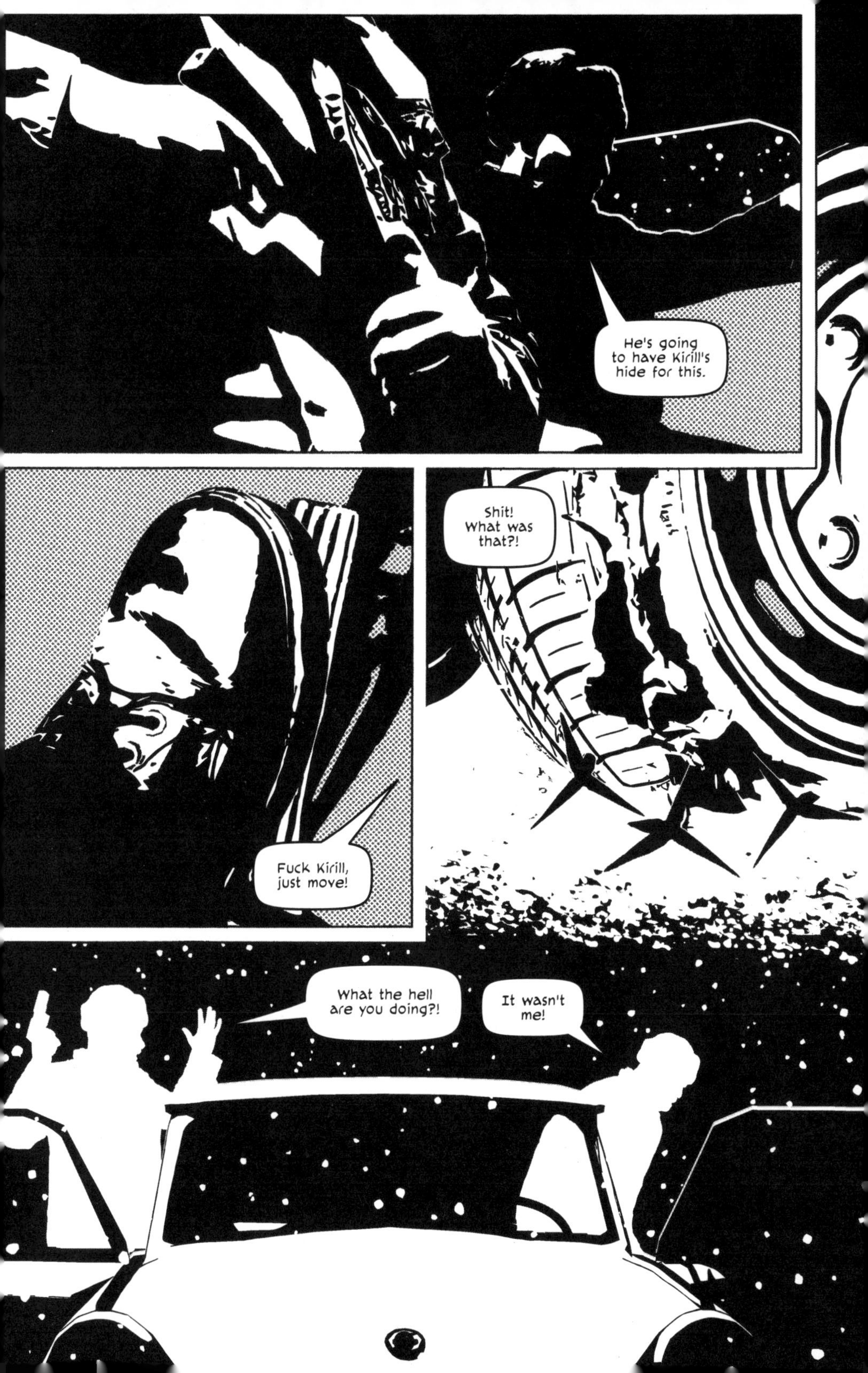
He's going to have Kirill's hide for this.
Shit! What was that?!
Fuck Kirill, just move!
What the hell are you doing?!
It wasn't me!

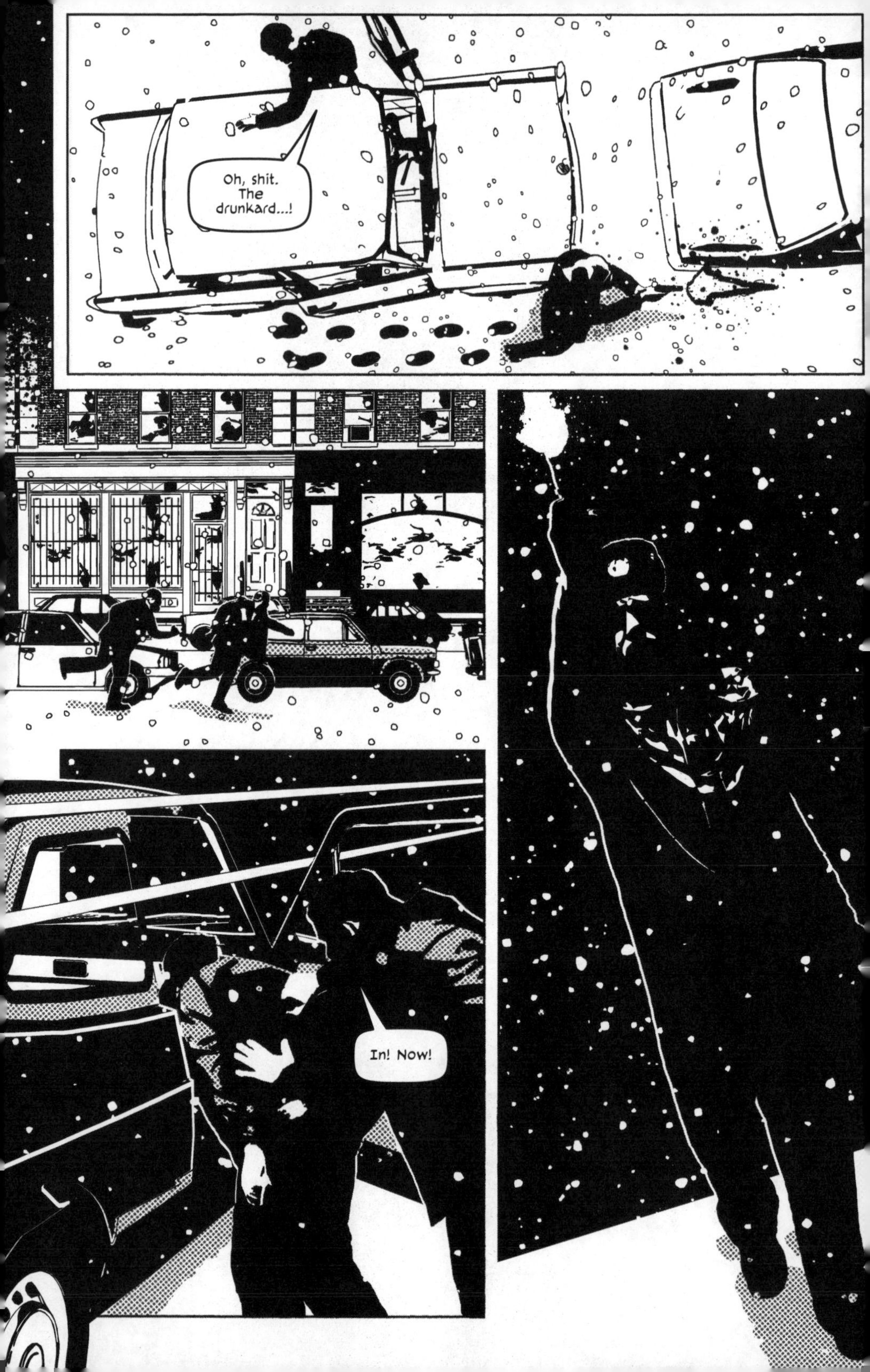
Oh, shit. The drunkard...!
In! Now!

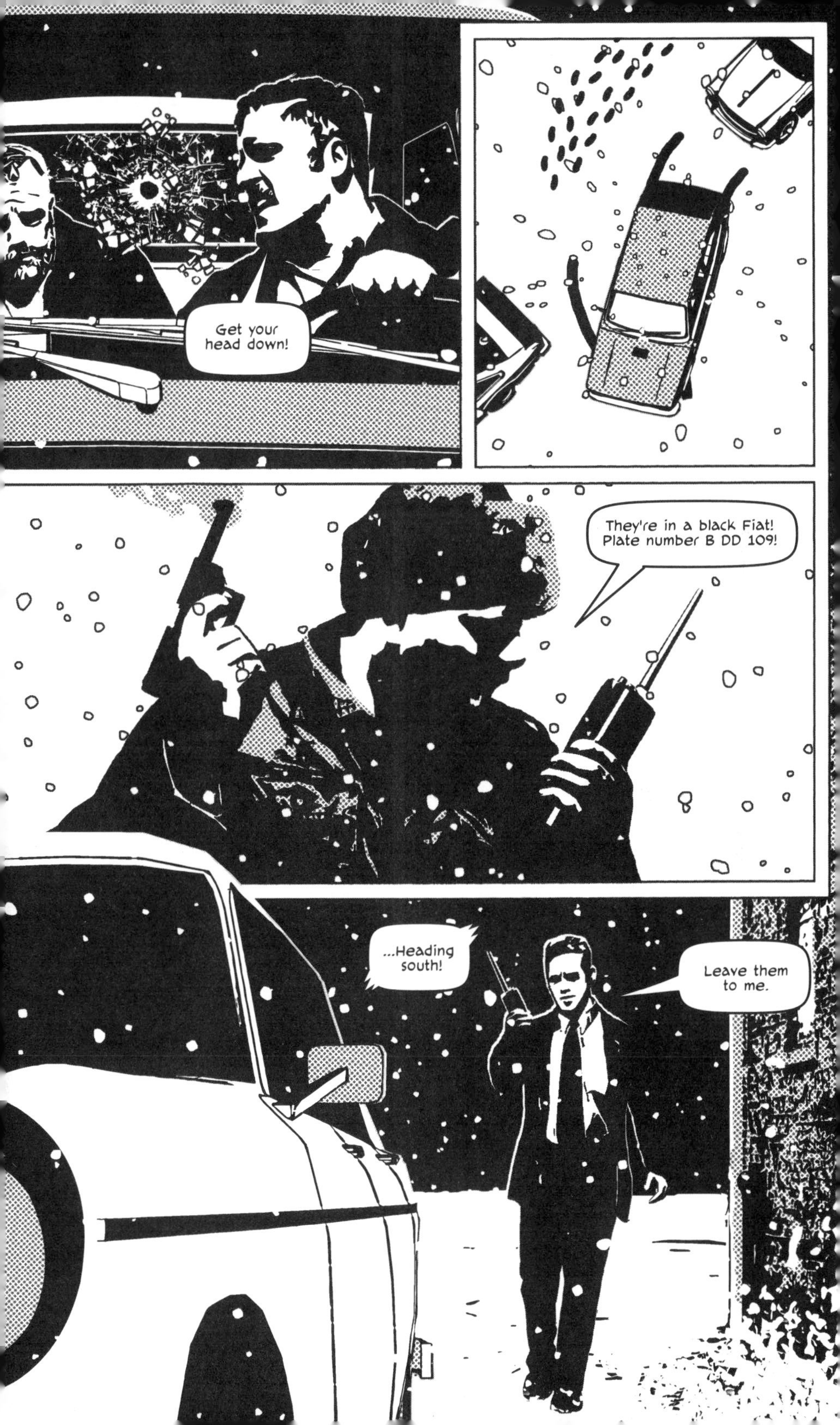
Get your
head down!
They're in a black Fiat!
Plate number B DD 109!
...Heading
south!
Leave them
to me.

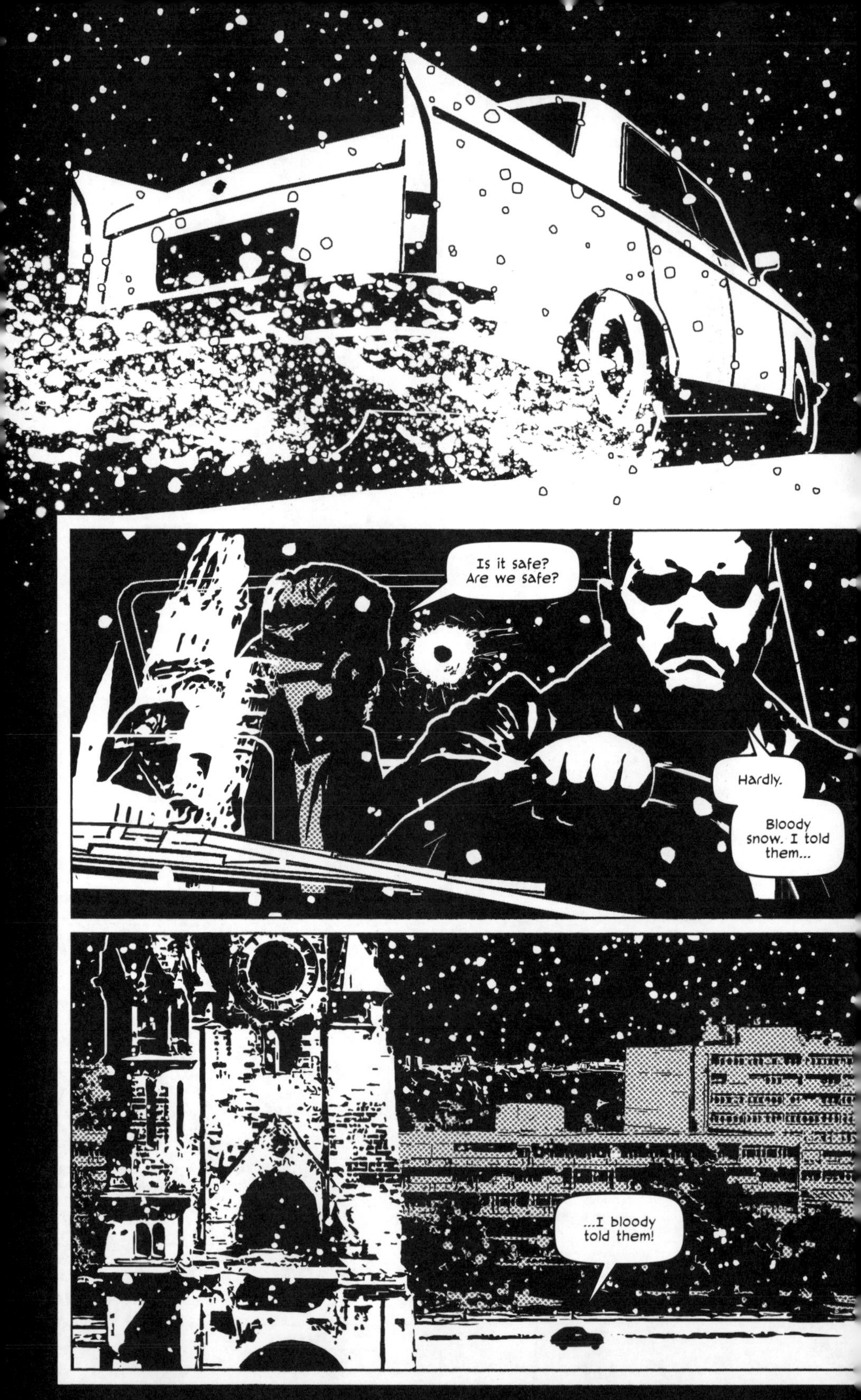
Is it safe? Are we safe?
Hardly.
Bloody snow. I told them...
...I bloody told them!

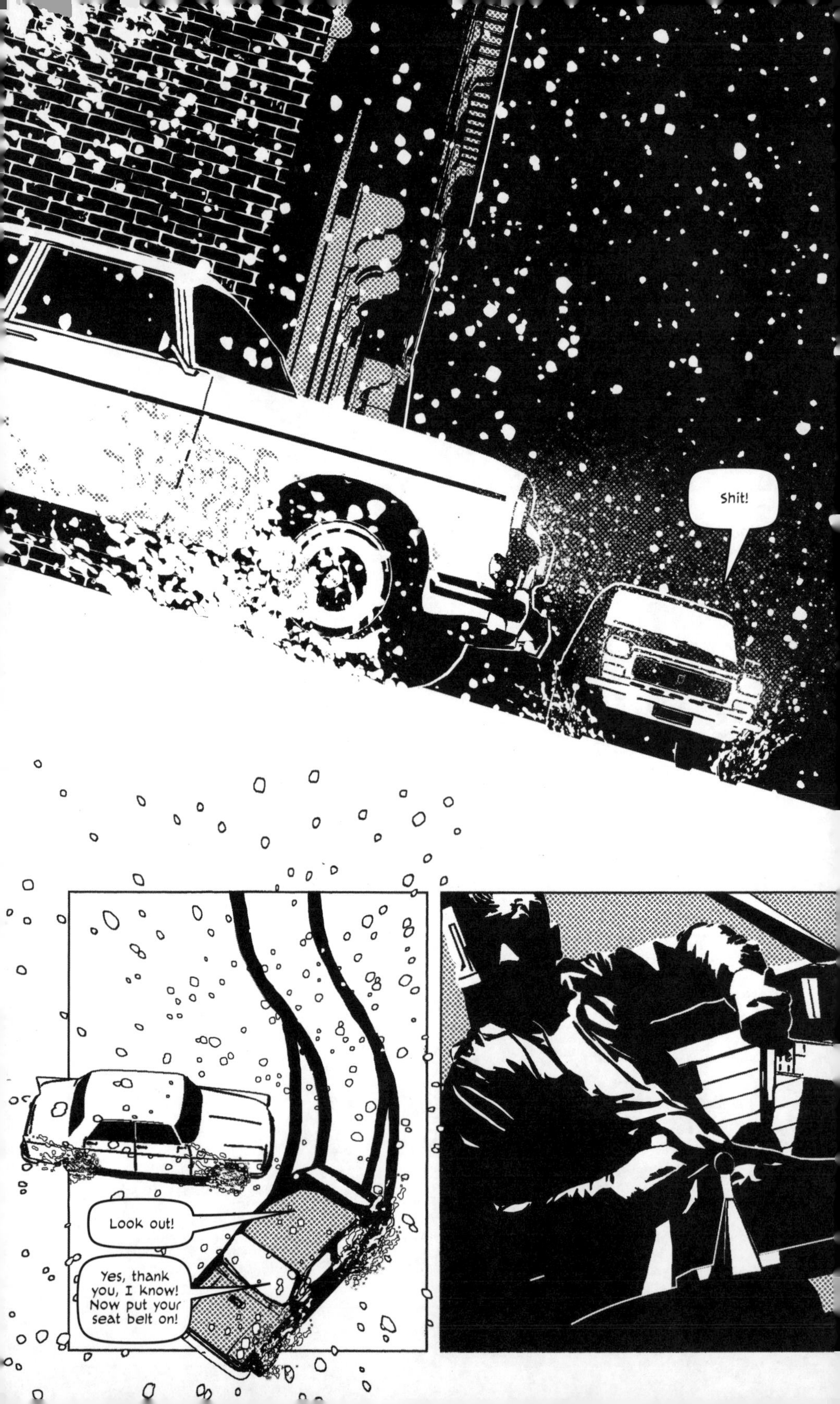
Shit!
Look out!
Yes, thank you, I know! Now put your seat belt on!

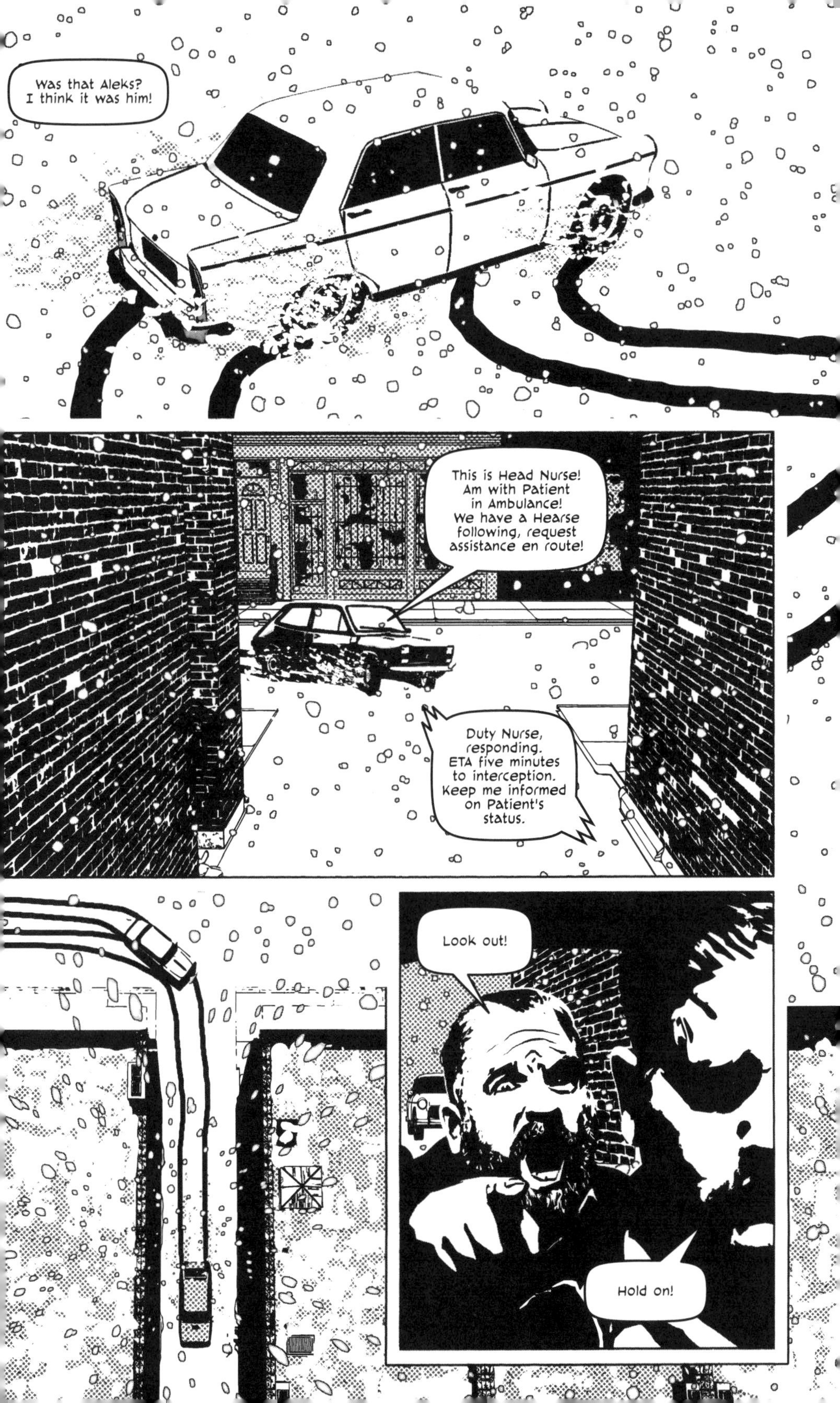
Was that Aleks? I think it was him!
This is Head Nurse! Am with Patient in Ambulance! We have a Hearse following, request assistance en route!
Duty Nurse, responding. ETA five minutes to interception. Keep me informed on Patient's status.
Look out!
Hold on!

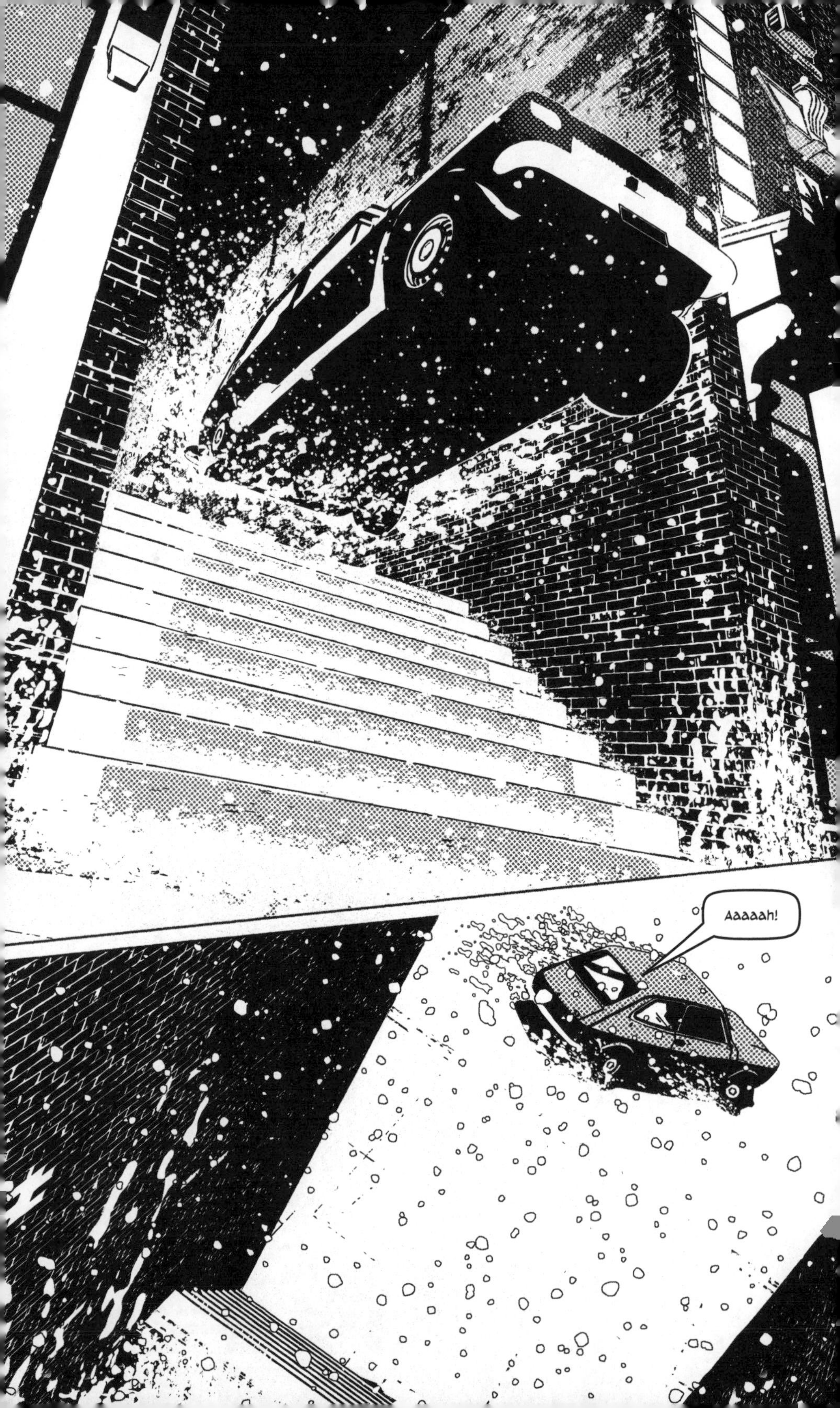
Aaaaah!

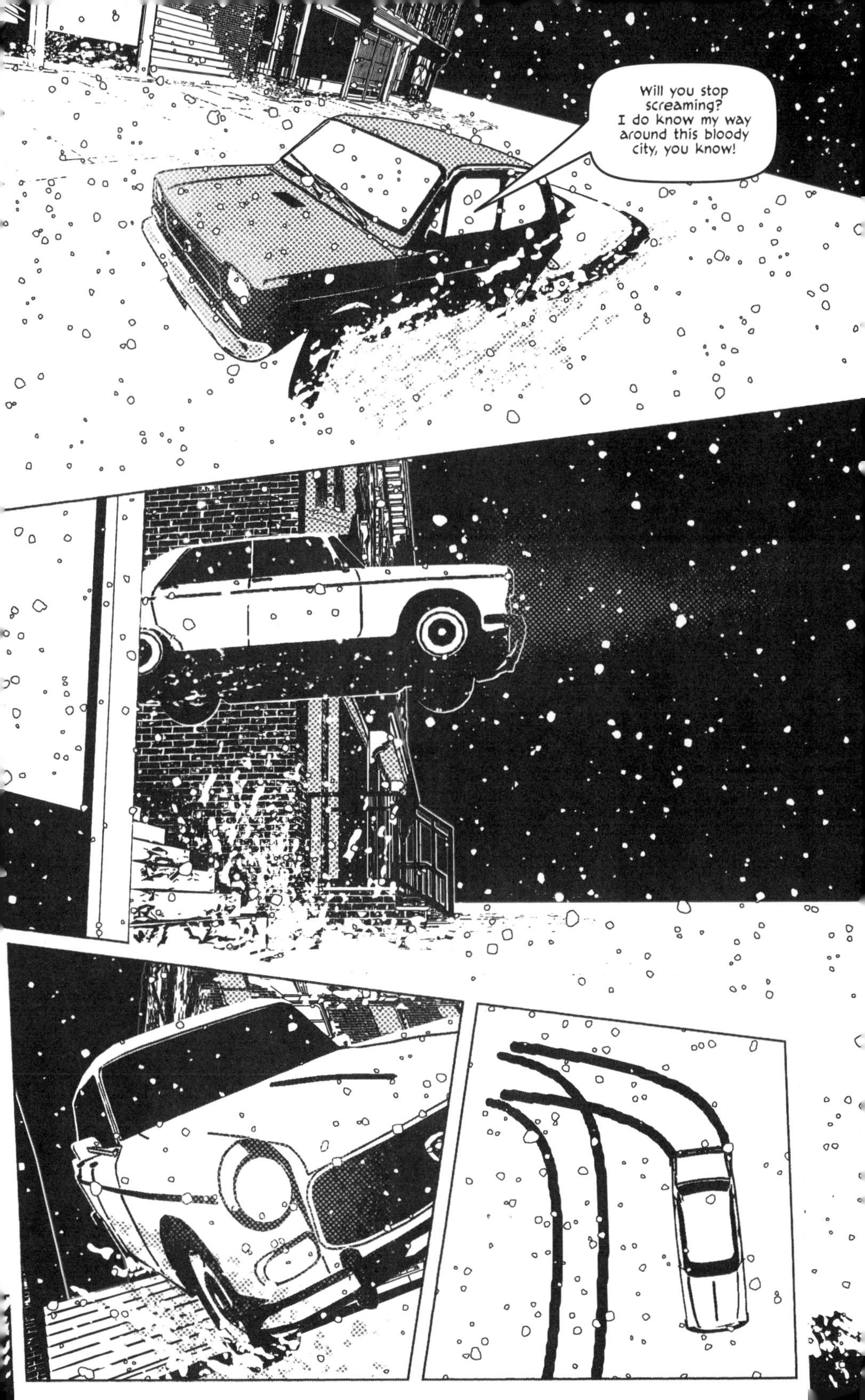
Will you stop screaming? I do know my way around this bloody city, you know!

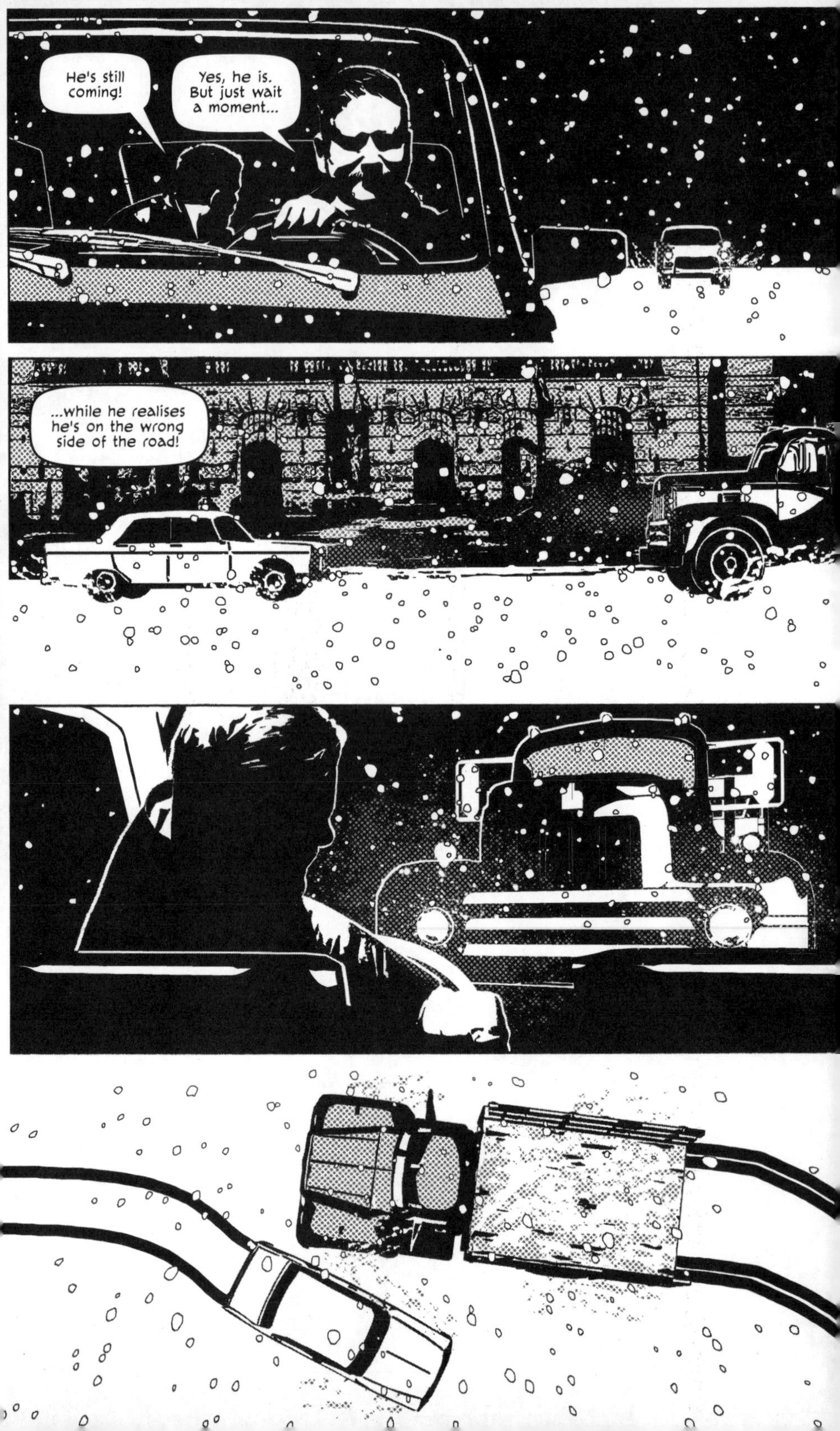
He's still coming!
Yes, he is. But just wait a moment...
...while he realises he's on the wrong side of the road!

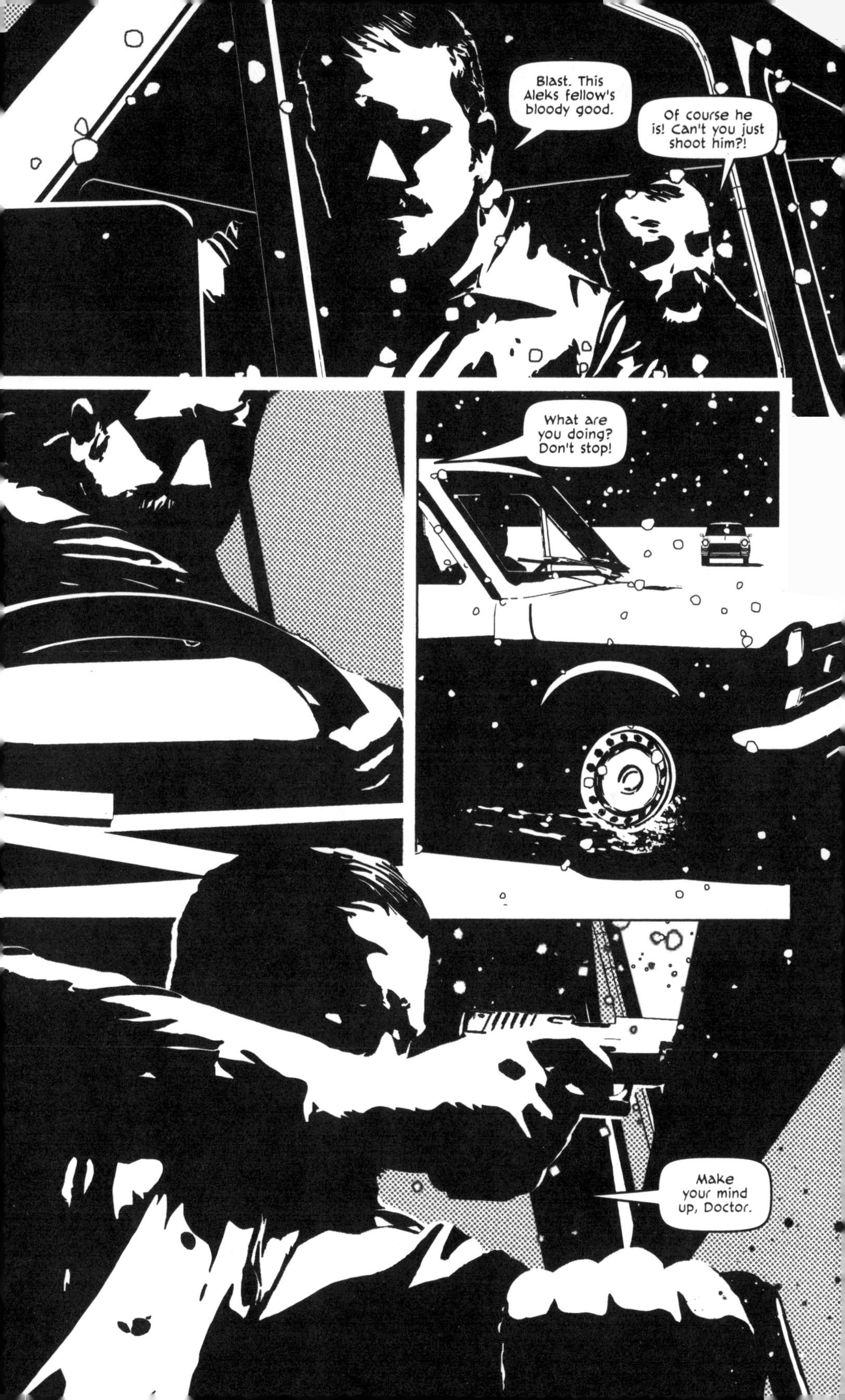
Blast. This Aleks fellow's bloody good.
Of course he is! Can't you just shoot him?!
What are you doing? Don't stop!
Make your mind up, Doctor.

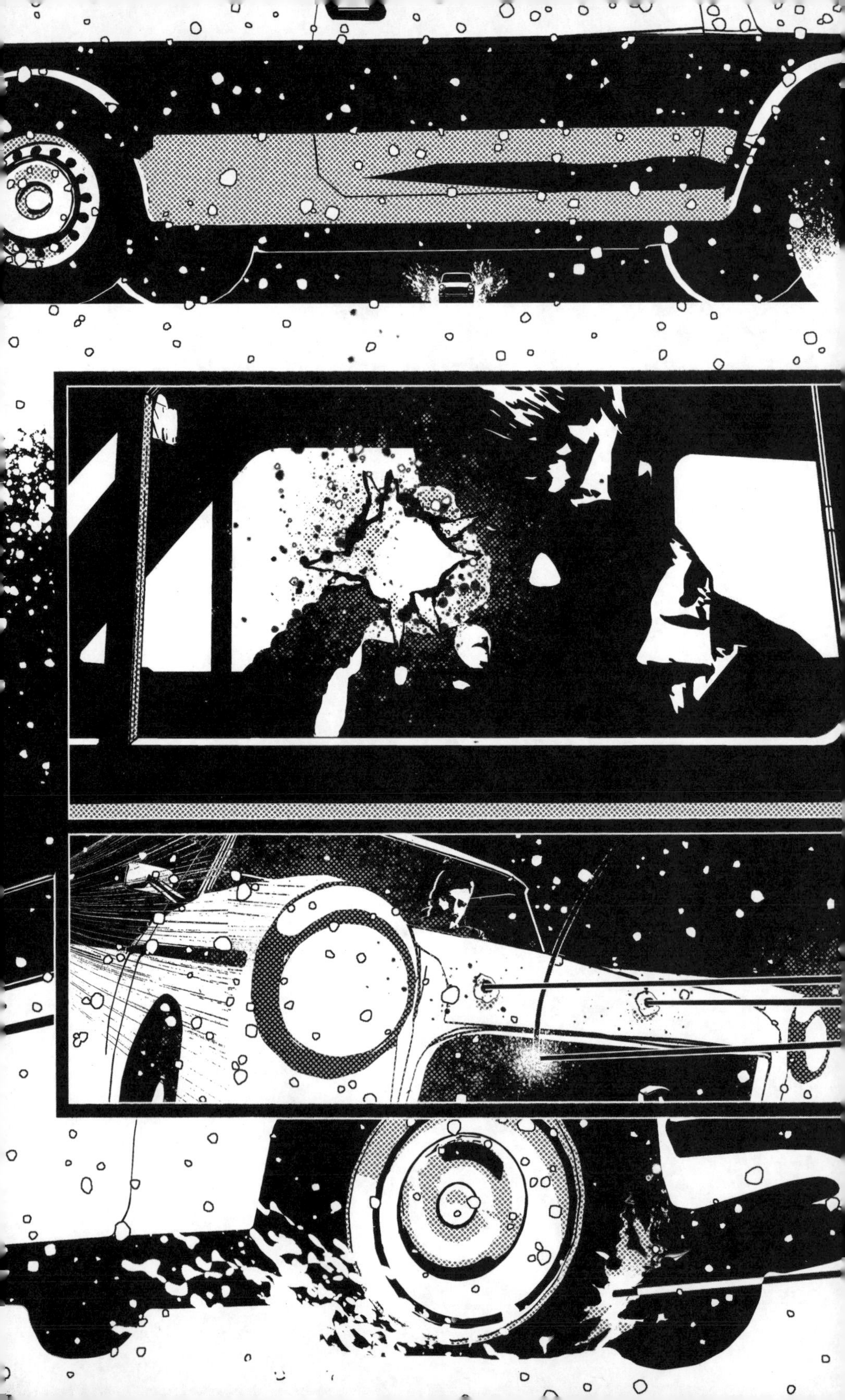

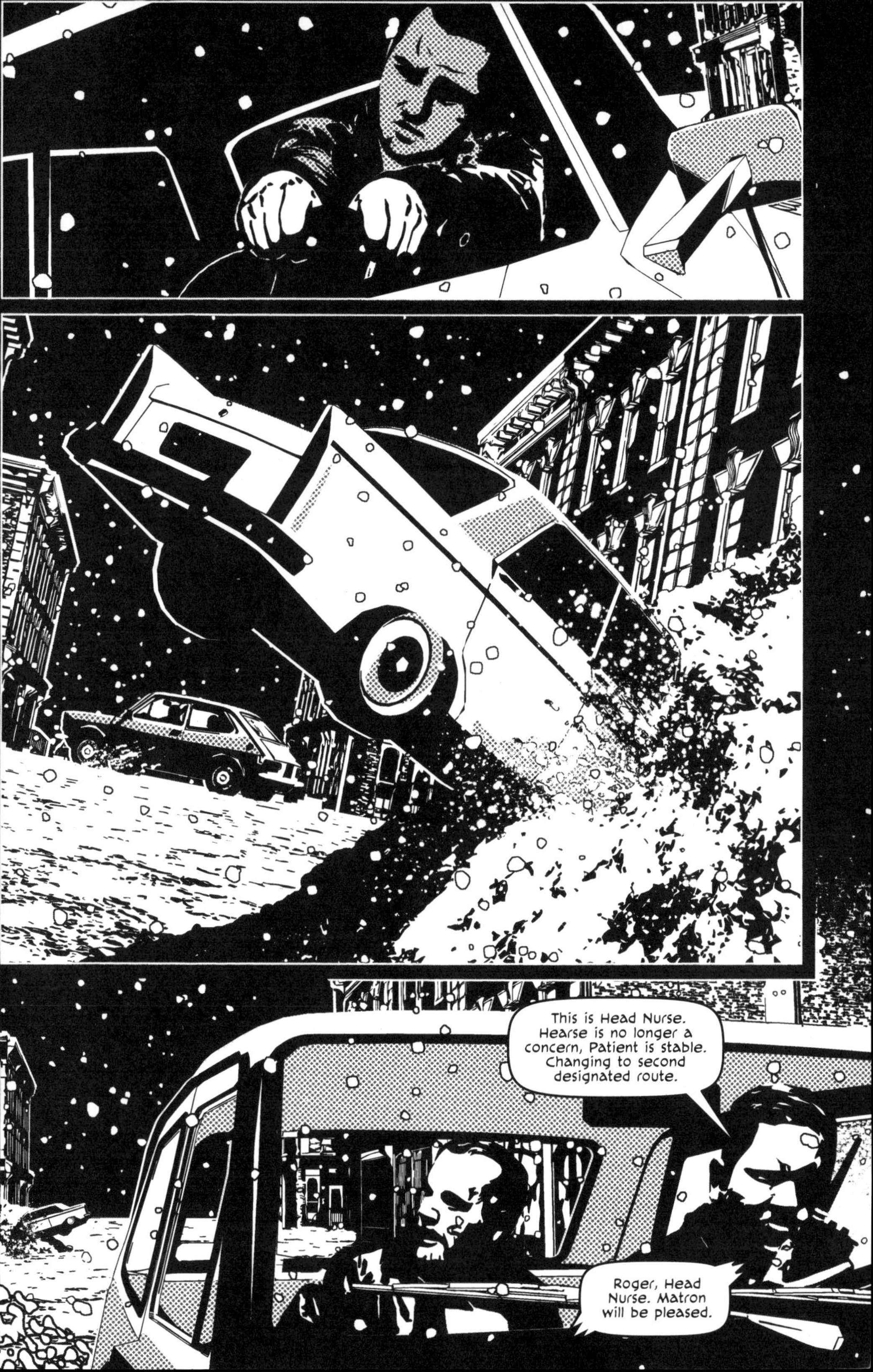
This is Head Nurse. Hearse is no longer a concern, Patient is stable. Changing to second designated route.
Roger, Head Nurse. Matron will be pleased.

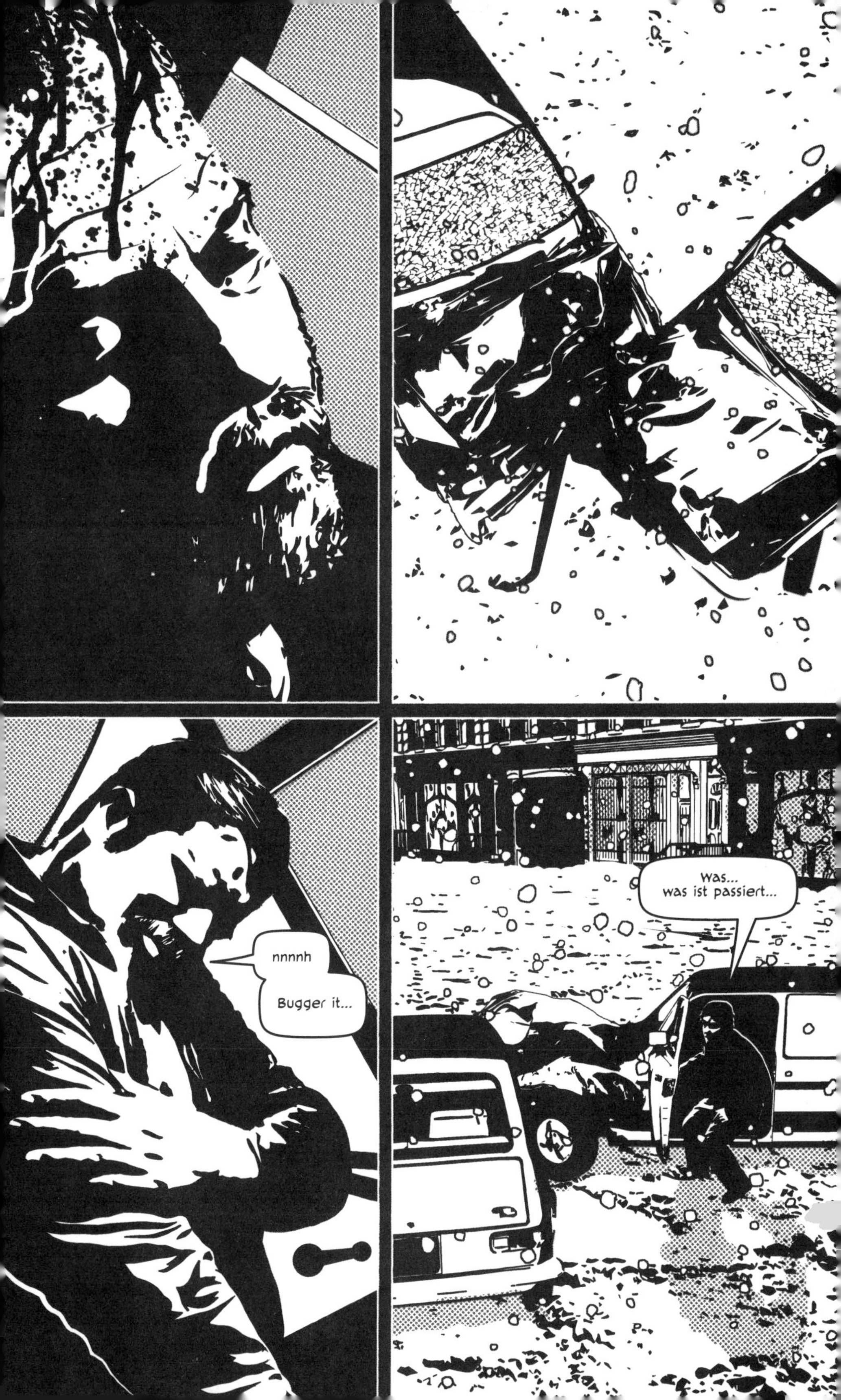
nnnnh
Bugger it...
Was...
was ist passiert...

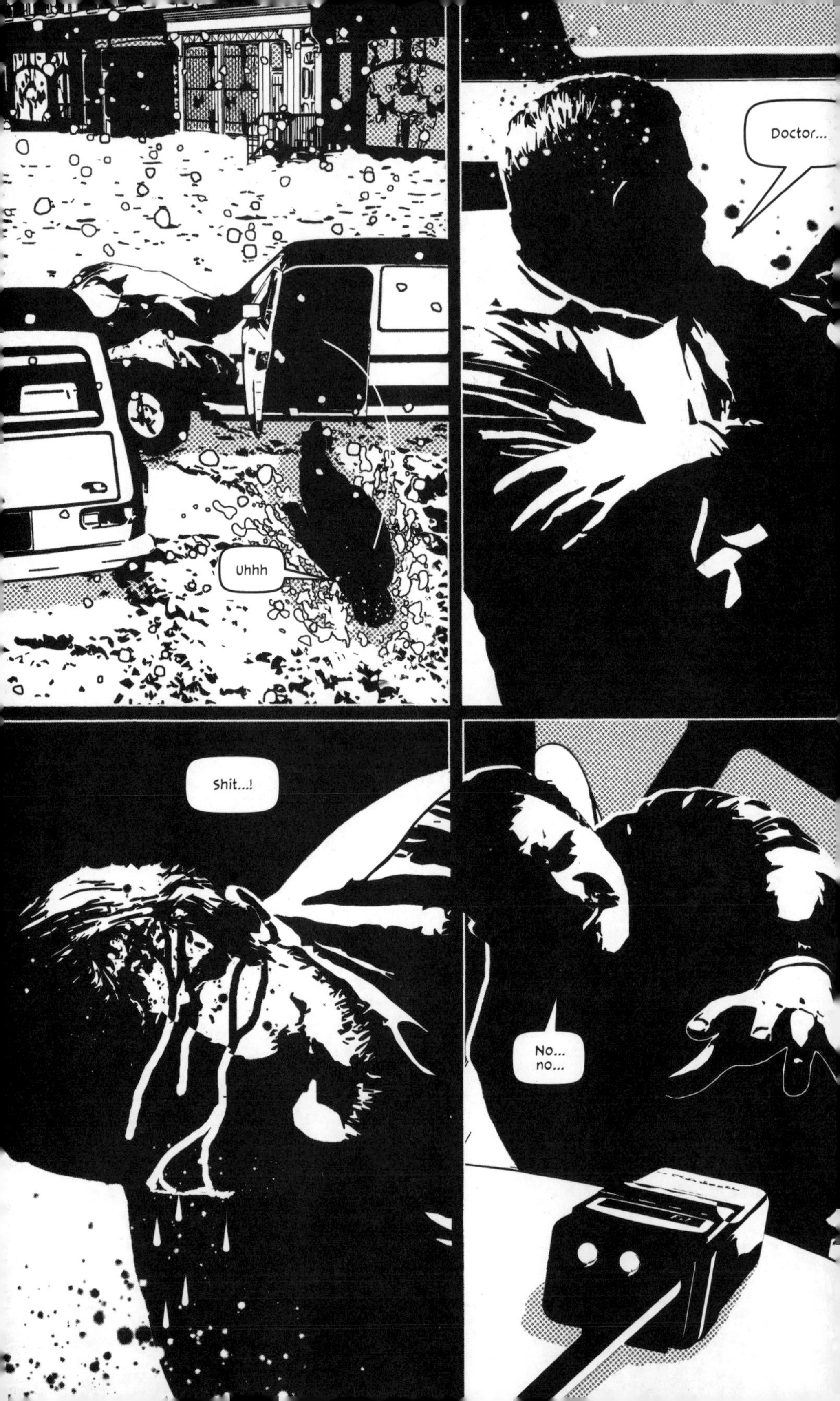
Uhhh
Doctor...
Shit...!
No...
no...

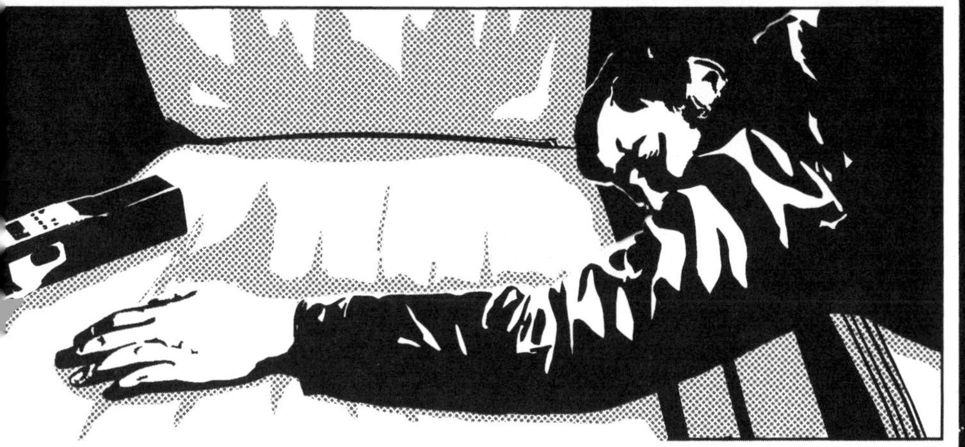
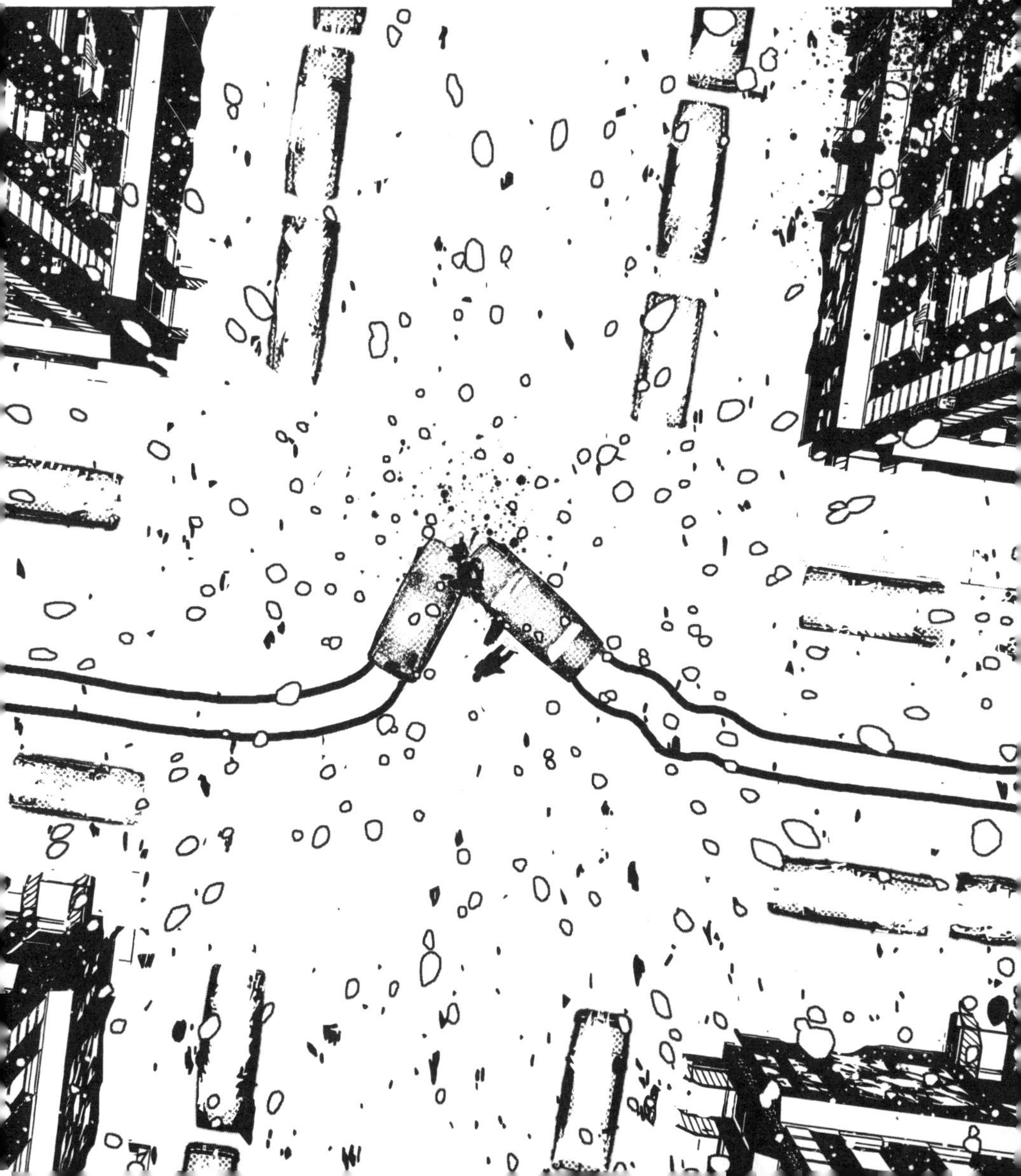

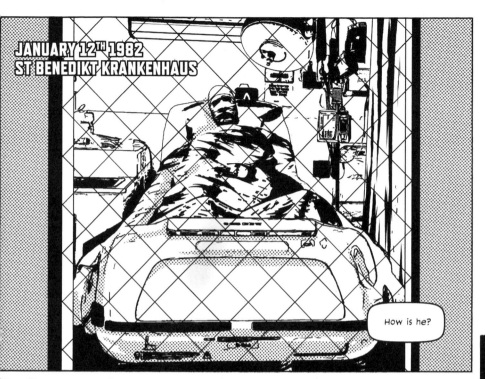

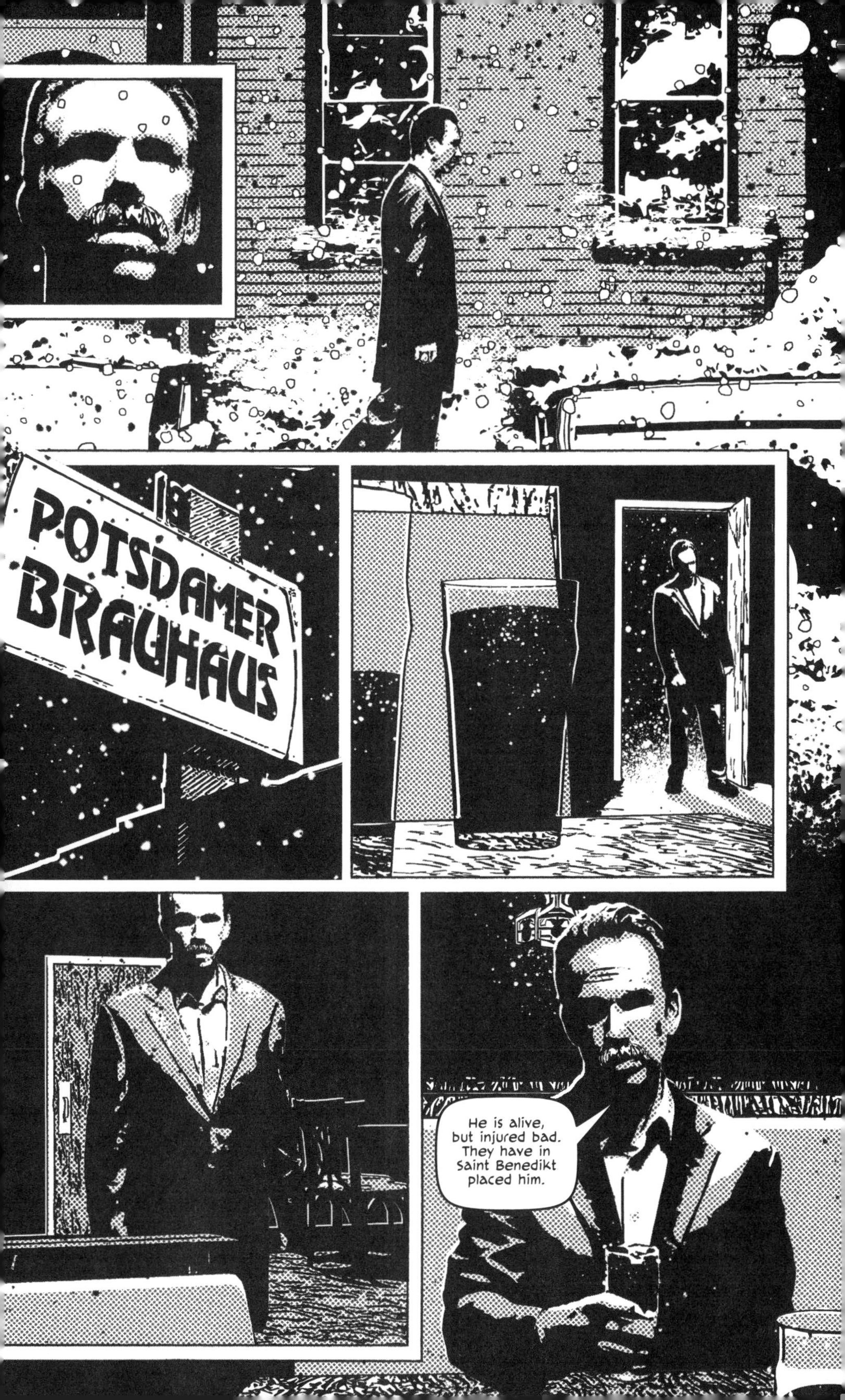
19
POTSDAMER
BRAUHAUS
He is alive, but injured bad. They have in Saint Benedikt placed him.

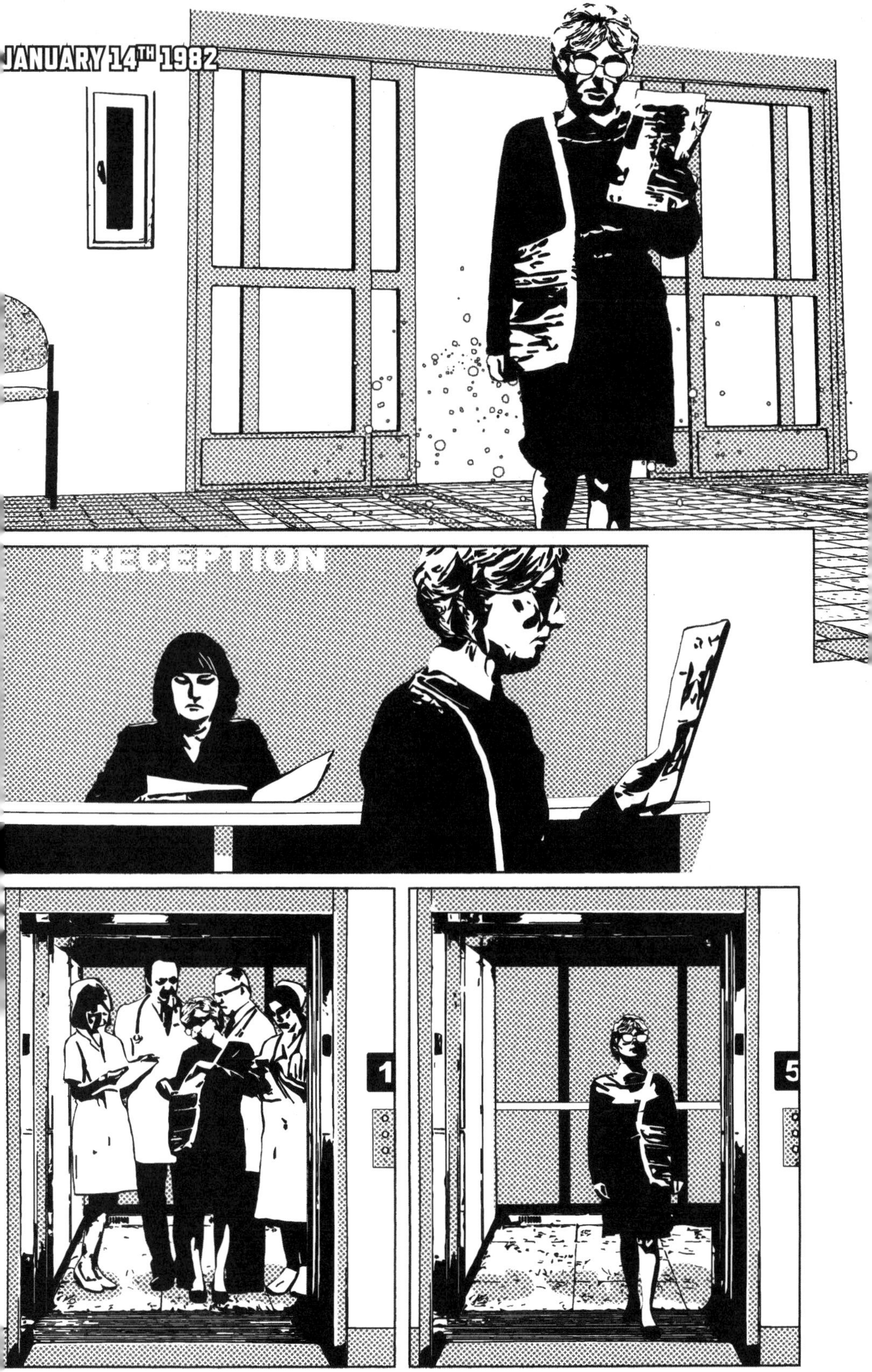

JANUARY 14TH 1982
RECEPTION
1
5

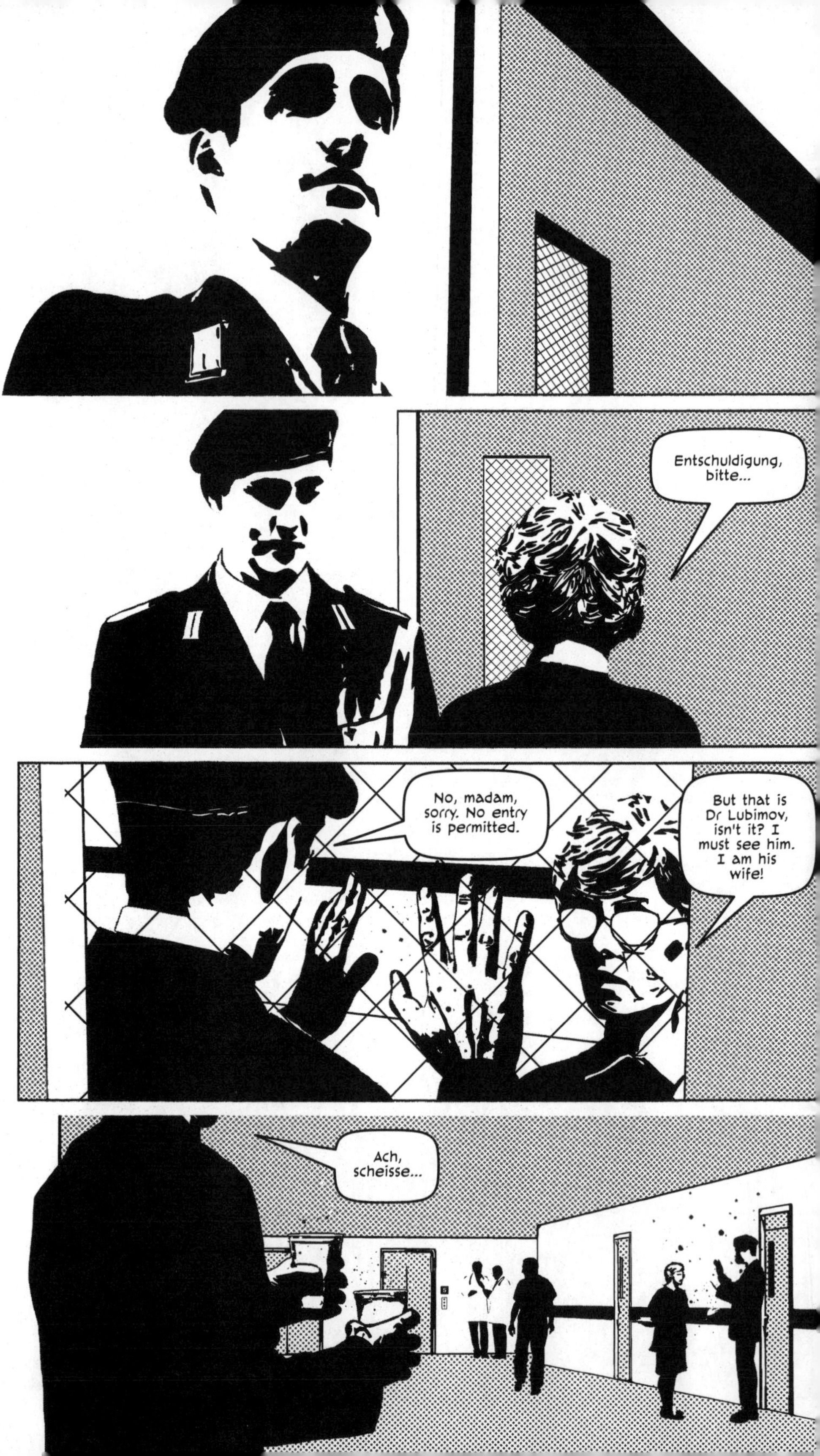
Entschuldigung, bitte...
No, madam, sorry. No entry is permitted.
But that is Dr Lubimov, isn't it? I must see him. I am his wife!
Ach, scheisse...

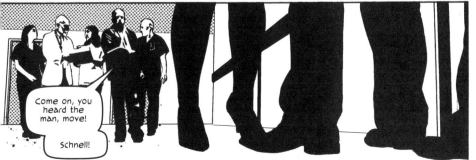

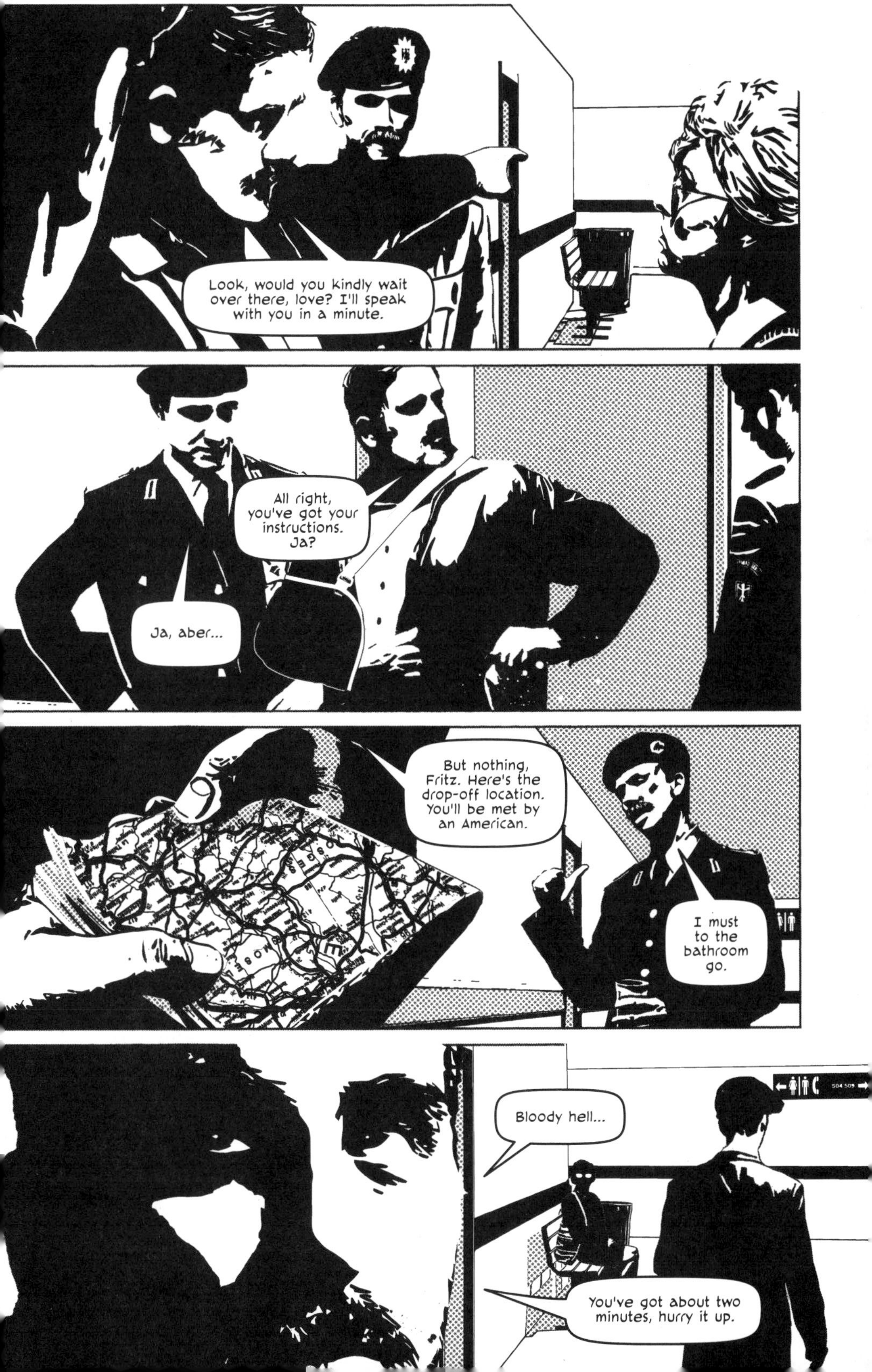
Look, would you kindly wait over there, love? I'll speak with you in a minute.
All right, you've got your instructions. Ja?
Ja, aber...
But nothing, Fritz. Here's the drop-off location. You'll be met by an American.
I must to the bathroom go.
Bloody hell...
You've got about two minutes, hurry it up.

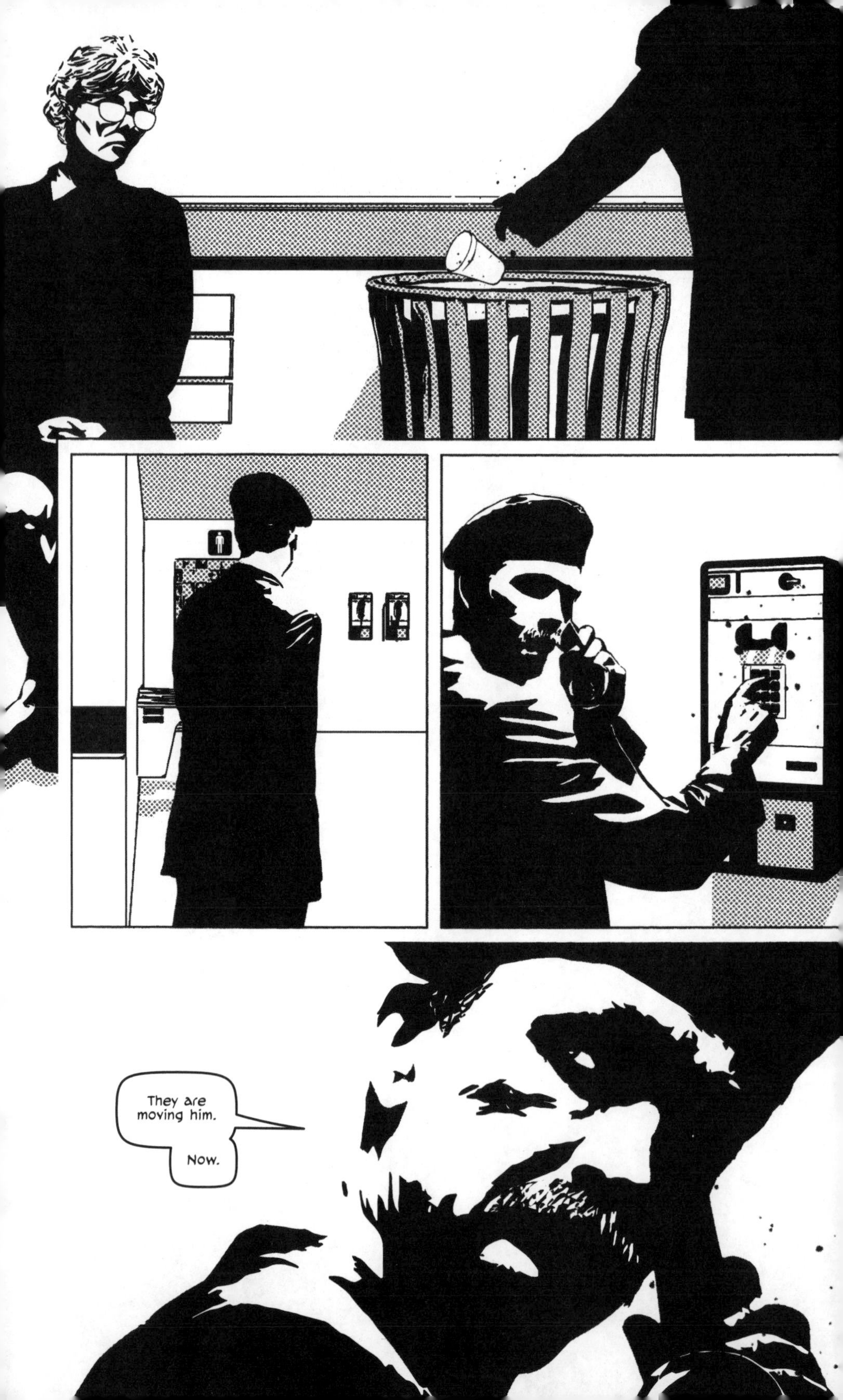
They are moving him.
Now.

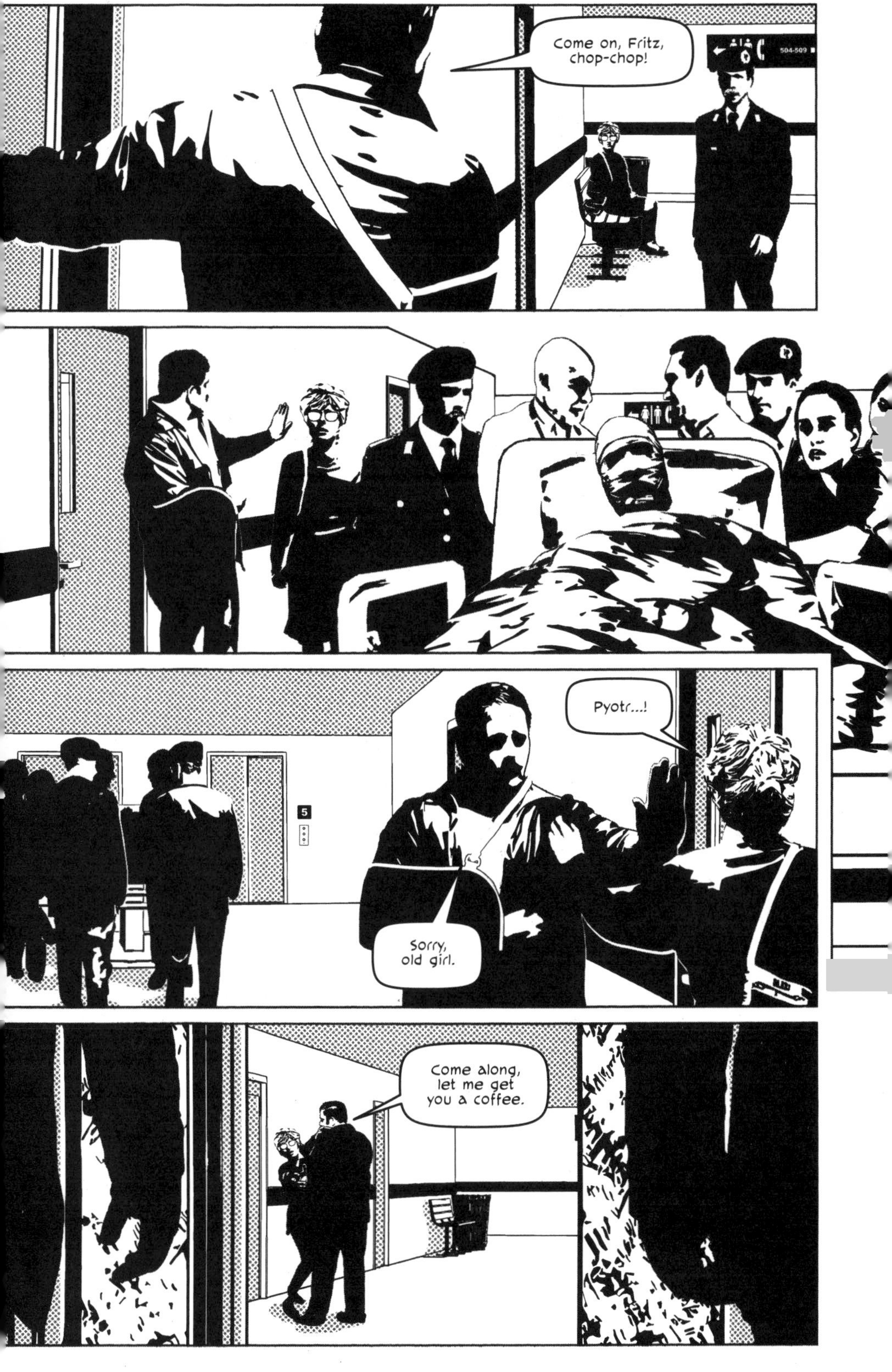
Come on, Fritz, chop-chop!
504-509
Pyotr...!
Sorry, old girl.
Come along, let me get you a coffee.

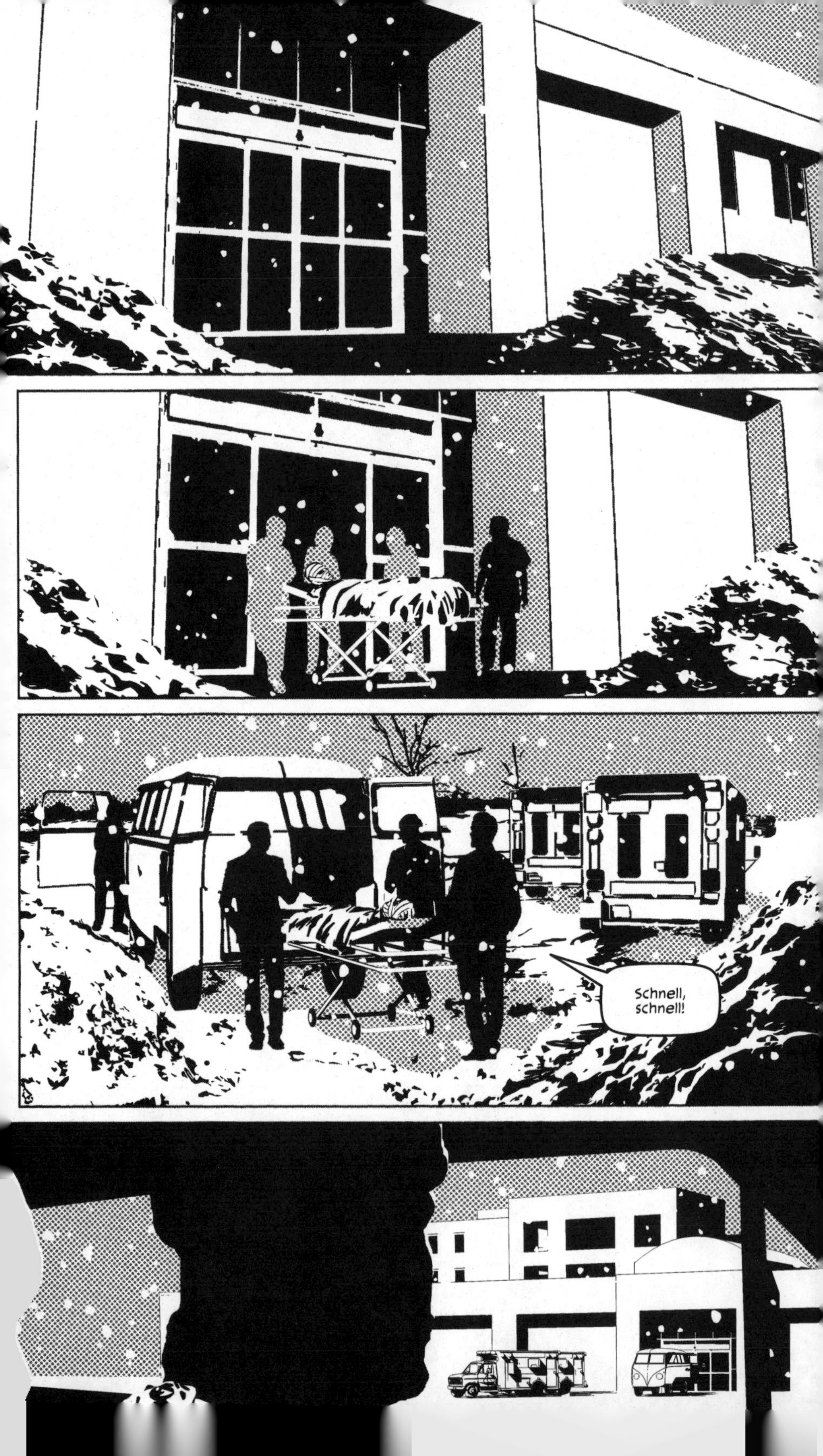
Schnell, schnell!

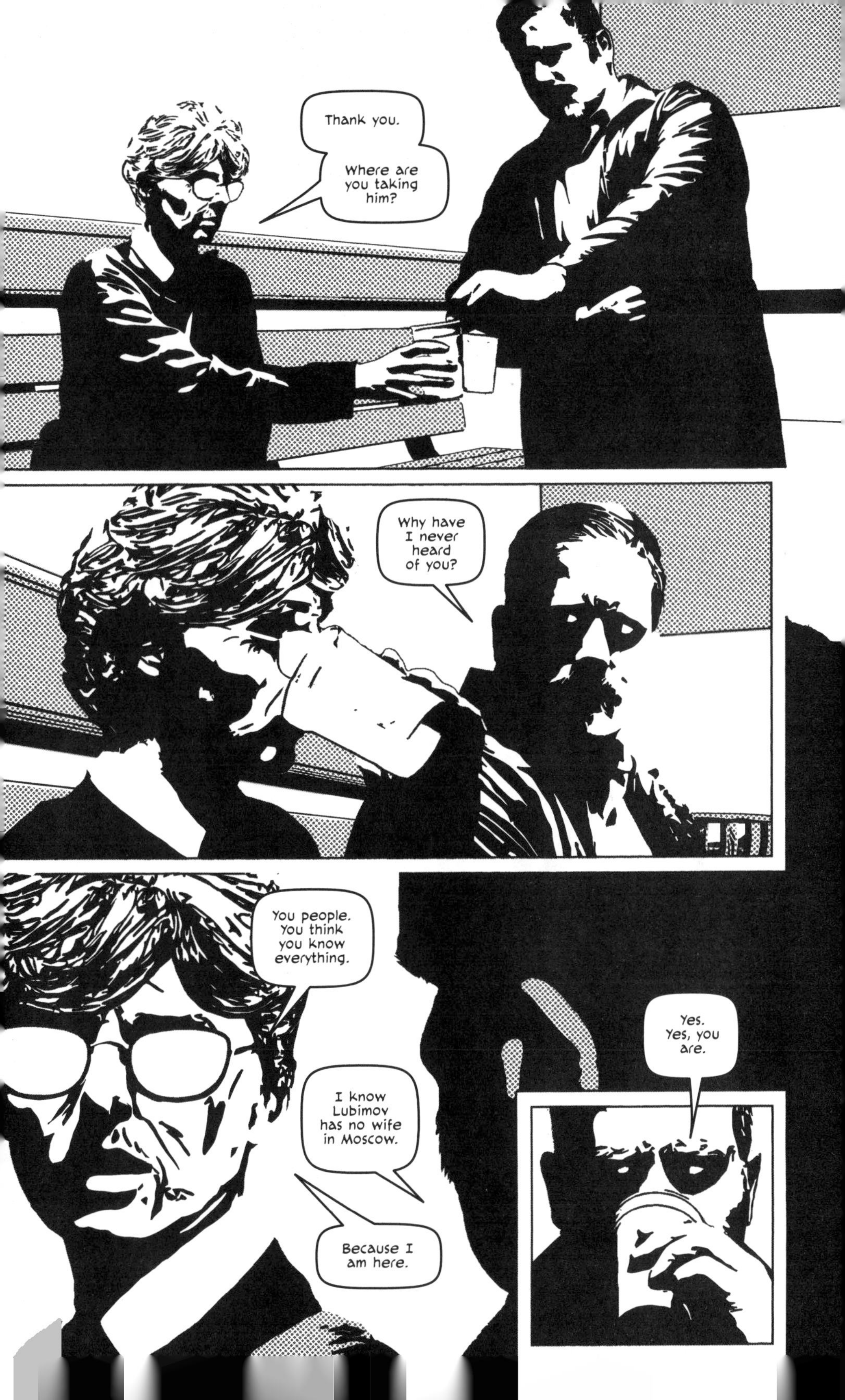
Thank you.
Where are you taking him?
Why have I never heard of you?
You people. You think you know everything.
I know Lubimov has no wife in Moscow.
Because I am here.
Yes. Yes, you are.

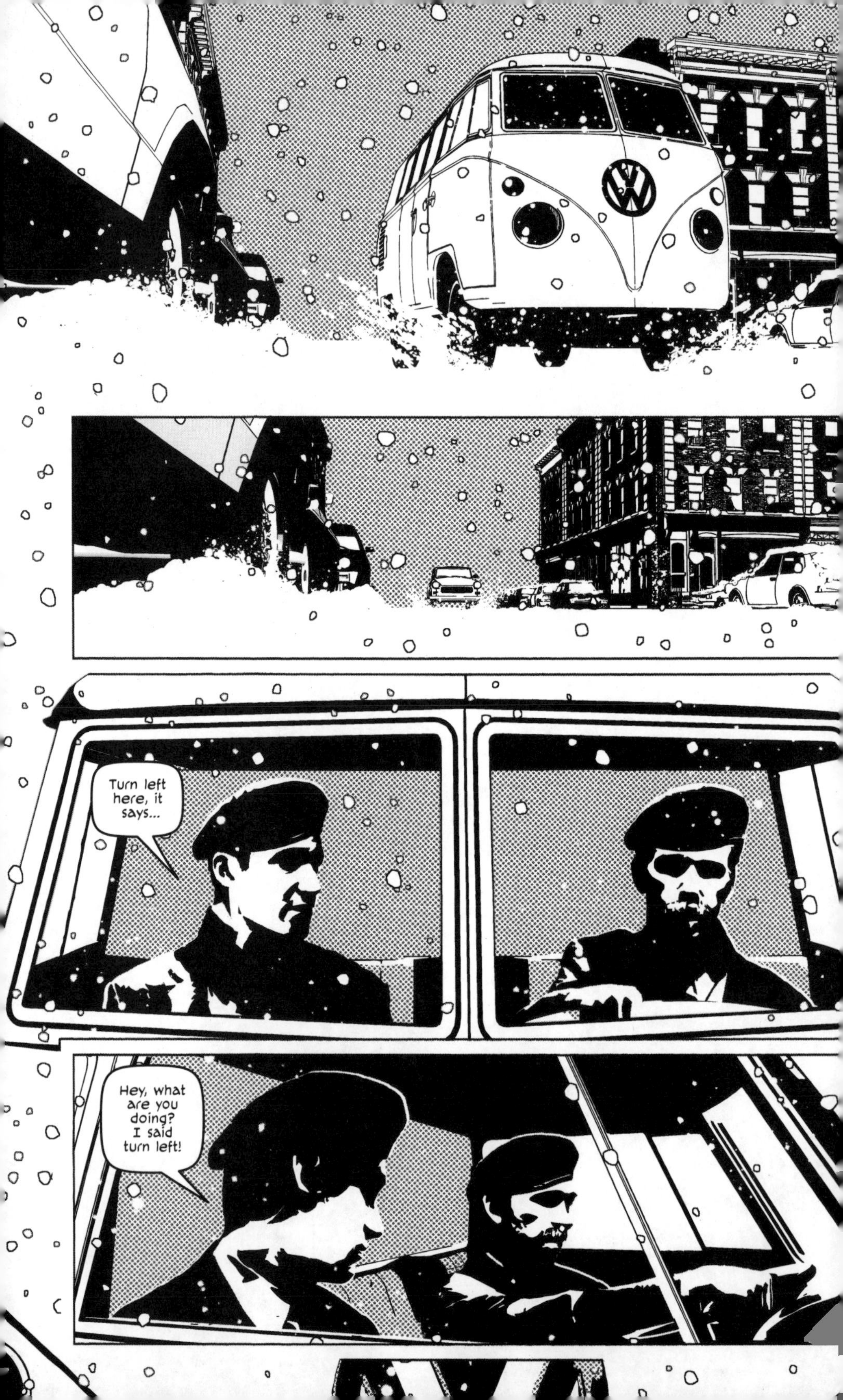
Turn left here, it says...
Hey, what are you doing? I said turn left!

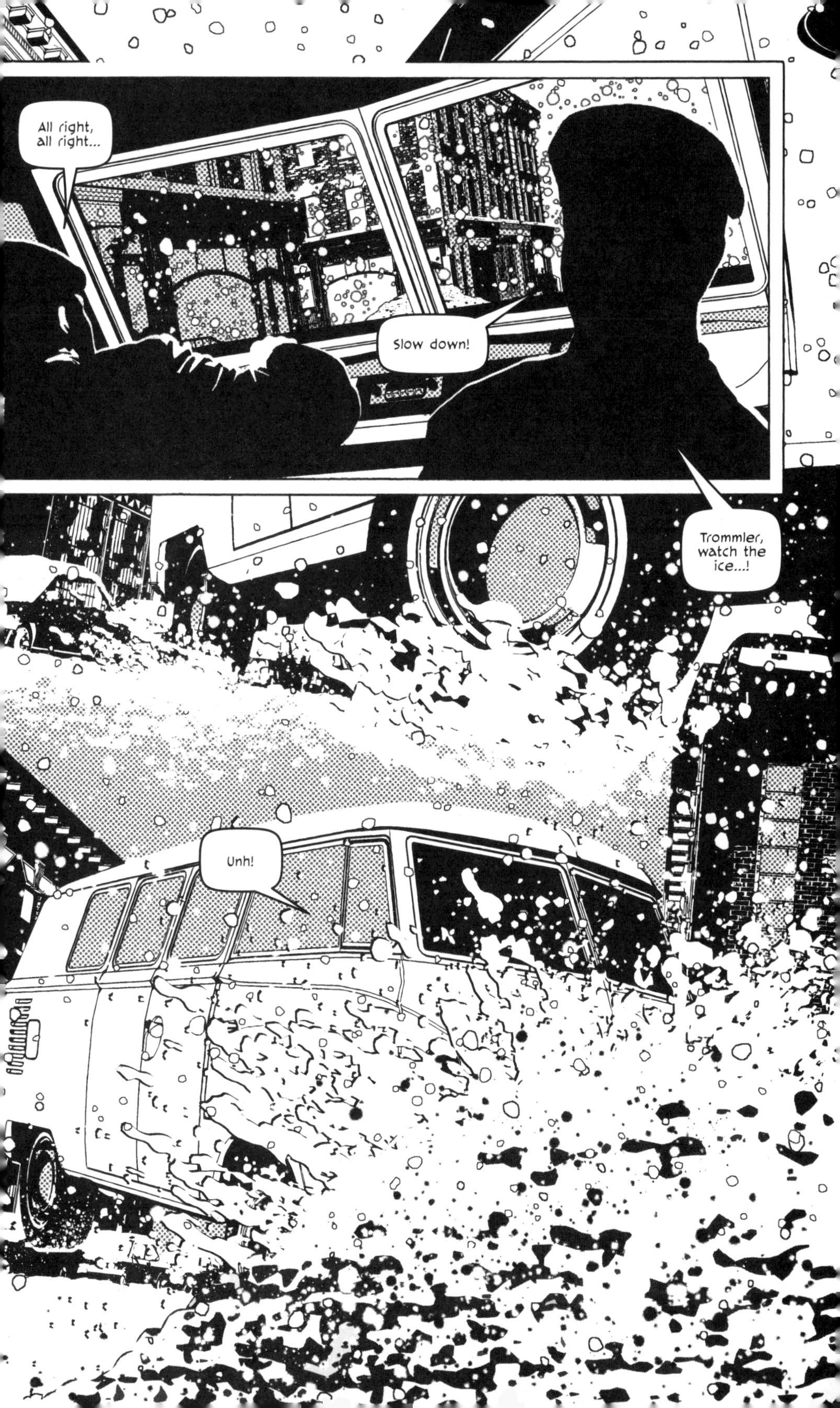
All right, all right...
Slow down!
Trommler, watch the ice...!
Unh!

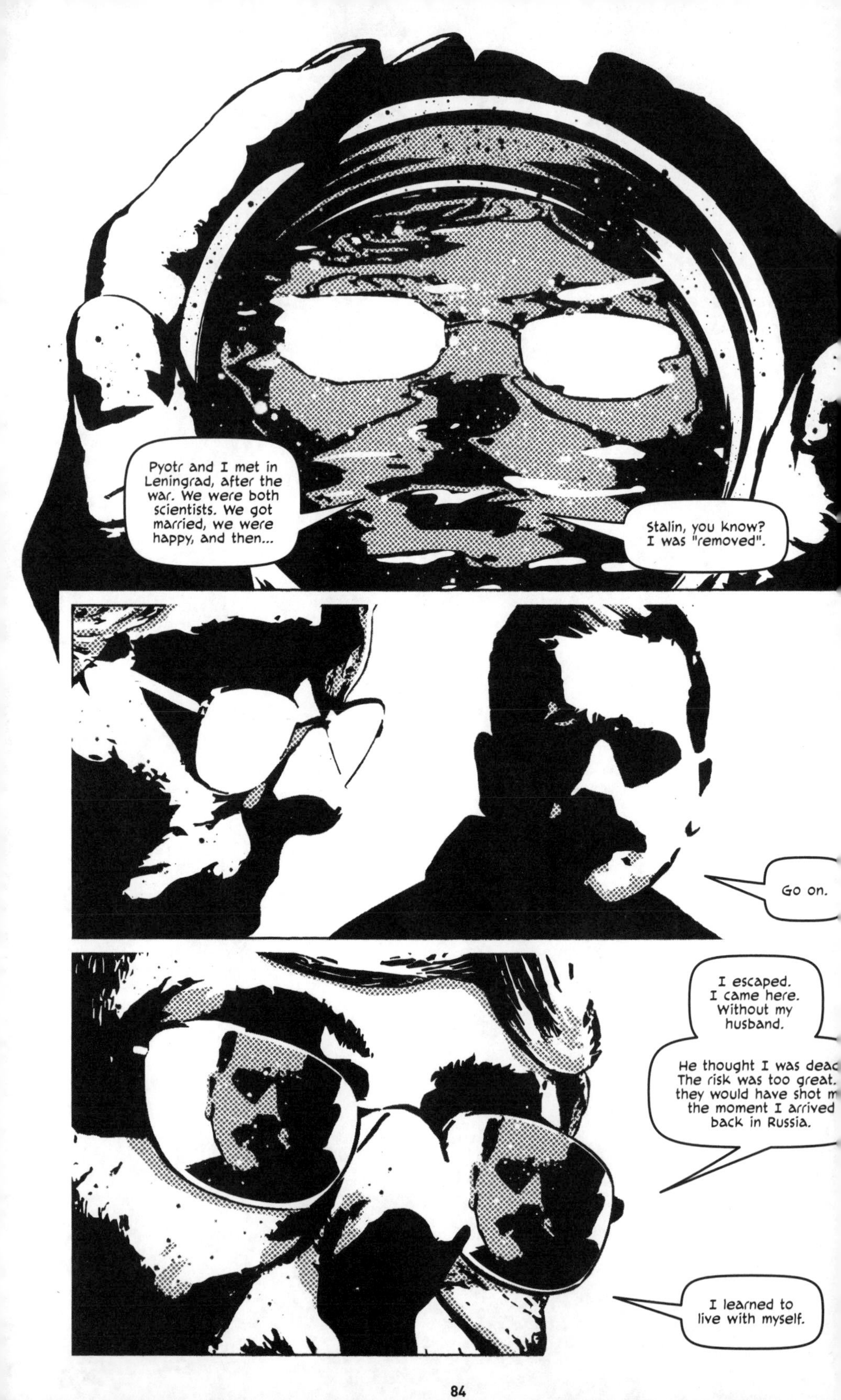
Pyotr and I met in Leningrad, after the war. We were both scientists. We got married, we were happy, and then...
Stalin, you know? I was "removed".
Go on.
I escaped. I came here. Without my husband.
He thought I was deac The risk was too great. they would have shot m the moment I arrived back in Russia.
I learned to live with myself.

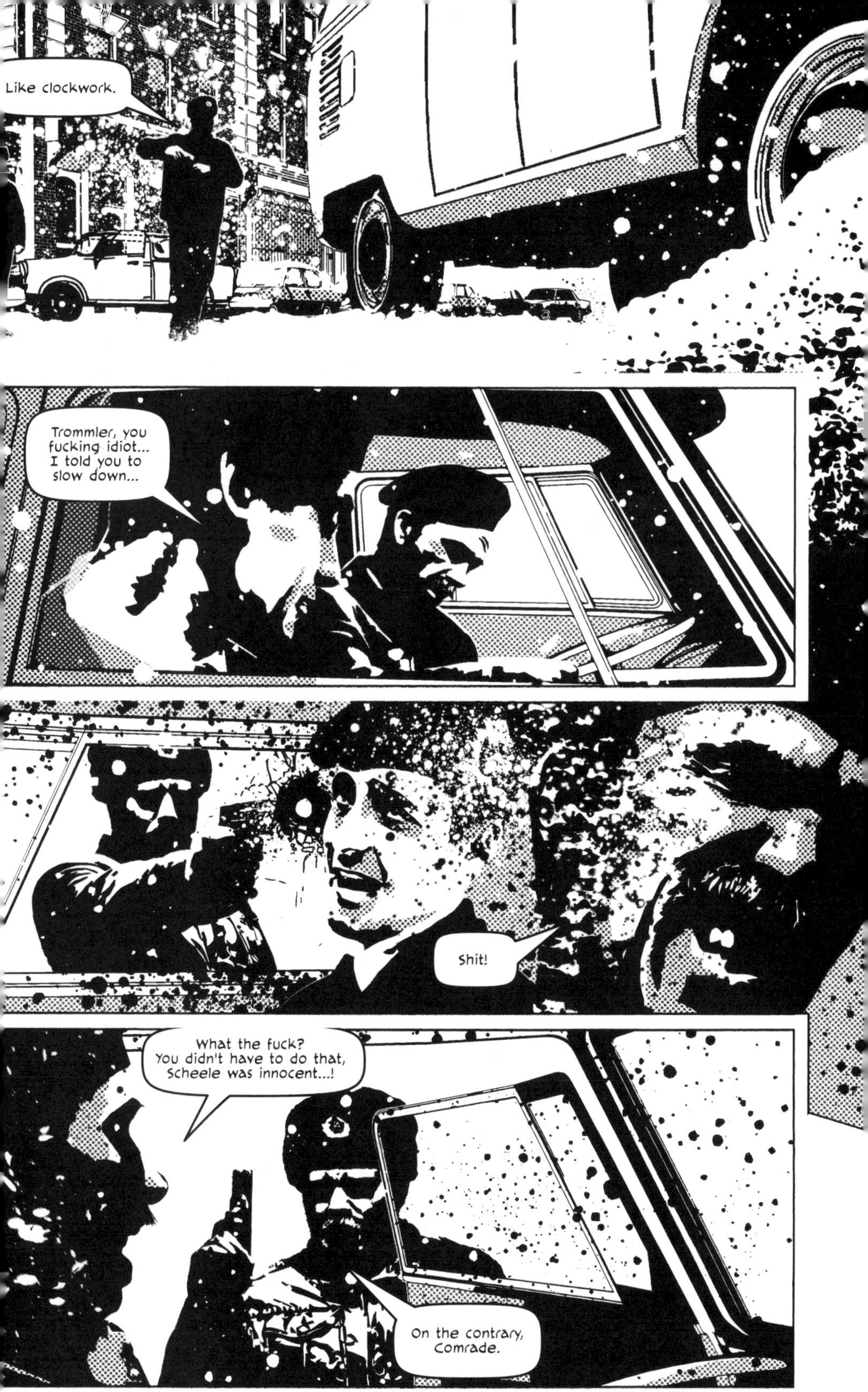
Like clockwork.
Trommler, you fucking idiot... I told you to slow down...
Shit!
What the fuck? You didn't have to do that, Scheele was innocent...!
On the contrary, Comrade.

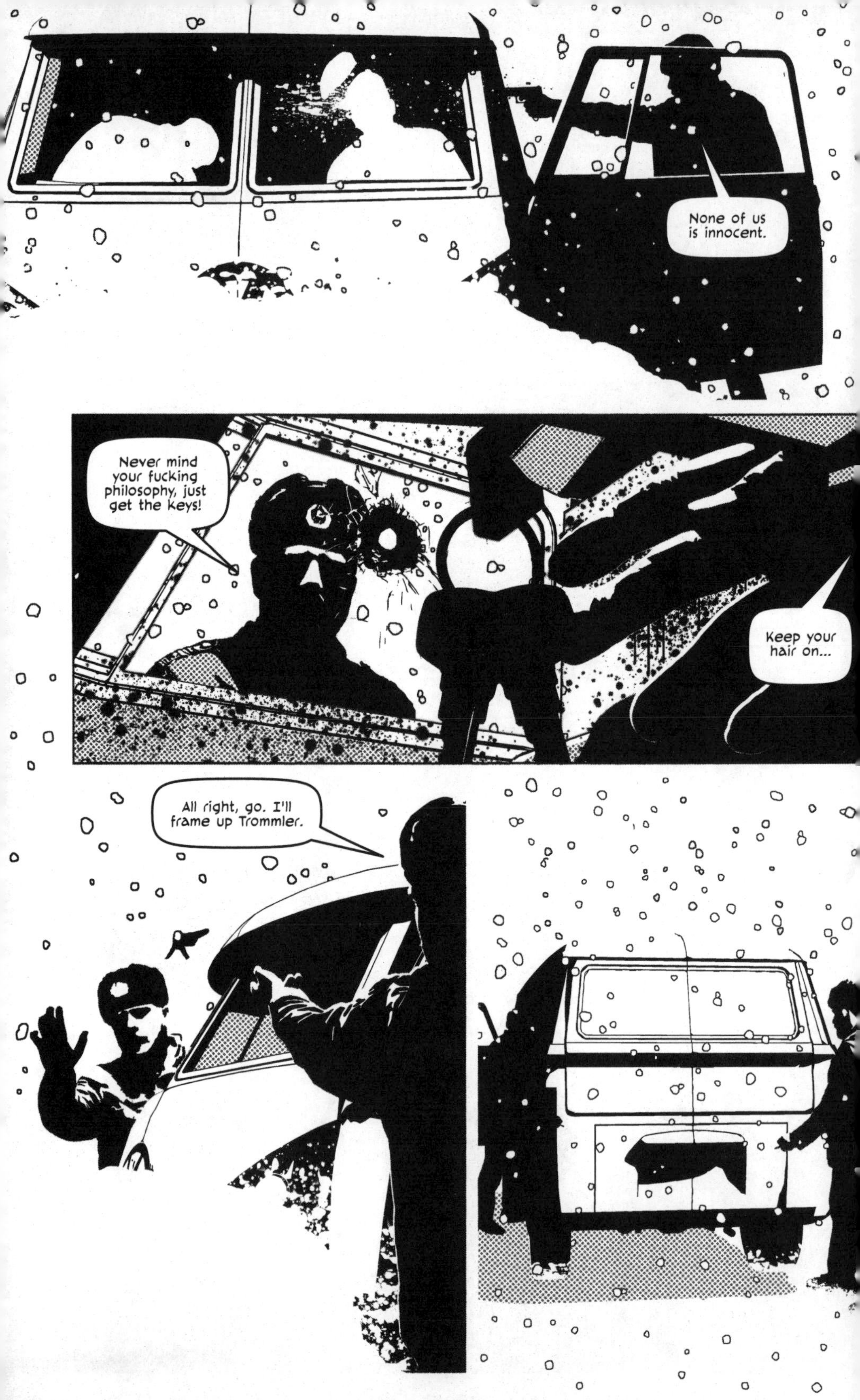
None of us is innocent.
Never mind your fucking philosophy, just get the keys!
Keep your hair on...
All right, go. I'll frame up Trommler.

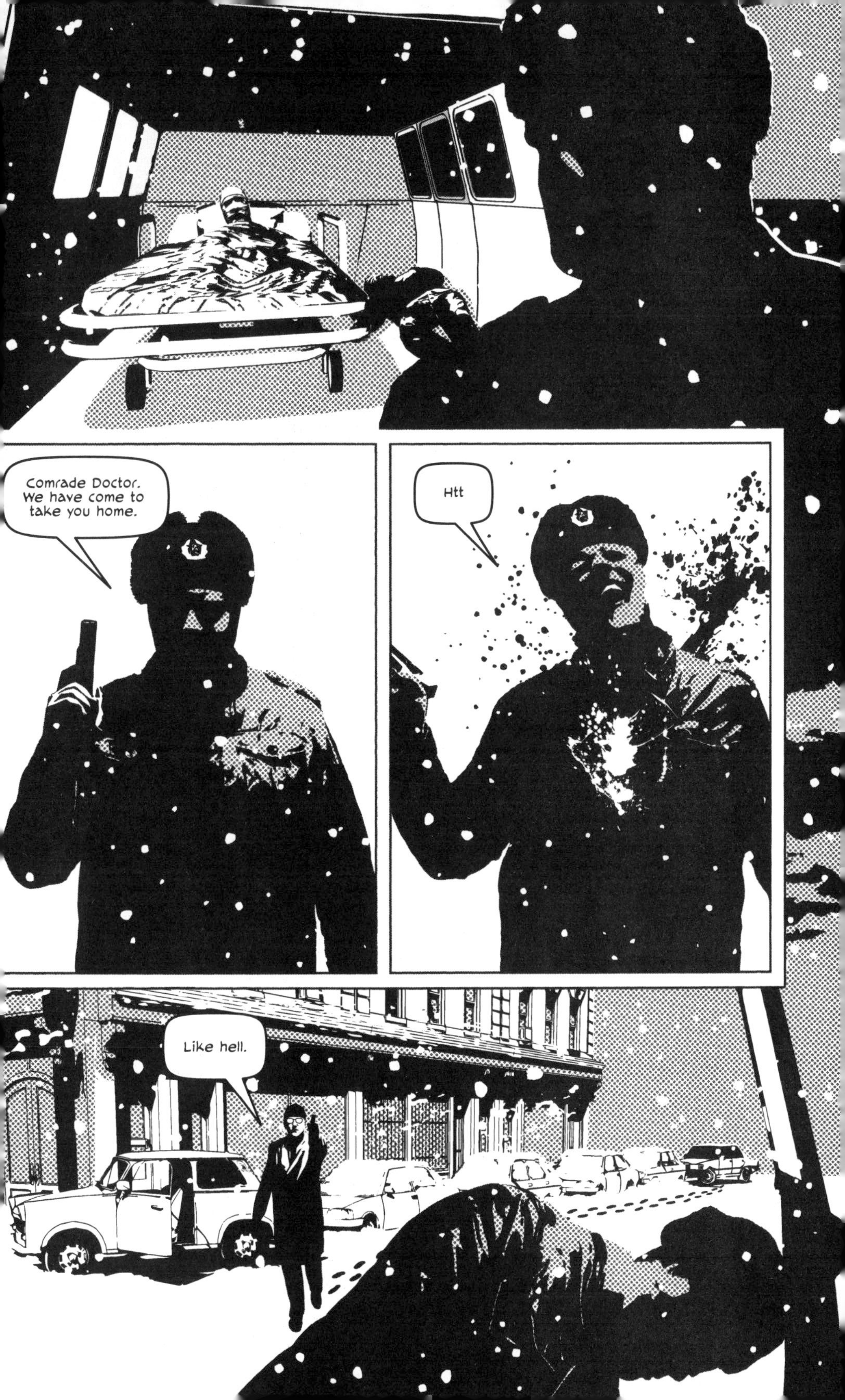
Comrade Doctor. We have come to take you home.
Htt
Like hell.

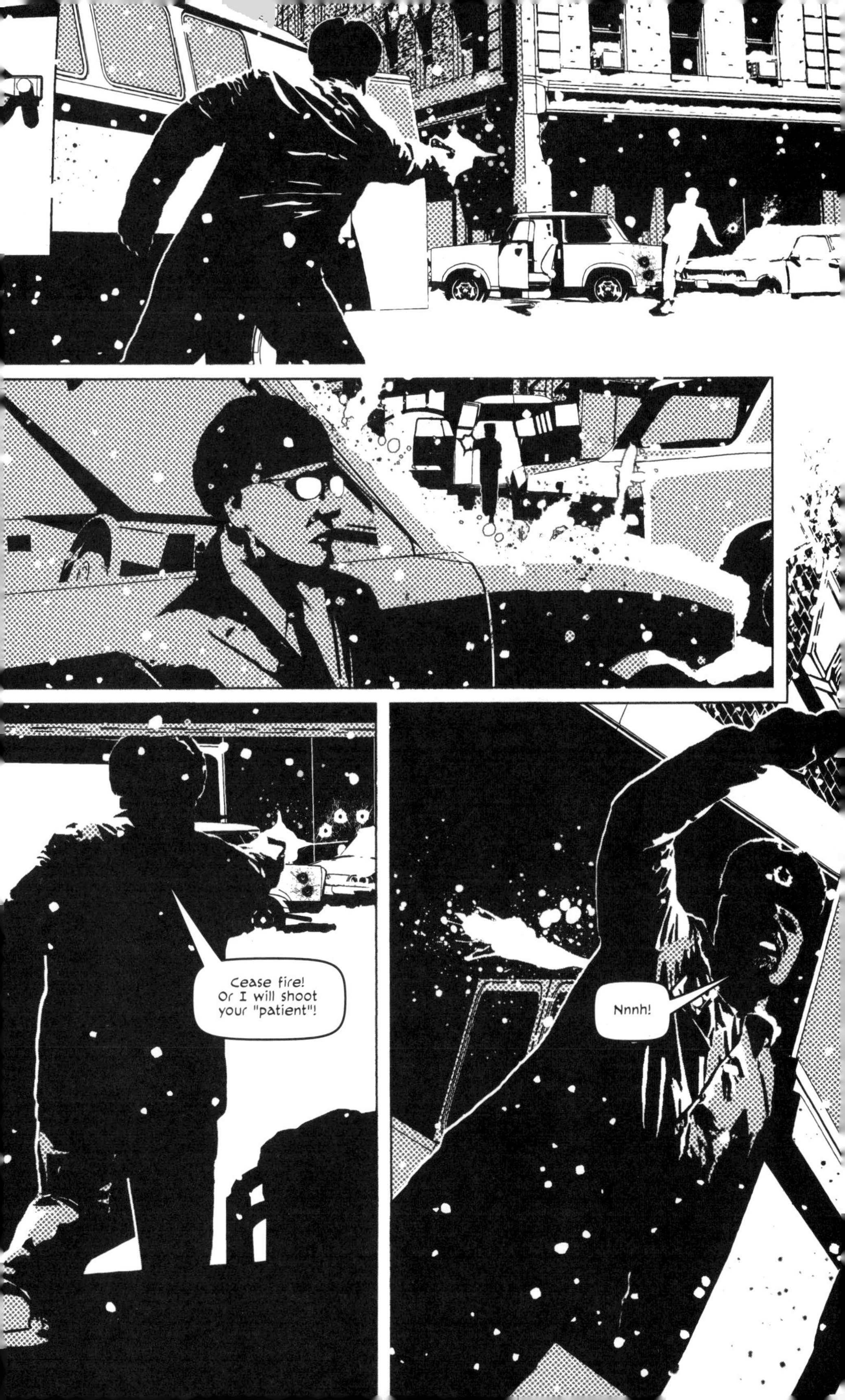
Cease fire! Or I will shoot your "patient"!
Nnnh!

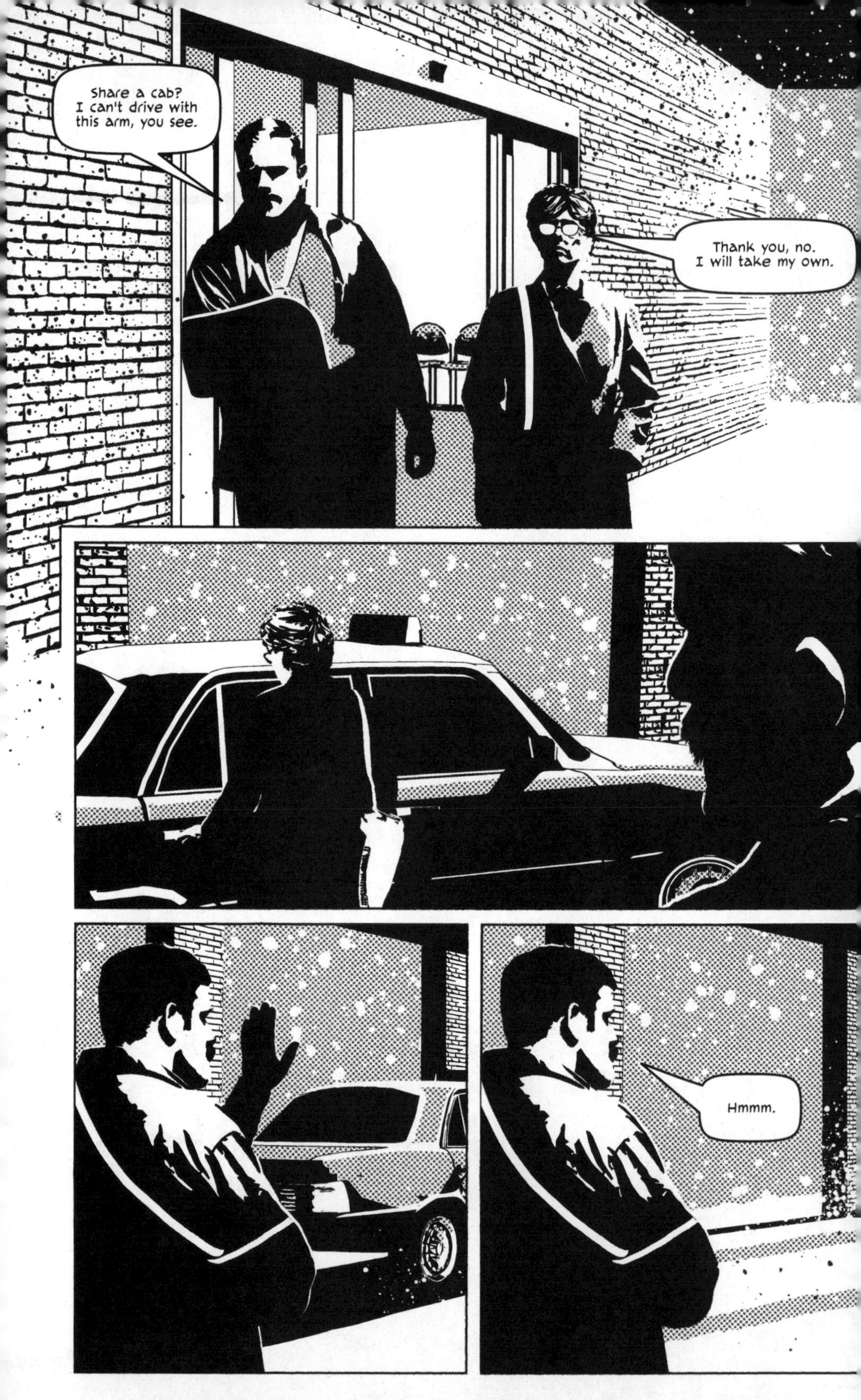
Share a cab? I can't drive with this arm, you see.
Thank you, no. I will take my own.
Hmmm.

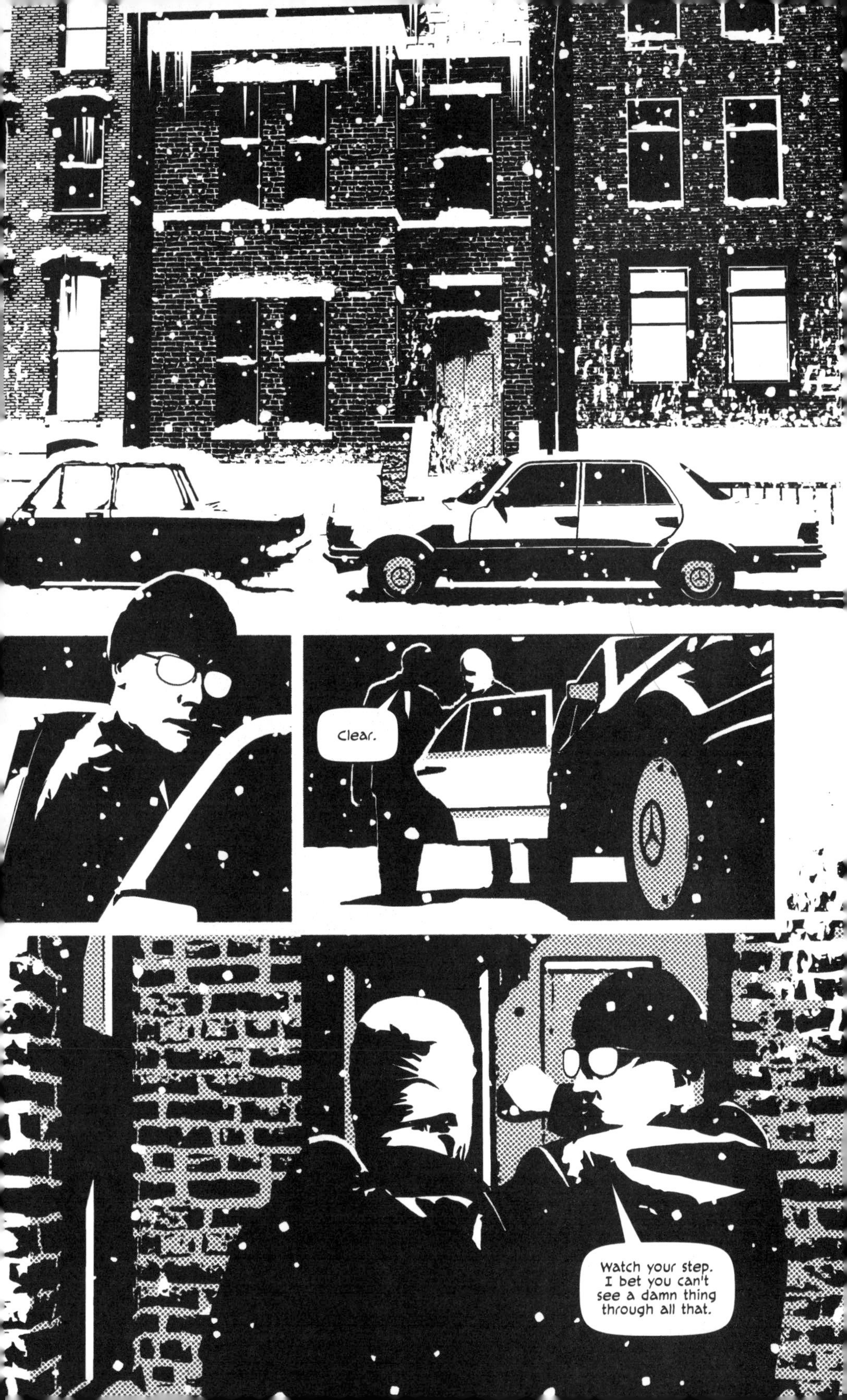
Clear.
Watch your step. I bet you can't see a damn thing through all that.

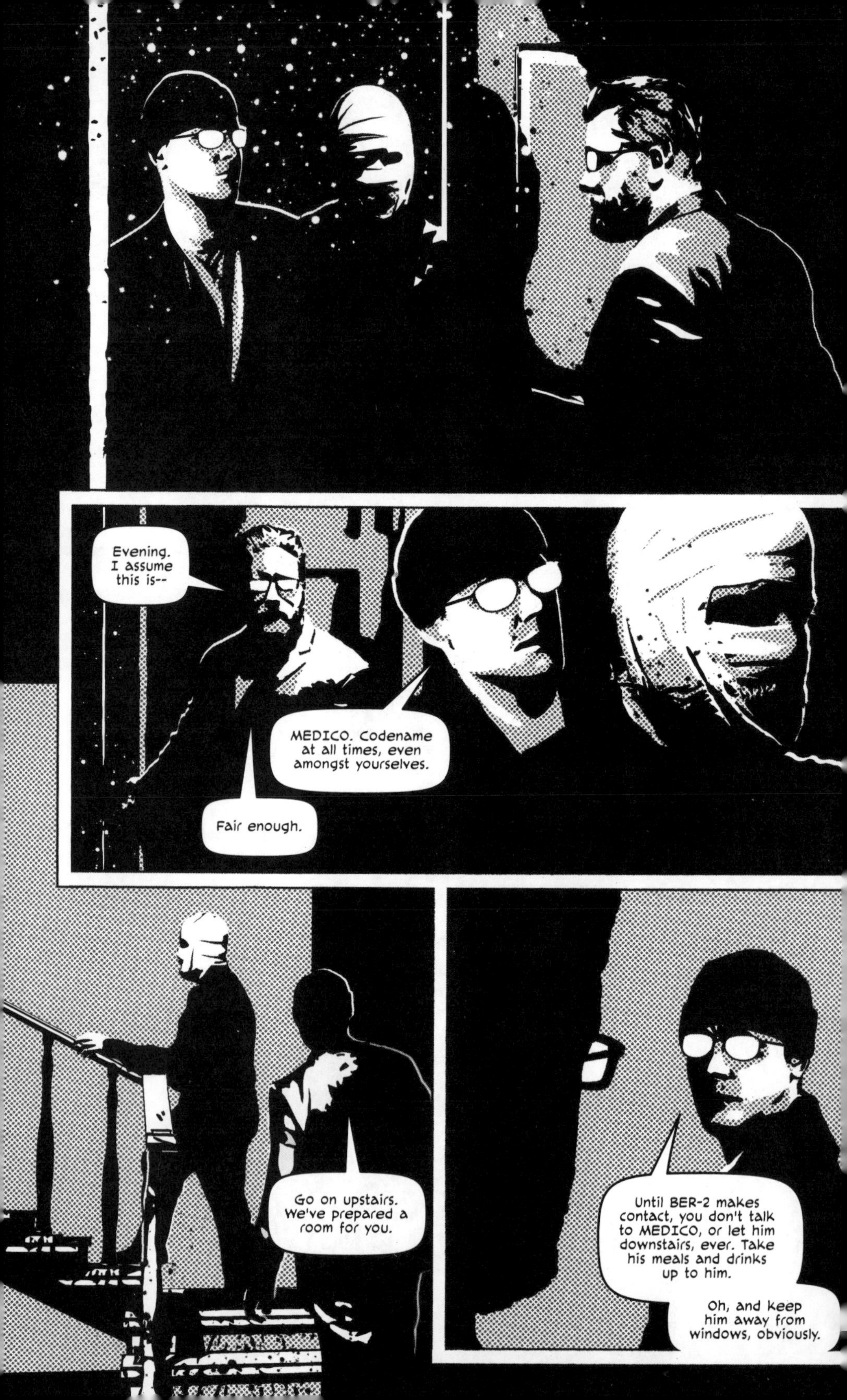
Evening. I assume this is--
MEDICO. Codename at all times, even amongst yourselves.
Fair enough.
Go on upstairs. We've prepared a room for you.
Until BER-2 makes contact, you don't talk to MEDICO, or let him downstairs, ever. Take his meals and drinks up to him.
Oh, and keep him away from windows, obviously.

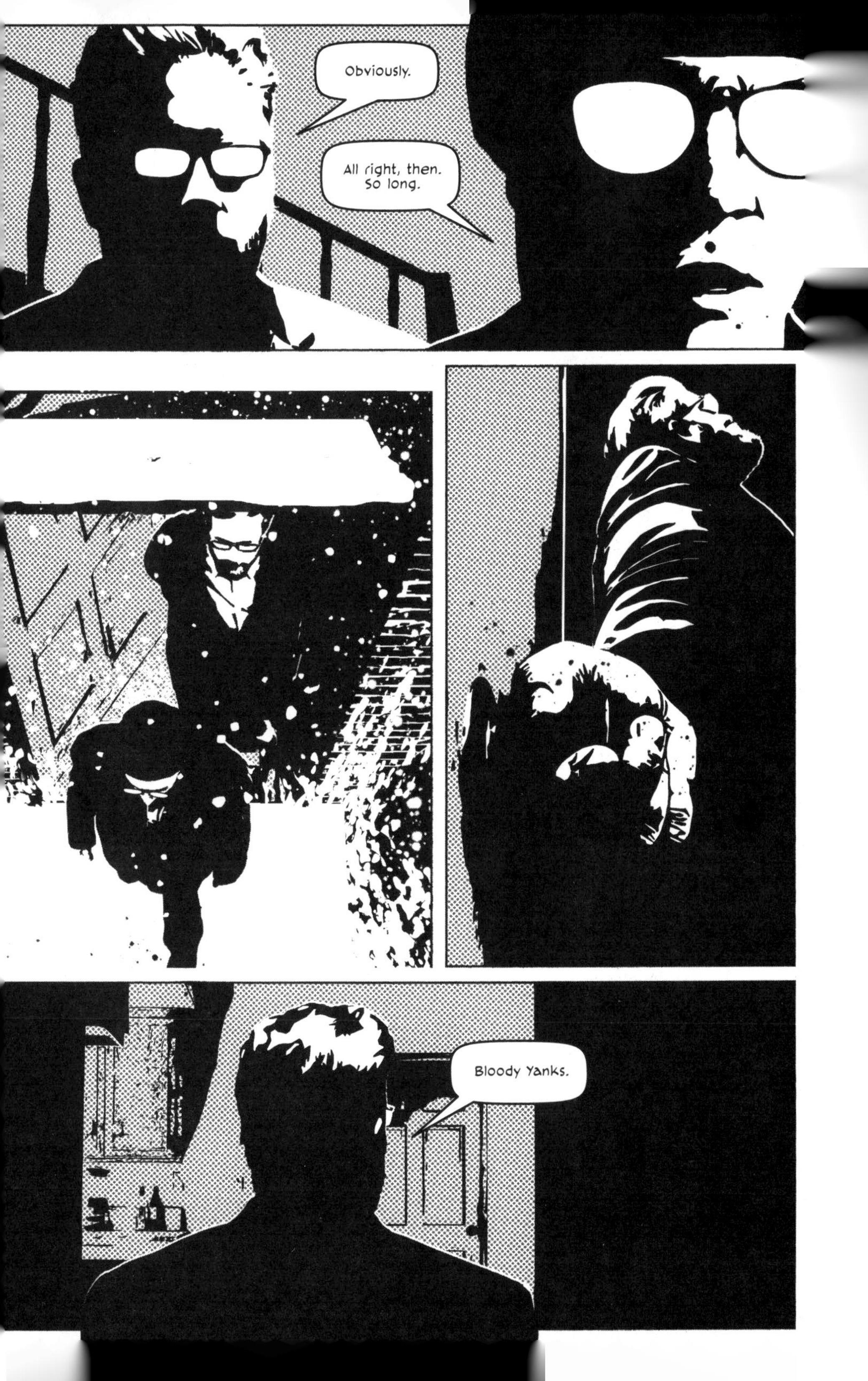
Obviously.
All right, then. So long.
Bloody Yanks.

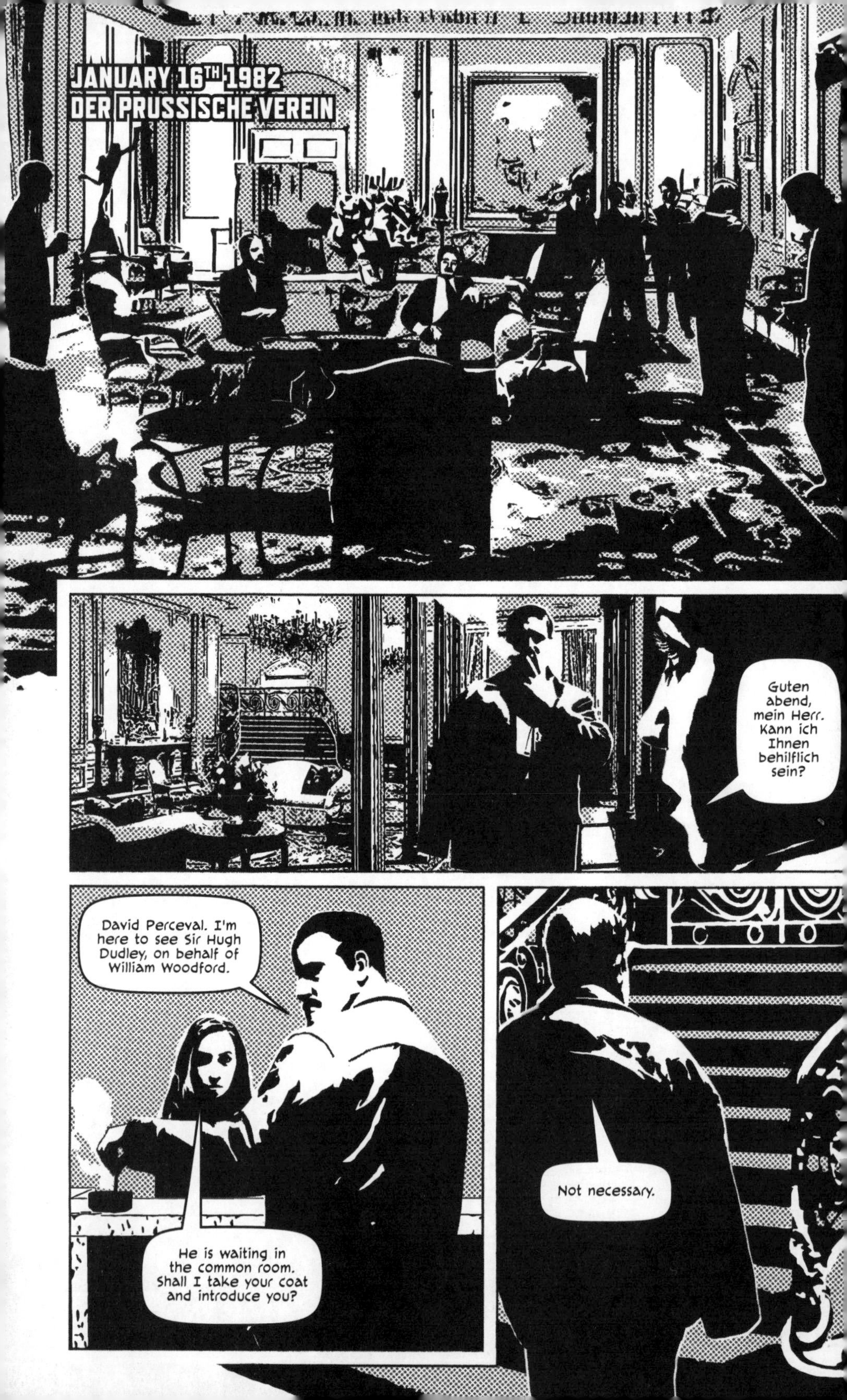
JANUARY 16TH 1982
DER PRUSSISCHE VEREIN
Guten abend, mein Herr. Kann ich Ihnen behilflich sein?
David Perceval. I'm here to see Sir Hugh Dudley, on behalf of William Woodford.
He is waiting in the common room. Shall I take your coat and introduce you?
Not necessary.

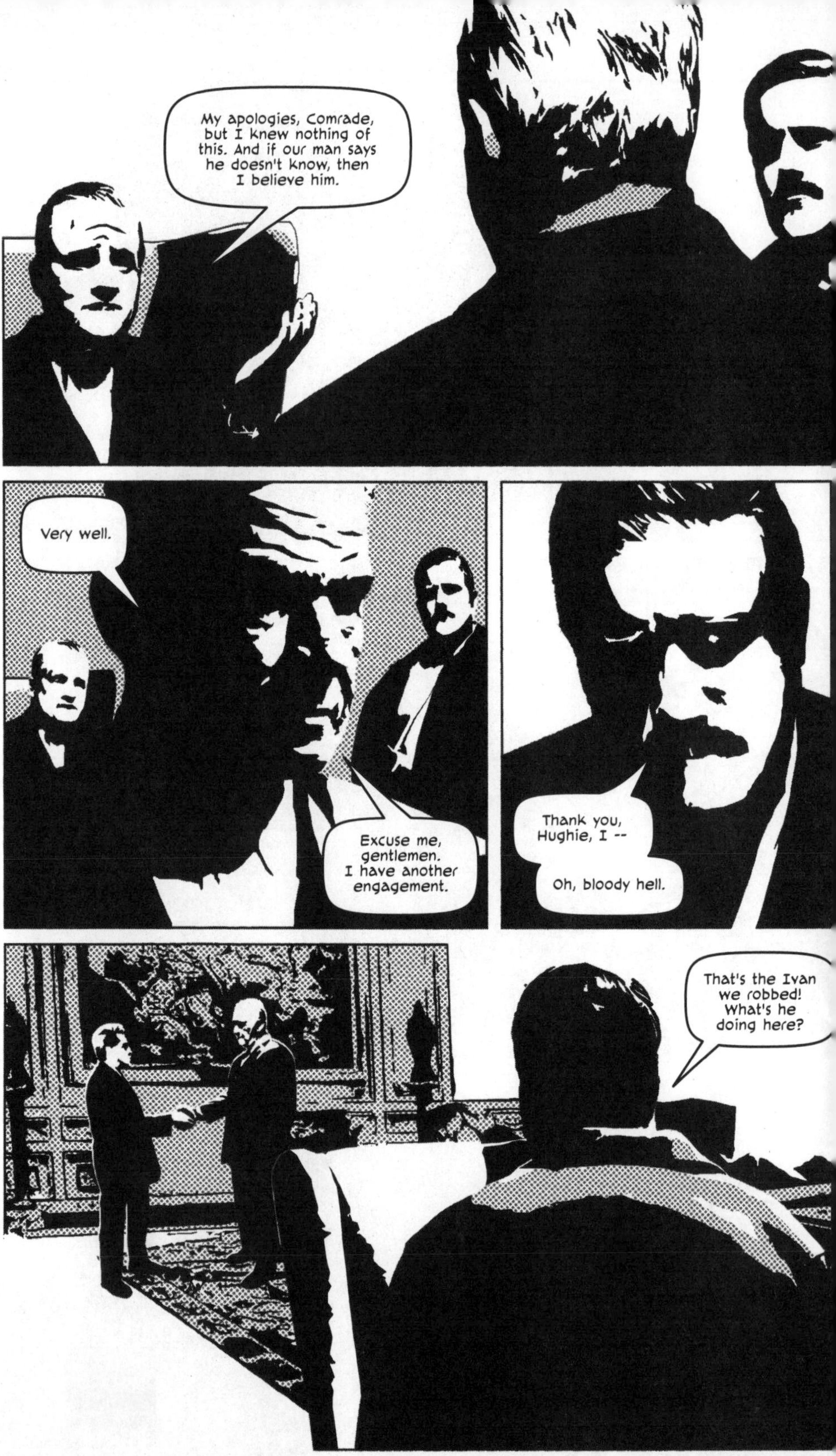
My apologies, Comrade, but I knew nothing of this. And if our man says he doesn't know, then I believe him.
Very well.
Excuse me, gentlemen. I have another engagement.
Thank you, Hughie, I --
Oh, bloody hell.
That's the Ivan we robbed! What's he doing here?

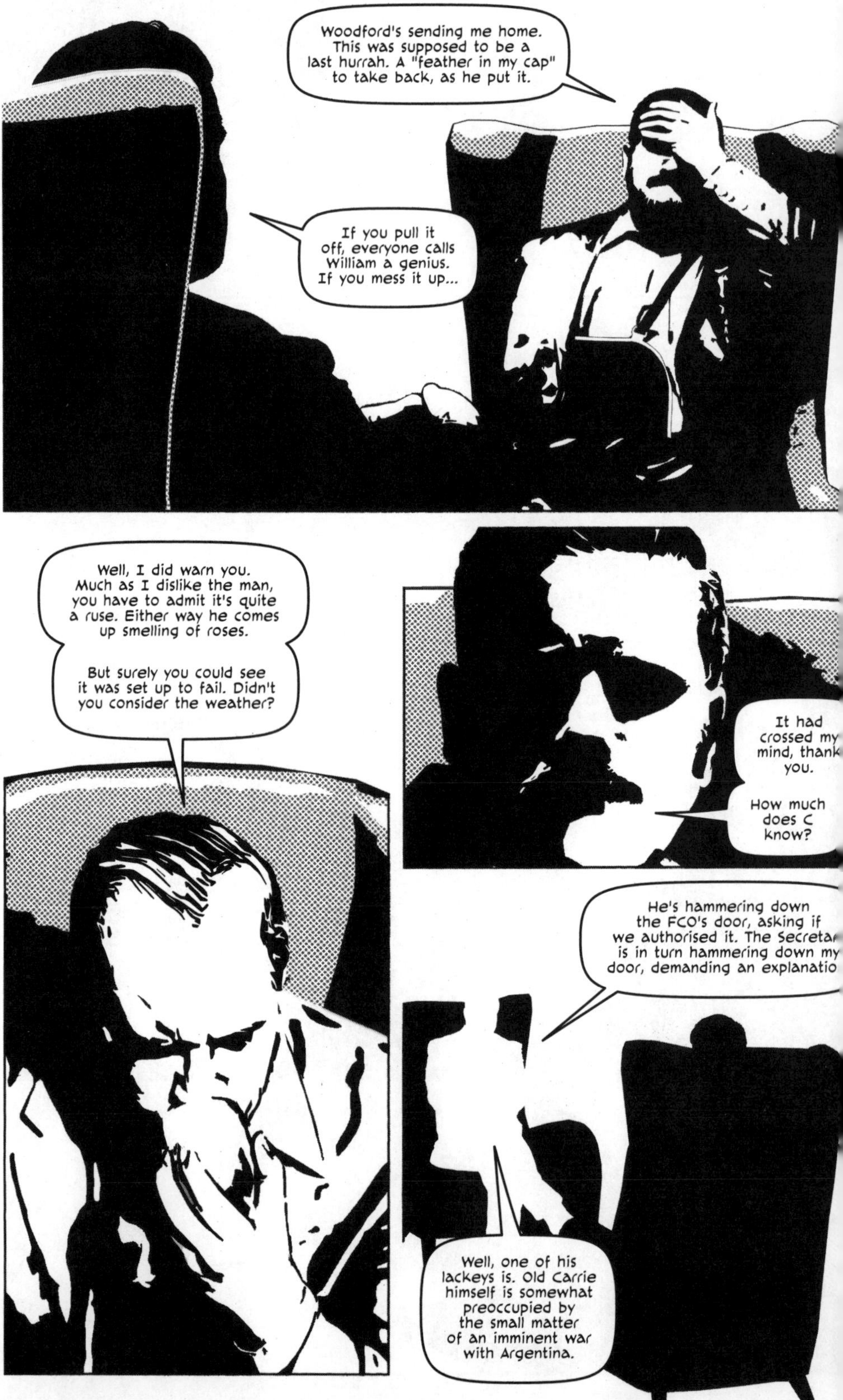
Woodford's sending me home. This was supposed to be a last hurrah. A "feather in my cap" to take back, as he put it.
If you pull it off, everyone calls William a genius. If you mess it up...
Well, I did warn you. Much as I dislike the man, you have to admit it's quite a ruse. Either way he comes up smelling of roses.
But surely you could see it was set up to fail. Didn't you consider the weather?
It had crossed my mind, thank you.
How much does C know?
He's hammering down the FCO's door, asking if we authorised it. The Secreta is in turn hammering down my door, demanding an explanatio
Well, one of his lackeys is. Old Carrie himself is somewhat preoccupied by the small matter of an imminent war with Argentina.

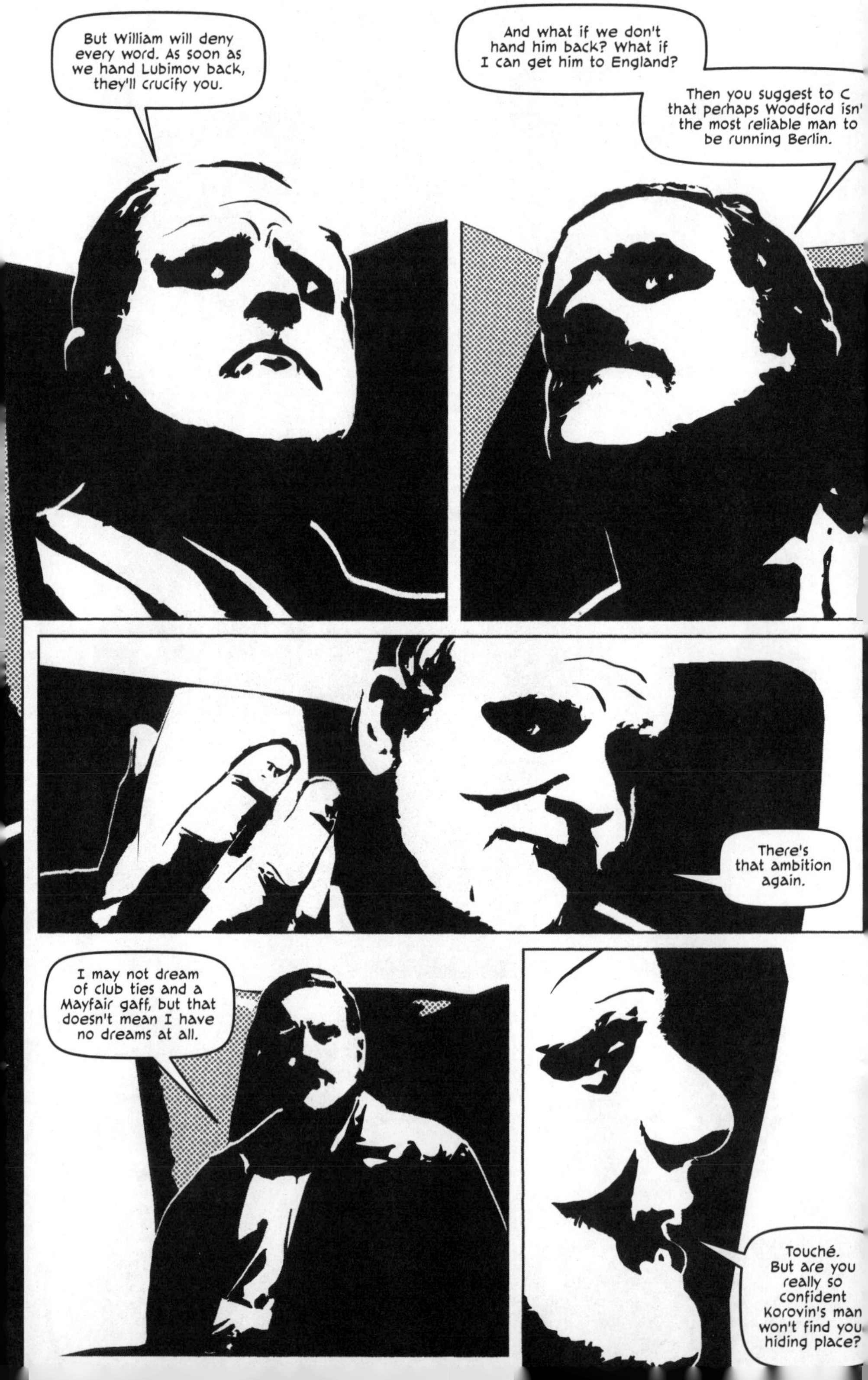
But William will deny every word. As soon as we hand Lubimov back, they'll crucify you.
And what if we don't hand him back? What if I can get him to England?
Then you suggest to C that perhaps Woodford isn' the most reliable man to be running Berlin.
There's that ambition again.
I may not dream of club ties and a Mayfair gaff, but that doesn't mean I have no dreams at all.
Touché. But are you really so confident Korovin's man won't find you hiding place?

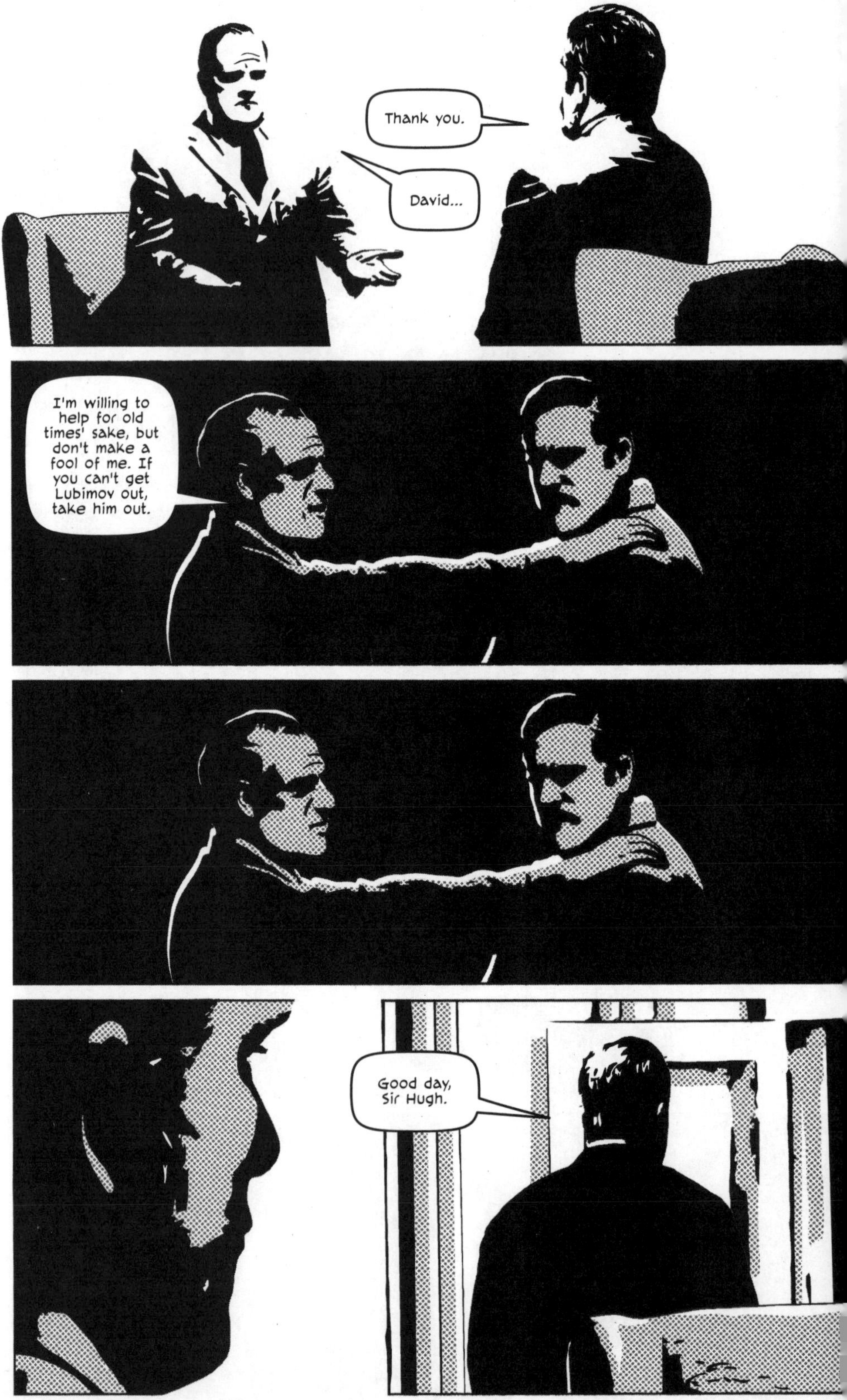
Thank you.
David...
I'm willing to help for old times' sake, but don't make a fool of me. If you can't get Lubimov out, take him out.
Good day, Sir Hugh.

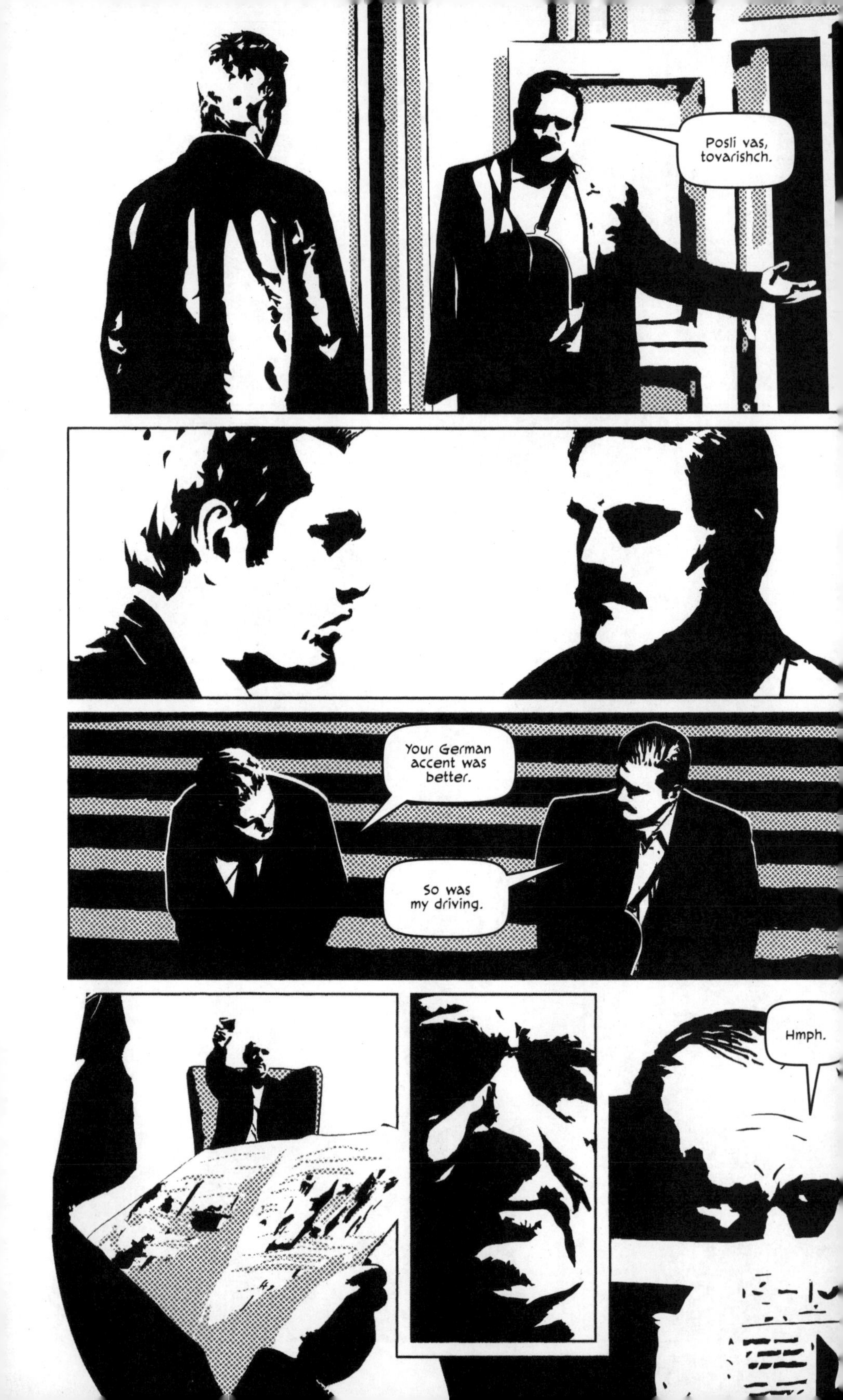
Posli vas, tovarishch.
Your German accent was better.
So was my driving.
Hmph.

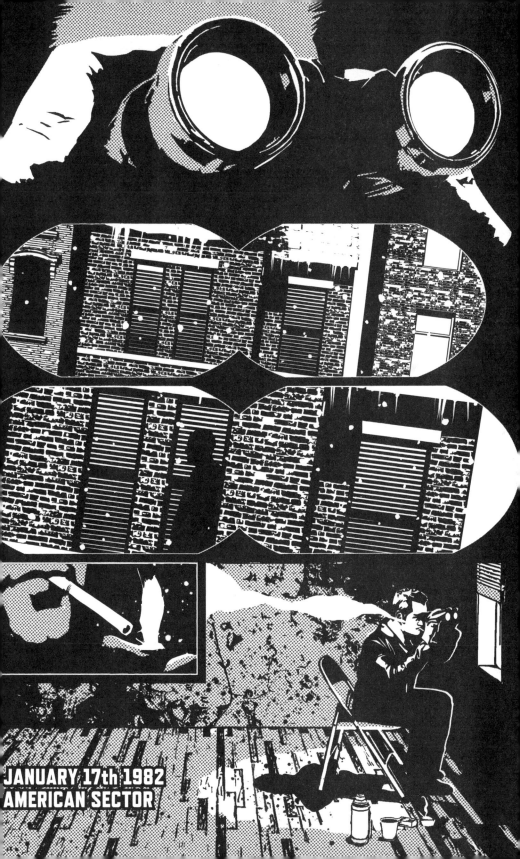

JANUARY 17th 1982
AMERICAN SECTOR

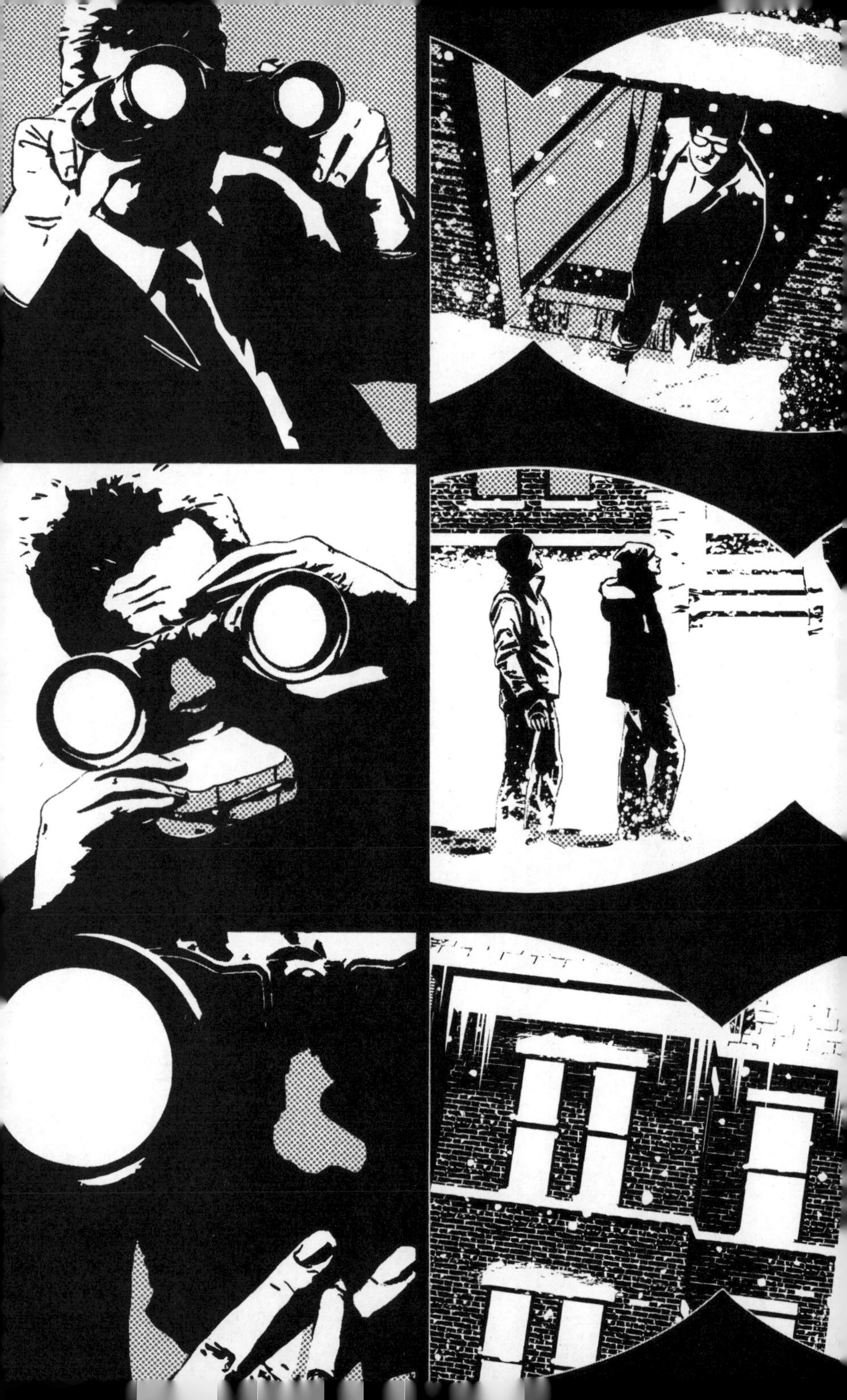

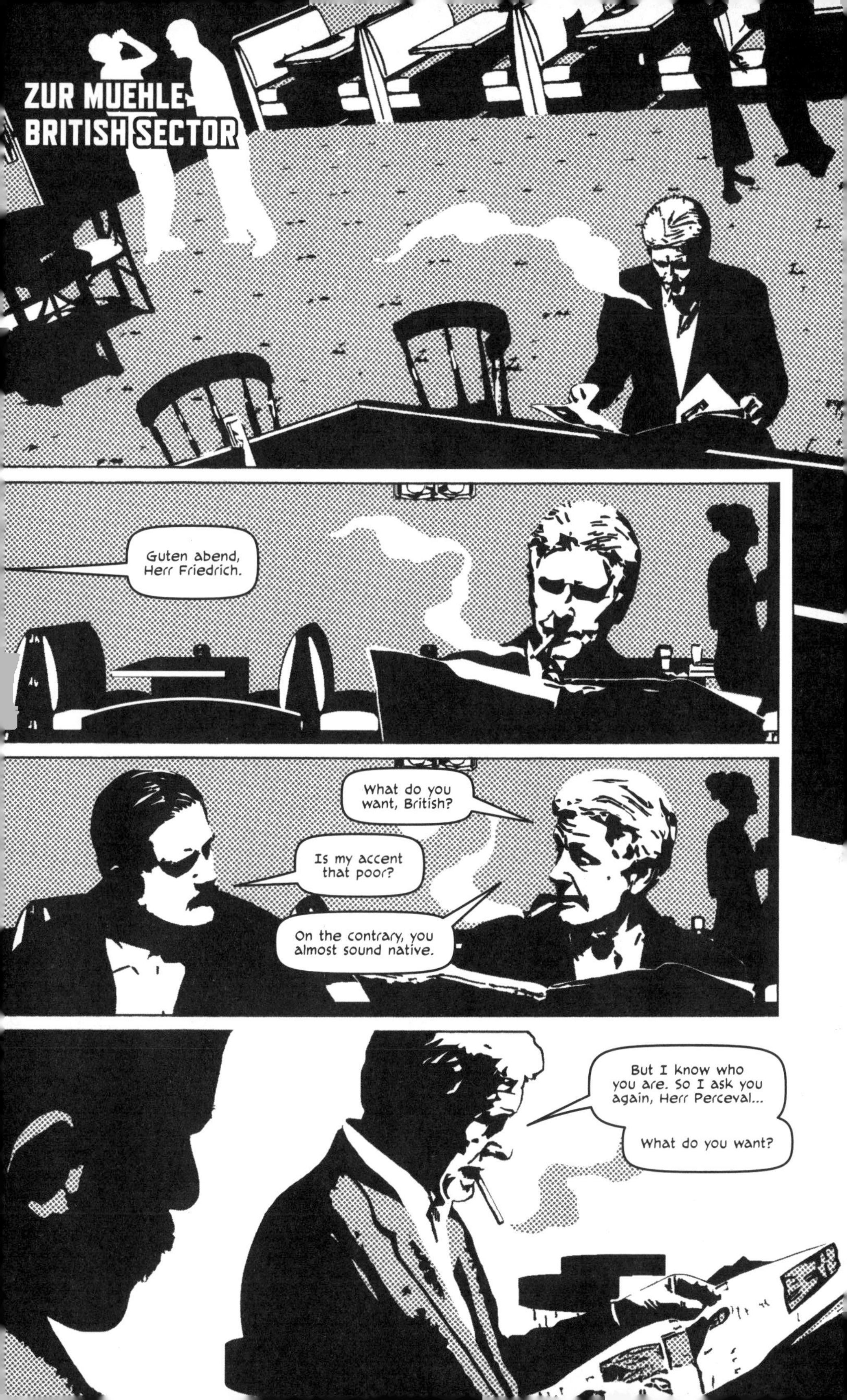
ZUR MUEHLE
BRITISH SECTOR
Guten abend, Herr Friedrich.
What do you want, British?
Is my accent that poor?
On the contrary, you almost sound native.
But I know who you are. So I ask you again, Herr Perceval...
What do you want?

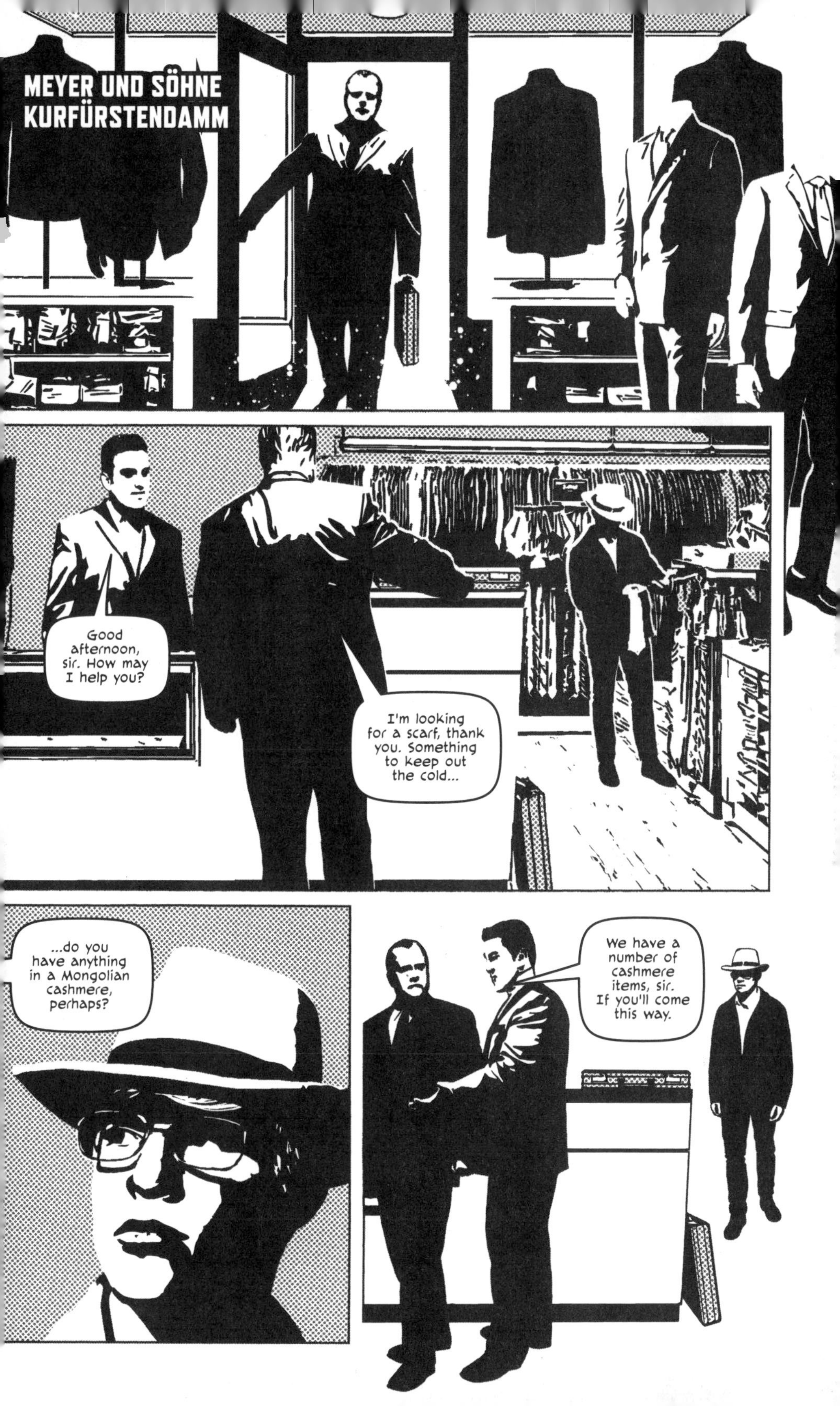
MEYER UND SÖHNE
KURFÜRSTENDAMM
Good afternoon, sir. How may I help you?
I'm looking for a scarf, thank you. Something to keep out the cold...
...do you have anything in a Mongolian cashmere, perhaps?
We have a number of cashmere items, sir. If you'll come this way.

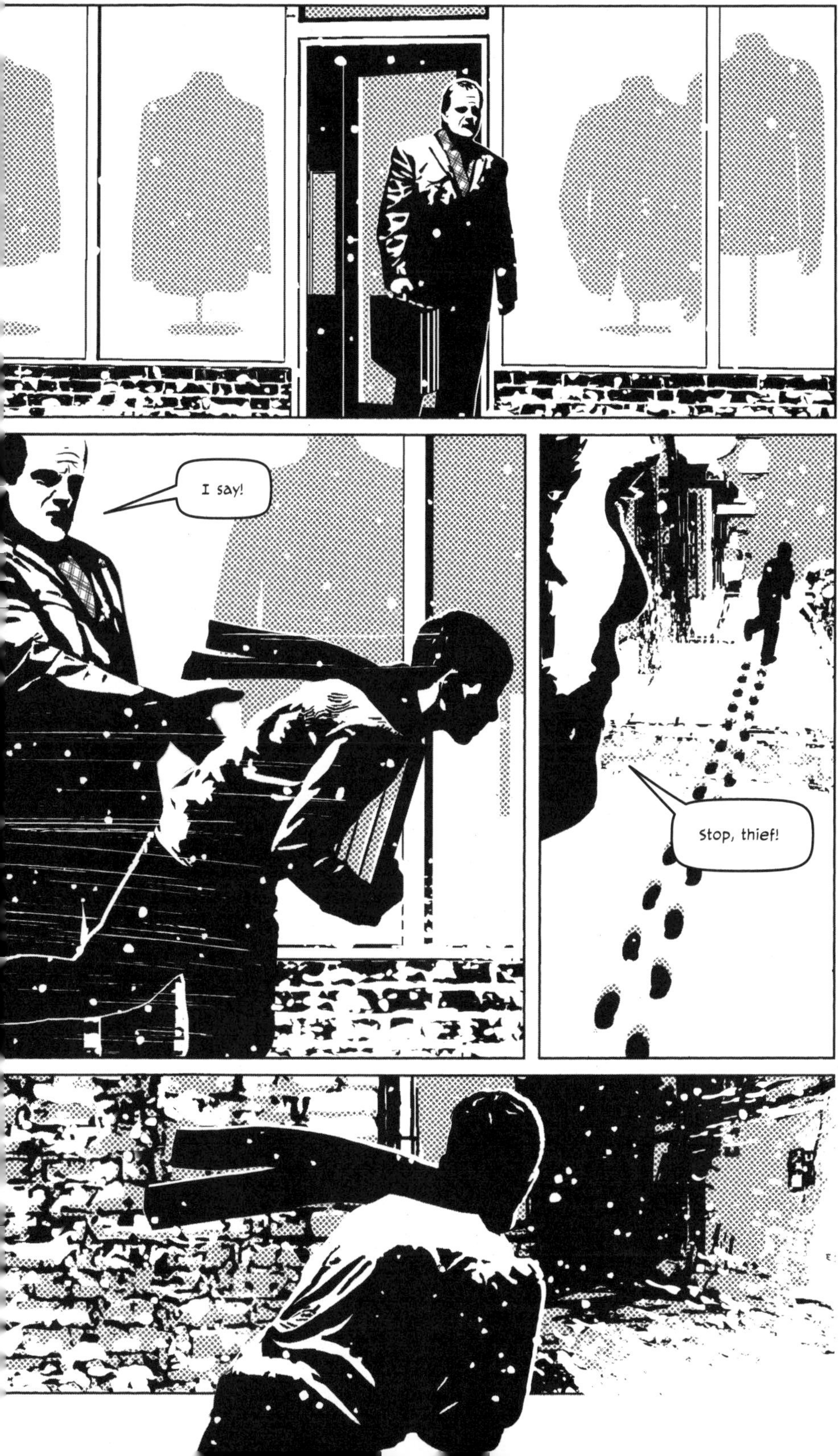
I say!
Stop, thief!

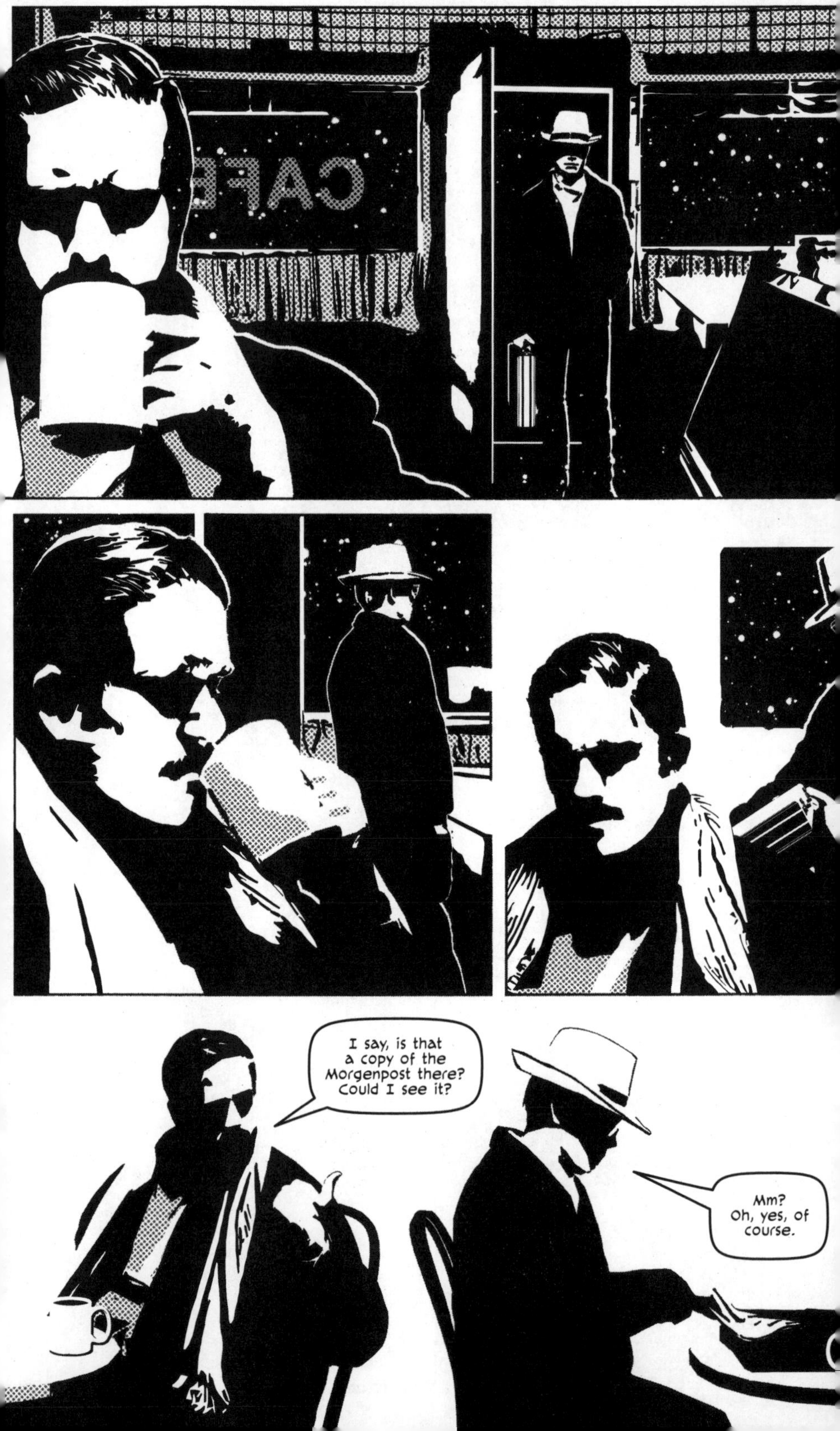
CAFE
I say, is that a copy of the Morgenpost there? Could I see it?
Mm? Oh, yes, of course.

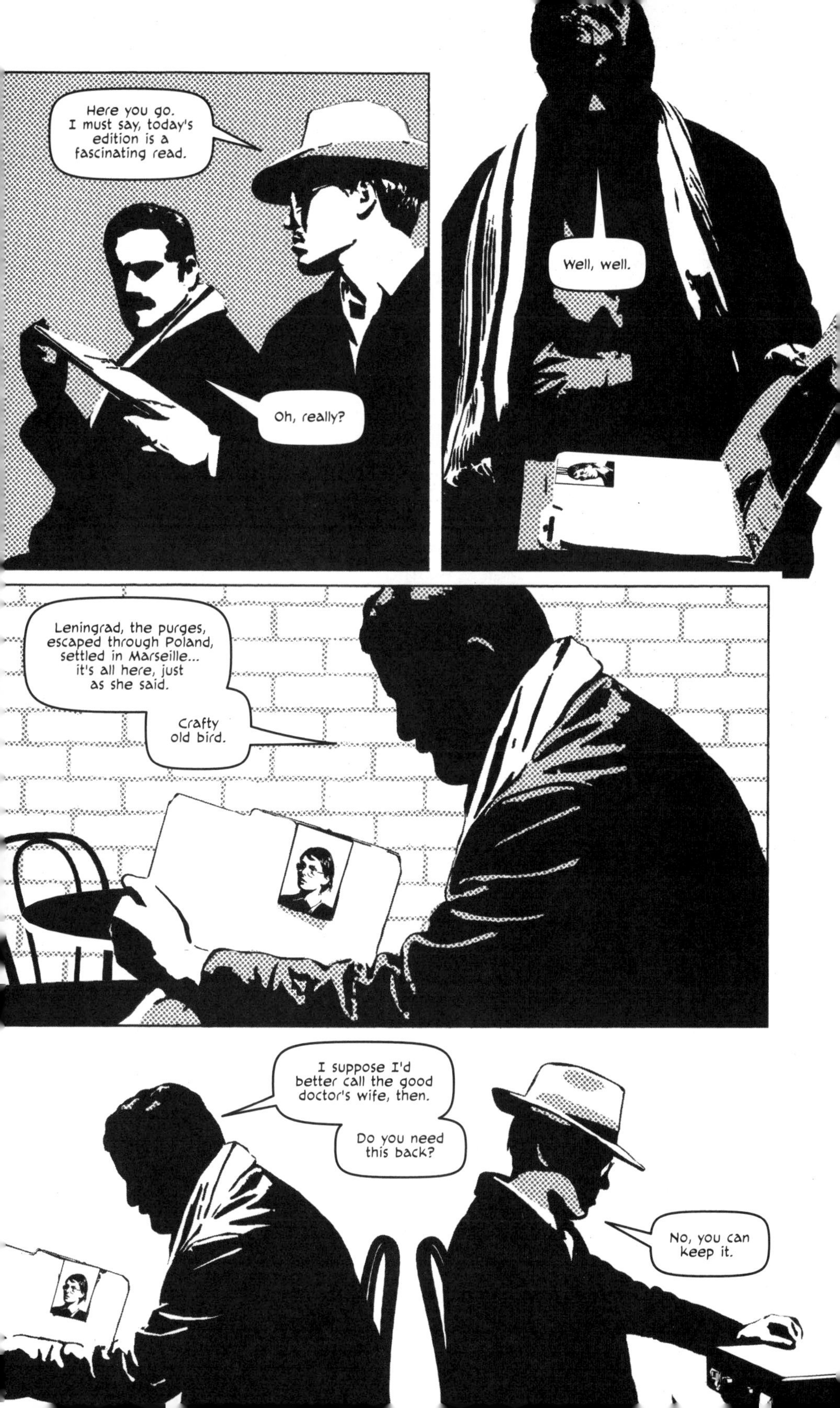

Here you go. I must say, today's edition is a fascinating read.
Oh, really?
Well, well.
Leningrad, the purges, escaped through Poland, settled in Marseille... it's all here, just as she said.
Crafty old bird.
I suppose I'd better call the good doctor's wife, then.
Do you need this back?
No, you can keep it.

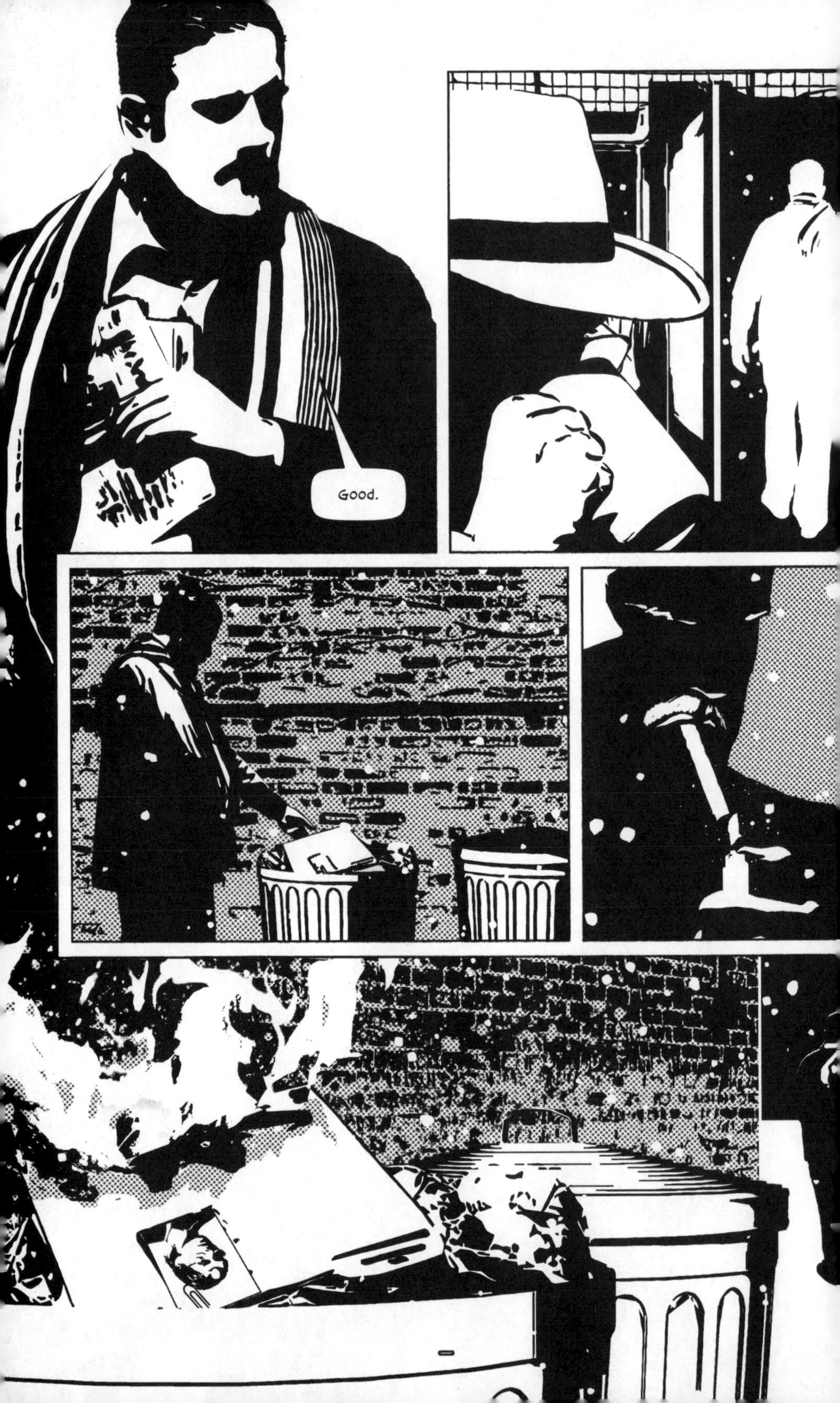
Good.

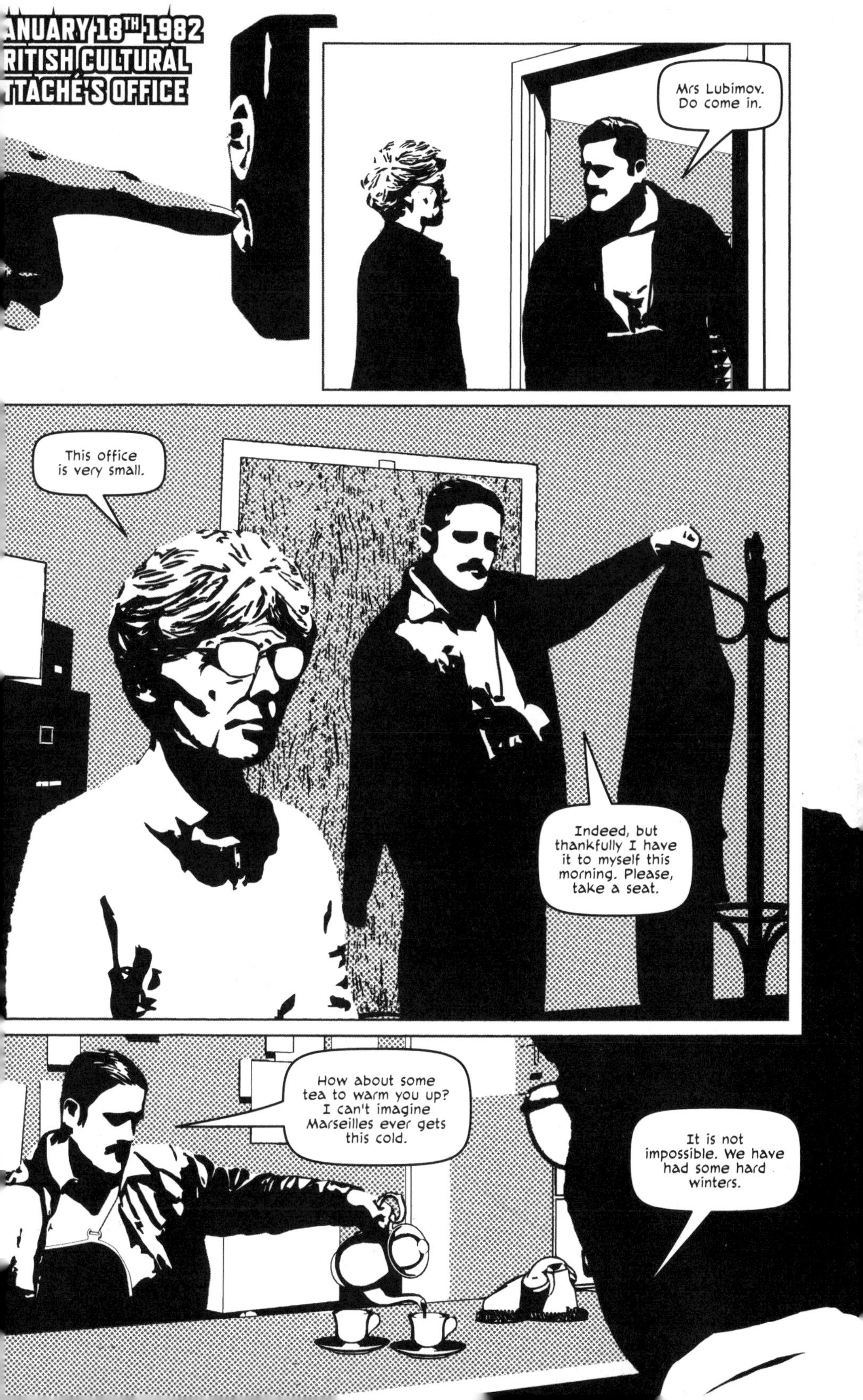
ANUARY 18TH 1982
RITISH CULTURAL
TTACHÉ'S OFFICE
Mrs Lubimov. Do come in.
This office is very small.
Indeed, but thankfully I have it to myself this morning. Please, take a seat.
How about some tea to warm you up? I can't imagine Marseilles ever gets this cold.
It is not impossible. We have had some hard winters.

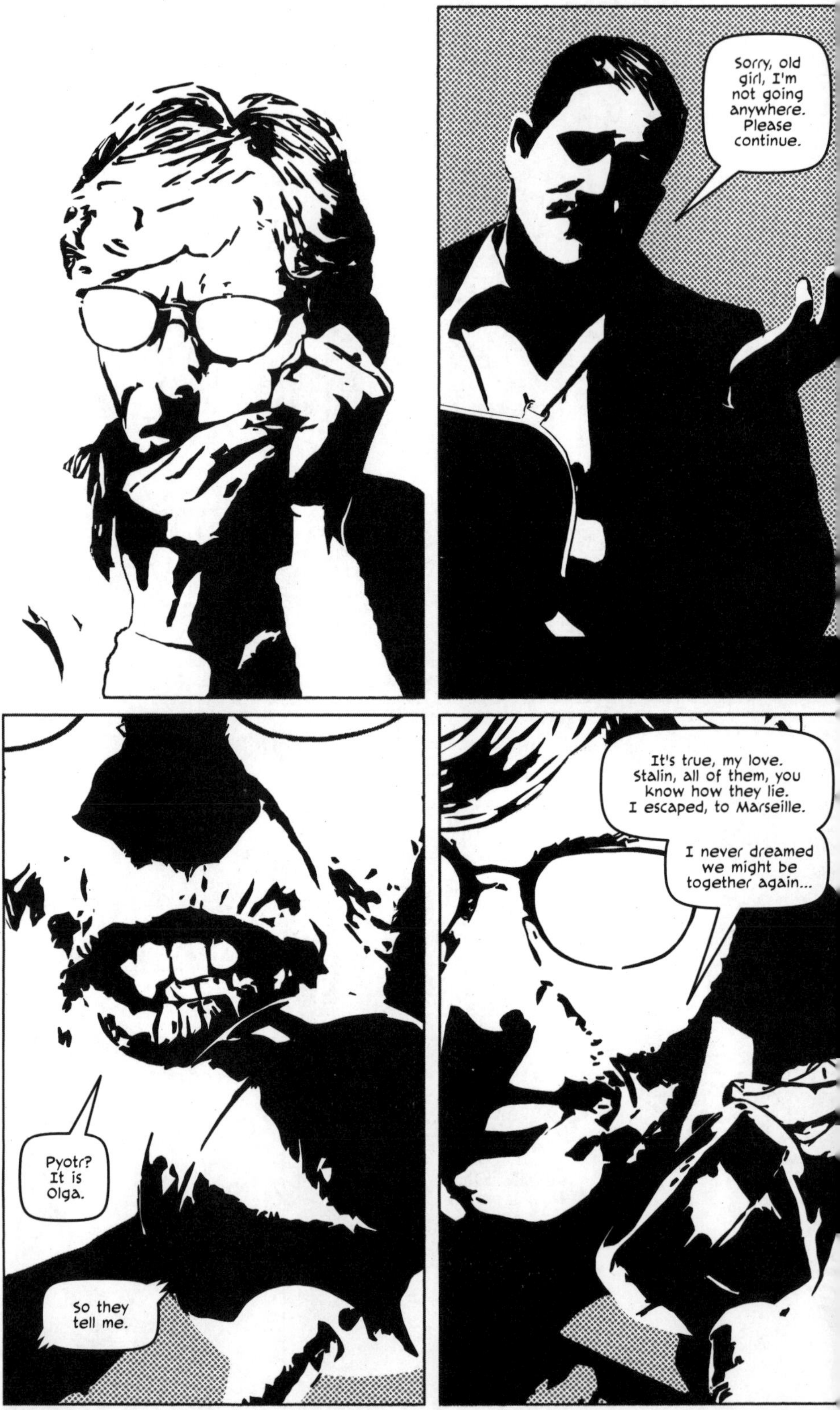
Sorry, old girl, I'm not going anywhere. Please continue.
Pyotr? It is Olga.
So they tell me.
It's true, my love. Stalin, all of them, you know how they lie. I escaped, to Marseille.
I never dreamed we might be together again...

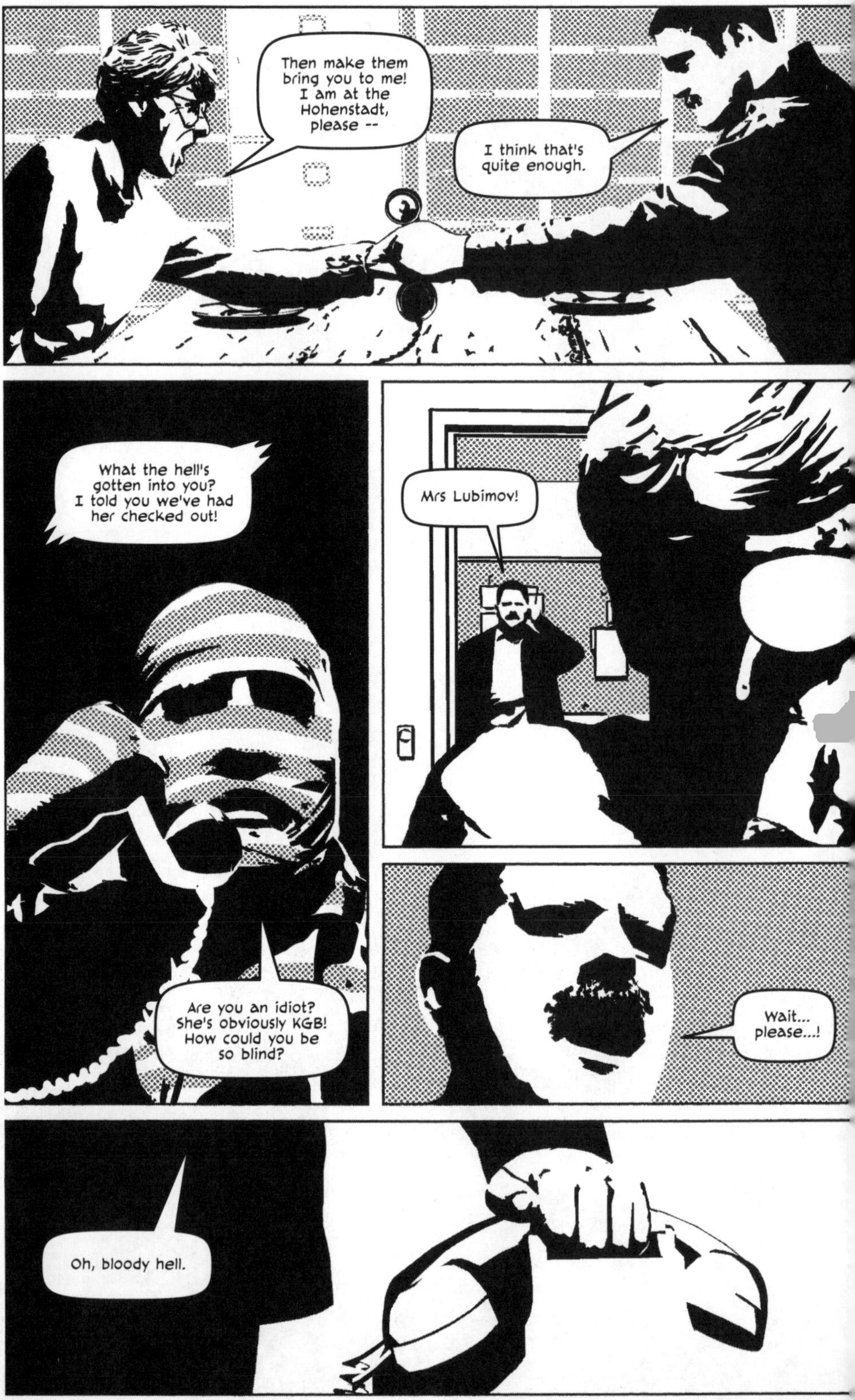
Then make them bring you to me! I am at the Hohenstadt, please --
I think that's quite enough.
What the hell's gotten into you? I told you we've had her checked out!
Are you an idiot? She's obviously KGB! How could you be so blind?
Mrs Lubimov!
Wait... please...!
Oh, bloody hell.

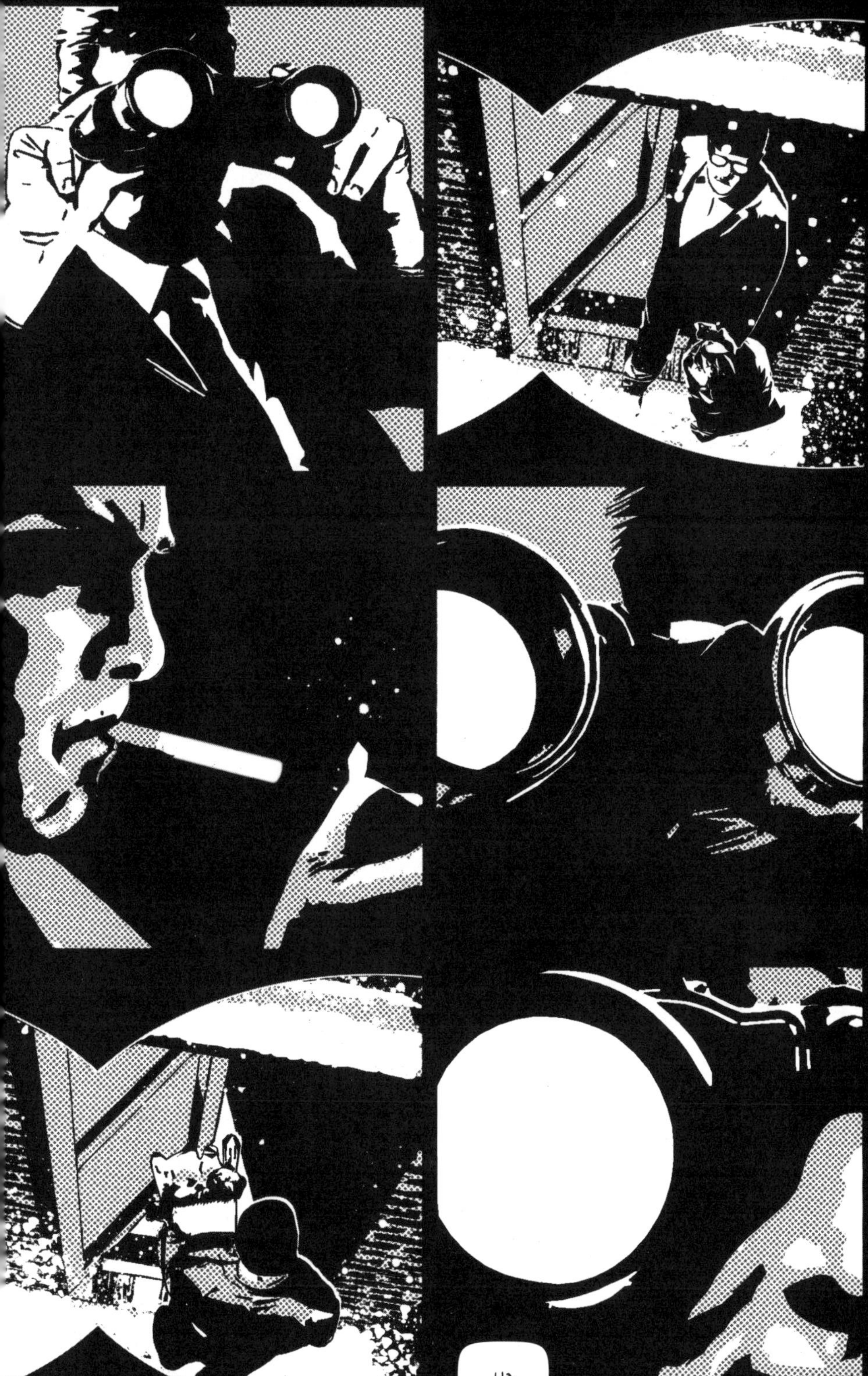
Ha.

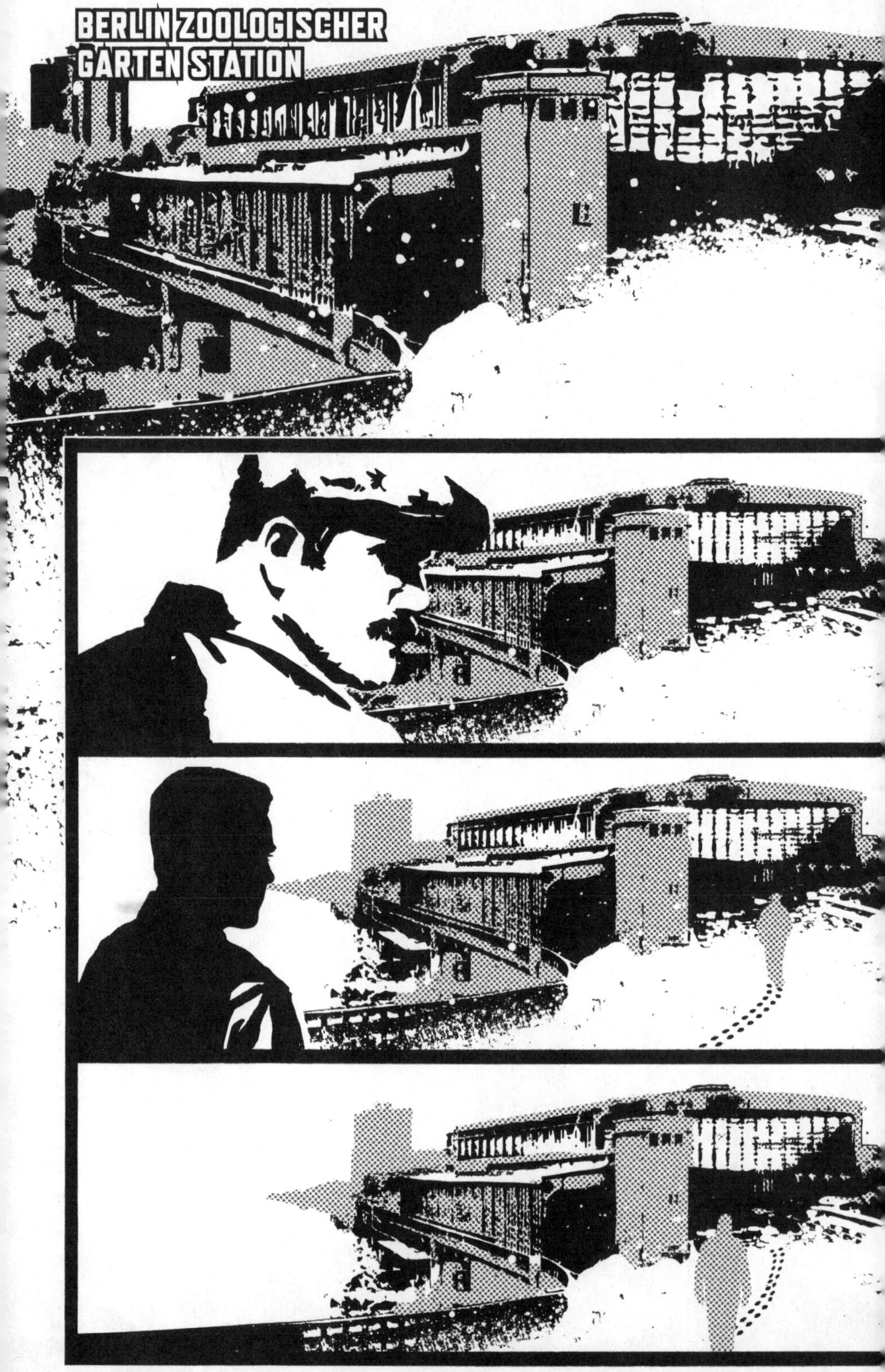
BERLIN ZOOLOGISCHER GARTEN STATION

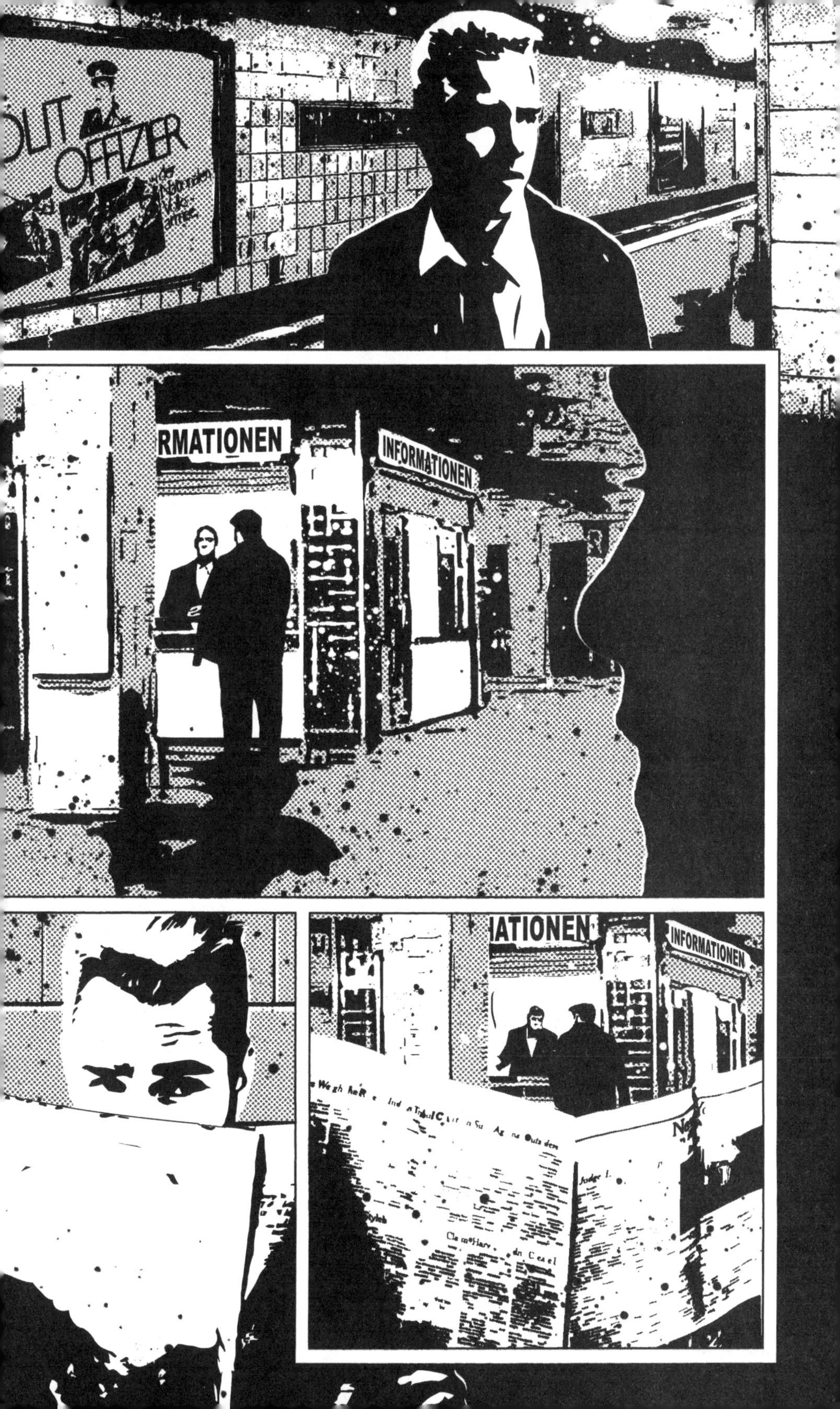

OUT
OFFIZIER
RMATIONEN
INFORMATIONEN
ATIONEN
INFORMATIONEN

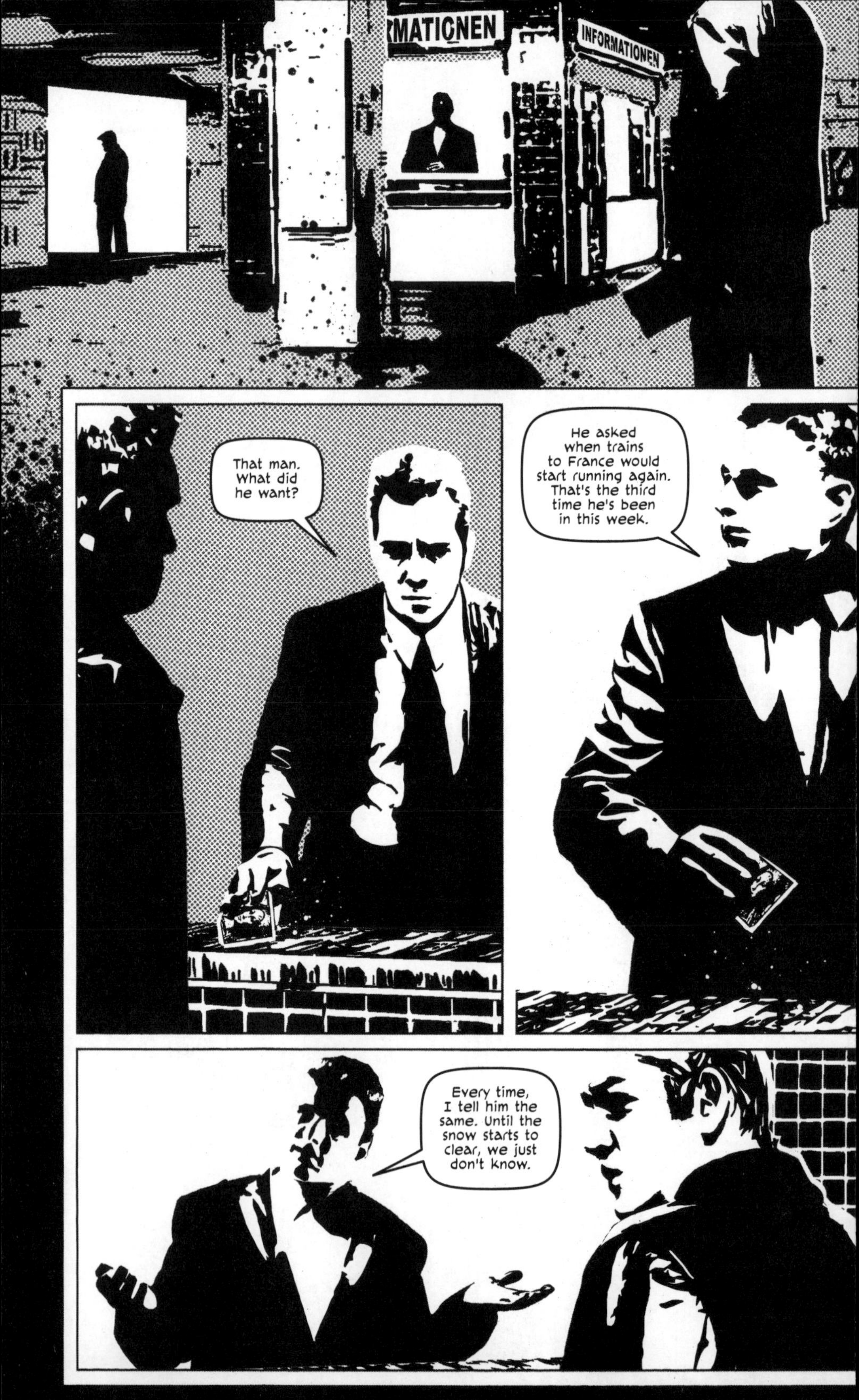

RMATIONEN
INFORMATIONEN
That man. What did he want?
He asked when trains to France would start running again. That's the third time he's been in this week.
Every time, I tell him the same. Until the snow starts to clear, we just don't know.

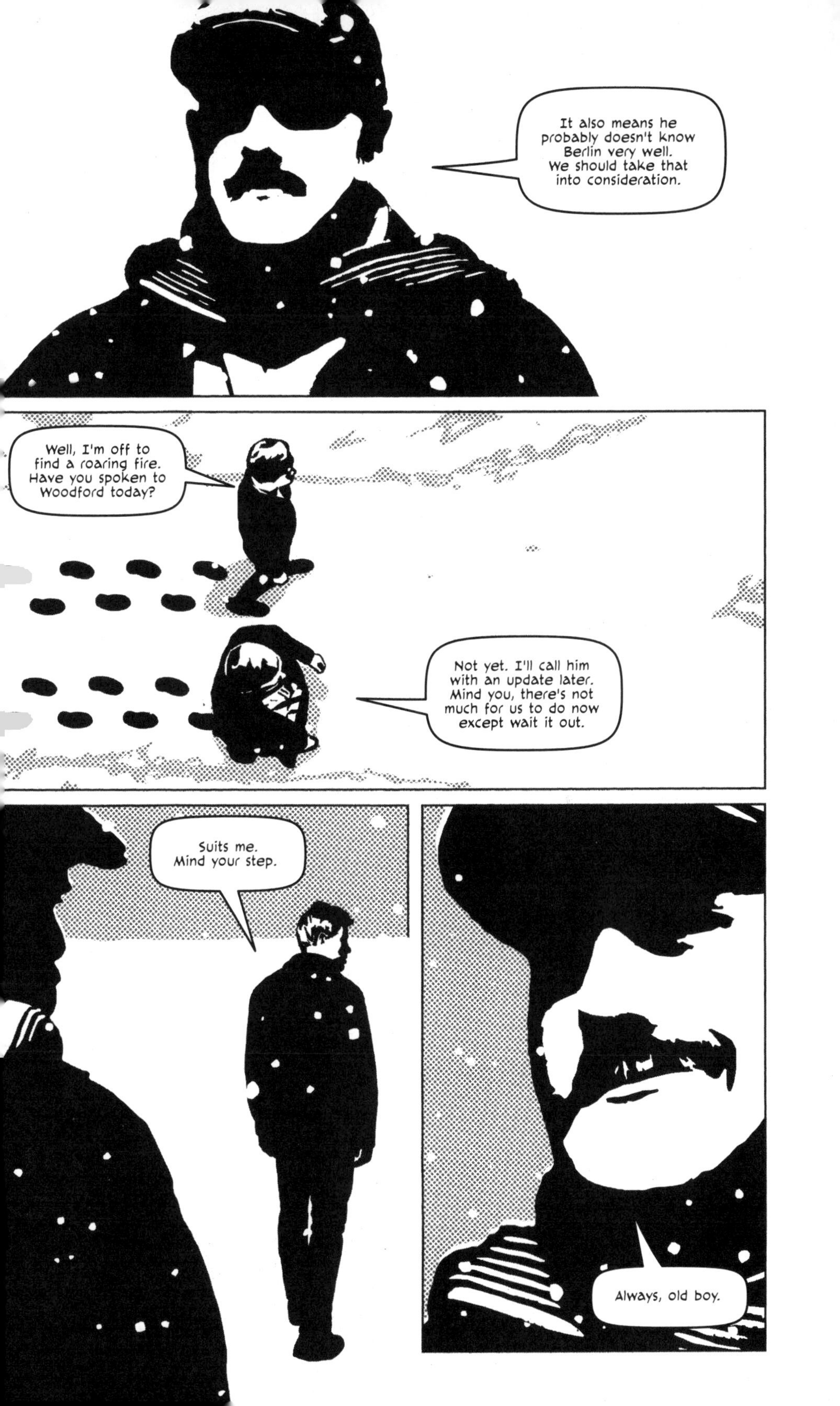

It also means he probably doesn't know Berlin very well. We should take that into consideration.
Well, I'm off to find a roaring fire. Have you spoken to Woodford today?
Not yet. I'll call him with an update later. Mind you, there's not much for us to do now except wait it out.
Suits me. Mind your step.
Always, old boy.

JANUARY 19TH 1982

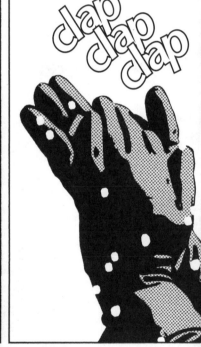

Congratulations, Yankee.

It was almost perfect...

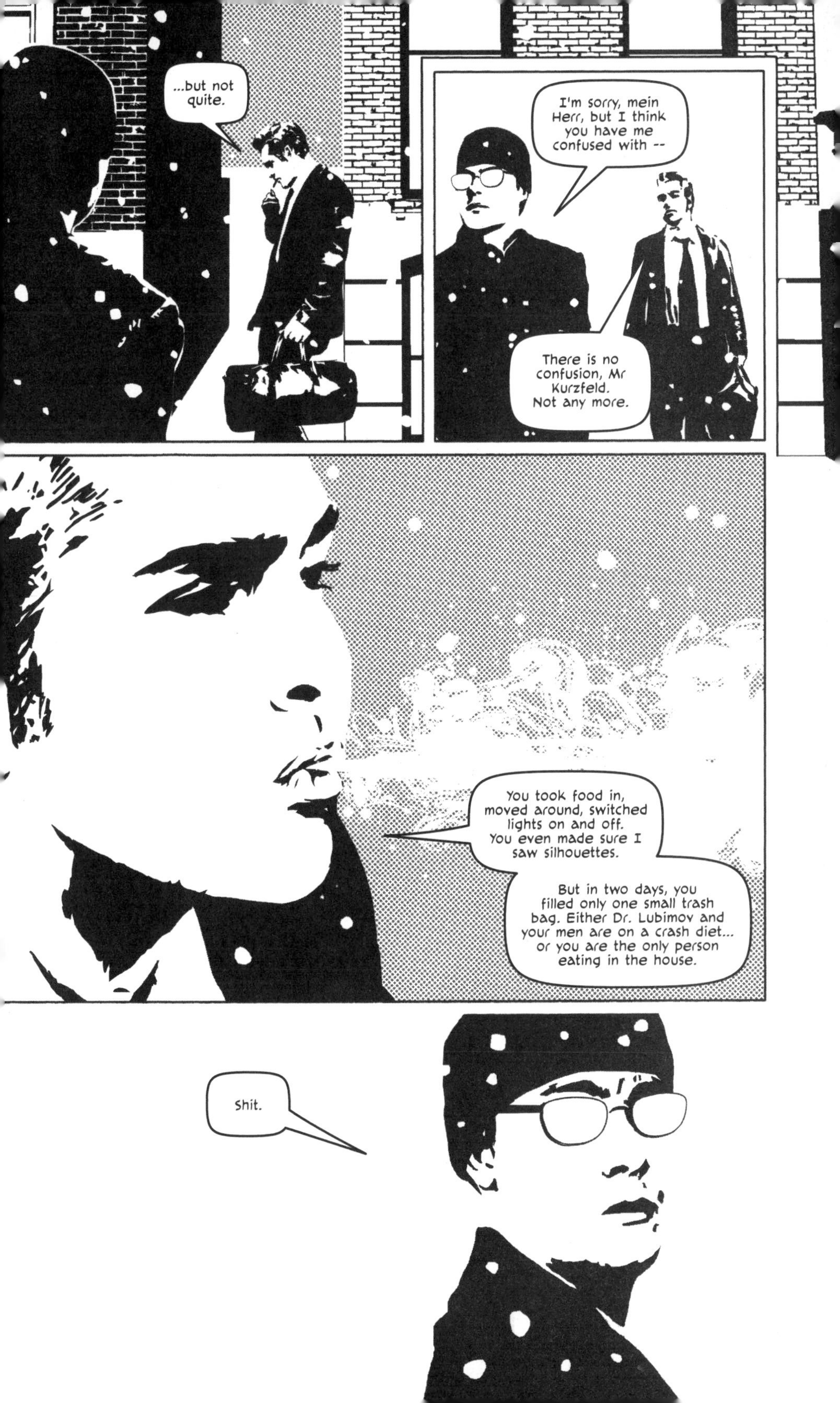

...but not quite.
I'm sorry, mein Herr, but I think you have me confused with --
There is no confusion, Mr Kurzfeld. Not any more.
You took food in, moved around, switched lights on and off. You even made sure I saw silhouettes.
But in two days, you filled only one small trash bag. Either Dr. Lubimov and your men are on a crash diet... or you are the only person eating in the house.
Shit.

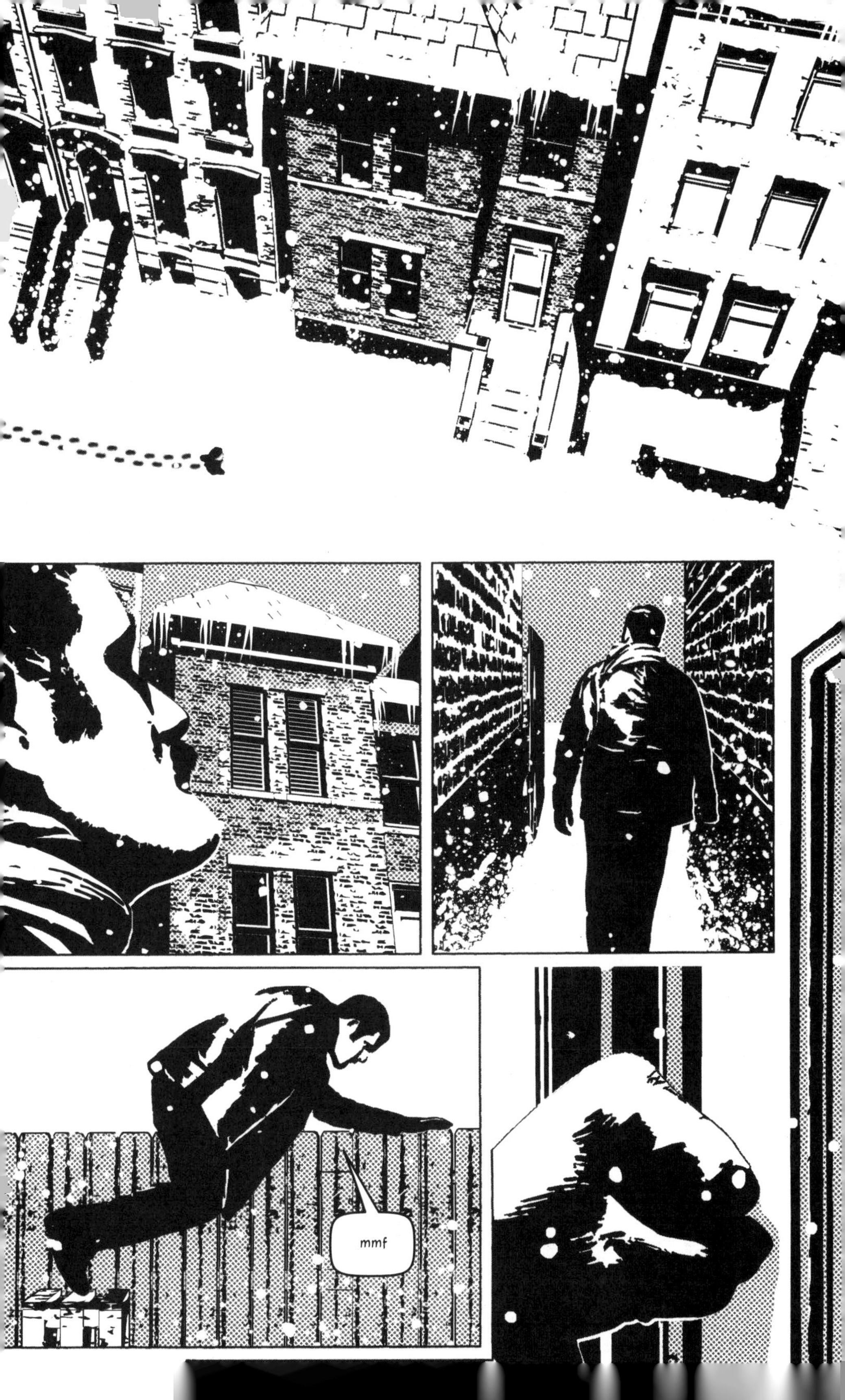
mmf

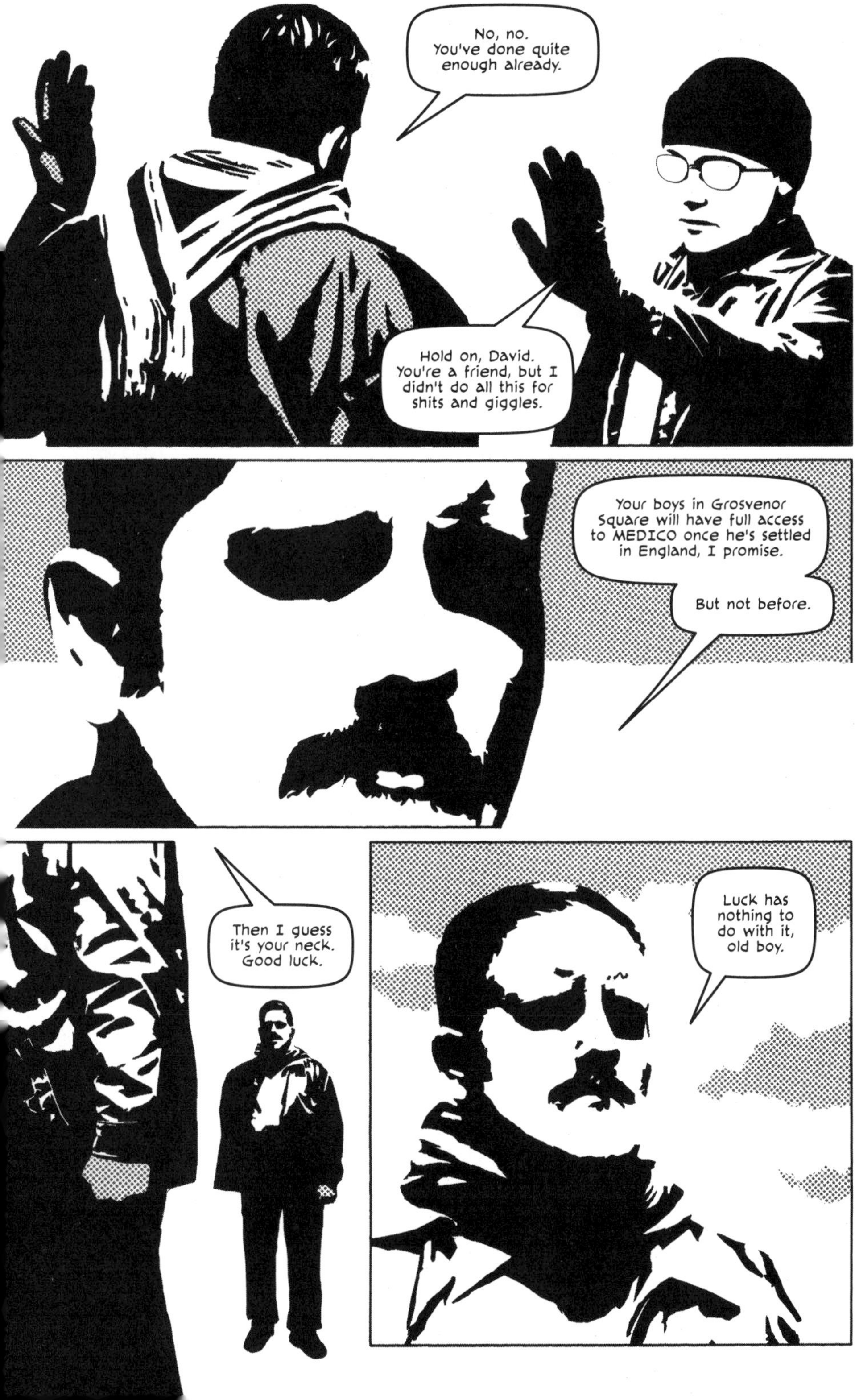
No, no. You've done quite enough already.
Hold on, David. You're a friend, but I didn't do all this for shits and giggles.
Your boys in Grosvenor Square will have full access to MEDICO once he's settled in England, I promise.
But not before.
Then I guess it's your neck. Good luck.
Luck has nothing to do with it, old boy.

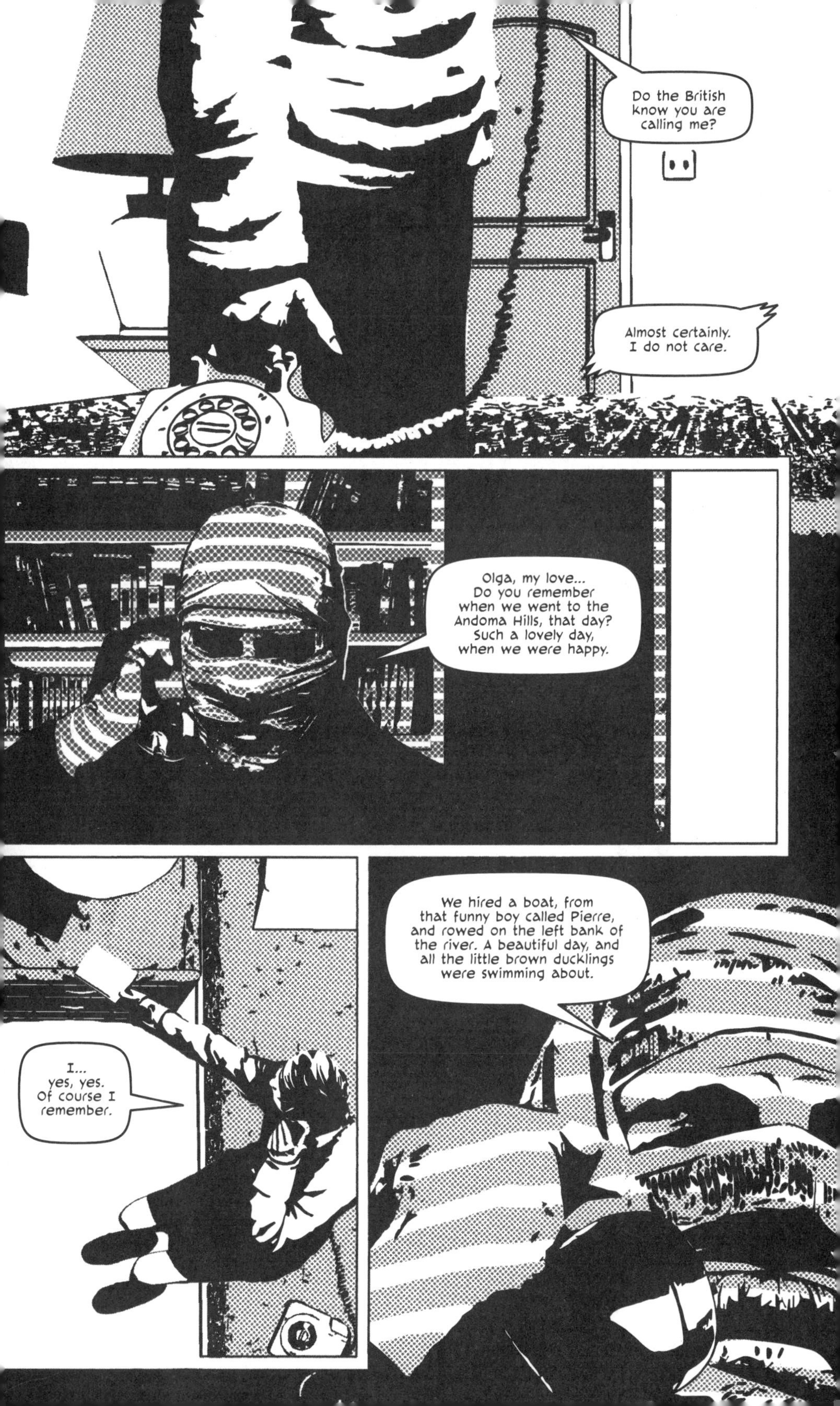

Do the British know you are calling me?
Almost certainly. I do not care.
Olga, my love... Do you remember when we went to the Andoma Hills, that day? Such a lovely day, when we were happy.
We hired a boat, from that funny boy called Pierre, and rowed on the left bank of the river. A beautiful day, and all the little brown ducklings were swimming about.
I... yes, yes. Of course I remember.

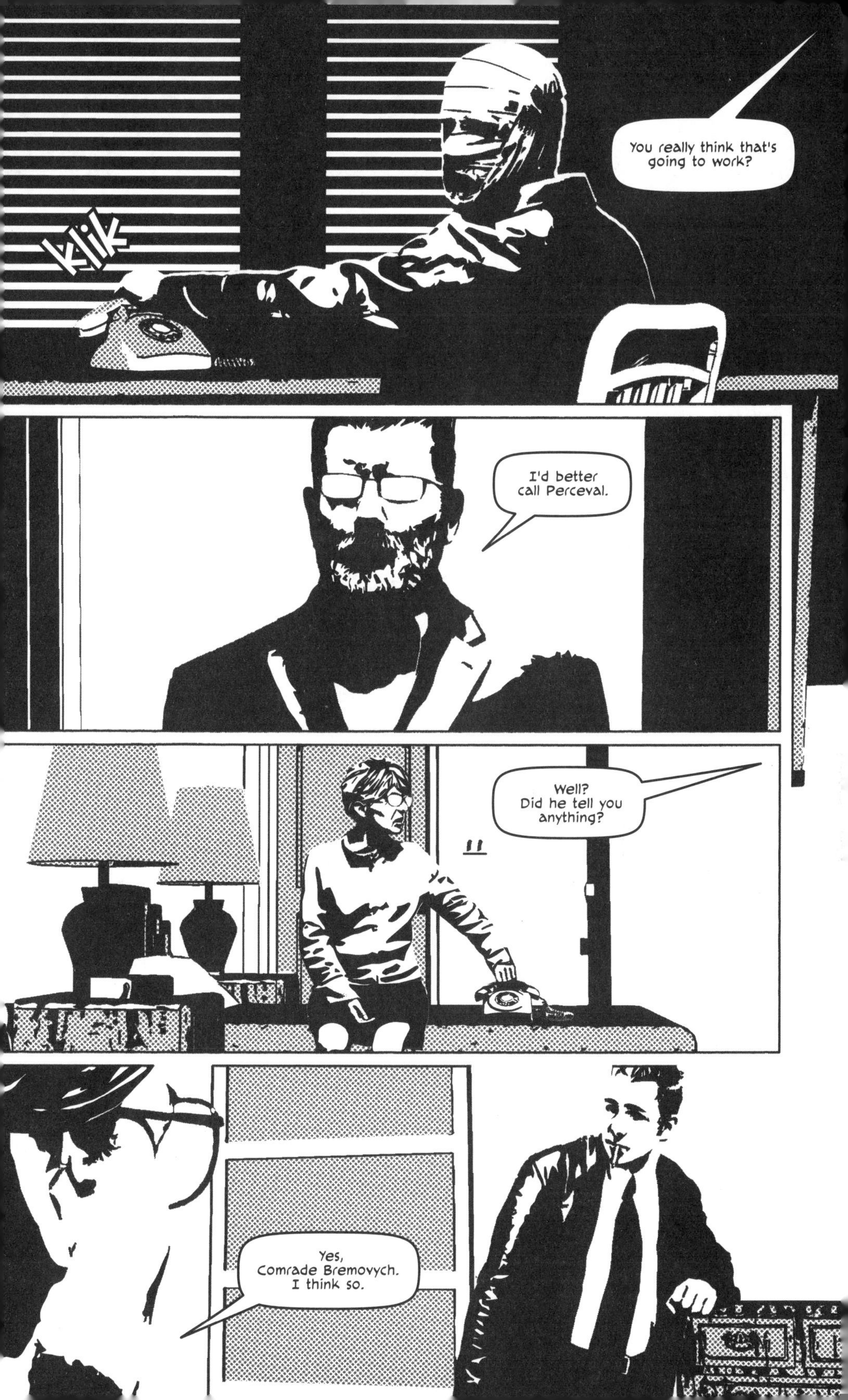
klik
You really think that's going to work?
I'd better call Perceval.
Well? Did he tell you anything?
Yes, Comrade Bremovych. I think so.

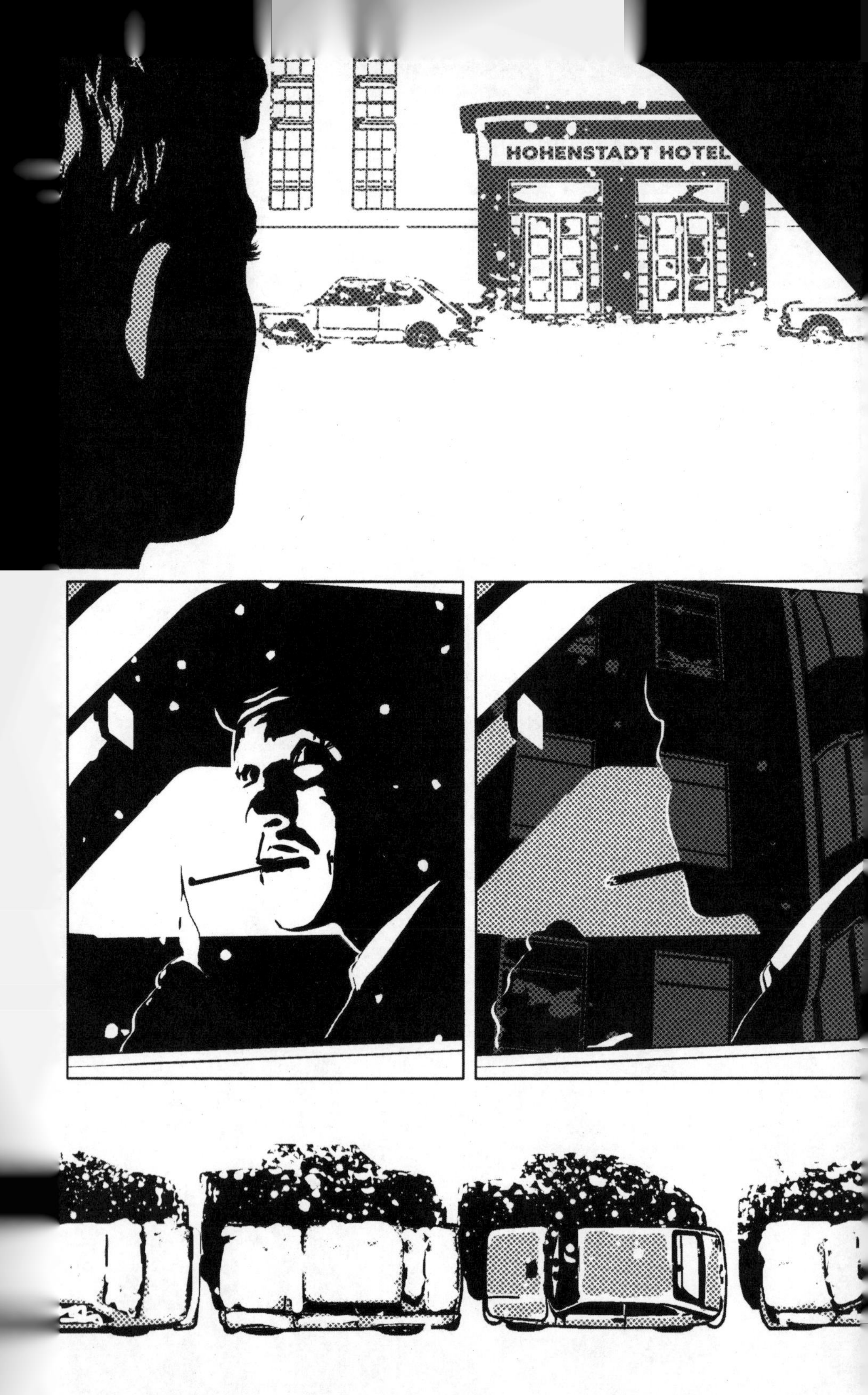
HOHENSTADT HOTEL

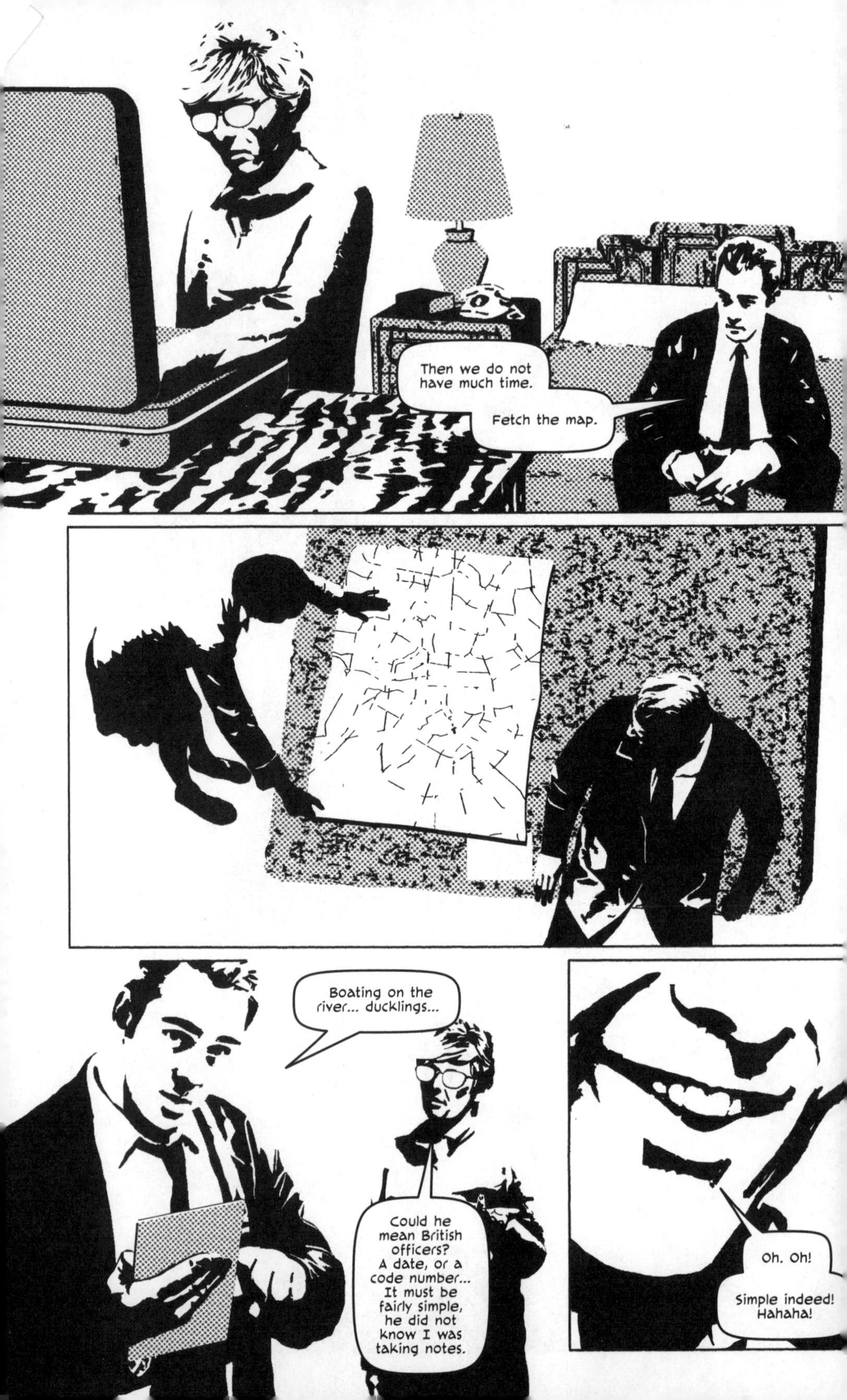
Then we do not have much time.
Fetch the map.
Boating on the river... ducklings...
Could he mean British officers? A date, or a code number... It must be fairly simple, he did not know I was taking notes.
Oh. Oh!
Simple indeed! Hahaha!

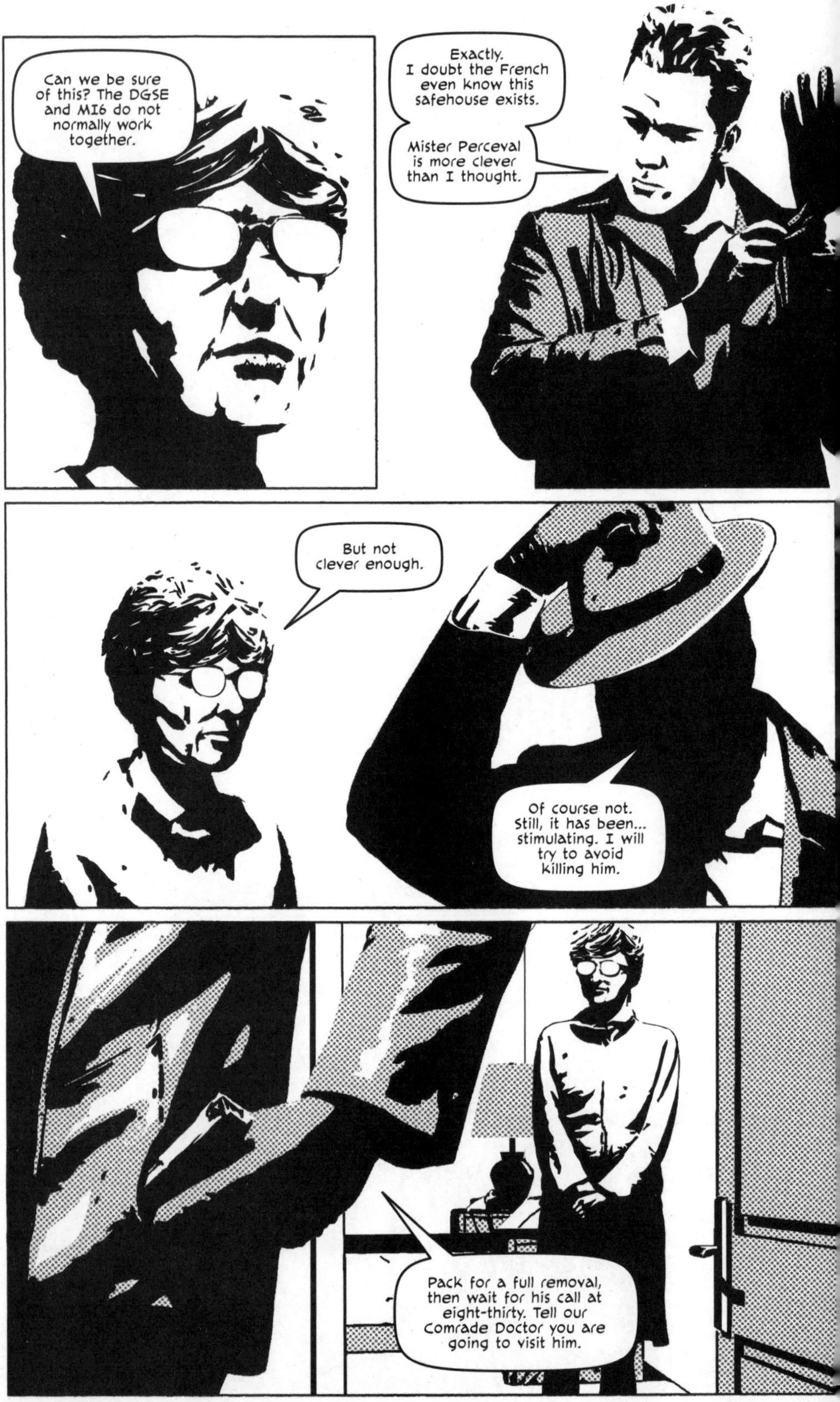
Can we be sure of this? The DGSE and MI6 do not normally work together.
Exactly. I doubt the French even know this safehouse exists.
Mister Perceval is more clever than I thought.
But not clever enough.
Of course not. Still, it has been... stimulating. I will try to avoid killing him.
Pack for a full removal, then wait for his call at eight-thirty. Tell our Comrade Doctor you are going to visit him.

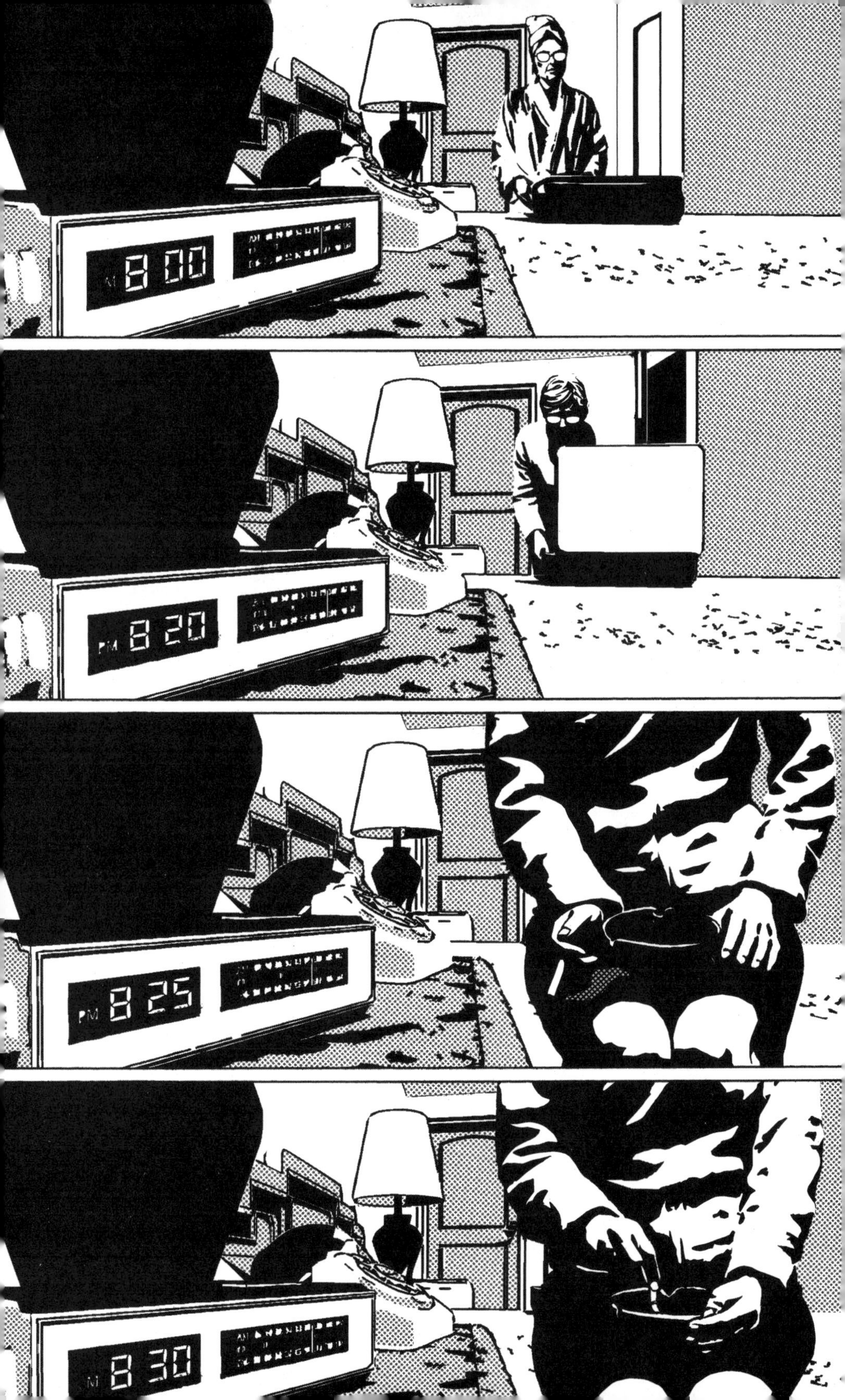
8 00
PM 8 20
PM 8 25
8 30

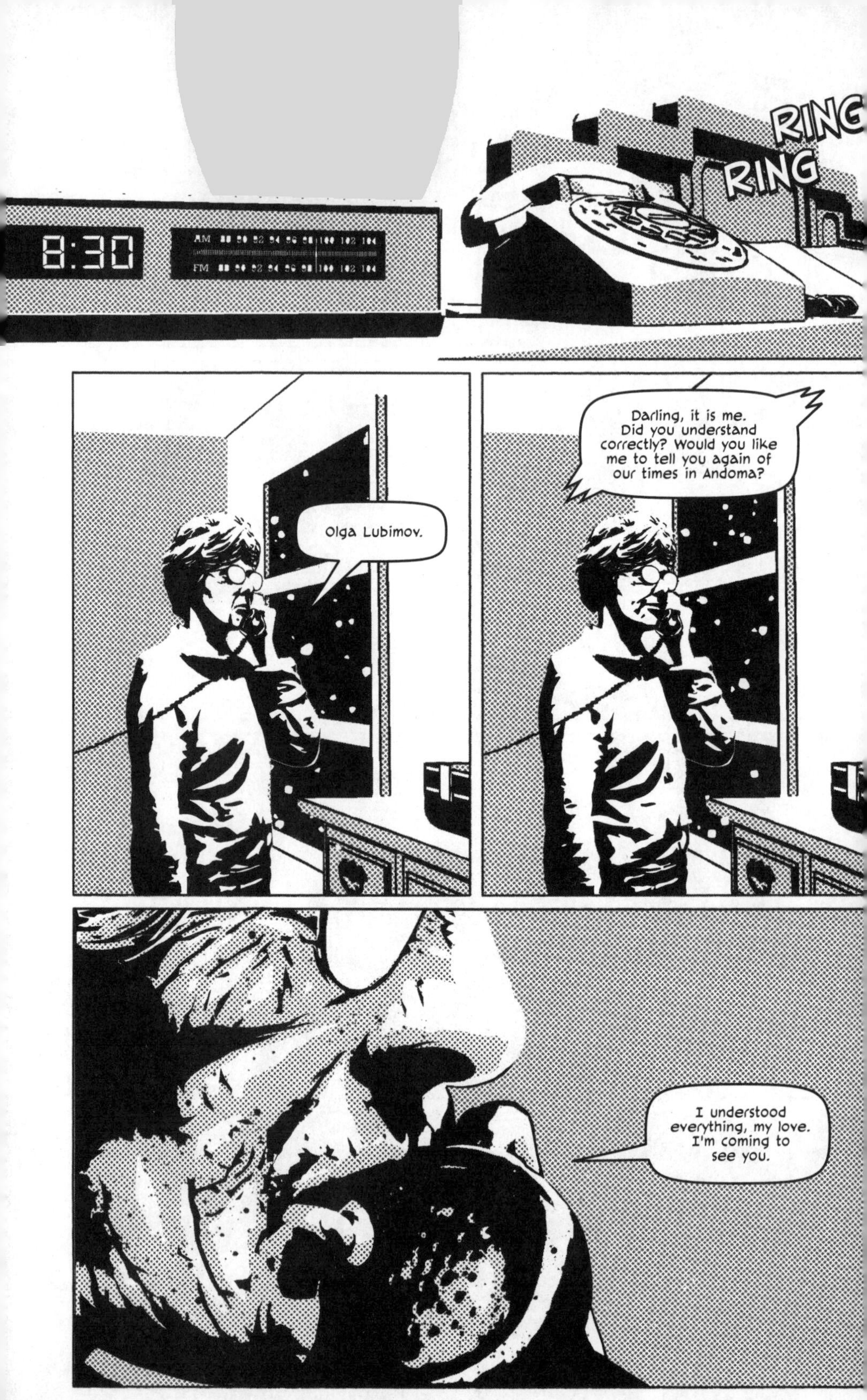
8:30
AM 88 90 92 94 96 98 100 102 104
FM 88 90 92 94 96 98 100 102 104
RING
RING
Olga Lubimov.
Darling, it is me. Did you understand correctly? Would you like me to tell you again of our times in Andoma?
I understood everything, my love. I'm coming to see you.

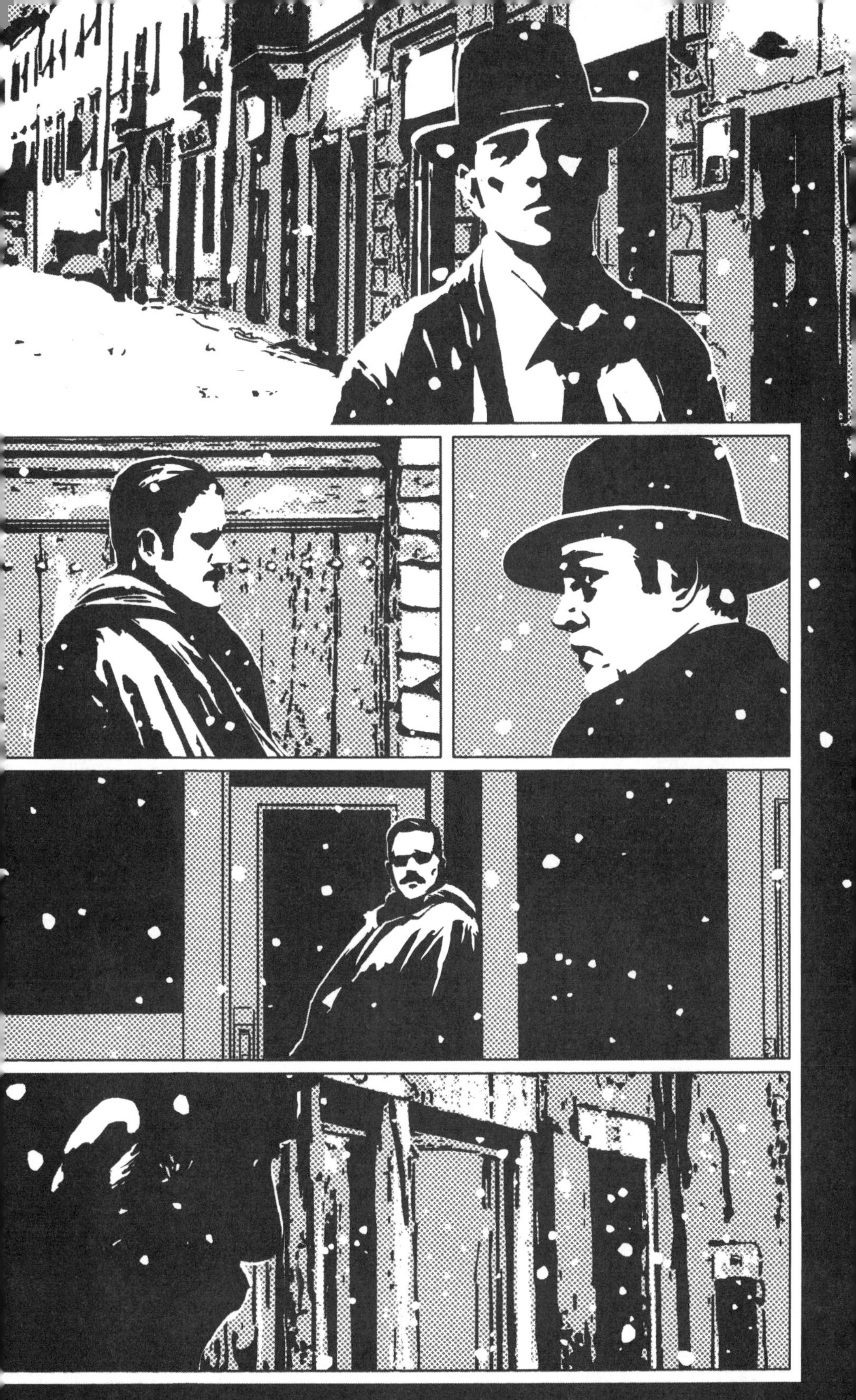

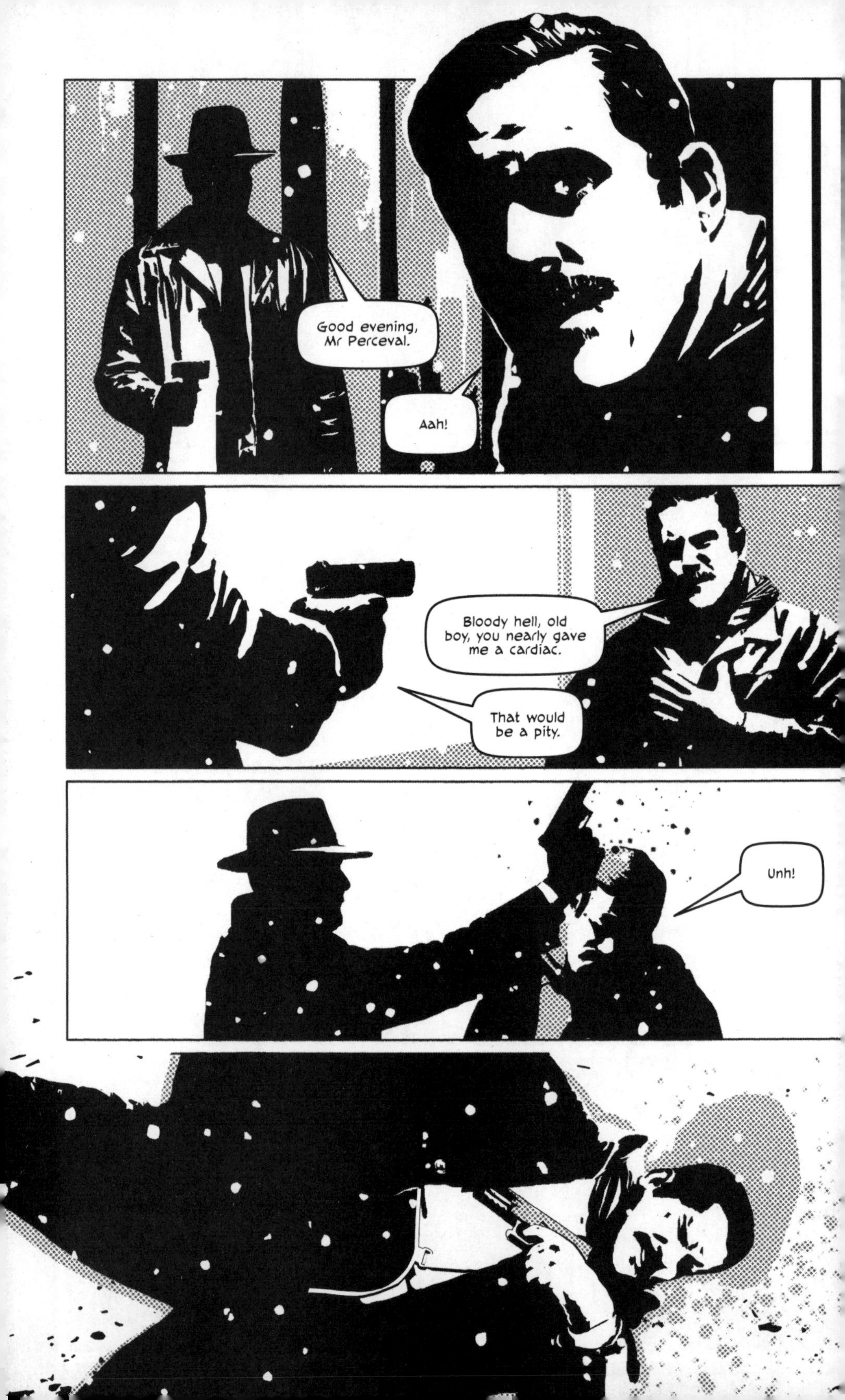
Good evening, Mr Perceval.
Aah!
Bloody hell, old boy, you nearly gave me a cardiac.
That would be a pity.
Unh!

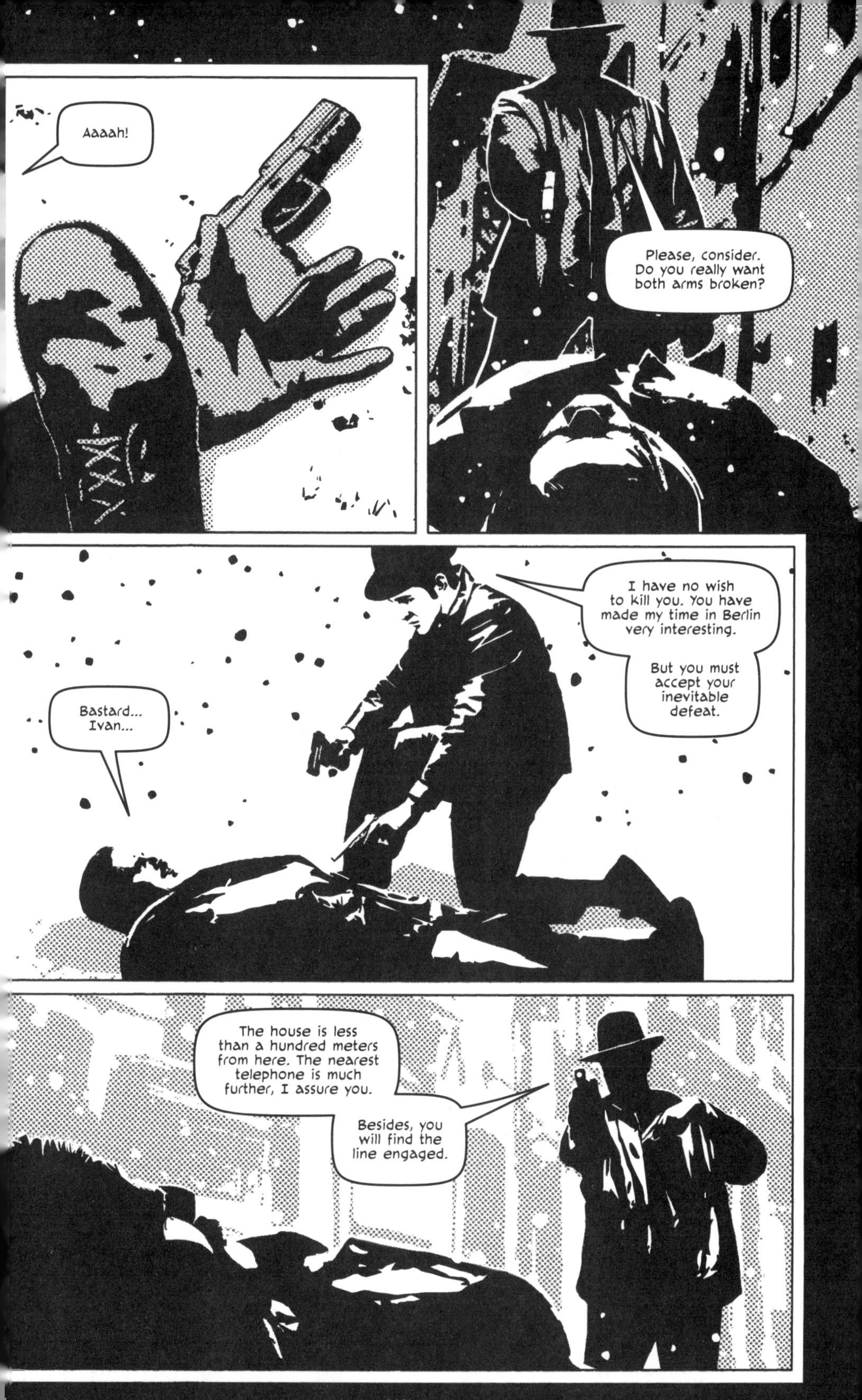
Aaaah!
Please, consider. Do you really want both arms broken?
I have no wish to kill you. You have made my time in Berlin very interesting.
But you must accept your inevitable defeat.
Bastard... Ivan...
The house is less than a hundred meters from here. The nearest telephone is much further, I assure you.
Besides, you will find the line engaged.

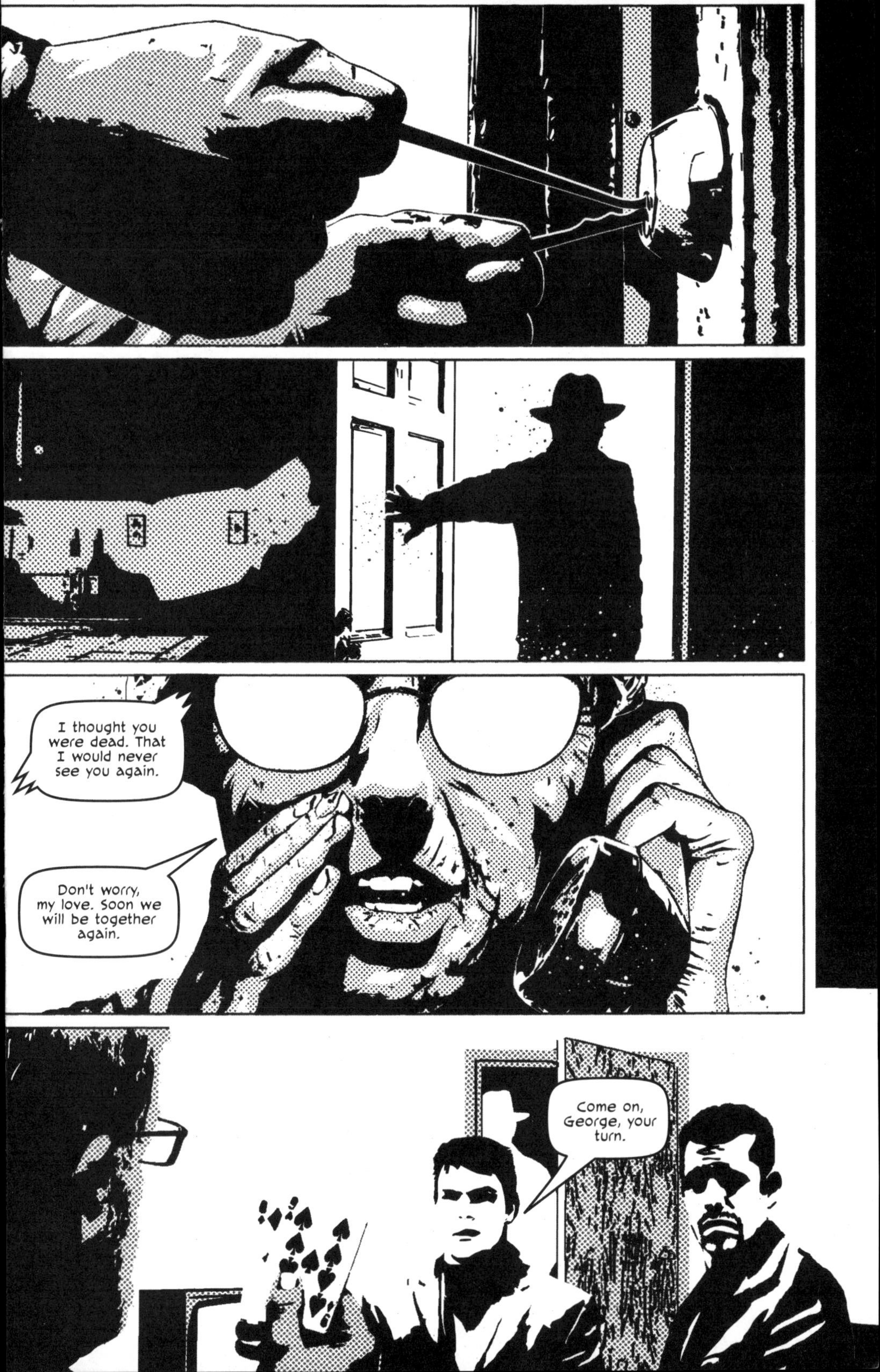
I thought you were dead. That I would never see you again.
Don't worry, my love. Soon we will be together again.
Come on, George, your turn.

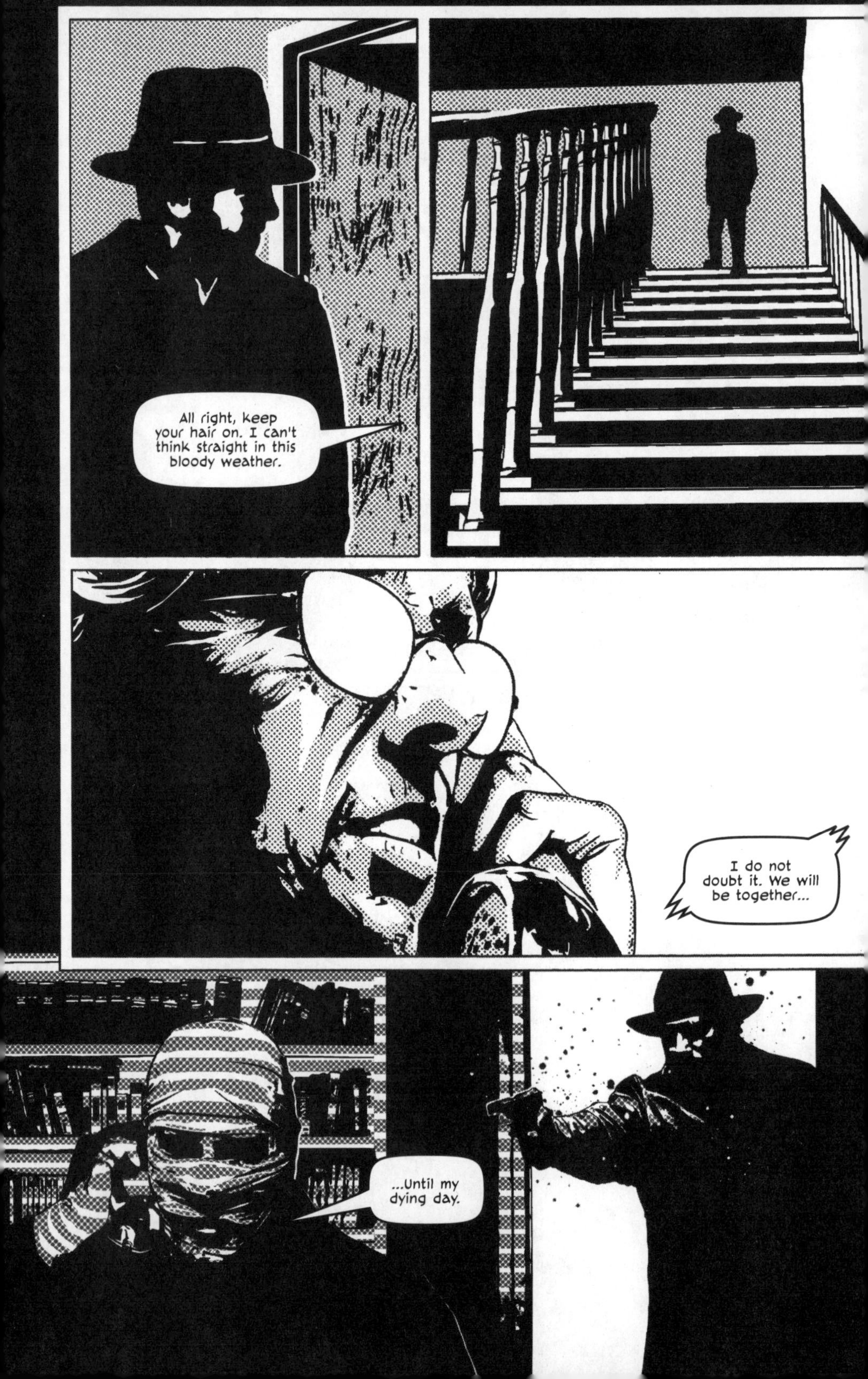
All right, keep your hair on. I can't think straight in this bloody weather.
I do not doubt it. We will be together...
...Until my dying day.

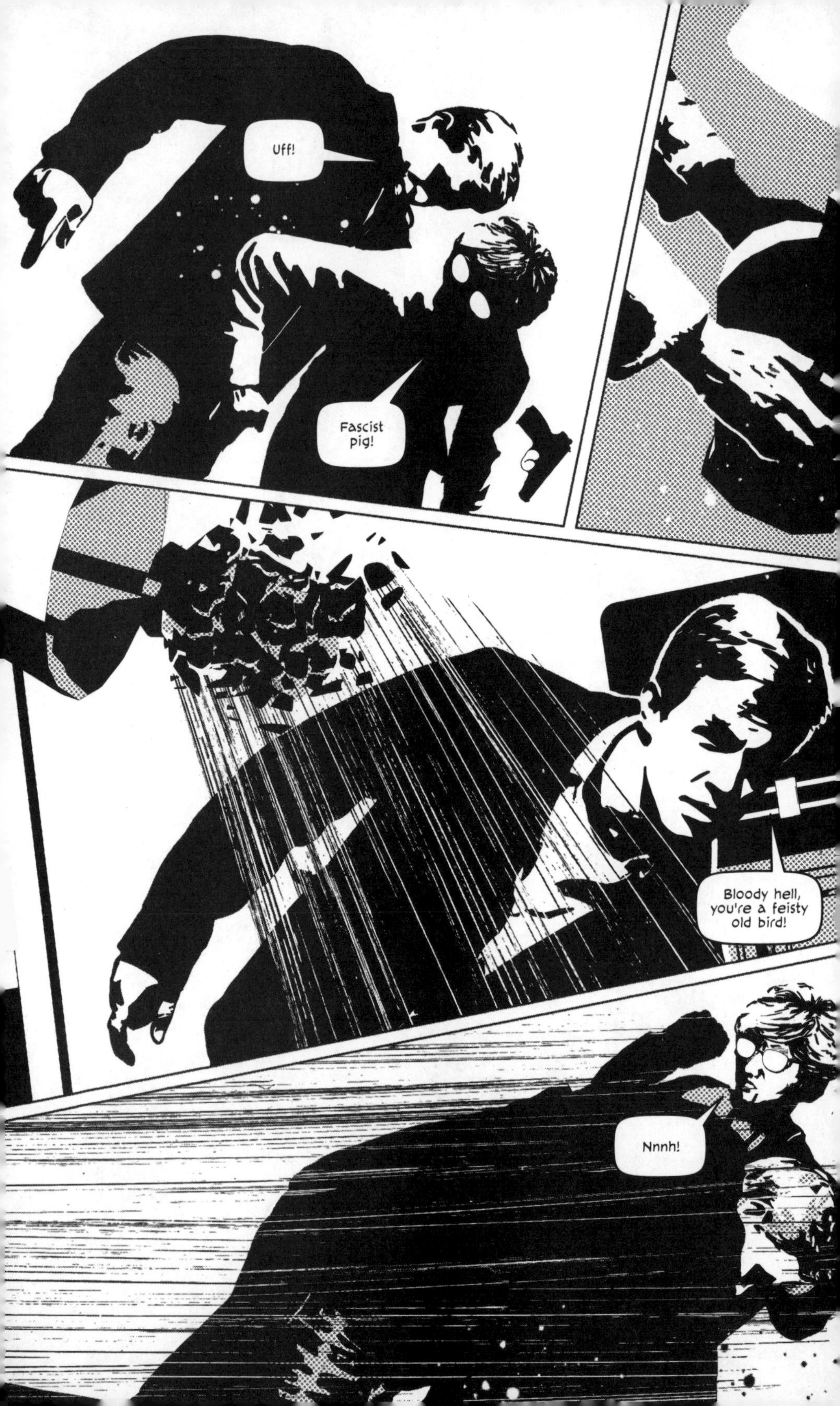
Uff!
Fascist pig!
Bloody hell, you're a feisty old bird!
Nnnh!

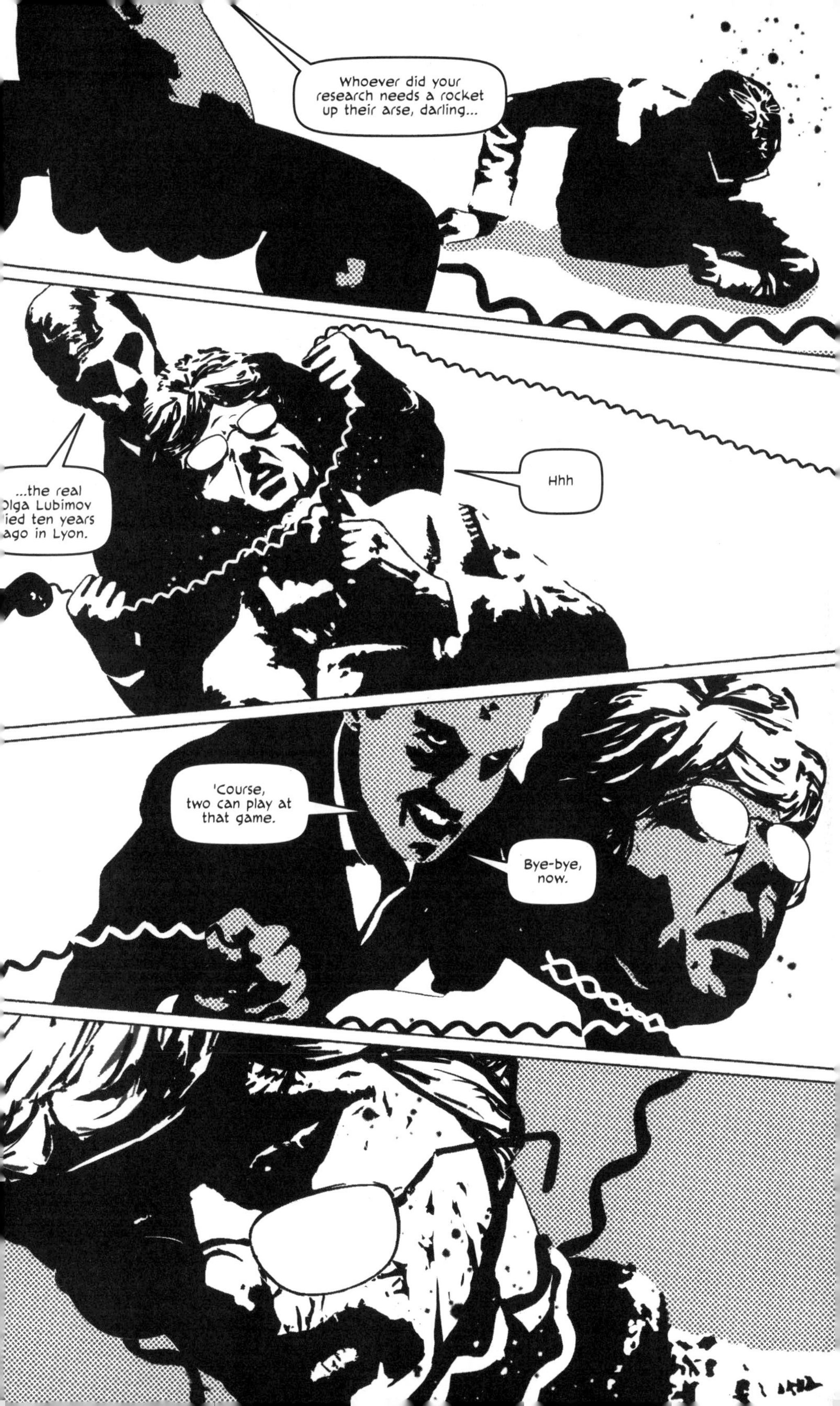
Whoever did your research needs a rocket up their arse, darling...
...the real Olga Lubimov died ten years ago in Lyon.
Hhh
'Course, two can play at that game.
Bye-bye, now.

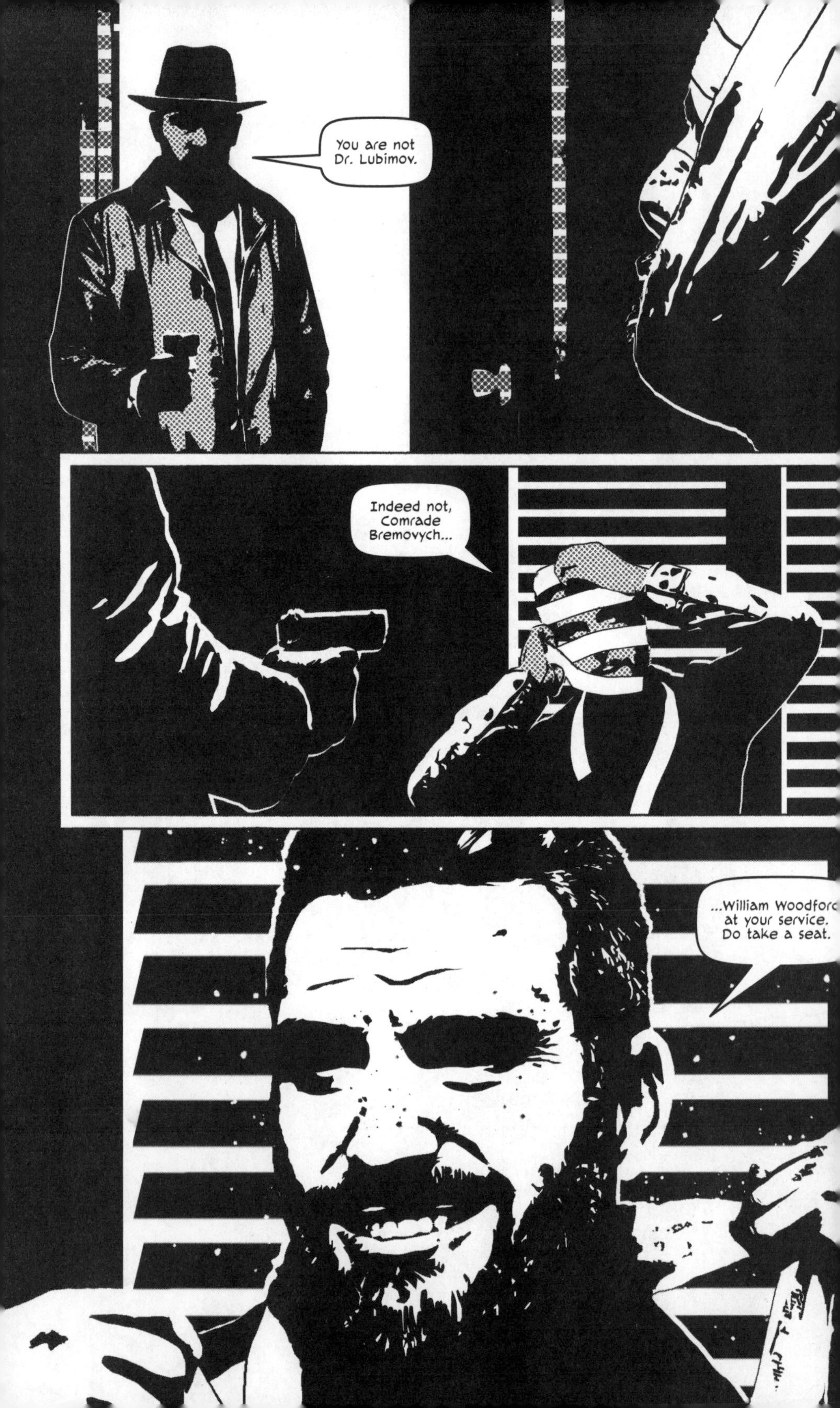
You are not Dr. Lubimov.
Indeed not, Comrade Bremovych...
...William Woodford at your service. Do take a seat.

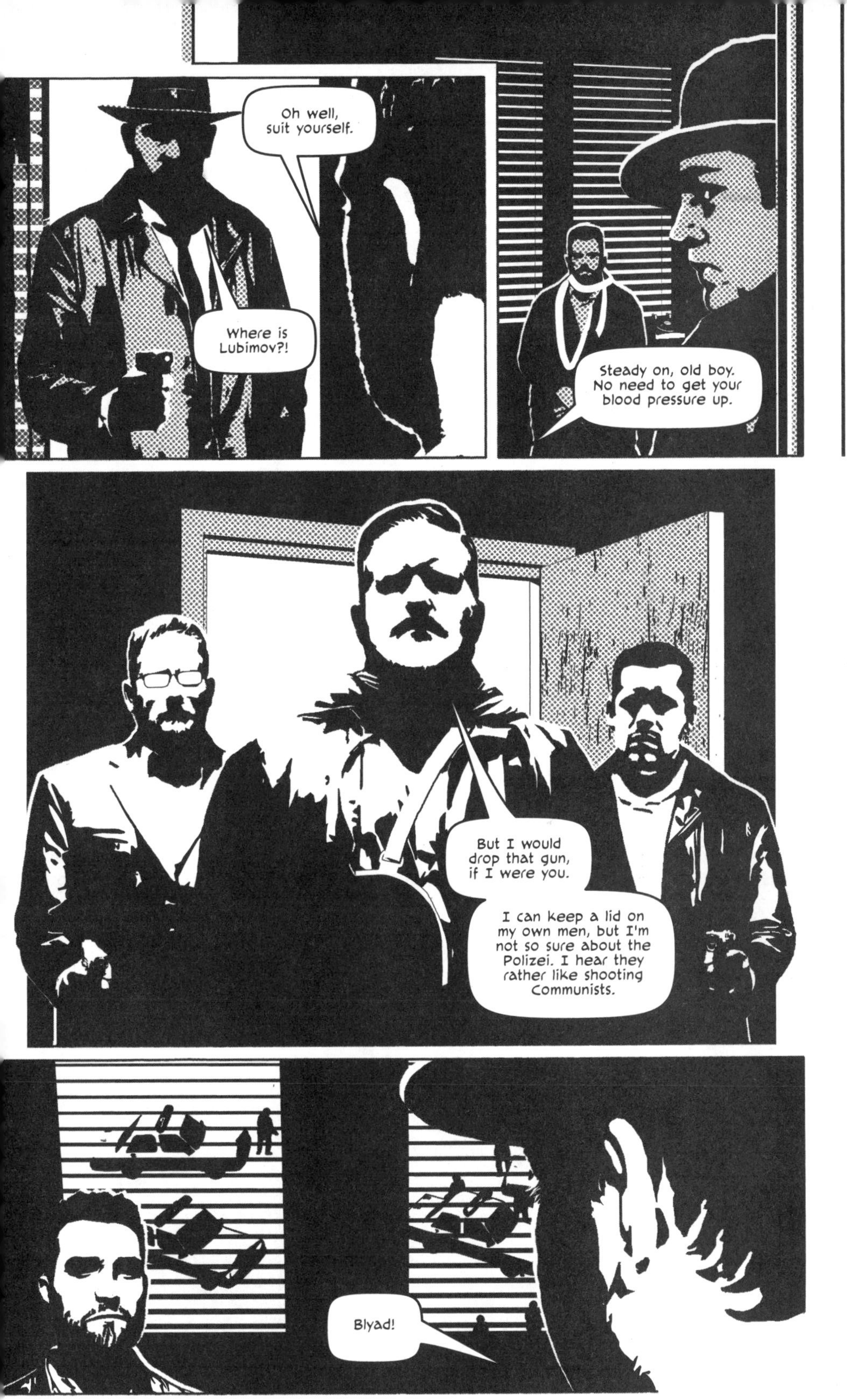
Oh well, suit yourself.
Where is Lubimov?!
Steady on, old boy. No need to get your blood pressure up.
But I would drop that gun, if I were you.
I can keep a lid on my own men, but I'm not so sure about the Polizei. I hear they rather like shooting Communists.
Blyad!

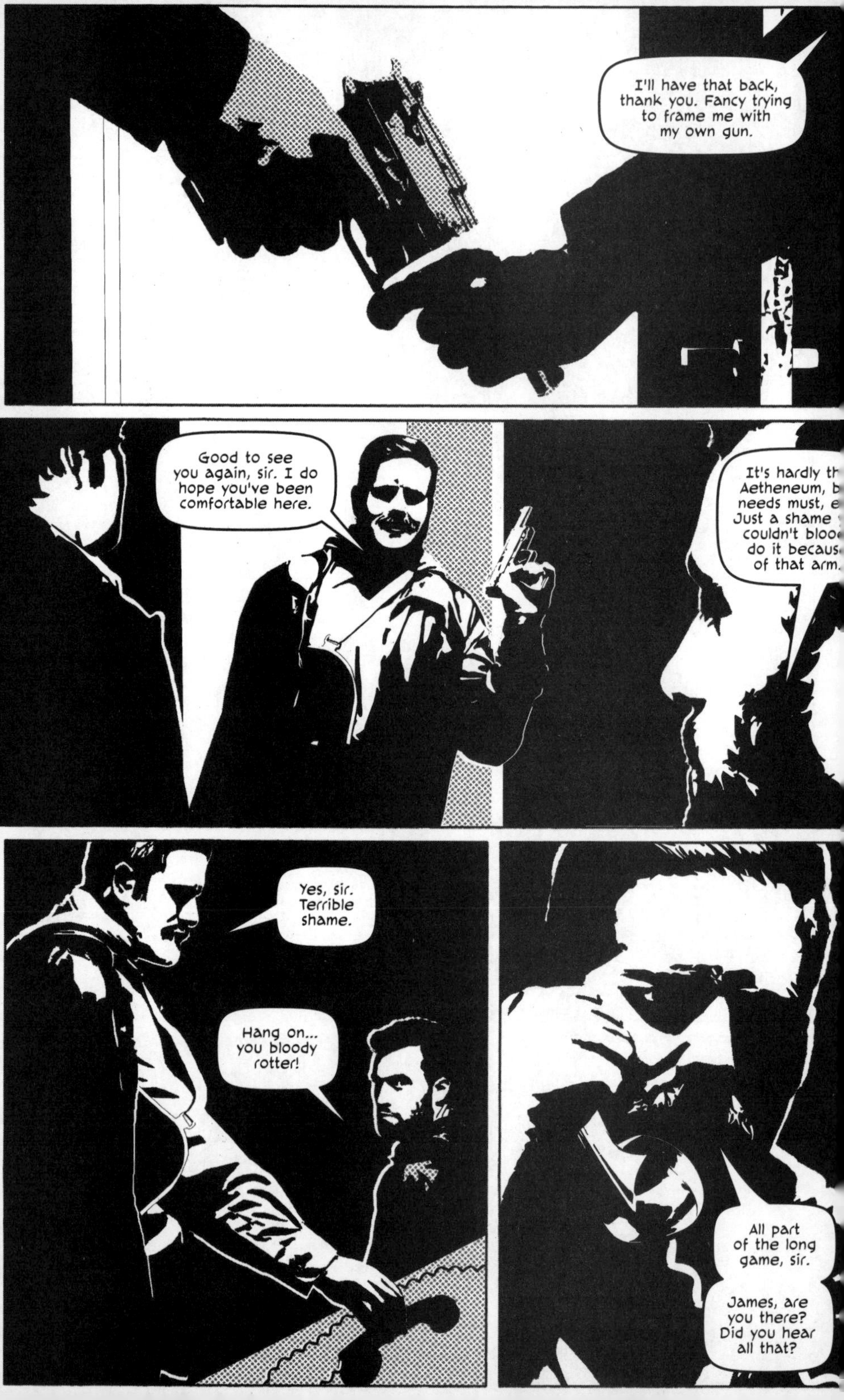
I'll have that back, thank you. Fancy trying to frame me with my own gun.
Good to see you again, sir. I do hope you've been comfortable here.
It's hardly th Aetheneum, b needs must, e Just a shame couldn't bloo do it becaus of that arm.
Yes, sir. Terrible shame.
Hang on... you bloody rotter!
All part of the long game, sir.
James, are you there? Did you hear all that?

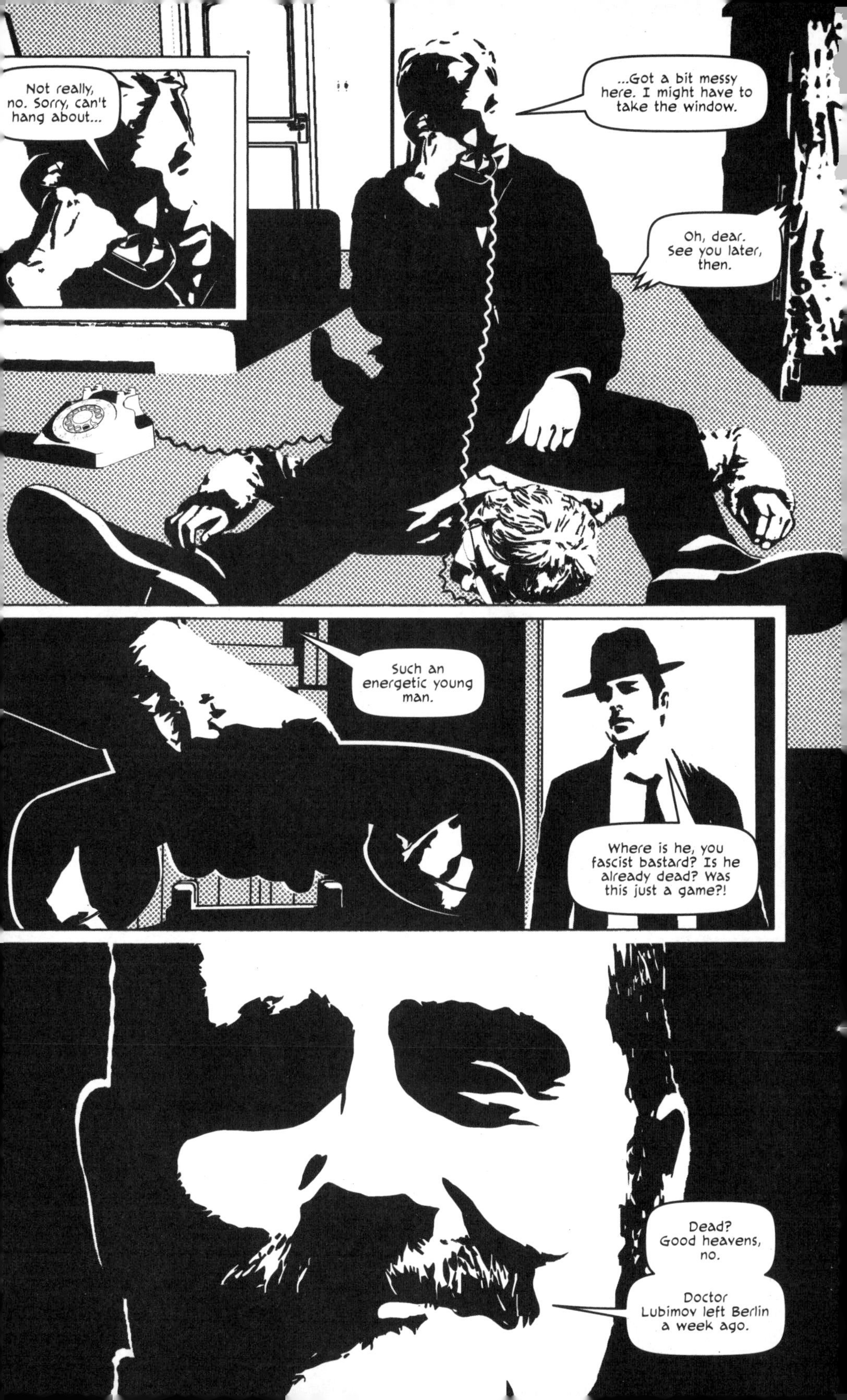
Not really, no. Sorry, can't hang about...
...Got a bit messy here. I might have to take the window.
Oh, dear. See you later, then.
Such an energetic young man.
Where is he, you fascist bastard? Is he already dead? Was this just a game?!
Dead? Good heavens, no.
Doctor Lubimov left Berlin a week ago.

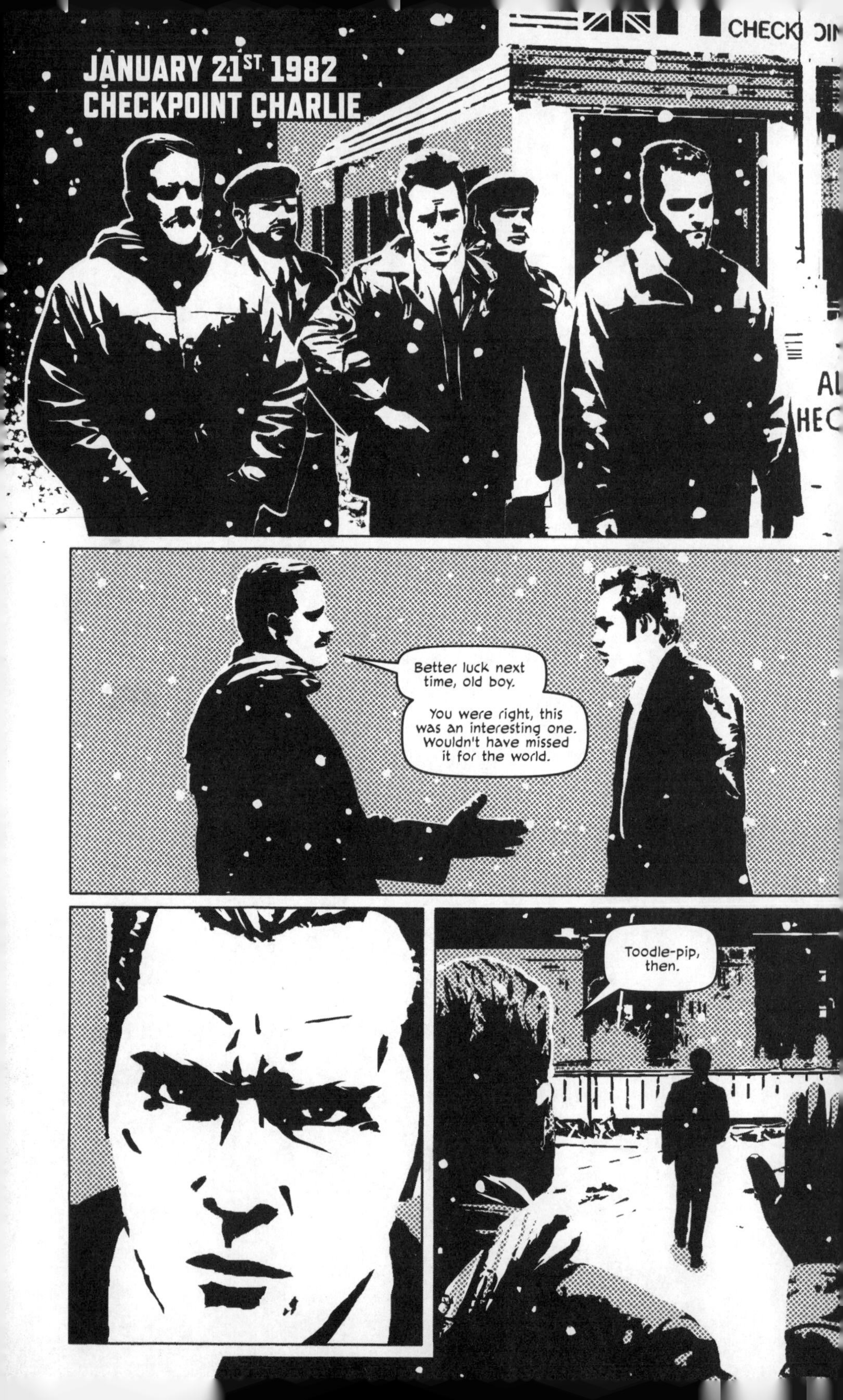
JANUARY 21ST 1982
CHECKPOINT CHARLIE
Better luck next time, old boy.
You were right, this was an interesting one. Wouldn't have missed it for the world.
Toodle-pip, then.

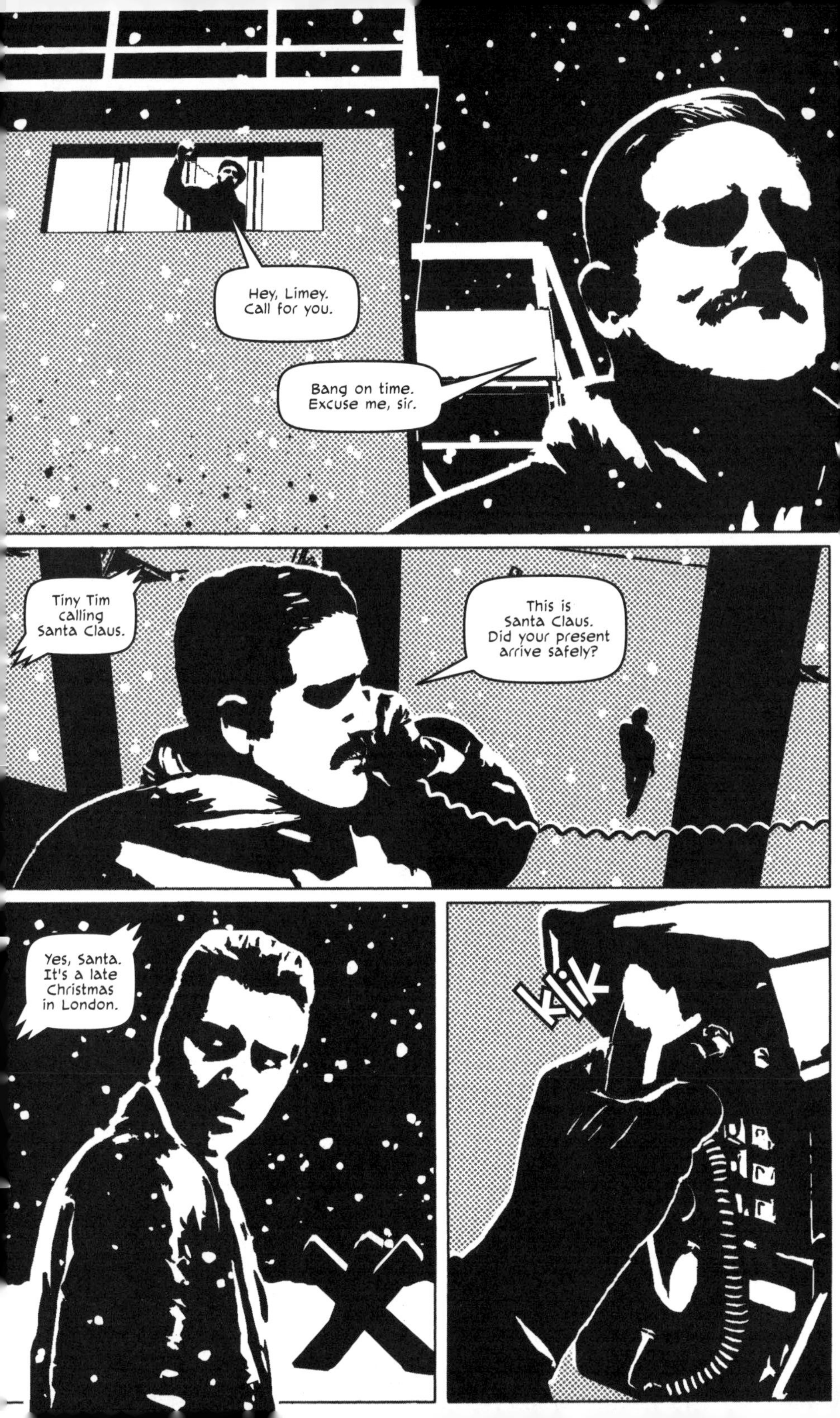
Hey, Limey. Call for you.
Bang on time. Excuse me, sir.
Tiny Tim calling Santa Claus.
This is Santa Claus. Did your present arrive safely?
Yes, Santa. It's a late Christmas in London.
KLIK

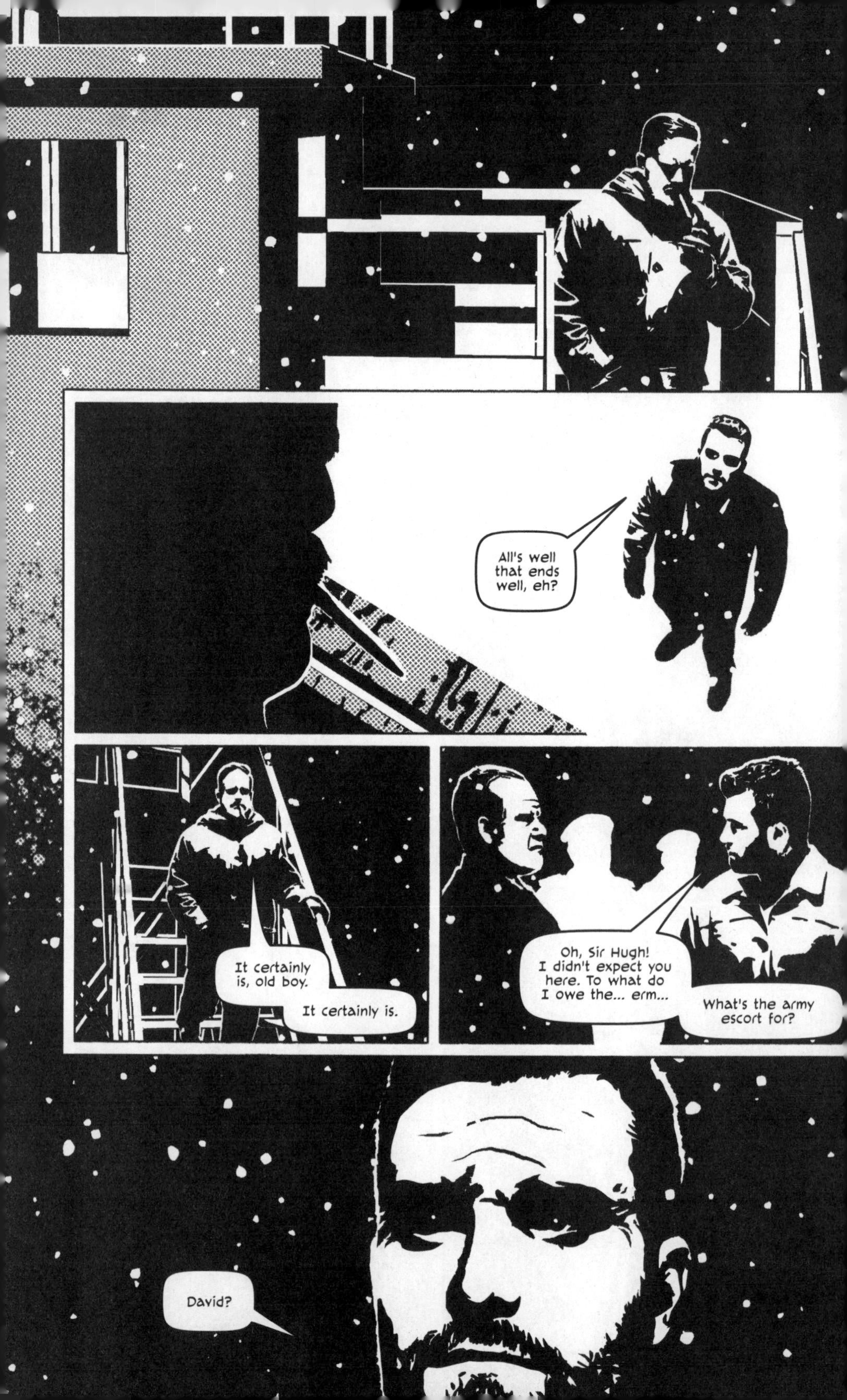
All's well that ends well, eh?
It certainly is, old boy.
It certainly is.
Oh, Sir Hugh! I didn't expect you here. To what do I owe the... erm...
What's the army escort for?
David?

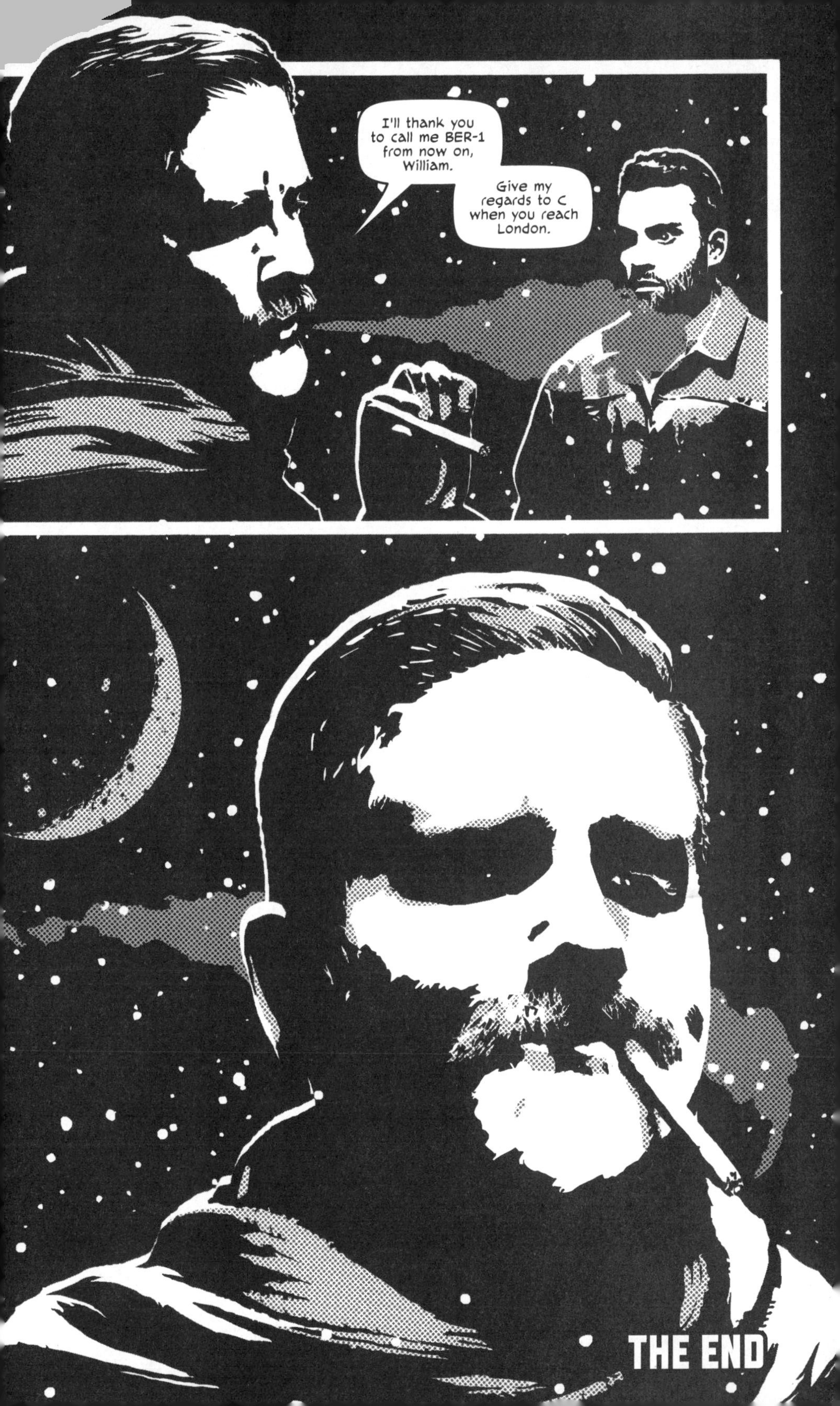
I'll thank you to call me BER-1 from now on, William.
Give my regards to C when you reach London.
THE END

WRITTEN BY
ANTONY JOHNSTON

ILLUSTRATED AND LETTERED BY
STEVEN PERKINS

THE
COLDEST
WINTER

DESIGN BY
KEITH WOOD

ADDITIONAL COVER DESIGN BY
DYLAN TODD

EDITED BY
CHARLIE CHU

THE COLDEST WINTER

BY **ANTONY JOHNSTON** & **STEVEN PERKINS**

Published by Oni Press, Inc.

PUBLISHER **JOE NOZEMACK** · EDITOR-IN CHIEF **JAMES LUCAS JONES**

SALES MANAGER **DAVID DISSANAYAKE** · PUBLICITY COORDINATOR **RACHEL REED**

DIRECTOR OF DESIGN & PRODUCTION **TROY LOOK** · GRAPHIC DESIGNER **HILARY THOMPSON**

DIGITAL PREPRESS TECHNICIAN **ANGIE DOBSON** · MANAGING EDITOR **ARI YARWOOD**

SENIOR EDITOR **CHARLIE CHU** · EDITOR **ROBIN HERRERA**

ADMINISTRATIVE ASSISTANT **ALISSA SALLAH** · DIRECTOR OF LOGISTICS **BRAD ROOKS**

LOGISTICS ASSOCIATE **JUNG LEE**

ONI PRESS, INC.
1319 SE Martin Luther King Jr. Blvd.
Suite 240
Portland, OR 97214
USA

onipress.com · facebook.com/onipress · twitter.com/onipress
onipress.tumblr.com · instagram.com/onipress
antonyjohnston.com · @AntonyJohnston · stevenperkinsart.com · @SPerkinsArtist

First edition: December 2016

ISBN: 978-1-62010-400-2 · eISBN: 978-1-62010-370-8
Library of Congress Control Number: 2016943123

10 8 6 4 2 1 3 5 7 9

PRINTED IN USA

ANTONY JOHNSTON

Antony Johnston is an award-winning, *New York Times* best-selling author of graphic novels, video games and books, with titles including *The Coldest City* (now the film *Atomic Blonde* starring Charlize Theron), the epic series *Wasteland*, Marvel's superhero *Daredevil*, and the seminal video game *Dead Space*. He has also adapted books by bestselling novelist Anthony Horowitz, collaborated with comics legend Alan Moore, and his titles have been translated throughout the world. He lives and works in England.

antonyjohnston.com

STEVEN PERKINS

Steven Perkins has been a professional comic book artist and writer since 2001. In that time, he's worked on projects such as *Silent Hill*, *Max Payne*, *CSI: Crime Scene Investigation*, *Se7en*, and *Credence*, as well as his original graphic novel, *Pacify*. Steven currently resides in Los Angeles, not far from the beach.

You can see more of his work at *StevenPerkinsArt.com*.

NOVEMBER 1989.

MI6 spy Lorraine Broughton was sent to Berlin to investigate the death of another agent, and the disappearance of a list revealing every spy working there. She found a powderkeg of mistrust, assassinations and bad defections that ended with the murder of MI6's top officer, as the Berlin Wall was torn down.

Now Lorraine has returned from the Cold War's coldest city, to tell her story.

And nothing is what it seems.

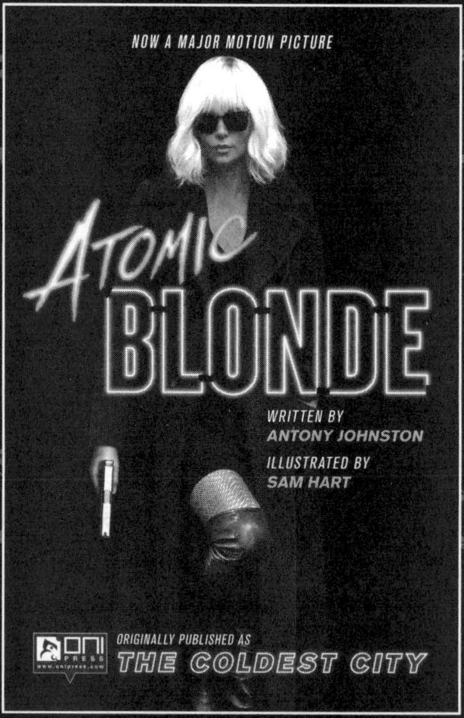
NOW A MAJOR MOTION PICTURE
ATOMIC
BLONDE
WRITTEN BY
ANTONY JOHNSTON
ILLUSTRATED BY
SAM HART
ONI PRESS
www.onipress.com
ORIGINALLY PUBLISHED AS
THE COLDEST CITY

176 PAGES
SOFTCOVER, BLACK AND WHITE
ISBN 978-1-62010-381-4
$14.99 US

ONI PRESS

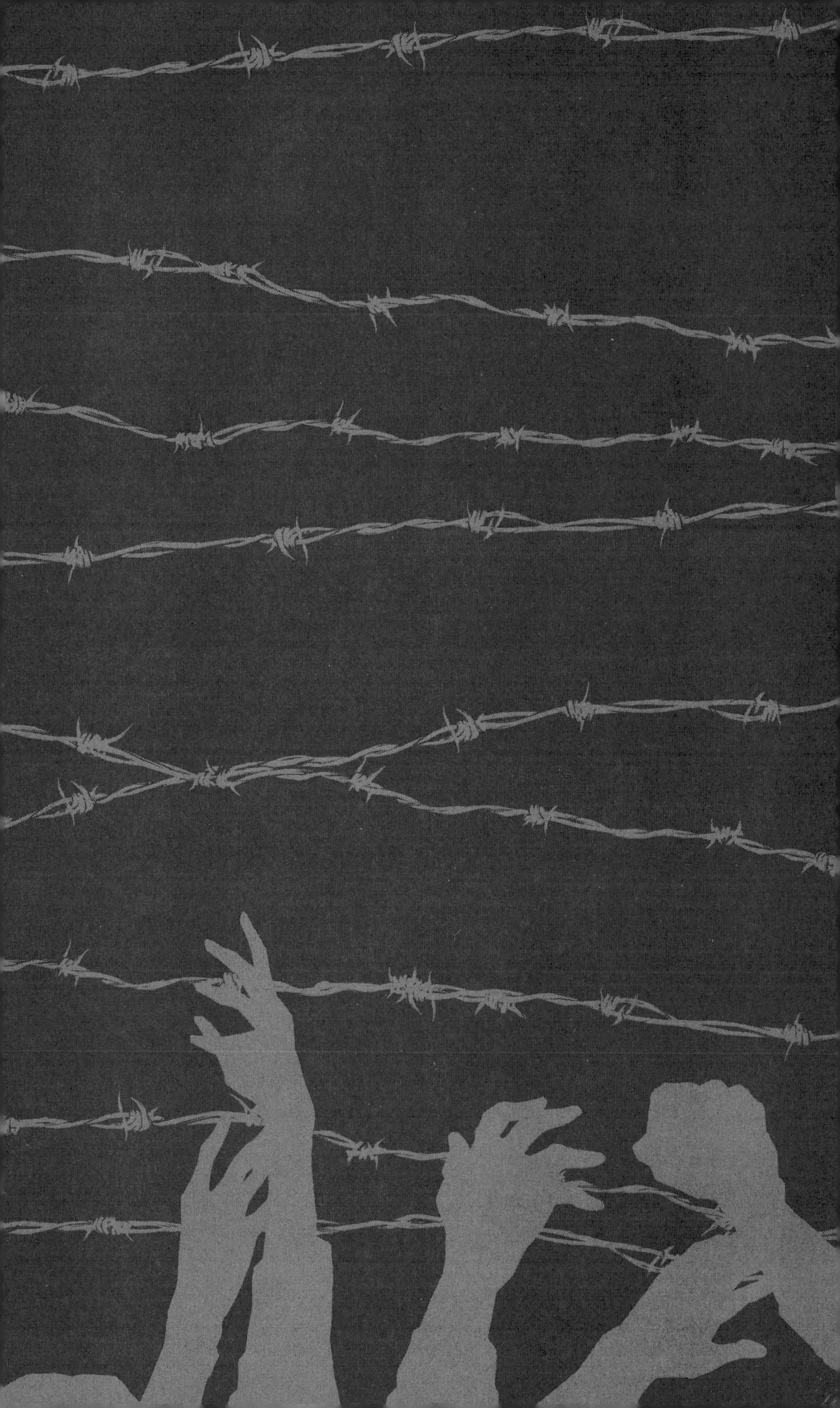

OTHER BOOKS BY ONI PRESS!